Dazzling romance . . .
White-hot passion . . .
**CATHERINE LINDEN'S**
**DIAMONDS IN THE NIGHT**

As she demonstrated in *The Baron's Woman* and *Wakefield's Passion,* Catherine Linden has a tremendous ability to tell wildly romantic stories. Her previous Leisure book, *Highland Rose,* earned a *Romantic Times* Reviewers' Choice Award Nomination and was hailed as a triumph.

"Reading *Highland Rose,*" they raved, "is like walking through a fragrant field of heather. Ms. Linden displays an intimate and deep appreciation of Scotland's turbulent history throughout her long and lavishly detailed story. This splendid blend of fact and fiction will remind readers of Karen Harper's and Mary Pershall's memorable novels."

Now Catherine Linden is back, with her most spectacular romance to date . . .

**DIAMONDS IN THE NIGHT**

Set in one of the most dramatic eras in history, *Diamonds in the Night* tells the story of an innocent woman lost in a dangerous country . . . a man as wild as the land he sought to tame . . . and a love more precious than a priceless jewel.

# DIAMOND BRIGHT DESIRE

"Knave!" Olwyn gasped, frantically trying to cover her nakedness as bold, mocking eyes roved over her body. "You—you are despicable, Justin Wentworth, and don't imagine—"

He sprang up and seized her in his arms and silenced her with a kiss, then tumbled her back on the bed, where Olwyn's struggles were swiftly subdued. Leaning over her, Justin caught her by the chin and looked deep in her eyes. "I'll tell you what I imagine. I imagine that you really want to stay here—"

"Never! I—I hate you!"

Slowly, maddeningly, he shook his head and went on as if she hadn't interrupted. "I also imagine—I know!—that I *want* you to stay."

"And I know why!"

"Oh?" His brows rose in that sardonic way that Olwyn found so infuriating. "Then we must think alike. That's a good start to our friendship."

Enraged at his audacity, at the sheer arrogance of the man, Olwyn again made a futile attempt to throw him off, but Justin simply let his weight rest a little more heavily on her and put his lips to her ear and whispered, "For a recent virgin you certainly know how to arouse a man, Olwyn Moore."

Other Leisure books by Catherine Linden:

HIGHLAND ROSE

# DIAMONDS IN THE NIGHT

## CATHERINE LINDEN

LEISURE BOOKS  NEW YORK CITY

A LEISURE BOOK

July 1989

Published by

Dorchester Publishing Co., Inc.
276 Fifth Avenue
New York, NY 10001

*In Nuruzambora you can hear the scorched
    earth cry
For the rain to green the brown land,
To drive away the drought, the death of growing,
They watch the dawn, but fire rises in the
    sky . . .*

—Griqua poem

◇

# Farewell Scotland

◇

—————◇————— 1 —————◇—————

*Glasgow, Scotland*
*November 1, 1868*

The three medical students huddled in the entrance to the Copper Jug, one of the more notorious coffee houses in Glasgow. They had the collars of their cloaks turned up against the evening chill and now and then stamped their feet to keep the circulation going. But neither the sleet, the gusting wind, nor the dank dreariness of the night could dampen their spirits as they chatted together in low, excited tones. All three were in fine fettle, never finer than when involved in some prank or another, and the one they were anticipating that night promised to be a topper, especially for Devlin Sproat, the ringleader.

After wagering on the outcome Roy Gilbertson peered down the dismal street. "What if she doesn't come?"

Sproat, tall and deceptively indolent, looked smug. "Miss Moore always walks home this way," he said. "I know; I've followed her."

The other two exchanged an uneasy look at this revelation. Devlin hadn't mentioned it before, and somehow it changed things a little. It occurred to both Gilbertson and Keith Moody that this wasn't the spur-of-the-moment idea they'd thought it was, but they quickly brushed their misgivings aside and swallowed the questions that arose in their minds. Both took their cue from Devlin. They admired and looked up to him and took great pains to stay on his good side. Great sport was to be had with Devlin; he had a positive genius for thinking up the most exciting pranks and entertainments, and generally paid for all their amusements. He was the only one with money to spend.

Devlin Sproat came from affluence. His father was one of the most renowned surgeons in Scotland and his mother was from that branch of the Osborne family prominent in steel, so he had wealth and powerful connections behind him. Further, his father was on the Board of the medical school. Gilbertson and Moody, on the other hand, hailed from a working-class background and had neither money nor connections of any kind, and their lives would have been very dull indeed without Sproat's friendship. Therefore, they were quite prepared to agree to all his suggestions, however wild—and Devlin had a rather bizarre side to his nature—even if it occasionally meant bending the school rules or, in the case of that particular evening, breaking them.

"Lud, I almost forgot!" Sproat thumped his chest with a clenched fist and gazed down at his thick wool cloak. "I'd better get rid of this before she spots me wearing it or our plans will be ruined."

With that he dashed inside the Copper Jug and removed the garment and hung it under a pile of similiar garments on the clothes rack, then hurriedly rejoined his companions outside. They all looked at each other and burst out laughing. It was going to be a spiffing lark! All the more exciting since they'd wagered on the outcome, Gilbertson and Moody wondering if Olwyn Moore would fall for Devlin's charm and both inclined to doubt it, even though Devlin was very successful with other women. *This* woman was different. She'd ignored their subtle advances up to now, pretending not to notice. She wasn't easily impressed, as so many other women were, by the fact that they were going to be doctors, possibly because she was fairly well educated herself and had attained a position far above most women, though all three were mystified as to how that had come about, considering she was from the slums.

They viewed Olwyn Moore as an enigma and a challenge. Devlin Sproat was secretly obsessed with the girl, who was as beautiful as she was bright, and determined to win her over and lay weeks and months of frustration to rest, yet he knew he had to be careful. The only reason he'd involved the others was to allay any suspicions Olwyn might have if he approached her alone.

The massive gray bulk of Glasgow with its shipyards, factories, and ever-rumbling mills, loomed all around them. The city lay prostrate on the banks of the River Clyde like a great waterlogged beast mired in the mud, struggling with its last breath to save itself from drowning. It had rained continuously for a month. During the last two days the rain had turned to sleet, the grim hand of winter already upon it. The lung troubles always simmering in the industrialized city now flared up to epidemic proportions, bringing work to a standstill and filling the wards and even the hallways of the Royal Infirmary. Many died, and some of these victims, those without relatives to claim their bodies, ended up in the dissecting rooms of Anderson's Medical College.

Olwyn Moore was not allowed in the dissecting rooms even though she had a great interest in medicine and would have been a nurse—like her heroine, Florence Nightingale—if circumstances hadn't ruined her plans. Now, instead of working with patients or attending lectures, she was employed as a junior clerk in the administration office of the medical school. That in itself lent her status at a time when few women worked outside the home, except as domestics and, just lately, in the factories and mills. There was potential for advancement in her job, in theory. In practice Olwyn had her doubts. She'd quickly realized that it wasn't enough to be capable and intelligent and willing to work hard; other less tangible obstacles could bar her from getting ahead.

"My dear Miss Moore, it's past six o'clock," said a long-suffering voice from across the room, a high-ceilinged room with battered oak cupboards and desks and green-shaded oil lamps. "You still have the Notice Board to clean out before we can leave," the petulant voice continued. "Already I'm going to be late home for supper."

Olwyn felt herself tense. She inhaled deeply and out of long habit fixed a pleasant expression on her face before raising it to the only other woman in the school—the one who had been there first.

"Yes, Miss MacCutcheon," she said. "I'll do it at once."

"Thank you." Enid MacCutcheon was invariably polite, Olwyn had noticed, even when she despised people, and rarely ever raised her voice. But she could infuse into that voice such a chill, such scorn, that she didn't have to raise it. She was the ladylike type who could drip malice with a smile on her face, and frequently did when people failed to come up to her high standards.

Enid lifted her head ever so slightly, peering at the girl from under her brows as Olwyn collected the batch of fresh cards to be tacked onto the notice board in the hallway outside the general office. "Hurry," she said, "if you please."

Everything about the young woman offended Enid's sensibilities; her shapely figure, raven-black hair, but most of all Moore's catlike golden eyes. As she'd told her sister Flora, "I declare she puts men under a spell with those eyes of hers. Why else would Mr. Kerr have hired her, considering her background?"

Flora had patted her hand soothingly. "Never fear, Enid, she can't possibly have a fraction of *your* ability. They'll find that out soon enough. Anyway, you still have the distinction of being the first woman to be hired at the school and no one can take that away from you."

Scant comfort, MacCutcheon brooded, when every man in the school was smitten with the little hussy!

Olwyn was from the Gallowgate, one of the roughest, poorest sections of Glasgow, and her immediate superior never let her forget it for a moment. To the senior clerk, Olwyn was an upstart from the slums, a bold young lady who often forgot her place and thought much of herself just because she had somehow managed to acquire a little education. MacCutcheon let it be known that an invisible gulf yawned between herself and the only other woman in the school; that it pained her to have to work with someone far less refined and genteel than herself. Under the circumstances she couldn't possibly recommend Olwyn Moore for promotion and hadn't in the two years the girl had worked at the school. Enid would have quickly found a way to get rid of Moore but the decision wasn't hers to make, unfortunately, and Mr. Kerr, old sop that he was, certainly wouldn't sack her. Now all she could do was wait and watch and hope the girl would do something serious that would bring her to the attention of the Board. If and when that happened, Mr. Kerr would have no say in the matter and out she would go!

In the hallway outside the office Olwyn opened the glass-fronted notice board and quickly pulled down the old cards, some advertising items for sale, others rooms to rent or vacant jobs. The last were of great interest to the students, most of whom had to work for part of the year to save money to attend school the other half, and when the new listings appeared at the beginning of each month—many advertising part-time work—they were eagerly sought out by the students.

Yet one such job offer had been shunned. It had been sent in two months ago by the Reverend James Scobbie, a local minister, who would shortly be leaving Scotland to take up his new post as a missionary to Nuruzambora in Africa. Scobbie was looking for an assistant to accompany him to Africa; a God-fearing young man with some medical knowledge. In essence his card stated that the candidate for the job should be at least eighteen years old, in sound health, and possess a cheerful willingness to work hard and help others. Then came the part that put everyone off. For the first year of employment the successful candidate would be on probation without pay, though room and board would be provided and his passage out to Africa paid.

Olwyn had overheard one of the students complaining, "It's not a God-fearing young man that Scobbie wants—it's a saint! I ask you, who in his right mind would consider taking a year out of his studies for the privilege of working for nothing, especially in a wilderness like Africa?"

Olwyn turned Scobbie's card over in her hand, thinking that if she had been a male and could have met the other qualifications, which, after all, weren't very stringent, she might have given it a try. She had always yearned to travel, and the thought of Africa conjured up an exotic, if vague, picture in her mind of azure skies and waving palms, of blazing sunsets and mysterious forests where dark-skinned people danced to the beat of weird music pounded out on drums hewn from hollow tree trunks. Every time she glanced at Scobbie's card as she walked past the notice board it fired her imagination, and she couldn't understand why nobody had taken him up on his job offer out of a sense of adventure if nothing else. All the students seemed to care about was setting up fashionable practices and making as much money as possible—

"Moore!" hissed an irritable voice from behind her. "How dare you waste precious time in daydreaming when there's work to be done." Miss MacCutcheon's protuberant eyes glinted spitefully, registering the guilty flush on the girl's cheeks that only emphasized her radiant beauty. "Mr. Kerr shall hear about this in the morning," the senior clerk went on. "And you can expect your wages to be docked accordingly. After all, you aren't paid to stand about with your head in the clouds."

For just a moment the pleasant, long-suffering mask dropped from Olwyn's face as an angry retort rose to her lips at the injustice of it all. The truth was that she worked twice as hard as Enid MacCutcheon! From the time she arrived at work at eight in the morning until she left at six at night, and often later, she never slackened and rarely lifted her head from the work MacCutcheon stacked on her desk. The older woman always went home for an hour at lunch time while she stayed in the office struggling to get through her various tasks—and many of the senior clerk's as well. More and more over the past year she'd inherited her superior's responsibilities, only to have MacCutcheon get the credit for them.

Olwyn's golden eyes flashed with resentment as she faced the older woman. From the time she'd first started at the school two years ago this woman had been hostile to her and had done everything in her power to undermine her in the eyes of Mr. Kerr. Olwyn was suddenly furious and tired of having to hold her tongue, but as she opened her mouth to protest she spied the malicious gleam in the other's eyes and realized that MacCutcheon was eager for a confrontation. Her next words proved it.

"Is there something you would like to say to me, Miss Moore?" Enid asked sweetly.

Olwyn clamped her lips shut and shook her head. Insolence to a superior meant instant dismissal and she was determined not to allow MacCutcheon to goad her into making a rash move that could cost her her job, well aware that it would be almost impossible to find another like it. When she could trust herself to speak Olwyn held out the Reverend Scobbie's card.

"What shall I do with this? It's been posted for two months already and—"

"Discard it," Enid snapped. "It should be obvious to you by now that nobody is interested in the job. Can't you think for yourself, girl?"

"Yes, but Mr. Scobbie is a minister, and out of respect—"

"Get rid of it!" MacCutcheon sniffed. "Scobbie might be a minister but he's a failure just the same. Why else do you imagine he's going to Africa— because the Hottentots are about the only people likely to listen to his sermons," she finished with a brittle laugh that set Olwyn's teeth on edge.

At six-thirty on that chilly Thursday evening in November both women left the building together and walked in silence to the front gates. It was long since dark and the neighborhood lamplighter had tried valiantly to chase the shadows away, but the watery yellow light he left behind had done little to penetrate the gloom or bring cheer to the dripping facades of the nearby buildings, or brighten the path ahead. An incandescent haze hung like a halo around the lamp-post outside the front gate. Beyond, darkness encroached, dismal and faintly menacing.

Miss MacCutcheon only lived two streets away in a pleasant terraced house she shared with her unmarried sister, and there she would sit down to a good hot meal in front of a roaring fire. Olwyn lived in the opposite direction and *her* destination was a tenement boarding house in the Glasgow slums where she shared a dingy little room with two other boarders and could neither look forward to a hot meal, fire, or a welcome of any kind. Her roommates held themselves aloof from her; they worked in the cotton mills and could neither read nor write; Olwyn was educated and spoke like "the nabbery"; therefore in their eyes she was a snob. They shunned her.

On the wet pavement the two women took leave of each other.

"Good evening, Miss Moore."

"Good evening, Miss MacCutcheon."

Olwyn watched the senior clerk march stiff-backed up the street and wondered how she'd ever imagined she could make friends with Enid MacCutcheon, indeed, with any of her ilk. Her father had been wrong in his assertion that education, hard work, and ambition were all that was required to change one's station in life. Olwyn was only eighteen years old but already realized that these things *weren't* enough. Education had only succeeded in distancing her from her own people, and as for the upper classes, they came no closer to accepting her either. They judged people by who they were and where they came from, and to them she was a product of the slums and lacked a pedigree, therefore was beneath their notice. If anything, these people resented her aspirations and were that much more determined to keep her down, where they felt she belonged. Even Mr. Kerr, though kind enough, still treated her in a patronizing manner. If he were ever forced to choose between Enid MacCutcheon and herself, Olwyn had no illusions about which one of them he would support.

"Old frog!" she muttered under her breath as the senior clerk vanished around the corner, and she suddenly hoped the woman would stumble into a puddle on her way home.

Olwyn sped wraithlike through the dark streets, keeping a close watch on every alley and wynd she passed. Now and then she had to leap into a doorway for protection when a coach thundered by, sending up a wave of filthy black spray from the gutter. Her serge mantle had seen countless winters and was now shiny and threadbare and there was a crack in her boots that let in water. Within minutes of leaving the medical school she was drenched, and each gust of wind made her flesh shrivel; it was almost as if she were naked to the elements. There were few pedestrians abroad on such a miserable night and those she passed had their faces buried in the collars of their cloaks, lending them a furtive, vaguely threatening appearance. Once, when Olwyn came upon a brightly lit window, she paused for a moment and glanced inside and saw a large family gathered around the supper table, the mother with her youngest on her knee, the children's voices chiming merrily like bells in the night.

Quite suddenly Olwyn felt desperately lonely, caught in the void between two worlds and unable to enter either. She had never known the comfort and security of a mother's knee since Anna Moore had died at her birth, and her father, Douglas, had been a quiet and undemonstrative man who discouraged outward displays of affection. He had been a printer to trade, a largely self-taught man with a mission, to see to it that his only child found a way out of the Gallowgate and a life of grinding poverty and hopelessness in the slums.

Moore astounded their neighbors by scraping together the money to send his daughter to a church-run school and also paying for elocution lessons to rid her of the "common twang" so prevalent in the Gallowgate. Then, when Olwyn was fourteen years old, he found her a job with a Dr. Gibb and through this man she heard all about the wonderful achievements of Florence Nightingale. When Queen Victoria endorsed Miss Nightingale's work and encouraged her to start a school in London to train others like herself, nursing immediately became a respectable profession. "There's talk of a similiar school starting in Glasgow," Dr. Gibb informed her one day, watching her closely, smiling when he saw the interest leap into her eyes. "As you know, I'll be retiring in a year or two," the elderly doctor continued, "and I'd like to think you have a good job to go to when this one is over, lass. You're a very clever girl," he praised, "and a hard worker, so I'm quite willing to undertake to prepare you to enter this school once it's established."

Olwyn had been thrilled and grateful to the generous doctor. Her future glowed with promise and she eagerly read all the textbooks Dr. Gibb gave her to study, and sat in attentively during his surgeries and accompanied him on his rounds, soaking up all the knowledge and experience she could get.

It all came to naught. One evening when Olwyn returned to her tiny "single end" home in the Gallowgate it was to find the entire building ablaze. Douglas Moore and ten other people died in the fire and they lost everything they had, and there was no question now of Olwyn going to nursing school.

Shortly afterward Dr. Gibb retired, but before he did he put in a good word for Olwyn with his friends at the medical school, and through this she was taken on as a junior clerk under Enid MacCutcheon, who soon made it clear that they could never be friends.

Friends . . . Olwyn turned the word over wistfully in her mind, wondering if she would ever have any and where they would come from. More and more often of late she was painfully conscious of something dreadfully missing in her life. How she longed for shared laughter and light-hearted conversation, for the companionship of people she cared about and who would care about her in return, but in the no-man's-land she trod she was completely alone. Suddenly it terrified her! She couldn't bear to think that it would always be like this, and in desperation asked herself what she could do to remedy the situation. All her attempts up to now had been spurned.

She crossed the street and turned a corner and spied the first of a group of coffee houses and taverns up ahead, bright lights splashing out of their windows to dance gaily in the puddles. Shivering and chilled to the marrow, they seemed so warm and welcoming to the girl, but Olwyn's landlady had warned her about such places, particularly those around the university and medical school. Mrs. Baird maintained they were hotbeds of social and political unrest, patronized by people with brilliant minds but without a shred of plain common sense between the lot of them. Further, women didn't go there on their own.

Olwyn paid no attention to the three figures stand-

ing in the doorway of the Copper Jug, but as she came
abreast of them a voice suddenly cried out, "Oh . . .
Miss Moore! Late tonight, aren't you?"

Olwyn stopped abruptly, peered at them in surprise, and recognized three students from the medical
school, senior students soon to graduate. Her eyes
lingered on the one who had spoken; the one she knew
best, or at least had seen the most. Devlin Sproat often
popped into the administration office for one reason
or another—his father was on the Board, she had
heard, and a friend of Mr. Kerr's—so she supposed
that was the reason. Young Sproat always gave her a
warm smile in passing. Sometimes Olwyn had the
impression that he would have liked to stop and chat,
but of course that was strictly against the rules.

She smiled at the group tentatively.

Sproat walked over and took her arm and drew her
into the shelter of the doorway. "Why, you're
soaked!" he said, gazing down at her mantle. "You'll
catch bronchitis at this rate, or the sickness going
around. What you want is a hot drink to warm you up,
my girl. Doctor's orders!" he finished with a grin.

Gilbertson threw open the door of the Cooper Jug
and waved her inside.

For a second Olwyn hung back, unsure what to do.
It was against the school rules to associate with the
medical students—but they weren't on school property now! Also, she didn't really know these young
men—but how could she get to know them if she
refused their invitation? Thirdly, she was nervous
about entering one of these establishments since she'd
never been in a public eating place in her life—but
there had to be a first time for everything.

Finally . . . she went.

## 2

Once inside, Sproat ignored the tables in the center of the room and led them to one of the more private booths lining either side. When a waiter appeared he ordered coffee for four and a tray of pastries, then smiled at Olwyn, seated directly across the table.

"You must sample the éclairs, Miss Moore," he encouraged. "I trust you like sweet things?"

She had never tasted an éclair in her life, or indeed anything but plain, simple food, but she nodded. "You are very kind."

"Nonsense! Everyone needs a little treat now and then."

The students could see she was awed by her surroundings and very unsure of herself as she glanced around. The coffee house was decorated in bright shades of red, gold, and green, and lit by lamps with glowing stained-glass colors that Olwyn thought quite beautiful. A fire blazed at one end of the room and the place was crowded, bustling with activity, the customers cheerfully chatting animatedly together or debating this topic or that with vigor and enthusiasm. Laughter rang out again and again.

While she examined the interior of the coffee house the three students examined Olwyn just as avidly, admiring at close range her shining black hair, the delicate perfection of her features, and the long, alluring eyes that sparkled like liquid gold in the lamplight, crystal droplets of rain trembling on her lashes.

Behind her back Sproat winked at his friends and held up two fingers in a victory sign as if to say, "The battle is already half won," and such was his confidence in himself that he firmly believed it. Nothing in his experience with women prepared him for defeat, and this one, he could see, was more innocent than most. He began to get very excited, anticipating the delights ahead.

To draw her out he said, "How can you abide working for old biddy MacCutcheon?" And before Olwyn could answer he went on, "Do you know what the students call the pair of you? Beauty and the Beast!"

The early part of the evening passed in a pleasant haze for Olwyn. Sproat plied her with coffee and cakes and all three stimulated her with amusing conversation; above all they made her laugh. Soon she thawed out and realized that she was having a wonderful time—the best in her life—and began to hope they could continue to meet now and then in the warmth and brightness of the coffee house. Next time, she told herself, she wouldn't be so awkward and nervous.

When it came time to leave Devlin Sproat announced that he would walk her home. "But first I'll have to pop back to my rooms for a cloak," he told her. "It's not far from here; just around the corner."

They parted from the others outside the Copper Jug. Olwyn shook hands with them gravely and thanked them for a lovely evening.

"The pleasure is ours," drawled Moody, and flicked a meaningful glance at Devlin Sproat.

As it turned out, Devlin lived not "around the corner" but three blocks away in one of the better old buildings in the neighborhood, and he had three whole rooms to himself, which astonished Olwyn. She and her father had lived in one small room and counted themselves lucky to have such space since most of their neighbors in the Gallowgate had lived eight and ten to a room, with most of them forced to sleep on the floor.

Devlin's flat was spacious, too, and in Olwyn's eyes, very well furnished, if a little untidy. The first thing she spied when he waved her into the sitting room was the enormous amount of books lying about, so many they overflowed the bookcases and lay piled up on the floor. At the sight of them Olwyn exclaimed in delight, for she loved to read and here was a veritable feast spread out before her eyes.

"Help yourself to whatever you fancy," Sproat offered casually before ducking into the nearby bedroom for his cloak, or pretending to.

Olwyn threw off her mantle with a feeling of relish and knelt down on the floor in front of the nearest stack, many beautifully bound in leather and with protective brass edges. She shook her head in wonder that anyone could treat such expensive possessions so carelessly, leaving them scattered about the carpet where they could be trodden on or kicked accidentally. Now, if *she* owned such an extensive library . . .

Devlin glided silently back into the archway between the foyer and sitting room and stood watching the girl for a moment or two as Olwyn picked up one book after the other, virtually caressing the engraved bindings with a slim white hand. He shivered and moistened his lips, imagining how those hands might feel caressing *him*; something he'd dreamed about for months now, lurid dreams that excited and tortured him through the long dark hours of the night.

Yet he was a little anxious. It was one thing to have a

fling with a girl of this type when there was no chance
of his father finding out about it, but quite another
when the girl worked at the school itself; what if she
boasted that she was having an affair with the son of
one of the Directors? Women were terrible gossips;
they couldn't keep a thing like that to themselves.

It never occurred to Sproat that Olwyn might reject
him. He was rich, well connected, and handsome, and
had always had great success with women. He was a
young man given to sudden, intense passions; love
and hate burned in him with equal fervor. Devlin
usually got what he wanted, and now that the girl was
here, in the privacy of his rooms at last—

Suddenly he was behind her, sinking to his knees on
the floor, his arms sweeping around her to draw her
close to him. The feel of her inflamed his long-
thwarted desire and immediately his body was hard
and eager, his senses pounding for release.

"If you only knew how much I've yearned to see
you alone!" he confessed breathlessly. "All those
excuses I made to go into your office . . . surely you
must have guessed why? Oh, Olwyn, dearest, tell me
you feel the same? Tell me!"

Olwyn went rigid with shock. The book she'd been
holding slipped from her grasp, the pages fluttering,
but not nearly as much as her heart.

With a sweating hand Devlin turned her face to his
and his greedy mouth was on her lips, his tongue
probing and thrusting. Even then, somewhere at the
back of his mind he *knew* he was being a little hasty, a
mite overwhelming, but he just couldn't seem to
restrain himself. She was so lovely and fresh and felt
so soft and warm in his arms that it made him go a
little mad.

He swept her back on the floor and leaned over her,
his face terribly flushed and his eyes glittering. He
kissed her again and again with mounting urgency, his
teeth nibbling and his tongue lapping her smooth
cheeks and ears, nuzzling her hair and the silky skin of
her throat while his free hand shuddered down the

tempting curves of her body. "Nobody need ever know about us," he babbled. "I'm a doctor, or soon will be, so if anything happens—you know—I can take care of you myself."

Before she guessed what he was about, Sproat wrenched her skirt up over her thighs, quickly freed himself, and fell throbbing upon her, encouraged that she hadn't uttered a word of protest or made a move to stop him.

Olwyn couldn't. She was paralyzed with fear, stupefied that the considerate young gentleman of such a short time ago had by some hideous metamorphosis changed into a beast with a scarlet, lust-contorted face and a body that kept butting her, animal-like, while at the same time his hand pushed at her roughly as he tried to force her legs apart. She was petrified. Sproat was like a different person and the change in him chilled her.

"You'll see . . . how good it feels," he gasped, and something fiery and rigid pushed hard against her thigh—and finally the ice encasing her mind and limbs shattered. Olwyn jerked away from him as if she'd been burned, the sudden movement upsetting his balance. She tried desperately to get to her feet but Sproat lunged and caught her and hauled her back into his arms where he stared down at her in surprise and resentment. Her golden eyes were filled with loathing and disgust. "Leave me be!" she cried, trying to wriggle free. "Have you gone off your head, Devlin Sproat?"

Her words and expression stung him to the quick. Never had a woman looked at him like that before. For a second Devlin considered arguing with her, trying to coax her, but something in her eyes told him it wouldn't work. Instead, he crushed her mouth under a brutal kiss and told himself that she had led him on and now must take the consequences. She was nothing but a teasing little slut!

A violent struggle ensued, and the stacks of books tumbled all about them. In desperation Olwyn seized one of them, a heavy volume of poetry with wicked brass tips put there to protect the expensive bindings. With all her strength she swung it back over her head. Sproat saw the danger at the very last minute and pulled back, but too late. It struck him a crashing blow on the forehead that rocked him back on his heels, where he teetered for a moment, then slumped sideways onto the floor.

The room went deadly quiet, the only sound Olwyn's harried breathing. There was an instant when nothing moved, then, sobbing, she sprang to her feet and scooped up her mantle and flew to the door, her only desire to get away, to escape the clutches of this weird creature who had once been Devlin Sproat and who had changed into a satyr before her very eyes. She was almost sick with terror.

Olwyn wrenched the door open and was on the point of making her escape when she heard a loud groan from behind her. She froze, her heart thudding so fiercely it threatened to suffocate her. Very slowly she turned around and glanced back at him. He hadn't stirred, but it was then that she noticed the blood trickling down his face, dripping off the end of his nose onto the carpet. Her heart gave a mighty leap of horror. She had wounded him badly! Perhaps he was dying! With that thought the grim specter of a gallows surfaced in her mind with herself swinging at the end of a rope, not a single soul about to mark her passing.

She trembled in a paroxysm of indecision—when Sproat moaned again, this time even louder. Pressing a fist to her mouth Olwyn walked back and stood gazing down at him, knowing she had to try to help him yet loath to touch him in any way.

Sproat's hand shot out and gripped her ankle.

She screamed, the blood draining from her face. Devlin exploded in a burst of hysterical laughter that was even more chilling than his silence had been. Still keeping a firm hold on her, he rolled over onto his back and lay grinning up at her, his eyes gleaming with triumph.

"Do you know what they do to women like you who dare attack a gentleman?" he asked her, and when she didn't reply, "They throw them into prison and leave them to rot there, but first, I've heard, the jailors have their fun with them. They say they're a filthy, debauched crew," he informed her with relish.

His smile broadened when he saw she was terrified.

"They especially enjoy comely young women like you, Miss Moore."

Frightened as she was, his gloating smile enraged Olwyn. "You forced me to strike you," she defended herself. "You behaved like a—a despicable beast!"

"Rubbish!" he sneered, and now he gazed up at her haughtily. "*My* deportment has never been in question, I assure you. Perhaps I should refresh your memory." He gave her a cold stare and went on, "I was good enough to treat you to a pleasant evening, which is more than most gentlemen would have done for a girl of your sort, and I even offered to escort you safely home afterward. Remember, if you will, that I didn't force you to come up here, now did I?"

Olwyn opened her mouth, then closed it again.

"Then, once you were in my rooms you tried to rob me when my back was turned; and when I caught you in the act you attacked me—"

"That's a lie!" Olwyn cried. "I did no such thing!"

Sproat laughed softly, propping himself up on an elbow. "Ah . . . but I imagine the police will take my word over yours. Besides, Gilbertson and Moody will back me up. Who do you have to stand up for you?"

A crafty look came into his eyes and with his free hand he began to caress her leg, running his fingers up to her knee, then her thigh.

"I can always change my mind about reporting you to the police," he said, his voice thickening. "I think you know how to persuade me if you try hard enough."

"You're wicked! Evil!" Olwyn screamed at him, and wrenched her foot free. She ran to the door with Sproat's threat ringing in her ears. "By tomorrow you'll be behind bars, you silly little fool. I won't rest until you're put away!"

The sleet was still falling outside when Olwyn ran from the building, and it was bitterly cold. A thin film of ice had formed on the pavement and she slid in her haste to get away, almost losing her balance, grazing her hand on a stone wall as she flailed wildly to save herself from falling. She hardly felt it, momentarily buoyed up with fury as she was. What a fool she had been to trust Devlin Sproat and his friends! Sproat had only been nice to her for a reason; a vile reason. To think he'd imagined she would willingly fall in with his plans! Had he expected her to feel honored at being singled out for his attentions? she wondered angrily. She a poor girl from the Gallowgate and he a fine gentleman from one of the best families in Glasgow!

All too soon her fury ebbed as grim reality set in.

Olwyn knew she was in terrible trouble. Sproat really *could* have her put in prison. Gilbertson and Moody would back up his lies and Sproat's influential family had powerful connections all over Scotland. How could she hope to stand up and defend herself successfully against such people? It was pointless to even try.

What was she going to do? The obvious answer was to get away from Glasgow before they came to arrest her, perhaps even away from Scotland itself! And she had to leave tonight, her mind rushed on, since it was dangerous to tarry.

Her entire savings amounted to a little under three pounds, a sum that certainly wouldn't take her very far or keep her for very long either, and how could she expect to find another job without a character reference from her present one?

Overwhelmed by the desperate predicament she was in, Olwyn stumbled into a dark close and sat down on a doorstep and put her head in her hands. Those hands were blue and numb with the cold, the bleeding cut on her wrist congealed and frozen over.

Her teeth chattered uncontrollably, and never had winter seemed so bleak or her future so grim. Perhaps the best thing she could do, she sobbed, was to lie down in the wet road and stay there until she froze to death. Nobody would even mourn her.

Self-pity only lasted a moment or two. There was a spark in Olwyn that refused to give up, that kept telling her that she *did* have a bright future ahead of her, that someday, somewhere, she would achieve the success that her father had always evisioned for her, aye, and even more important, love and happiness too.

She took her hands away from her face and sat up alertly. Think! she prodded herself. There had to be some means of escape, to get far enough away from Glasgow that the Sproats couldn't find her . . .

Had she only been a male, she mused, she might have applied for the job with the Reverend James Scobbie. It wasn't so far-fetched, Olwyn reasoned. She was the right age and even had a little medical knowledge through working for Dr. Gibb and studying the textbooks he had given her, and as far as she knew Scobbie still hadn't found anyone to fill the post. Africa was certainly far enough away! She had to smile a little at that. The authorities wouldn't search all that distance to find her, not for the Sproats or the Queen herself!

If she'd only been born a boy.

$$\diamond \quad 3 \quad \diamond$$

The *Randolph,* bound for Cape Town, left London on November fourteenth. It was a relatively new vessel of close to two thousand tons, its modern screw-propelled engines fueled with good British coal, the belching funnels mingling with the pall of smoke always hanging over London.

Two days after embarking most of the passengers crowded the main deck to take their last faint look at their island home, now just a darker blue line astern against the lighter blue of the sea. Many raised brimming glasses in a toast of farewell, gulped the contents, and threw them overboard, and others wept openly, vowing that one day they would return.

Amid the other passengers a tense little party of five stood at the ship's rail. This group included the Reverend James Scobbie, his wife Hannah and two young sons, and Scobbie's medical assistant, Oliver.

Hannah Scobbie was devastated at leaving home and far from enthusiastic about what lay in store for them in Africa.

"I shan't see Scotland again," she predicted morbidly, her plump face mottled with weeping. "Oh dear"—she pressed a hand to her heart and turned mournful eyes on her husband—"I must sit down at once or I fear I shall swoon."

"Oliver!" Scobbie motioned his helper forward and together they assisted his wife to the nearest bench, where she slumped down dejectedly and commenced taking great gulps of the chilly sea air until a little color returned to her cheeks. Oliver in particular watched her anxiously, wondering if the first medical crisis was about to erupt so soon, and quailing inwardly at the thought of it.

Hannah Scobbie *would* have swooned if she'd known that her husband's new employee was a wanted person—and not a lad at all! Far from being sad at leaving home, Olwyn felt overwhelmingly relieved to get away. Only now, with the island of Britain swallowed up in the sea mist, did she feel really safe. Devlin Sproat couldn't touch her and the authorities couldn't reach her. She was free!

The past two weeks had sped by in a whirl of activity. From the moment the idea of turning herself into a male had popped into her mind, Olwyn hadn't hesitated. To hesitate was to invite cowardice. Once the decision was made on that freezing Thursday evening after she left Devlin Sproat's rooms, Olwyn rushed home and threw her few belongings into a burlap sack, retrieved her savings from a hiding place under a loose floor board, and spent the rest of the night in a derelict warehouse, her only companions a stray dog and whole family of curious rats. Up at dawn the following morning, she paid a visit to the local rag-picker the moment his shop door was opened, and there she purchased the necessary masculine attire. With that done she hacked off her waist-long hair, crying a little as the silken tresses fell softly about her feet and, once dressed for the part, boldly presented herself at Scobbie's church door before she could lose her nerve altogether.

The minister turned out to be a plain, direct sort of man without affectation or pretensions of any kind, and that had helped greatly. Though he spoke well enough, his voice had the rough burr of the Glasgow Olwyn knew best, and somehow that eased her too. He was in his late thirties, on the short side, with close-cropped brown hair and small hazel eyes and features that could only be described as lumpy. To Olwyn he looked more like a dock worker than a vicar, especially when he opened the door to her in his shirt sleeves, his clerical collar conspicuously missing.

Naturally, he'd been taken aback to find her standing on his doorstep since they'd had no prior contact of any kind, but he'd invited her into his dusty manse behind his mean little church and there proceeded to interview her. By then Olwyn had passed beyond the stage of overt nervousness to a plateau of cold, brittle calm, a curious state where her entire being was concentrated on only one thing—getting the job. She was from Edinburgh, she informed Scobbie, and had worked there under a doctor while preparing to enter medical school, only to have to abandon her plans through lack of funds.

"And how did you hear about me all the way over in Edinburgh, lad?" the minister asked her curiously.

Olwyn had been prepared for the question.

"I happened to be in a coffee house one evening and got into conversation with some students from Glasgow," she replied. "They mentioned you, Mr. Scobbie, and told me about the job. Is it"—here she'd gulped—"still available?"

He nodded, eyeing her quizzically, his first impression that she was rather small and slight for a youth of eighteen, though a fine-looking boy in a somewhat effeminate way, with brilliant amber eyes that his tabby-cat might have envied. From the state of her attire he could well believe that she was lacking funds, and felt a touch of sympathy, always having been short of money himself. Leaning forward over his desk he queried, "And what of your family, Master

Moore? What do they think of this notion you have of going to Africa?"

"I'm an orphan, sir," Olwyn replied politely, "so I've no one but myself to consider."

Scobbie reassessed her and began to like what he saw. She was very courteous, well spoken, and looked one straight in the eye, but before he put off any more time in discussing it he decided he might as well be blunt, and it was at this juncture that all the other candidates had gotten up to leave.

"I won't be able to pay you anything for at least the first year," he told her. "You see, the Free Missionary Society doesn't budget for medical assistants for their missionaries." He paused and smiled thinly. "They seem to feel we can manage quite well muddling by on our own, and many do, mind you, but I'm not prepared to risk it since I'll have Mrs. Scobbie and the children with me in Africa."

Olwyn nodded. "Yes, I understand."

He peered at her. "You're still interested?"

"Yes, Mr. Scobbie, I am." It was at that point that Olwyn began to feel really hopeful, and she could hardly contain her excitement.

His homely face broke into a vast smile. "That's fine, then, Oliver. It's heartening to know that some people aren't motivated by money. Now, there's just one more thing . . ."

The "one more thing" almost proved her undoing. Scobbie pawed about in a desk drawer and brought out some tests. At the sight of them Olwyn blanched and her hopes disintegrated. She almost burst into tears.

"Just do the best you can, lad," the minister instructed kindly, catching sight of the dismay on her face. "I understand that you've had no formal training and don't expect perfect marks."

Perfect marks! Olwyn doubted that she'd gotten a quarter of those questions right—yet James Scobbie had hired her! Of course no one else wanted the job and by then he was desperate, with only two weeks remaining until he had to leave, so he had taken her on. She had been ecstatic, and still was.

Olwyn had gotten to know Scobbie a little during the two weeks prior to their departure, while she helped with all the preparations for their move. It was patently obvious to the girl that the minister had married out of his class. The son of a poor farmer—one of ten children—James had married the daughter of a mine owner, once upon a time a working man himself, but Harold Ramsay had quickly risen in the world to the point where he had bought the mine he once labored in as a youth, and now lived in a large house in the Bearsden area of Glasgow in the rarefied atmosphere of the gentry. Though Mrs. Ramsay and her son and daughters visited the manse in the time leading up to departure, Mr. Ramsay didn't show his face. Olwyn sensed that Ramsay and his son-in-law didn't get on, and from things that were said she gleaned that Ramsay was very much against James becoming a missionary and taking his daughter and grandchildren away to Africa.

Where James was forthright and outgoing, his wife was quiet and reserved. Hannah Scobbie was as tall as her husband, and inclined to be plump, with soft fair hair and round blue eyes that filled with tears constantly during the two weeks leading up to their leave-taking. Young Harold took after his mother's side of the family. He was a very handsome lad and exceptionally tall for his thirteen years and quite unlike his little brother Jamie, who favored his Papa's lineage. Once or twice, while at the manse, Olwyn had turned to find Harold watching her with a certain disdain and superiority on his face, as if to say that he wasn't at all impressed with his father's puny assistant who was little taller than he was for all that Oliver was eighteen years old.

At that time Olwyn was more concerned about her new job and what lay ahead for them in Africa than in the faint hint of animosity she felt coming from

Harold—or Hal as he was called—though this was to cause her problems later.

Their first port of call would be Cape Town, James informed her, and there they would stay for about a month to recuperate from the long sea voyage and make arrangements for the trip into the interior. Their final destination was Nuruzambora, six hundred miles northeast of the Cape, where the mission station was already established.

"Basil Erskine and Robert Sloan were sent out there two years ago," said James as they were packing books into wooden crates in his study, "so the groundwork has already been done for us." He frowned and pursed his lips, confiding, "Unfortunately, the Society has reason to be dissatisfied with Sloan and Erskine, hence the reason they are sending me out to join them. You see, they are supposed to send regular reports home to the Directors, and both men are very remiss in their duty. Sometimes many months go by without word from them, and even when they do write the information they include is sparse."

Scobbie waved to an official-looking document on his desk.

"That's a letter from the Society; I'm to carry it to them personally so they can't claim they never received it," he went on soberly. "I gather they are being severely reprimanded for their negligence—as well they should be! After all, the Society pays their wages and sponsors them, so it's the least they can do to keep in touch. As it is, we hardly know much more about Nuruzambora now than we did before they were sent there; it's very annoying and not much help to us."

Scobbie broke off and glanced at his study door, which was closed, and added in a low voice, "Don't mention any of this to Mrs. Scobbie. She's a dreadful worrier and upset enough as it is."

Hannah might have come from a privileged background, thought Olwyn, but it didn't take her long to realize that their present mode of living was quite poor. The manse was shabbily furnished and, cold as it was outside, they rarely had a fire in the grate. The only hospitality she was offered in their home was a simple cup of tea, and Olwyn could see that this embarrassed Hannah, who had obviously come down in the world through marrying James.

Snow started to fall a few days before they left Glasgow to board ship in London. When she went to the manse, as she did every afternoon, Olwyn found the house as cold as a tomb. James was standing at his study window bundled up in an old tweed cape and with a woolen muffler about his neck. By then, hiding out in the tumbledown warehouse, Olwyn too had a miserable cold.

Glowering at the weather on the other side of the window, James said, "Just think, Oliver, soon we'll wake up every morning to sunshine and heat! For breakfast we can pluck the ripe fruit off the trees and hunt all the meat we want for supper. And Oliver, we will tread land where white men have never trod before, and there will be no one to tell us what we can or cannot do, or where we can or cannot go. Isn't that a stirring prospect?"

"Oh yes, Mr. Scobbie!" She smiled. "It does sound grand."

James sighed and hunched his shoulders. "I love Scotland in many ways, Oliver, but I think I'll love it even more from a distance. Say what you like, it's inhibiting here. The common man just can't make headway at all. Class distinction is the curse that will eventually bring Britain low, make no mistake about that! In Africa we'll have none of that nonsense to hinder us."

When she left the manse that afternoon Olwyn took a good hard look at Scobbie's church, and a mean little church it was, the gray granite stones black with grime and spattered with pigeon droppings, huddled forlornly between two towering tenements dominating it from either side. It was in the Gorbals, every bit as wretched and poor as the Gallowgate. Gazing back at it, Olwyn could well understand why Scobbie sought new, hopefully more salubrious pastures to preach in. He seemed almost as desperate to leave as she was.

Now they were safely away and Britain had vanished behind them. That part of her life belonged in the past and Olwyn looked forward enthusiastically to the future. She'd signed on with the missionary for a year. When that time was up James had promised to review her performance and, if possible, start paying for her services. She was satisfied. In fact, delighted. Her only concern now was to keep in mind who she was supposed to be—*Oliver* Moore! It meant pitching her naturally husky voice even lower. She had to take care not to say or do something typically feminine, and made a point of studying other males closely, observing their habits and mannerisms, then trying to copy them. In lots of ways it was highly amusing, like acting out a role in a play, though she could never let down her guard for a moment except in bed at night, where she would lie smiling to herself in the dark, feeling quite proud of the way she had carried it off, her confidence in herself soaring.

The only immediate problem Olwyn had to contend with were the sleeping arrangements on board ship. With the *Randolph* being a fairly new vessel the cabins even in steerage class were clean and modern, if spare, furnished with two bunks separated by a small oak chest on which sat a metal pitcher and bowl for one's toilet. A curtained recess at one end of the room provided some privacy for bathing purposes, and the rail above could also be used for hanging clothes, with space below for storing on-board luggage.

Hannah and James had a cabin to themselves but Olwyn had to share hers with the two boys, with them in one bunk and herself in the other.

Their first night on the *Randolph* was very difficult for Olwyn.

Both boys threw off their clothes and pulled on nightshirts and jumped into bed, Jamie to fall asleep at once, but Harold propped himself up on an elbow and lay watching Olwyn inquisitively.

She lay down fully clothed on her own bunk and picked up a textbook given to her years ago by Dr. Gibb. Olwyn could feel the boy staring at her.

Finally he said, "Aren't you going to get undressed, Oliver?"

"Later. I have studying to do."

"Oh, I shouldn't bother about that," Harold said airily. "I wouldn't touch a book if I didn't have to; I hate reading. When I found out we were going to Africa I thought I wouldn't have to ever again, but old preaching Papa arranged for me to have lessons even while we're away, which is just like him."

Olwyn turned shocked eyes on the boy, amazed at the disrespectful way he'd referred to his father. Hal just laughed. "Well, he *does* preach a lot and he *is* my Papa, so what's wrong with putting the two things together?"

"It's not very nice, Harold."

His clear blue eyes, so like his mother's, looked her up and down.

"You know, I was rather hoping you'd be a big, jolly sort of chap, not a bookworm!" he said with a touch of contempt in his voice. "Look at this"—he raised his arm and flexed his muscles proudly—"I'm younger than you are but I'm much stronger. I always beat everyone else at sports at Murchison, where I went to school," he explained. "I especially like boxing. My grandfather Ramsay taught me all about it; we're very close, you see. He feels that every boy should know how to defend himself." He eyed her consideringly, then added, "Perhaps some day *we* can have a go. Are you game, Oliver?"

Olwyn felt a touch of uneasiness. Young as he was,

Harold Scobbie was already aggressively male, the type anxious to prove it at every opportunity.

"Oh, I doubt your father would like that," Olwyn replied as casually as she could.

He gave her a smug look, as if he felt her disquietude for all that Olwyn tried to hide it, but he said no more on the subject and to her relief lay down to sleep. She glanced at him from the corner of her eye and saw that he looked like an angel now, more beautiful than the homely little brother curled up behind him, his chestnut curls rumpled and his smooth cheeks as rosy as a milkmaid's. His appearance was deceptive. Olwyn made a note to herself to be extra careful with Hal and, if possible, to try to win him over. She was very anxious to have good relations with all the Scobbies since they would all be living so close to each other at Nuruzambora.

Cautiously she rose from her bunk, carried her nightshirt into the alcove, and quietly drew the curtain. In near darkness she undressed and loosened the bandages wrapped tightly around her breasts to flatten them. Once they were off Olwyn stretched and sighed in relief and wondered idly when she could be a woman again. Not for at least a year, certainly; as long as she worked for James Scobbie.

She bathed quickly, pausing now and then to listen for movement in the outer room, then hastily pulled the nightshirt over her head and tip-toed back to bed and doused the lamp. Olwyn smiled to herself in the darkness and gave herself a mental pat on the back at how cleverly she had pulled everything off, though she was a little ashamed at having had to lie to Mr. Scobbie—not that she'd had much choice.

She was up well before the children in the morning, and this became her usual routine while aboard ship. It all worked out very well, or had so far.

A week after they embarked trouble broke out between Harold and his father. Olwyn was soon to learn that this was nothing new. The teenager was outgoing and adventurous and, as little Jamie remarked drolly, "Hal speaks to everybody."

That night he was an hour late for supper and his parents had been very worried. "From now on I want everybody back in their cabin by six o'clock," said James, after treating his oldest son to a stern lecture. "This ship has over a thousand passengers, people from all walks of life, and we have to be wary of who we associate with. After dark it's like a floating Sodom and Gomorrah," he continued darkly, "with drinking, dicing, and all manner of wicked things going on." He shook his head and sighed. "It would fair burst your heart to observe how they cavort and engage in sinful pleasures without giving a thought to the accounting that must come later when He"—here James nodded to the ceiling—"brings them to Judgment. I think it's about time I passed the pamphlets out; then they can't say they haven't been warned." He glanced at Olwyn. "You can help me, Oliver."

Later, in their own cabin, Harold grumbled, "My father's an old grouch. He spoils all the fun. Yes, and he makes an idiot of himself, too, passing out his silly pamphlets—"

"What pamphlets?" Olwyn interrupted, remembering James saying that she had to help him with this task.

"Oh, just a lot of silly religious rot," the boy replied irritably. "My grandpa Ramsay used to call them Hell Fire and Brimstone trash, warning people about the horrible things that would happen to them if they didn't mend their sinful ways and follow Christ instead of Satan; that sort of thing." His face flushed with resentment as he went on, "Papa embarrassed the family by handing them out in the street and outside taverns and music halls. Sometimes people laughed at him and threw things." He shuddered. "It was awful!"

Suddenly his face cleared and he laughed. "He

wants *you* to help him! What a hoot that will be!" he choked, hugging himself and rocking back and forth with mirth. "I'm just glad he didn't ask me, for I'd have refused, yes, even if it meant a beating. What are you going to do now, Oliver?"

What *could* she do but agree? Mr. Scobbie was her boss, and though she'd been hired as his medical assistant, still . . . she could hardly refuse, considering all Scobbie had done for her.

They began making their rounds of what James called the "pleasure pits" the very next evening, bundles of religious tracts tucked under their arms, Scobbie resolute and quite cheery and Olwyn pale and diffident, but determined to do the best she could, bolstering herself by thinking that she'd had to do far more trying and difficult things in her life and managed to pull them off quite well.

They chose the steerage tavern first. Before they entered James caught her arm. "Now here's our chance to get to know a lot of the passengers," he said. "Many of them live in Africa and are returning there after a visit home, so always ask where they're from, Oliver. With so many people on board there are bound to be some from near Nuruzambora. Find out all you can about the area. It could prove to be helpful."

She nodded. "I'll do my best."

"Good lad!" He slapped her on the back. "You work the left side of the tavern and I'll take the right. God grant you success!"

With that Scobbie boldly entered the noisy tavern, Olwyn trailing behind, her eyes immediately blurring and watering in the smoky atmosphere reeking with alcohol fumes. The place was packed with roistering customers who didn't take kindly to being reminded of their shortcomings, as the girl quickly found out. One enormously fat lady in a bright red dress mistook Olwyn for a gypsy lad and was most annoyed to be handed a gospel pamphlet instead of having her fortune told, and cuffed her on the ear, grumbling, "Who are you to tell me I'm a sinner? I'll not be preached to by a tinker's whelp half my age!"

"Gan awa wi' ye!" cried a drunken Scot when Olwyn pressed a tract into his hand. "We want nae Bible-bashers here. Get oot afore a hurl ye overboard tae the sharks!"

James fared considerably better, but then he was the one wearing the clerical collar. Besides, he was older, thicker-skinned, and more experienced. Most of them, if grudgingly, accorded him some respect, and quite a few engaged him in conversation, which was what he had hoped for.

They spent an hour in the tavern, one of the longest in Olwyn's life.

"Splendid, wasn't it, Oliver?" James smiled when they met again outside. "Oh, it's downright astonishing the wonderful people you meet when engaged in the Lord's business. I spoke to people from Natal, Port Elizabeth, and even a tiny place called Hopetown," he told her enthusiastically. "Hopetown isn't so very far away from where we are going, lad."

Then he announced that their next stop was the Gull, the tavern in the first-class section of the *Randolph*. Olwyn's heart sank. In desperate hope of dissuading him she said, "But . . . are you sure we're *allowed* in first class?"

"Och, aye, laddie, never fear." James grinned at her, guessing how she felt, and broke into the broad Scots dialect that he often used when his wife wasn't about, and which he knew usually brought a smile to Olwyn's lips.

He draped an arm about her shoulders and peered into her doubtful face, saying encouragingly, "I'd expect the folks in the Gull to be a mite more polite and considerate than the rabble in there"—with a nod to the Beacon, "and as for being allowed in, well . . ." he touched his collar, "my badge of office works wonders. Few would dare to stand in the way of an emissary of the Lord."

The Gull was three times the size of the tavern they had just left and ten times more elegant. The rich oiled-walnut wainscotting glowed, the plentiful brass shone, and there were fine paintings of ships and hunting scenes on the walls. The customers, too, were better attired, Olwyn noticed as she took a quick glance around, once they opened the door, and she could see no women in this room at all. But the Gull shared a few things with the other watering hole. It, too, was dimly lit and smoky and almost as noisy, with a crowd of men standing four deep around the bar. James waved her to that side of the room and struck off in the other direction. Olwyn could see that he was enjoying himself, never happier than when acting as spokesman for Christ.

Left standing alone, she inhaled staunchly and squared her shoulders and pulled her old cloth cap down over one eye, which she felt gave her a rakish appearance, a devil-may-care look that she was far from feeling, but at that point she needed all the confidence she could get. That done she strode up to the nearest table on her route to the bar, where an elderly gentleman was sitting alone and looking somewhat glum, and greeted him briskly. "Good evening to you, sir! Be kind enough to accept this little token of goodwill."

Olwyn set the pamphlet beside his wineglass on the table.

The old fellow, a portly gent with curling white whiskers, looked at the tract, then up at Olwyn, squinting the better to see her in the gloom.

"Eh . . . what's this, boy?" he barked, cocking his right ear at her. "Confound it, I cannot hear you in all this din. Sit down, sit down"—he waved to the vacant chairs around his table—"and tell me what the deuce you are talking about."

Olwyn hesitated, then sat down, thinking that this was much better, that Scobbie was right when he surmised the customers in the Gull would be more polite. As James had instructed, she smiled brightly and immediately tried to draw the man into conversation. "Are you going out to Africa for a visit, sir?"

He leaned closer, and Olwyn realized that he was hard of hearing. "A visit, d'you say?" And when she nodded, "No, no, I live there. Cape Town."

He picked up the tract and took his eyeglass from his vest pocket and read the caption. "Repent or Perish. Blessed is the transgressor who forswears his evil ways and casts off the yoke of Satan . . ."

Olwyn flushed and took a quick, surreptitious look around, wondering if anyone was listening. While the elderly gentleman looked frail, he had a surprisingly strong voice, and Olwyn saw a few heads turn in their direction. Though she knew it was wrong, she couldn't help feeling embarrassed, and for a moment was sorry she'd sat down at all.

Shortly she changed her mind. Though he seemed gruff and unfriendly, the old man—Mr. Wainwright, he introduced himself—turned out to be quite pleasant, and, she thought, rather lonely. He asked her lots of questions and when he discovered she worked for a missionary bound for Nuruzambora his bushy brows shot up and he turned in his chair until he was facing the bar.

"D'you see that big fellow yonder?" Wainwright jabbed a finger at a tall, golden-haired man lounging against the bar, his back to them. "That's the chap you ought to speak to," he said. "Name's Wentworth. Got a place on the Cape. But he also runs a trading post in Teragno," and at Olwyn's blank look he explained, "That's quite close to Nuruzambora, not more than a few miles away. I've heard him mention the name at the Club." Mr. Wainwright tugged at his whiskers and smiled. "Wentworth has some rare stories about the interior. Keeps one on the edge of one's seat. I'd have a word with him if I were you."

Olwyn thanked the old man and rose and glanced around for Mr. Scobbie, eager to tell him about Wentworth and sure James would like to speak to him himself, but at that moment he was otherwise engaged on the opposite side of the room, holding forth with a large group of men around a table. Olwyn shrugged and decided to approach Wentworth herself, bolstered as she was with her success with Mr. Wainwright, who had turned out to be most cordial.

She walked up to the bar confidently, her tracts in her hand. The trader was with several friends, all with brimming tankards in their hands, and some of them, she could tell from their flushed faces and loud, boisterous laughter, were slightly worse for wear with what Scobbie called "demon drink." Olwyn had to push her way past them to reach Wentworth, whom she greeted by name. When he didn't hear her in all the noise going on about them she touched his arm, saying in a louder tone, "Sir, may I have a moment of your time?"

The big man swung around, frowning, and peered down at her as if she'd been a troublesome insect bent on annoying him, and a daunting sight he was. Gazing up at him, Olwyn was reminded of the pictures she'd once seen in a Glasgow museum depicting the barbarous Norsemen who long ago had attacked the coast of Scotland, raping, pillaging, and reducing her countrymen to slaves. In the paintings they too had been exceptionally tall and broad, with the same darkly tanned skin and flowing golden hair, and fierce blue eyes that were hard and penetrating. The Norsemen might have been this man's ancestors, she thought uneasily, and probably were.

"What do you want?" His voice was deep and curt—but at least he was Scottish.

Flustered, and wishing now that she'd waited for Scobbie, Olwyn thrust a pamphlet into his hand, babbling, "Please accept . . . this is a little token of—it's a religious message, sir," she finished in a rush.

He stared at her, his razor-sharp eyes raking over her meager figure clad in a shabby jacket and breeches that were shiny with wear, at her raggedly chopped black hair tied back with a string, and the jaunty cloth cap pulled down over one eye, and a distinctly feline eye it was, bright and inquisitive. To Justin Wentworth she looked cocky and wise, like a street urchin, and he couldn't imagine how such a scamp had been permitted to enter the Gull.

One of his tipsy friends tapped Olwyn on the arm. "What are you touting, boy? Let's have a look."

Turning to the heavy-set man who had spoken, Olwyn nervously handed him one of her pamphlets and, when other hands shot out, gave the rest of them one too. They were all around her now with herself in the middle, like a pack of hounds around a hapless fox, and she cringed when the heavy-set fellow began to read the tract aloud, then broke into amused laughter. "This isn't a church, sonny! You'll make no converts here. We all enjoy our evil ways too much to forswear them, eh, lads?" he finished with a wink to his friends.

Olwyn began to feel hot and claustrophobic and very nervous, hemmed in by them as she was, and she began to back her way out of the group—when Justin Wentworth suddenly pounced and grabbed her by the arm.

"Check your pockets, lads," he advised his friends. "Something about this Bible-spouting rogue doesn't quite ring true. Look at him!" He had hold of both her arms and thrust her out in front of the others, all of whom were frowning now and examining her more closely. "Note his ragged clothes and general air of disrepute," the trader went on, his fingers like iron as they bit into Olwyn's tender flesh. "I'd guess he's a stowaway, a common beggar or a gypsy, but I have to admit that the religious angle is a clever trick."

For a second, as the men hastily rifled through their pockets and patted their vests to make sure their watches and chains and money were where they should be, Olwyn was too stunned to utter a word in her own defense. She could tell at a glance that these men were all rich and powerful, for by now she equated money with power, and each and every one of them could make serious trouble for her if they chose. It was the old story all over again, the poor at the mercy of the rich! Just when she felt herself begin to cower in apprehension, the specter of Devlin Sproat and what he had done to her swelling in her mind, a sudden burst of defiance blazed up inside Olwyn, the determination not to be taken advantage of again.

"I'm not a thief!" she cried angrily, twisting around to glare up at the man who held her. "You have no right—I demand that you release me at once!"

A flash of strong white teeth lit up his tanned face and he chuckled mockingly. "You demand? Stowaways, boy, are in no position to demand anything." He shook her a little when she glared at him. "You'll stay right where you are until these men ascertain that none of their possessions are missing—then we'll investigate to see whether or not you've paid your passage to Cape Town, which I doubt."

When Wentworth's friends nodded to say that everything seemed to be intact, Olwyn said smugly, "You see! Like all your ilk you judge a book by its cover. Now"—she cranned around to peer up at Wentworth—"kindly take your hands off me."

He gazed down at her, amazed and faintly amused by her spunk, even while a little annoyed at her insulting remark about judging a book by its cover.

"What have you got in your pockets?" he demanded suddenly, thinking that she needed to be taught a lesson. "A watch or a purse or two, I'll warrant."

"I—I have not!" Olwyn spluttered, getting red in the face. "Let me go!"

Justin winked at his friends above her head. "I think we'd better make sure. He's already gone the rounds of the other passengers. They might well have been taken in with the religious angle."

Then he said something that sent a bolt of pure

horror through the girl he was holding. "Right, lads, let's strip him down!"

Olwyn screamed then. She forgot the role she was playing and shrieked at the top of her lungs, shrill, piercing, and womanish, chilled at the thought of being exposed for the charlatan she was.

# 4

Justin nearly let her go. It jolted him badly when her scream rang out. He had never heard a lad shriek quite like that before, and he spun Olwyn around to face him and gave her a searching look, for the first time noticing her delicacy and beauty. He also saw frightened tears sparkling in her eyes. The sight of those tears had Wentworth's mind reeling in confusion. What kind of lad was this? he asked himself in wonder, and at that moment he sensed something very odd about her. "Look here, boy," he began—and got no further.

Fortunately for Olwyn, James Scobbie saw her plight and came bustling over to the bar, and James was afraid of no one. Wagging an admonishing finger around the group, he informed them coldly of who he was and stated that Olwyn was his assistant.

They all gaped at Scobbie and his bold way of addressing them. Finally one fellow mumbled, "Your pardon, sir, we meant no harm. 'Twas just a bit of sport, you understand—"

"No, I don't understand," James interrupted brusquely. "You had no right to pick on a defenseless boy."

James draped an arm around Olwyn's shoulders when he noticed how she was trembling, and said to her, glaring at the men, "And we think of the savages at Nuruzambora as uncivilized! I wouldn't be at all surprised if we receive better treatment from them."

"Nuruzambora?" Wentworth repeated. "What do you mean?"

James looked him up and down, his eyes flinty. "I am going there, sir, as a missionary for Christ."

"I know the area well—"

"Do you, indeed?" Scobbie responded frostily, then he added something that brought a gasp from the men's lips, all of them except Wentworth. "I sincerely hope," James went on, "that your manners don't rub off on the natives."

There wa₃ a second when Wentworth's vivid blue eyes narrowed, when he gazed down at James haughtily, then the tension snapped and Justin burst out laughing. Inclining his golden head slightly, he made Scobbie a little bow. "I try not to contaminate them," he said, then sobering, "Seriously, please accept my apology and allow me the pleasure of buying you a drink?"

Olwyn felt James relax a little. She heard him refuse the drink, saying that alcohol was never allowed to "soil his lips." Then she fully expected that they would leave. All her anxiety came surging back when James said, "But I *will* accept a cup of coffee. I'm most curious to hear all you can tell me about Nuruzambora."

She almost swooned. She shot Scobbie a look of surprise and dismay but James didn't notice. All his attention and interest was now fixed on the trader.

In moments they were seated at one of the tables with coffee before them. He divided his time between Cape Town and a remote area called Teragno, Wentworth explained. The latter was about ten miles upriver from Nuruzambora. Teragno was the site of his main trading post, he went on, and he had built it into a kind of fortified village. From all over the territory he collected the likes of ivory, beeswax, indigo, and even ostrich feathers and exported them to Europe. He had lived in Africa for five years, he said, now and then sending an amused glance to Olwyn, who gazed back at him stonily and in silence.

James put down his cup and leaned forward eagerly. "You must know my fellow-missionaries, Sloan and Erskine?"

An almost imperceptible change came over the trader; a sudden detachment. "I know them." He seemed reluctant to admit it, thought Olwyn, watching him. "But I wouldn't say well," he added. "I travel a lot in business and it leaves little time for socializing. They, too, have been busy since they arrived two years ago—clearing land, digging wells, and constructing more permanent buildings than the simple mud huts they lived in when they first arrived."

"And what of God's work?" James querried. "How successful have they been in converting the natives?"

There was a pause. Wentworth looked at James from under his brows, as if sizing him up. Then he gave a shrug. "I'm afraid I can't answer that question, but this I *can* tell you; nothing happens fast in Africa. The natives are naturally suspicious of the white man. It takes time to win their trust. The white man, for his part, often has a difficult time coming to terms with native culture. You see, practices that might seem cruel, even diabolical to our eyes are quite normal to these people. They have their celebrations, initiation and fertility rites, even their wars"—his white teeth flashed in a grin—"and there are lots of those. It's ludicrous to expect them to change overnight," he said quite firmly. "There are those, of course, who take the view that we have no right to change them at all."

"There are also those who don't care," James said dryly. "But I dare to hope that I might be instrumental in showing them the Light, as laid down in the scriptures. From what you've just told me about their mode of living I'd say that the poor souls are floundering in a pit of darkness. Initiation and fertility rites! In the name of goodness!" He shook his head and sighed.

Olwyn glanced at the trader and saw laughter glinting in his eyes, but he sobered and then looked exaggeratedly grave when he saw her frowning at him.

James sat thoughtful for a moment, tapping his saucer with the head of his spoon, then said, "Well, I hope my compatriots have at least tilled the soil and planted the Good Seed at Nuruzambora. That would be a start."

Olwyn could tell that Wentworth found them highly entertaining—and that angered her. She eyed him surreptitiously while his attention was on Scobbie. He was well set up in his expensive clothes, she observed. His voice was deep and cultured, even though he had the manners of a barbarian; his manner assertive and self-assured. It was clear to Olwyn that he was well-bred—at least in some ways—and very prosperous and used to the finer things in life, yet now and then, when he spoke about his life in the hinterlands of Africa, she sensed a subtle change coming over him. Behind the polished, sophisticated facade at such moments emerged quite a different person; a tough, flint-eyed man of the frontier as he laughed—laughed!—about wars and the diabolical practices of the natives and questioned that anyone had the right to expect them to change. Oh, she thought, he was hard as iron! Under that charming smile he was heartless!

Suddenly he was looking at her curiously. "And what will your duties be at Nuruzambora, Oliver?" he asked her.

When informed that she would be Scobbie's medical assistant his brows shot up in astonishment. Then he gave her a dubious look that Olwyn found very insulting. His next words were even *more* insulting. "Once you arrive at Nuruzambora I'm going to have to introduce you to Hero," he told her. "You might learn something from him. He's the local witch doctor in the area and tries very hard to live up to his name. His philosophy is that the more painful the treatment, the quicker the cure. His patients rarely return to him for a second consultation."

Scobbie laughed heartily at this, but Olwyn wasn't amused to be told she could learn something from a primitive witch doctor, and had to force a smile when James said, "That's a clever trick, eh, Oliver? You must remember that the next time you're stuck for a cure."

They finished their coffee and stood up to leave.

"There are so many things I wanted to ask you," James said, eyeing the tall man hopefully. It worked. Wentworth graciously consented to meet with him again for further discussions, and then added, "Don't hesitate to send for me if you need help of any kind, once you reach Nuruzambora."

Scobbie was delighted by this show of friendship and parted from the trader in fine spirits, very pleased with the contact they had made, even if his young assistant wasn't. Olwyn was far from happy that Wentworth was going to be their neighbor, though fortunately not a very close one. Ten miles, she told herself, was still quite a long way away, especially in a wilderness country without roads of any kind. That thought brought her some small comfort.

Wentworth left the tavern himself shortly thereafter. The meeting with the new missionary had exasperated him. He saw Scobbie as an idealistic prig, a man who was shockingly uninformed, unprepared, and naive about the area he was going to, though in all fairness he supposed the missionary society was to blame for that.

Justin wondered if he should have been more candid with Scobbie. As he walked back to his stateroom it occurred to him that it might have been kinder in the long run to prepare him for what he would find at Nuruzambora, then he shrugged the thought away. It was not his concern. Better that he maintain a certain distance from the mission station. Besides, he had important matters of his own that shortly would occupy all his time and attention.

He unlocked the door of his stateroom and closed and locked it behind him, then stepped into a small foyer that opened out into a spacious sitting room that was plush and ornate in the latest Victorian fashion, with an overstuffed sofa and two matching chairs upholstered in gold brocade and a marble-topped cocktail table in the center of the seating arrangements. The walls were hung with several mirrors and seascapes in carved mahogany frames, and there was an elegant leather-topped desk against one wall. From this room an archway led into a bedchamber done in the same white-and-gold theme, much of the space taken up with a magisterial canopied bed.

Justin saw no reason why he shouldn't travel in comfort during his annual business trips to Europe, a nice contrast to the harsh, primitive accommodations he often had to endure while moving around southern Africa. At Teragno, too, he liked to maintain some semblance of civility, even while recognizing that there was no place for softness on the veld. Yet it was so easy to degenerate into a barbarian in keeping with one's surroundings, and he'd tried to avoid that. When he'd first gone to Africa five years ago he'd felt it happen to himself before he checked it, and he'd watched the transformation in progress with others from Europe.

It always amazed Justin how quickly the trappings of civilization fell away and how rapidly the more basic instincts took over under the right—or rather, the wrong—stimulus. He knew of many who were little better than the savages they'd once looked down on when they first arrived; who were lower and crueler than the wild beasts howling beyond the thorn fences at night and who no longer would be recognized by the relatives and friends they'd left behind in Europe.

Some intangible barrier once crossed made it impossible to go back. He'd stepped away from that barrier himself just in time, but even so, the harshness of life in the interior of Africa had changed him, though he supposed that change had begun even before he left Scotland.

Wentworth threw off his jacket, sat down at the desk, and picked up a leather valise from the floor nearby. Since the day was dull and little light came in the small porthole, he lit the lamp, then extracted a doeskin pouch from the valise and emptied the contents onto the desktop. They were like small pebbles, eight in all. Justin picked up the largest of them and turned it slowly, consideringly, under the light. It was whitish, opaque, except for the spots where friction had abraded it, and at these spots it flashed and sparkled like blue fire.

He'd gone to Britain with others that were even bigger. Those he had sold off in London during his visit home, and how eager the buyer had been to know where they came from! Justin, naturally, hadn't told him.

Smiling, he recalled the day he'd found the first of these rare pebbles on the banks of the Orange River at a spot on the very edge of his own land at Teragno. Yes, and more and larger were yet to be found there, he was convinced of it! The moment he returned to Africa he planned to buy up all the land in that vicinity—land presently belonging to a poor Boer farmer—then he'd form a company, all legal and airtight, and in that way he'd control the new industry about to emerge, an industry that would make itself known around the world with the speed of a meteor.

Bemused, Wentworth placed the pebble he was holding on the back of his hand. The white stone glinted and stood out against the deep bronze of his skin like a gem placed on dark velvet. These remaining eight stones were the ones he'd found on that very first day, and they'd led him to search for the others, which were larger. The original eight represented the foundation of his new company. He would never sell them. One day he would have them embedded on a plaque that would take pride of place in his office. They were the trailblazers to a fortune. Men had killed for far less. These rocks, he reflected, made all his other enterprises pale by comparison. Justin Wentworth, dealer in ivory, cotton, indigo and other sundry goods, would in the near future become a dealer in the world's most prized commodity.

Diamonds.

Secrecy was imperative. For this reason he had by-passed the gem dealers in Cape Town and taken his finds to London. Now Justin was impatient to get back to Teragno to buy up as much land as he could afford, if possible all the diamondiferous land bordering on his trading post where these stones had come from. Only after all this was accomplished would he shout his astounding news to the world, and the mad stampede would begin, but by then he'd be firmly in control.

Justin contemplated the idea of staggering riches, to be in a position to buy anything his heart desired, anything at all. Even people. Yes, they, too, could be bought. As his father used to say, everyone had a price. Everyone!

Christina came into his mind.

His expression hardened.

Vast wealth meant being able to buy off Christina, the stepmother responsible for having him disinherited from the Wentworth Cotton Mills in Scotland, and turning his father against him. In a curious way the diamonds reminded him of his stepmother; they were the hardest mineral on earth.

He gazed into the lamplight, his mind going back to another time. His father's second wife was one of the most beautiful women he had ever seen, and certainly the most scheming and remorseless. Into his mind rose a vision of milk-white skin soft as rose petals, and titian hair like spun copper, eyes the color of smoke. He could still smell her perfume, musky and stirring, and still see her body, taut-breasted and as sinewy as a serpent. Only six years older than he was—and his stepmother!

They had no contact now, but he'd glimpsed her now and then during his yearly visits to Scotland and saw that she was as bewitching as ever. Through friends he heard the rumors of her spending and lavish entertainments, also that she was still merrily slashing her razor-sharp path across the lives of anyone who stood in the way of her objectives, and still imperiously directing her empire from Wentworth Lodge, the mansion that had been in his family for generations.

Three years ago his father had died without their being reconciled. He left the mills and all his considerable assets to his beautiful second wife without as much as a mention of Justin in his will. His last words to his only son had been spoken in anger. "Never darken my door again! Fend for yourself if you can, but I predict you'll never amount to anything without the Wentworth fortune behind you—but you'll never get your hands on it after what you've done!"

Justin had been twenty years old at the time, nearly six years ago now. Soon afterwards he'd left Scotland for southern Africa, relishing the challenge of a little-known frontier, the more distant the better. Teragno hadn't disappointed him. In the early days it had taken all his wits, courage, and determination just to stay alive, but he quickly saw the untapped potential there and gradually began to prosper until, five years later, he was a moderately rich man in his own right. Now, with the discovery of diamonds, he'd outstrip anything his father had achieved and shortly leave him far behind, like a donkey in the wake of a racehorse.

Then he'd bide his time and wait for the right moment, and sooner or later those moments always came. He'd buy back Wentworth Lodge, the home of his ancestors, and the mills and factories and all the rest of it, and Christina would learn to her sorrow the meaning of the Latin inscription over the portal of her home—which she'd never bothered to ask about. Only the True Blood Here Reside. She would pay for lying that he'd tried to entice her into his bed.

That house, Justin had promised himself, would one day be passed down to his son, yes, even if he himself never lived in it again, and the interloper would be ousted. Of that he was determined.

He had time. A legitimate heir didn't figure in his immediate plans. First came his diamond-mining company, an enterprise that would require all his energy and concentration, but eventually . . . a wife.

Normally he was a man who moved swiftly. Ponderous deliberation was foreign to his nature. But in the case of a wife, Justin knew he could not afford to be impetuous. If temptation ever reared its head he need only remind himself of Christina, beautiful on the outside but vile inside, lying and cheating with a pretty smile on her face. This poisonous flower had cost him his birthright and the love and respect of his father, something he wasn't likely to forget. An honest woman, as James Scobbie might have put it, was more precious than rubies—or even diamonds, thought Justin with a rueful smile.

Young Harold Scobbie laughed uproariously when he heard about Olwyn's problems while handing out the pamphlets, so much so that his father wheeled on him and snapped, "Wheesht, ye gallus wee eejit! In future *you* can help me and we'll see if you can do better."

Hal sobered instantly and a sullen expression replaced the mirth on his face. He was angry at James sticking up for Oliver, and though he certainly didn't identify with his pious father, still . . . he was jealous of the closeness he'd noticed developing between the missionary and his young assistant. When Harold met Justin Wentworth for himself two days later he was greatly impressed and, inquisitive as he was, would have asked him lots of questions if his papa hadn't hogged the conversation. Just the same, he managed to get one up on Oliver by inveigling an invitation to visit Mr. Wentworth in his stateroom at a later date, a request that earned him a scolding later.

"You'll stay away from Mr. Wentworth's quarters," his father warned him once they returned to the cabin. "I won't have you making a pest of yourself."

Harold's fair skin reddened. "But he said I could go!" he protested.

"And I say you cannot!" James stabbed at his chest with his thumb. "I'm the one you'll obey."

"Oh, for goodness sake, can we not have a little peace in this family?" cried Hannah, pressing a hand to her breast and at the same time throwing her husband a chiding look, for James was always so quick to jump down Harold's throat. "It's natural enough that he'd want to make friends with Mr. Wentworth since he's going to be our new neighbor," she said, "and since *he* doesn't seem to mind why should you make a fuss, James?"

"I know Harold," he replied darkly.

Any slight to her darling offended Hannah and brought out her protective instincts, even to the point where she would gainsay her husband. She put an arm around the boy's shoulders and soothed, "Perhaps once we get to know him a little better the children might pay a brief social call to his stateroom." When Scobbie glowered at her she added placatingly, "You could take them, dear, or even Oliver. That way you could keep an eye on them."

"We'll see," her husband snapped sulkily.

Olwyn knew nothing of this conversation, which was just as well. She'd have been very much opposed to visiting Wentworth in his stateroom or anywhere. She thought of him as the arrogant Norseman, and Olwyn had a sneaking suspicion that he didn't think too highly of missionaries. Certainly he hadn't been at all anxious to talk about Sloan and Erskine, the men already at Nuruzambora, though he must have sensed that James was eager to hear all about these men. He had practically snubbed James when he kept probing.

Scobbie didn't seem to notice, which surprised Olwyn. The day after their meeting with the trader in the Gull, he took her aside, saying, "I'm very glad to have met Wentworth. It's comforting to have his compound at Teragno not too far from Nuruzambora should trouble of any kind ever arise. I'm thinking of Mrs. Scobbie and the boys."

Olwyn didn't say anything but her face tightened, wishing she could share his enthusiasm but feeling only antipathy instead. James turned and looked gravely into her eyes. "I want good relations with Wentworth, Oliver," he said, leaving her in no doubt of what he expected of her. "It could be advantageous to us in countless ways; besides, he's a countryman of ours and it's natural that we should all be friends." When she was still silent, a mulish pucker about her mouth, he suddenly grinned and threw an arm about her shoulders and went on coaxingly, "Forget the little, ah . . . altercation you had with him and his friends. Blame it on the demon drink, a poisonous brew that turns grown men into naughty children; they didn't know what they were about."

Olwyn disagreed, but she kept her thoughts to herself.

"I know you'll do everything in your power to help the friendship along," the missionary added, thumping her heartily on the back, but serious nevertheless. "With Erskine and Sloan so undependable it will be good to have a capable man like Wentworth in the vicinity."

Olwyn almost choked. Scobbie had, in essence, ordered her to be nice to Justin Wentworth and she could hardly refuse!

Soon Olwyn had something else to worry her and take her mind off the trader. Once the *Randolph* was out in the open Atlantic the weather roughened and they encountered the first storm of the voyage. Towering waves as cold as death broke over the vessel again and again until it shuddered and groaned, pitching and bucking while the passengers hung onto anything riveted down, sure they were going to end up at the bottom of the sea. Many people were seasick, including Hannah and little Jamie, and as soon as the worst of the gale was over and it was safe to move about, Scobbie, naturally, turned to Olwyn for help. "What can you do for them, Oliver?"

Her moment of truth had come, the time to demonstrate that the claims she'd made were justified. For a moment Olwyn was almost sick herself as she contemplated exactly what she'd taken on. It was one thing to brag about what she could do, quite another to have to work with real, live patients!

When James frowned at her, wondering why she was hesitating, Olwyn struggled to control her nerves, her mind skittering back to the time she'd worked for Dr. Gibb. Many's the time she had watched him treat dyspepsia and various kinds of stomach upsets, and thinking of that she ran into her own cabin for her shiny new black medical bag—paid for and stocked by James to the specifications of his doctor back in Glasgow—and lifted out the ingredients she would need. These included carbonate of bismuth, magnesium, and bicarbonate of soda, all of which she mixed with a little fresh water. This potion she coaxed down the throats of her first patients three times a day. Within twenty-four hours both Hannah and Jamie felt much better.

Hannah Scobbie clung to her hand in gratitude. "I've never been so sick in my life!" she said, her cheeks still wan. "I'm ashamed to say that there were moments when I wished for the release of death. But now . . ."—she managed a weak smile—"I feel ever so much better. Thank you, Oliver, dear. What a treasure you are!"

Harold watched all this morosely. It seemed to him that Oliver was only doing the job he'd been hired to do, and he was irritated at his mother for being so appreciative. Hal was very close to his mother and it twisted him up inside to watch her clinging to Oliver's hand—then to call him a treasure! He felt like shoving him away from the bed, and he might have, too, if his father hadn't been watching, beaming at the pair as if the sight of them being so chummy pleased him. At that moment Harold didn't know which of them he despised more, his papa or Oliver Moore.

Scobbie *was* pleased, and he silently congratulated himself for bringing Oliver along. He proceeded to boast about the lad in the half-empty dining saloon, so many of the passengers still ailing in their cabins. James went so far as to compare Olwyn favorably with the ship's doctor, a man who was terribly overworked at that time and about ready to collapse in bed himself. The result was that Olwyn suddenly found herself with scores of new patients on her hands, so highly did James recommend her doctoring skills.

She was suddenly an important personage, rushing out of the cabin she shared with the boys at dawn, her medical bag in her hand, sometimes not returning until late at night. "He's getting swollen-headed," Hal grumbled about her to his little brother. "He's puffed up like a balloon."

Then came the final betrayal. "I like Oliver," said Jamie, an endearing little boy with an infectious smile, who normally looked up to his older brother in all ways. "I think he's nice, and very clever too."

"He's a milksop!" Harold spat, hurt and angry that Jamie, too, had been won over. "I could whip him with one hand tied behind my back—and one of these days I shall. Why, he looks like a common gypsy, and you know how tricky they can be."

Jamie thought about it for a minute or two. "It's his clothes," he said with a decisive nod. "Mama said they're little better than rags. She's going to make him new ones to wear before we get to Cape Town."

"What?" Harold howled indignantly, his face flooding with angry color, jealousy eating into him that not only his father but his mother liked Oliver so much

. . . perhaps, at least in his father's case, more than he liked him. "Why should Mama make him clothes?" he choked. "He's only a—a servant."

The smaller boy considered, then shrugged. "Mama likes to sew."

For a week Olwyn hardly saw the Scobbies as she labored over her patients, dosing them, washing them, and moving from cabin to cabin in an atmosphere redolent of sweat and vomit. The more seriously ill were handled by Dr. MacKay and the ship's nurse, also a male, but there were so many of them that the medical men were glad enough of her assistance. She was constantly running back to her cabin to consult her textbooks when the usual cures didn't work, always, of course, checking with Dr. MacKay before trying something new. Countless passengers were suffering from colds and influenza on top of the seasickness, and this made them very weak. Olwyn was devastated when one old lady of seventy-five died, in spite of their strenuous efforts to save her.

The loss of this patient drove home to Olwyn the seriousness of the job she had taken on for Mr. Scobbie. It prompted her, once she asked Scobbie's permission, to ask Dr. MacKay if she could continue to work with him for the remainder of the voyage; to sit in on his cases if nothing else, anything that might increase her knowledge and experience. She also decided to read her four bulky medical textbooks from cover to cover.

$$\diamond \quad 5 \quad \diamond$$

A week later they were invited to dine with Justin Wentworth and his friends in the Grand Saloon.

"No, you cannot go," Scobbie told his older son when Harold kept badgering him. "You and your brother will stay with the Beatons in the cabin next door, and you will mind your manners while you're about it."

Hal almost wept at the injustice of it all. The Beatons were in their sixties and sober and dry, even more pious than his father, if that were possible.

"I'm almost fourteen," he burst out, though his birthday was still several months away. "And I'm nearly as big as Oliver. I don't see why he can go and I can't. After all, I'm your son—"

Hal sped from the room when he felt tears rushing into his eyes, banging the door shut behind him.

Olwyn was in the Scobbies' cabin at the time, being measured for the new clothes Hannah was sewing for her so that she would look "presentable" when they arrived in Cape Town. Her new breeches were already finished and now Hannah was working on a jacket, though it wouldn't be ready to wear to Wentworth's dinner.

Olwyn was terribly embarrassed to be caught in the middle of a family fray, and said quickly, "I wish you would let Harold go in my place, Mr. Scobbie. Really, I don't mind. I'll stay and watch Jamie."

"You will do no such thing!" James fairly shouted, furious as he always was when Harold argued with him. "You are going, Oliver"—he shot an angry glance at Hannah, whom he blamed for spoiling the boy—"I wouldn't take Harold to a circus with the deportment he has."

It was a subdued little party that left to join Wentworth in the Grand Saloon a few nights later, James sober in his best Sunday suit, a garment that was shiny with wear, and Hannah pale and silent in a refurbished gray taffeta gown with a little new cream lace added to perk it up. Olwyn, however, looked very smart and handsome in the new black breeches and white shirt that Mrs. Scobbie had made for her. Since her own jacket wasn't yet finished, she'd had to borrow one of Harold's—the last straw where the latter was concerned. But he'd find a way to get his revenge, vowed the seething youngster as he watched them leave, totally unaware of Olwyn's offer to let him go in her stead. Oh, yes, Hal simmered, he'd find a way to get back at Oliver, who it seemed to him had all the fun, all the respect, too, from the people around them, especially his father.

Olwyn and the Scobbies were overwhelmed with the Victorian opulence of the first-class dining room, with its rich burgandy-red carpet, crystal chandeliers, and massive floor-to-ceiling gilt-framed mirrors. The mirrors reflected the elegantly dressed diners, the snowy-white damask table linen, and fine china and glassware, all glowing in masses of candlelight. On a raised dais in one corner of the large room smartly uniformed musicians played genteel chamber music

for the edification of the large assembly, just loud
enough to mask the various conversations going on
but not so intrusive as to force anyone to raise their
voices. The aroma of fine food was mouth-watering.

But Olwyn was even more overwhelmed at the sight
of their host in his black evening clothes, with stark
white at throat and cuffs, so flattering to his tall,
broad-shouldered frame and Nordic coloring. Staring
at him as he came forward to meet them, Olwyn felt
something flare and spring to life inside her, and flood
her with the strangest sensations, feelings that she
couldn't have described to anyone, and that she had
never experienced before.

Justin greeted them warmly and since they knew
none of his other guests, seated them close to him at
the head of the long table he had reserved for his
party, ten in all. He sensed that the Scobbies and
Oliver might feel a little out of their depth in such
elegant surroundings, and was anxious to put them at
their ease. After all, he thought, they were going to be
neighbors, and though he had no intention of seeing
much of them at Nuruzambora, he saw no reason why
they shouldn't be friendly.

Justin soon saw that he needn't have worried about
Scobbie being tongue-tied. James was like his older
son in that respect; he was naturally outgoing and
garrulous, perhaps a little opinionated. He immediately engaged a Major Kestler in conversation, while
Hannah began to chat to Kestler's drab wife, a
middle-aged lady with thin gray hair and a very sallow
complexion, thanks to the hot sun of the Cape, where
the couple had lived for the past fifteen years, the
major in service at the garrison.

Olwyn was placed slightly up-table from the
Scobbies, directly across from a heavy-set gentleman
with a narrow face and the sharp features of a rat, his
thin face and portly body at distinct odds with each
other. At her own side of the table she was seated
between two men, but after the first nod and smile she

hardly paid them any attention. Her eyes were riveted on a woman seated on Justin Wentworth's right; she was suddenly convinced, from her position at table, that the woman must be his lady friend, perhaps his sweetheart.

Olwyn was totally unprepared for the sinking feeling that swept through her. She could only nod mutely when Wentworth introduced the lady as Anne Carswell, from Cape Town. Anne had fair hair piled high in the latest London fashion. Her obviously expensive peach-colored gown was a shimmer of satin and lace—and so shockingly low-cut that Olwyn, and the men about her, could see most of her bosom!

Turning to the woman, Justin explained, "Oliver is the Reverend Scobbie's medical assistant."

Anne Carswell looked dumbfounded. So astonished was she that she forgot her manners and blurted, "Oh . . . you jest! That boy—"

"It's quite true." Wentworth seemed a little embarrassed.

Anne peered across the table at Olwyn so intensely that the girl's initial dismay changed to annoyance. She had seen that look before. Enid MacCutcheon had worn it often.

"Surely you cannot truly be a doctor?" Anne said to her.

"No, not truly," Olwyn replied sarcastically, resenting the superior expression on the lady's face.

The next minute Olwyn was ashamed of herself. More cordially, she explained that she wasn't fully qualified. "Good gracious!" Anne's plucked brows shot up in twin arches of surprise. "Then indeed we must hope that the Scobbies remain in good health at Nuruzambora, under the circumstances. Most irregular!"

With that the woman promptly lost interest in her and leaned over, her breasts flowing, to favor Wentworth with all her attention. Olwyn gave a start when a low voice at her side hissed, "Anne Carswell is a witch! God help Wentworth if she succeeds in getting her hooks into him. She drove her poor bugger of a first husband into the grave."

Olwyn swung her head around to stare at the young man seated on her left.

He nodded. "She's a widow on the prowl, and of course our host is an excellent catch. Lucky for Anne that they belong to the same social set on the Cape."

Olwyn's mouth fell open at such outspokenness. The first thing she noticed about Maury Howell was his grin, wide and devil-may-care. The next was his eyes, bright, curious, and a clear green.

She ended up having a very interesting conversation with Howell.

Maury began by politely asking her a few questions about the sort of work she'd be doing for Scobbie, but quickly turned to his own affairs. He was a junior engineer, he told her, working for the British Government at the Cape.

"I may be working for the government," he said in his frank way, "but in this world it's every man for himself, if you take my meaning? There's lots of opportunity out here in Africa for young fellows like us; it's just a matter of keeping your eyes and ears open. Whenever I can I'm going to make an expedition into the interior, just nose about and see what's what."

"How long have you been in Africa?" Olwyn asked him curiously.

"Two years. This was my first trip home. Africa is the place, though," he went on, his green eyes glinting. "You hear lots of rumors . . . there's talk of gold in the Transvaal, but the bloody Boers there make it difficult to sniff about."

"Boers?"

"It's the Dutch word for farmers. The Boers fled to Africa because they were oppressed at home." He laughed suddenly. "They settled at the Cape at first, then had to flee again to avoid the meddling of the Brits. They're a funny lot, the Boers, very independent and basically antisocial. Anyway, they trekked far out into the hinterland of Africa to find peace, and they don't take kindly to strangers poking about in their territory.

"Listen, Moore," he leaned closer and dropped his voice, "I know I have no right to say this, but I honestly think you are wasting your time working for a missionary. Look at it this way: The natives don't want Christianity. Aside from that, well, there's no future, no gain in mission work. I don't know about you but I for one intend to make a name for myself in Africa. It's a cracking spot with everything just starting up. You ought to think about it, you really should."

Maury Howell left Olwyn blinking and breathless at the way he rushed on. All his talk about making a name for himself, about Africa being just the place to do it, about the possibility of gold in the Transvaal—wherever that was!

Olwyn didn't know quite what to make of Howell, with his rosy cheeks and unruly mop of black curls that kept falling over his forehead, giving him a boyish appearance. One thing was obvious, he was full of drive and ambition. He had determination and enthusiasm, all traits she could understand. She found herself liking him; there was something attractive and very stimulating about the young man.

"How old are you anyway, Moore?" he asked her.

"I'm twenty-three."

"Eighteen."

"You look younger."

It was then, while giving her an appraising look, that Howell suddenly noticed the beauty of the "youth" sitting next to him at the table. He saw eyes that were long and luminous as honey in the candlelight, skin like a babe's, and features that struck him as being far too delicate for any man. Maury felt a touch of pity, thinking that it was a curse for any man to look so pretty. But he found Moore's interest flattering. The boy hung on to every word he said, and that pleased

Maury. He liked nothing better than to be the center of attention.

"We must keep in touch," he suggested. "I get about, you know, and might get up near the area you are going to one day." He grinned. "I'm apt to turn up on your doorstep, just like the proverbial bad penny."

"Oh, I do hope we meet again," Olwyn told him feelingly. She felt she had made a friend tonight. Then she did something without stopping to think. She reached over and squeezed his arm while smiling at him warmly, her expression a combination of wistfulness and hope.

Howell instantly recoiled at her touch. His eyes dropped to the soft white hand resting on his arm and he stiffened, flushing. Maury glanced furtively up and down the table to see if anyone had noticed this revealing bit of by-play, which would be bound to give them the wrong idea, and at the same time he felt a hot spurt of anger, sorry now that he had ever spoken to the pretty boy. He felt sick when he noticed Wentworth looking at them.

Justin had been amused when he saw the pair deep in conversation. Howell was well known on the Cape for being a braggart, a born enthusiast known to exaggerate his importance quite shamelessly. He was fond of drinking and gambling and throwing his money about, constantly having to tap somebody or other for a loan. Every Friday night, like clockwork, Maury could be found ensconced with his friends at Big Ben's, one of the better taverns on the harbor, owned by a Londoner, and there he would hold forth, trying to lure the unwary traveler into one of his card games, or into investing in one of his many wild and improbable schemes. Aside from his official job, Howell always had something or other going on the side. Justin had been about to warn Moore in a teasing way not to let Maury throw gold dust in his eyes, for there was something of the Pied Piper about the fellow. Then he spied the awkward interchange between the pair.

Suddenly he, too, was staring hard at Scobbie's medical assistant. He had never really looked closely at the youth before, but he recalled Moore's woman-ish scream that day they played in the Gull, and his own conviction then that there was something odd about the boy.

Through the candlelight Wentworth gazed upon undeniable beauty, but so very effeminate that he, too, felt a stab of pity for the youth. Most women would have given all they had to possess it, but a man—

When Anne Carswell leaned over and said some-thing to get his attention Justin gazed at her in exasperation. He had been dismayed to find they would be traveling on the same ship but felt obliged to spend at least some of his time with her, considering that they moved in the same circles in Cape Town. But he knew well enough what Anne was after, and knew, too, that she was destined to be disappointed.

Olwyn was left reeling in confusion at the sudden change in Maury Howell, wondering what she had done, how she could have offended him.

He had all but turned his back on her now and pretended not to hear when she attempted to speak to him. Embarrassed and hurt, Olwyn gazed into the candles, fighting back tears. What was it about her, she asked herself, that she couldn't seem to get close to anyone? Was it possible that she could be trying too hard?

Suddenly she sensed Wentworth looking at her.

He lifted the bottle of wine from the silver bucket at his side and motioned for her glass. When she passed it to him Olwyn saw a touch of sympathy, or was it pity, in his eyes? She felt like jumping up and dashing from the room.

## 6

I 'll take you on a tour of the ship," Harold Scobbie offered magnanimously. "You want to see everything before we reach Cape Town, don't you, Oliver?"

Olwyn glanced up from the book she was reading in surprise.

Hal went on. "You see, now that I'm friendly with the crew, I'm allowed into places where the regular passengers never go, and they're really interesting. I know you'd hate to miss them."

The change in the boy's attitude to her should have warned Olwyn that he was up to something. Never before had Hal professed any desire for her company. But Olwyn's immediate response was one of relief and pleasure, happy that their relationship seemed to be improving. "Yes," she nodded, setting her book aside. "I'd like that very much, Harold."

In about a week they were scheduled to arrive in Cape Town. The weather was hot now, enervating to people not used to it. For the past two days they had wilted and dripped in an atmosphere that was heavy and still and thunderous. The sea had become eerily calm. The ever-present breeze had disappeared. Below deck the cabins were airless, humid, and unbearably oppressive, and inevitably tempers flared as everyone waited tensely for the tropical storm that had been predicted.

Olwyn welcomed any distraction to take her mind off the heat, so they set off on the tour with Hal leading the way, she following behind with Jamie. The older boy did indeed know every nook and cranny of the *Randolph*. Nothing, it seemed, was off-limits to Harold. Confident and outgoing as he was, doors opened magically to young Scobbie. Jamie liked the engine room best, with its steamy atmosphere, coils and wheels and rumbling boilers, all the workings kindly explained to them by a marine engineer who was already well acquainted with inquisitive Harold. From there they climbed up and down the promenade decks and in and out of the lifeboats, and in the enormous ship's kitchen were treated to a sample of that night's dessert, freshly baked apple dumplings. They peeped into the Grand Saloon, which Olwyn had already seen, then into the equally grand but smaller Ladies Saloon, both of which were in the first-class section.

Finally, when they were exhausted, Hal turned to them with a gleam in his eyes. "Now this is the best part," he announced. "We are going to visit a friend of mine."

"Who?" both Olwyn and Jamie asked in unison.

Hal put a finger to his lips. "Oh, it's a secret. I want it to be a surprise."

They followed him along a hushed corridor in the first-class area. Here there were thick carpeting underfoot and shining brass lanterns on the walls, together with paintings of ships going back to the earliest times, including a few elegant clipper ships. All along the corridor were doors leading into the staterooms. Only people with lots of money could afford to travel in such style, and Olwyn wondered who on earth Hal could know among this group, though anything was possible with Hal. Perhaps some of the boys he played with on deck lived in this section, she mused.

He stopped before one of the doors and turned to her, saying under his breath, "Remember, if Papa finds out where we've been, say it was your idea to come here, Oliver. He wouldn't allow Jamie and me to come by ourselves."

"My idea?" She looked at him in confusion. "But I don't know your friend."

"Oh, yes you do." He grinned. "It's Mr. Wentworth."

Olwyn grabbed his hand when Hal made to knock on the door.

"We're not going in there!" she hissed, her face flushing a bright pink at the idea of barging in on Justin Wentworth, forcing themselves on him when he couldn't possibly be interested. The thought of it appalled her.

Harold's face reddened, too, but in anger. "Why not?" His hands clenched and unclenched at his side. "There's no harm in it," he added, glowering at her.

"No!"

When he made to knock again Olwyn pounced on his arm and tried to drag him away. In a flash they were scuffling, pushing and pulling each other, then Hal lost his temper, seized her by the front of her new white shirt, ripping it as he sent her crashing against Wentworth's door with all his might, panting, "That'll teach you! You'll think twice before you try to fight with me again."

The crack of Olwyn's head striking the door was very loud. Transfixed, both boys watched her slide down the wood surface to the floor, and sprawl there in a heap. There was a moment of shocked silence, then Jamie wailed, "Oh, Hal, look what you've done! He isn't moving—"

White in the face, Harold turned and sped away as fast as he could down the corridor and, after a moment's hesitation, his brother followed him.

Doors banged open up and down the hallway, some of the people disturbed from their afternoon naps. An elderly lady gasped when she saw the unconscious figure and cried, "Good Lord! And I thought this was a respectable ship. What on earth have they done to him?"

"It's a doctor that's wanted here," a man said, bending over Olwyn.

Wentworth wrenched his door open and gazed down. He had been working at his desk when he heard the commotion. Like everyone else he was suffering from the heat and had divested himself of his clothes to make himself more comfortable, so he'd had to take the time to pull on breeches before stepping outside to investigate. Now, when he appeared stripped to the waist, his bronzed torso exposed to view, the elderly woman had a further shock, though a pleasant one this time. "Glory be!" she gasped, staring at Justin. She might be old but she wasn't so old that she couldn't appreciate a splendid male specimen when she saw one. She promptly began fanning herself instead of Olwyn.

"I know this lad," Justin told the little group clustered about him. "I'll take care of him."

He carried Olwyn into his stateroom and deposited her on his own bed. The sky outside the porthole had darkened to a premature twilight, clouds thickening as the storm moved closer. The room was dim. Justin quickly lit the lamp, the better to examine young Moore and try to revive him. Hearing a distant roll of thunder and feeling the ship start to sway a little in a sudden gust of wind, the trader cursed under his breath. He had no wish to be stuck with Moore for the duration of the storm, and once they had some light he immediately leaned over the bed, slapping his face lightly and calling, "Moore! Wake up, lad. I warn you, I make a very poor nurse."

The youth lay on his back with his eyes closed and his face as white as the pillow behind him. His shirt, so recently made by Hannah, lay about his chest in tatters, half the buttons missing. Staring at him, Justin spotted the bandages held together with a pin, and frowned, thinking that the lad was indeed accident-prone as he gazed at what he thought was evidence of an older injury.

The boy's breathing, Justin noticed, was very shallow—and no wonder! The bandages about his chest looked very tight, hardly leaving him room to draw breath. They would have to come off, he decided, at least temporarily. Moore's lungs must have space to expand.

As he got onto the bed and straddled Olwyn, Wentworth wondered if Maury Howell could be responsible for the beating. Howell, as he knew, had a violent temper and had gotten himself into trouble before through fighting.

Kneeling over Olwyn, he slipped an arm under her body, raised her up, and with his free hand proceeded to unwind the bindings. In seconds an untidy heap of linen strips piled up beside them on the bed, then straggled over the side onto the floor. Whoever had treated him for this injury, Justin thought grimly, should be whipped, so tightly were they wrapped around him.

As the last of the coils loosened, the rest slipped snakelike down Olwyn's body and her torso lay bare. Justin started when he found a warm, full breast resting against the arm supporting her. Glancing down, he froze in shock. The next minute he threw her back against the pillows and leaped off the bed as if the touch of her had burned him.

"Christ!" he breathed, staring at her dumbfounded from several feet away. "Christ in heaven!"

He stood there with his head reeling for a moment, then almost warily returned to the bed and stared down at her in wonder, half-expecting to have her transformed back into a male at the blink of an eye. For a second Justin thought he was hallucinating; that the stifling heat had affected his brain.

His eyes widened at the sight of firm, round breasts

glowing like creamy marble in the lamplight, the nipples dusky as a rose. Slowly his eyes moved up to her face, and very closely now Justin studied features that were pure and without fault. Her long black lashes cast a razor-thin shadow across the smoothness of her cheek, and all about her on the pillow, hair black as ebony.

A woman, no mistake about that! A very beautiful woman . . .

She had tricked them all, James Scobbie included!

Why on earth had she done it? Justin asked himself, torn between admiration for her beauty and annoyance at having been duped.

He gave a start when he saw her eyelids flutter. She was breathing much more naturally now, he saw, with the bandages undone. Yes, he thought grimly, she would live to tell the tale—and he was determined to pry the truth out of her and find out what she was up to.

When he saw that she was starting to come around he hastily got back on the bed, deciding to give *her* a surprise this time.

Olwyn regained consciousness to feel an erotic tingling on the points of her breasts as Justin's warm breath whispered over her naked flesh. Frowning, she started to raise a hand to her chest when her wrist was seized and held in a grip of iron.

Her eyes opened then to find Justin Wentworth bending over her.

Olwyn's mind registered a dozen thoughts at once as she lay staring up at him in horror—Harold and his surprise, fighting with the boy, the fact that she was inside Wentworth's stateroom, naked, or nearly so, and worst of all—Justin Wentworth knew her secret now! He had ruined everything for her.

Olwyn went berserk.

She writhed violently beneath him, the suddenness of it taking Wentworth by surprise, and Olwyn managed to get both hands free. Scratching, clawing, twisting, she battled him, but some instinct warned her not to scream. To scream might bring more people into the room to witness her deception. All her fury, dismay, desperation, and fear she vented on the man leaning over her; a man she wanted to hurt as much as he had hurt her. She hated him!

Yet . . . something strange happened, something altogether unexpected. Olwyn could never have foreseen it, innocent and inexperienced as she was, so she had no way of knowing what to guard against. It began when, bolting upright, her naked breasts came in contact with the hardness of Wentworth's chest. A sudden, shocking thrill went through her when her nipples brushed against the crisp golden hair there. Olwyn shivered, gasping in surprise, then something equally astounding happened. She was fighting him tooth and nail; at any second she expected him to strike her, to at least give her a few hard slaps to make her stop. Instead, Justin leaned forward and kissed her.

It startled her, and Olwyn went absolutely still, staring up at him in wonder.

"You are so beautiful," he told her, holding her eyes with his. "It's a sin to hide such beauty under a shirt and breeches." As he spoke Justin moved his fingers languorously through her hair, gently stroking the lump that was rising painfully at the back of her head, his touch oddly soothing. Then the warm fingers found and caressed her ear, the delicate curve of her chin, and traced the bowlike outline of her lips while Olwyn lay rigid, watching him suspiciously.

"You should wear satin and lace," he went on in that deep, hypnotic way. "With diamonds here"—he touched the hollow of her throat—"and here"—he playfully tugged the lobe of her ear—"and here." He lifted one of her hands from where it had been poised to claw at him, and kissed her on the wrist.

"A white gown cut like this." His tanned finger made a low, scooped line just above her nipples, and in spite of herself Olwyn inhaled sharply, a shiver going through her. "Fitted smooth and snug under here." Justin drew the back of his hand lightly across the area under the fullness of her breasts, though he didn't touch them—and suddenly Olwyn wondered what it would feel like if he did. Ashamed of the thought, she asked unsteadily, "What—what about your lady friend, Anne Carswell? What would she think of . . . of this?"

"She means nothing to me."

Suddenly he bent his head and lightly circled a nipple with his tongue, his touch sending an electrifying jolt through the girl, bringing a weak gasp of protest from her lips. "Don't . . . please, don't . . ."

Justin paid no attention, aware now of what a good actress she was. He took masterful control of her then, kissing her more deeply, passionately, his hands invading her body, touching her in all her most intimate places, each touch igniting a spark like fire within her. She squirmed when he cupped her full breasts in the palms of his hands and bent to run the moist heat of his tongue over the tips, making them spring up eagerly. Then his hands were at her breeches, pulling them down over her hips.

"No!" Olwyn cried, feebly trying to slap his hands away. "You can't—"

She started, her body arching when she felt the strong masculine hand slip between her bare legs, his fingers probing her most private areas; then finding what he sought, those sensuous fingers began to move back and forth rapidly.

Olwyn's lips parted to scream at him to stop, to leave her alone, but no sound came out. It was as if she'd fallen into a trance wherein she had ceased to think and was alive only to sensation. She felt a moistness, a surge of heat, then a shuddering thrill coursed through her, so intense that she started to cry out, only to find her lips silenced under a bruising kiss. When he did pull away Olwyn moaned and reached for him frantically. Her glazed eyes saw him stand up and pull off his breeches. They widened in shock at the sight of hard, upthrust flesh rising from a nest of golden hair. Then Justin was back against her, poised for an instant between her legs, then driving down. Olwyn felt a fiery stab of pain as he entered her.

Oh, but the pain wasn't as intense, as compelling as the need he had awakened inside her. She wanted to feel all of him now, her hands fluttering to touch his hair, the hard muscles of his shoulders, the taut firmness of the hips rising and plunging above her. Grasping his hips, she drew him to her, unable to get enough, wanting . . . wanting . . .

A fierce burst of rapture swept through her. "Oh . . . God!" she cried. "Oh . . . dear God . . . don't stop . . ."

But the ecstasy was ebbing, and much as she clung to him it wouldn't come back. Justin smiled at her, his teeth so white against his dark skin, all his features strong and regular, his thick golden hair rumpled now, glinting in the lamplight by the bed. Such a handsome man! So commanding, exciting . . .

Dear God, what had she done? No, what had he *made* her do?

The tension shattered and Olwyn burst into tears, pushing Wentworth angrily aside when he tried to put his arms about her. Her head was pounding. She felt confused one moment; the next her mind was crystal clear. "So this," she choked, "is the price you made me pay for keeping my secret?"

Justin's smile faded and with it his contented look.

"Don't talk nonsense," he said. "You were more than agreeable, and I didn't force you to stay here—"

"I wanted to talk to you, that was all!" Olwyn accused, her face very pale now, her eyes huge. "I had to find out what you meant to do, to try to reason with you, if necessary."

"Reason?" Justin shook his head and laughed, his gaze burning down over her body. "I don't make a practice of reasoning with women when they are lying naked under me. It tends to interfere with my thought processes." Then he added something that both frightened and infuriated her, considering what he'd done. "And I don't recall promising to keep your secret."

"Swine! You—"

Justin held up his hand, his head turning to the porthole window. They could hear the wind howling now and, with their own storm over, feel the bucking and plunging of the ship. The walls of the room tilted, and a picture fell off the wall and landed with a crash on the floor. Justin's boots skidded across the carpet, and suddenly, as torrential rain thrashed against the window, they could hear splintering sounds from the deck above, things tumbling over in the room beyond. Justin rose and reached for his breeches. "Get dressed," he said, pulling them on while Olwyn kept her face averted. He turned and pulled her out of bed, steadying her as she was hurled against him as another wave struck the ship. "No, don't bother with these," he said impatiently as Olwyn stretched down with one hand to pick up the pile of bandages, still forced to hang onto him with the other or risk being thrown about and possibly injured. But when she bent down Justin had a view of the bed behind her. He saw the spots of blood on the sheet.

At first he couldn't believe his eyes. As Olwyn struggled into her shirt and breeches, while he kept a supportive hand at her waist, he couldn't take his eyes off those tell-tale stains. It wasn't possible! he thought, wanting to shrug the obvious away and beginning to feel an emotion suspiciously like self-disgust. She had seemed so wise, so designing, the type who was out for all she could get and wasn't too particular about what she had to do to get it. But—the blood spoke for itself. At that all his preconceived notions about her crumbled and only a void filled with questions remained in his mind.

Sober now, Justin quickly scooped up the rest of her things himself—her cap, boots, and the bandages, and with an arm about her hurried Olwyn into the sitting room and deposited both her and her belongings on the sofa, a heavy piece of furniture unlikely to budge. But the rest of the room, he saw, was in a shambles. Ornaments, pictures, bric-a-brac all lay scattered about, and more kept falling with every wave that struck the ship. Olwyn immediately curled up into a ball on the couch, her arms protectively over her head, her body trembling from top to toe.

All of a sudden Justin felt sorry for her. He felt like a cad. She looked so helpless and vulnerable sitting there, hiding her face in her arms, as much to avoid having to look at him, he didn't doubt, as to protect herself from flying objects. Sighing, he sat down beside her, and instantly Olwyn flinched and tried to move away. Very firmly Justin reached for her and drew her close to him, saying, "Don't worry, I won't hurt you. And the storm will burn itself out soon enough; they always do." Then, close to her ear, "What's your real name?"

She didn't answer, but kept her face buried in her arms.

Justin reached for her arm and drew it away from her face. He felt a pang when he saw the tears in her eyes and leaned forward and kissed her on the forehead, furious with himself now for having dared to judge her, someone he hardly knew. "A little while ago you said you wanted to talk. Well . . . why don't we start with your name?" He smiled slightly. "I can't go on calling you Oliver, not now."

Olwyn eyed him nervously, sensing a change in him. He didn't seem quite so hard now, so arrogant. Suddenly she began to hope.

"It's Olwyn." Then in a breathless rush, "Are you going to tell Mr. Scobbie about me?"

"Why in God's name did you do it? Why would a beautiful girl like you want to pass herself off as a man?"

Olwyn glanced away. "I did it to get the job with

Mr. Scobbie. You see, I—I'd lost the one I had . . .
there was a little trouble. I wanted to get out of
Glasgow."

Nothing on earth would have made her tell him
about Devlin Sproat!

"That was a very radical thing to do just to get a
job," he said, not sure whether he believed her or not.
"What kind of trouble were you in?"

It was hard to talk now. They practically had to
shout to be heard over the sounds of the storm. As he
waited for her to answer his question Justin glanced at
the heavy brass clock on the wall behind the desk,
startled to see that it was almost half-past five. At
six-thirty he had invited several shipboard friends to
his stateroom for pre-dinner drinks. If the storm was
over by then there was a good chance that they would
come.

Olwyn thought quickly. "I had a misunderstanding
with—"

A boom like a cannon going off resounded throughout the ship. Olwyn threw both arms around Justin's
back and buried her face in his neck, certain they were
doomed. She could hear crashing, banging, splintering
sounds as items not nailed down were hurled about
the cabin, and raising her head in terror, half-
expecting to see the waves roaring in about them, she
watched as everything was swept off the desk. Papers
flew through the air all about them. The contents of
Justin's leather valise spewed everywhere. Among
them was a small leather pouch, and when it struck
the wall tiny objects like pebbles burst out, scattering
in all directions.

Justin took her head and brought it back against his
shoulder. There was no point in attempting a conversation now. Trembling, Olwyn was glad of his strong,
warm body against hers at that moment, his hand
stroking her hair, his breath on her cheek. She forgot
about everything as she curled up against him and
prayed for the storm to end, for the ship to come

through it safely. If I die now, she thought, it will be as Oliver Moore, but at least I will have *his* arms around me. It was better than dying alone.

She lost track of time. Perhaps fifteen or twenty minutes passed before Justin put his mouth to her ear to whisper, "It's passing. You'll live to see Cape Town after all."

When everything calmed down Olwyn felt a giddy sense of relief. She expected Justin to start questioning her again. Instead his eyes went to the clock and he stood up and began searching about the mess littering the floor of the sitting room. Olwyn watched him curiously as he got down on hands and knees to peer under furniture, pushing things aside to look underneath. She saw him pick up several of the tiny pebbles and return them to the pouch.

"What are they?" she asked inquisitively.

He glanced at her over his shoulder. "Oh . . . just graphite. From my place in Teragno."

"Are they valuable?" He certainly seemed very intent on finding them!

He shook his head. "Not really, but they could hurt if you stepped on them with bare feet."

Justin was anxious to find the gems and lock them away before his guests arrived. He couldn't risk one of them finding a stone and starting to ask awkward questions, so he had no option but to forget the girl for the moment. With Olwyn looking on, he painstakingly examined the entire room and recovered seven of the stones, but one of them evaded him.

Olwyn began to fret, sure the Scobbies would be wondering what had happened to her by now, and certain Harold wouldn't have enlightened them. She was anxious to know where she stood with Justin Wentworth—but he seemed far more interested in his silly pebbles! She pulled her boots on and stuffed the pile of bandages inside her cap, then stood up. "I must go now," Olwyn announced.

Justin, worried about his missing diamond, gave her a distracted glance.

"We'll talk again before we reach Cape Town," he said, then at the worried look in her eyes he walked over and stood looking down at her. There were many questions he wanted to ask her, many things he wanted to say, but it was the wrong time. Smiling, he lifted his hand and touched her face. "Your secret is safe with me," he said.

# 7

Olwyn found the missing diamond, or graphite as she thought it was, only minutes later, but didn't bother to return it since Wentworth had assured her it was worthless.

She had more pressing claims on her time, namely to clean herself up before the Scobbies saw her and started asking awkward questions about where she'd been during the storm.

In spite of all the crashing and battering going on during the gale no serious damage had been done to the *Randolph*, and by the time Olwyn sped away from Justin's stateroom the clean-up crews and repairmen were already busy, scurrying about with their tools. In all the hubbub nobody paid her the slightest attention.

Olwyn stopped at a fresh-water pump and washed her hands and face and smoothed back the tangled mass of her hair as best she could, wishing she had a brush handy. At least her cap would hide most of it, she reasoned, and pulled the wadded-up bandages out of it to put it on—when something small and hard fell out and landed with a ping on the planks at her feet.

Stooping, Olwyn spotted the stone in the light of the lantern over the water pump as it lay winking up at her. She picked it up and stared at it for a moment, then thrust it into her pocket and promptly forgot about it.

In a closet off one of the laundry rooms she pulled off her torn shirt to rewind her bandages, her heart fluttering nervously lest somebody come by and catch her in the act. Once she'd replaced the shirt, fixing the garment as best she could considering its condition, she cautiously stepped out of her hiding place, her mind busy thinking up an excuse to explain her disheveled appearance to the Scobbies, finally deciding to blame it on the storm.

Olwyn came upon Harold hanging about the companionway leading down to the steerage cabins, obviously waiting there to intercept her. He wasn't so cocky now, she noticed. Instead he looked diffident and apprehensive. At the sight of him fury bubbled up inside her. This boy was the cause of the predicament she now found herself in. Thanks to him she had lost her virginity and even then, had no guarantee that Justin Wentworth would keep her secret. Wentworth knew the truth about her now, a powerful weapon he could wield over her.

Hal shrank away from the rage he saw burning in her eyes.

"I'm sorry, Oliver," he mumbled. "I'll never do it again, I promise. Please don't tell my father!"

Quite suddenly the anger drained out of her, leaving her exhausted and resigned. What was the point of ranting and raging at Harold now, she thought wearily, when the damage was done? Just the same, Olwyn eyed him sternly.

"You know, I hoped once that we could be friends, Harold—"

"Oh, we can, Oliver!" he cried, hope leaping into his eyes. "I'd like that very much, really I would."

"I wonder . . ."

He grabbed her arm, pleading. "Please give me another chance, Oliver? You won't be sorry. I—I know I haven't been very nice," he admitted, shame-faced, "but I'm not usually a bully. I always stuck up for the cow—the quiet lads at school."

"I'm not afraid of you, Harold," Olwyn told him firmly, looking him right in the eye. "And I'm not a coward, which you'll soon discover if you ever try anything like that again."

Uncertainty flickered in the round blue eyes that now sized her up with new respect as Olwyn faced up to him boldly. After a minute he nodded and sur-prised her by thrusting out his hand. Hiding a smile, Olwyn took it and they shook solemnly, man to man.

"I always keep my word; you'll see," Harold assured her.

The following day Justin searched every inch of his stateroom for the missing gem, reasoning that it couldn't have *walked* out of his quarters. He almost took the place apart, even poking inside ornaments and other hollow objects and running his fingers around picture frames, peering and digging into each tiny hole and crevice in his suite, all with no success. Once he had ascertained to his complete satisfaction that the stone was no longer in his stateroom his mind turned to Olwyn Moore, who had left the previous afternoon in such a hurry.

In the morning he sent a discreet messenger with word that he must see her at once and, after loitering about the vicinity of the Scobbies' cabins for almost three hours, the seaman finally managed a word with Olwyn in private. "Mr. Wentworth wants to see you immediately," the man told her. "It's very impor-tant."

In some trepidation, Olwyn made her way to Wentworth's suite. He had hardly been out of her mind since the afternoon of the storm, each detail of that afternoon etched in fire in her brain and senses.

Much as she despised the man because of what he had done to her, he was still the most exciting thing ever to come into her life, arousing a whole new set of emotions inside her that left her breathless even to contemplate, stronger and more compelling than the shame she felt at what had taken place between them.

So obsessed was Olwyn with the fascination of the man himself that all thought of the "graphite" had slipped her mind. As she made her way to his stateroom, her heart beating fast, the diamond remained tucked away in the pocket of her breeches where she had thrust it, completely forgotten.

Wentworth was waiting for her, pacing about his sitting room. The moment she knocked on his door he wrenched it open and drew her inside, banging it shut behind her. He too was in some state of agitation and Olwyn quailed at the sight of his grim face. It wasn't so much the loss of the gem itself that worried Justin, as what would happen if the girl were to show it to someone—someone more aware and knowledgeable than she was. Maury Howell, for instance.

His vibrant blue eyes raked over Olwyn's face as she stood before him trying to look cool and unconcerned, her dark head tilted back at a proud angle, her beautiful face cold. "Why did you send for me?" she queried, some instinct warning her not to show the turmoil she felt or allow herself to be intimidated by his hard expression, even though it hurt her, considering what had happened between them.

"I think you have something belonging to me," he growled.

Olwyn was startled. "What?"

Justin smiled sardonically, his eyes still cold, not in the least taken in by her pretended innocence. This was the girl who had audaciously turned herself into a male to deceive James Scobbie into giving her a job, he was remembering; the girl who admitted, even before that, to being in trouble of some kind in Glasgow, resulting in the loss of her job, even to having to flee Scotland! She had lied before, he thought angrily, and was lying now, and at that moment Justin was too worried to be tactful; worried about her, too, and what might happen to her if she casually revealed the gem to the wrong eyes.

"I want it back, you little thief!" he snarled, seizing her by the arm and giving her a little shake. "Where is it? What have you done with it?"

Olwyn turned pale, her eyes widening as she gazed up at his angry face. She had absolutely no idea what he was talking about, though she gleaned that something valuable had been stolen from his stateroom—and he was accusing *her* of stealing it!

The unfair accusation stung and injured tears flooded into her eyes. She had been right about him the first time, Olwyn thought bitterly. He was an arrogant beast and totally heartless! The tender, passionate lover of two afternoons ago had merely been a ploy he'd assumed to get what he wanted from her.

"I didn't take anything of yours!" Olwyn spat indignantly, trying to tug her arm from his grasp. "I wouldn't want anything belonging to you, Justin Wentworth, and I'm sorry I ever met you at all! If one of us is a thief it's you!" she hurled at him, her eyes blazing. "The thing you took from me two days ago can *never* be replaced—"

"You gave it freely enough," Justin interrupted with a smile that seemed more like a sneer to the girl watching him, then he shocked her further by adding, "You're the hottest virgin I've ever had in my bed."

With her free hand Olwyn slapped his face.

"Brute!" she screamed as Justin dropped her arm and touched his hand to his cheek, her temper boiling over, her nerves cracking under the stress and strain of the last few weeks. "I despise you!" she cried, and bolted for the door where she turned back to add, "And I hope I never have to set eyes on you again."

Justin started after her with the intention of catching her and shaking the truth out of her, if necessary, as he should have done years before with Christina, but after a few steps he halted. Perhaps he was a fool, he thought, but where Olwyn Moore was concerned the tiniest seed of doubt lurked at the back of his mind. When he'd challenged her the girl had seemed genuinely puzzled—or perhaps she was just a very good actress. There was certainly a lot more to Olwyn than met the eye, he mused, and he was *still* determined to find out all about her, for practical reasons if for nothing else. If she did indeed have his diamond then she was in considerable danger—and his future plans were in danger of being ruined. Justin made up his mind to keep a close eye on the reckless little wildcat, certainly the most intriguing and bizarre woman he had ever met, and the most infuriating.

An idea occurred to him, a way of keeping the Scobbie party in his sights.

"Land!" the excited cry rang out two days later. "Land on the horizon!"

The alert sent everyone galloping for the deck rail to point and exclaim in relief and wonder, most by now heartily weary of life on board ship and eager to test their balance on dry land once more, though two more days were to pass before this could take place. During those two days a carnival air prevaded the *Randolph*, the passengers gay and expectant, the meals festive, a ball held in both the steerage and first-class areas of the ship.

The Scobbies, naturally, didn't attend the ball. Listening to the music and watching the crowds flock to the saloon in their best attire, flushed and happy and bent on enjoying themselves, Olwyn experienced a sharp pang of envy. She should just be glad, she told herself dryly, that James didn't suggest they go there to pass out religious tracts.

On the day land was spotted Olwyn came across Wentworth's funny little pebble snuggled in the seam of her trouser pocket, but even then she didn't think too much about it or attach any special significance to her find. Whatever it was that he had lost must have been quite valuable, she reasoned, since he had stirred

up such a fuss about it, and this pebble—graphite—
was nothing worth bothering about, or so he had told
her, if not in so many words.

She started to throw it overboard but, noticing how
the strong sunlight reflected off the stone, here and
there making it sparkle, Olwyn decided to retain it
instead, quickly assuring herself that she had no
intention of viewing it as a keepsake to remind her of
the first time a man had ever made love to her. Far
from it! She was anxious to forget Wentworth, not
remember him.

Still, she *did* think of him. She lived in dread of
what he might do during those last few days on the
*Randolph* and feared he might seek retaliation following their fight. After a sleepless night Olwyn tried to
resign herself to the worst and stop torturing herself.
If Wentworth told James the truth about her there was
nothing she could do, and if for some reason he didn't,
then she could go on as before. Whatever happened
she would just have to accept it.

Hannah was in a flurry of activity preparing their
clothes for when they disembarked, anxious that they
should all look as smart as possible. As her husband
liked to joke, she had brought enough material with
her to sew her way around the globe—flawed fabric
bought cheaply from the Glasgow mills, but servicea-
ble nevertheless—and Hannah's fingers seemed per-
manently attached to a needle and thread. Already
those industrious fingers had stitched a new front
panel to Olwyn's torn shirt, finished the jacket she was
making for her, and sewn her an extra pair of
breeches.

Overcome with gratitude, Olwyn hugged her impulsively. "I've never owned so many clothes in my life!"
the girl admitted—and it was the truth.

Harold surprised her by approving. "You look very
grand in your new jacket, Oliver. It makes you seem
bigger and more muscular somehow."

Olwyn smiled at him, touched, well aware that this
was the finest praise the boy could think of. He had

been unusually subdued since their altercation. Sometimes she'd turn to find him watching her speculatively, almost as if she'd become a different person in his eyes and he was anxious to take her measure, but so far his attitude to her had definitely improved and for that she was thankful.

Passengers milled about the decks as the *Randolph* steamed into Table Bay, the dominating presence of its famous landmark, Table Mountain, looming ahead and overshadowing everything else, white buildings snuggled about its base, the crystal green of the sea like an apron all around. They could feel the waves of heat radiating out from the land and smell, faintly on the breeze, the tropical vegetation, pungent and somehow stirring, like a whiff of something exotic and rare. Olwyn caught the tang of an aroma like cloves and cinnamon and laughed at the dugout canoes of the natives, black as night, paddling madly out to meet them. Her heart gave a fierce leap of excitement that left her breathless.

As she stood leaning over the rail, Africa seemed to beckon to Olwyn. Even then she felt its warm, seductive lure, which many a stranger had felt before her, the magnetic tug of its wild and often savage beauty and the constant surprise of the new and different, the feeling of being an explorer in a land of ever-changing magic and boundless freedom, a place where anything was possible.

Olwyn recalled Maury Howell saying in his candid way, "I'm out to make a name for myself over there, and Africa is just the place to do it with everything starting up. It's a cracking spot for young men like us."

Would it also be a cracking place for a young woman? Olwyn mused with an upsurge of the old ambition instilled in her from childhood by her father.

Beside her Hannah Scobbie was growing restless. She turned to her older son fretfully. "Where on earth has your father gone now?"

The boy pointed down the deck a little way and, turning, they could see the missionary deep in conversation with Justin Wentworth. Olwyn felt a jolt of alarm. This was just the time, when they were about to disembark, that Wentworth might choose to tell James the truth about her! She was instantly terrified, for all that she'd tried to convince herself to stay calm, and clung to the rail until her fingers turned numb as she waited for Scobbie to finish his conversation and return to them.

When he did he was beaming. Olwyn stared at him askance.

"Well, that's a great load off my mind!" Scobbie announced, his smile taking in all of them. "We'll be traveling from Cape Town to Nuruzambora with Mr. Wentworth, and much the safer for it too. It was very decent of him to suggest it." James grinned. "It saved me the trouble of asking him!"

# Burnished
# Land

# 8

"Metse! Metse!"

*Africa
1868*

A native vendor with a face as black and shiny as wet coal—one of many peddling their wares among the teeming crowds milling about the docks—panted up to the Scobbie party with his cart and thrust the shell of a gourd into Olwyn's sweating hand. Hot and thirsty as she was, she grasped it eagerly and was about to raise it to her lips when an Englishman standing next to her knocked it away.

"Never touch the water!" he warned, almost shouting to be heard over the noise. "It's contaminated and 'twill make you ill unless it has first been boiled for several minutes. Aye, and never touch the food either until it has been cooked to a frazzle." He patted his stomach and added ruefully, "Believe me, I know."

Olwyn thanked him for the advice, and made a note to herself to remember that in future.

The blazing sun, heat, the sounds and smells and general chaos attendant on the arrival of a major steamship at Cape Town made conversation impossible. While the Scobbie boys exclaimed and pointed at their first glimpse of the natives, whose color ranged from rich cream through coppery tan to deepest black, depending on where they were from, Hannah fanned herself vigorously, alternatively amazed and frightened by the new sights revealed to her startled eyes. James looked about keenly, anxious to make contact with Walter Hogg, the church elder and merchant they would be staying with while in Cape Town.

Olwyn found it all very bewildering but exciting nevertheless; the steamy heat and blinding sunshine, the dazzling white robes of some of the natives and the vibrant color and sheer confusion seething all about her.

Quite soon she saw that Cape Town was a study in contrasts, from the orderliness and quaint charm of the residential part of town, much of it built by the Dutch, though the British were now in control of the Colony, to the teeming squalor of the native section with its crowded shanties and narrow, dusty streets, countless intriguing little shops—most of them run by Arabs—and the vague air of danger and mystery that pervaded this area of the city, if city it could be called.

It was nothing like as big as Glasgow, Olwyn noticed once Walter Hogg arrived to whisk them away from the docks to his home in the hills, though to her wondering eyes, considerably more exotic. Thrilled by what she glimpsed through the carriage window, Olwyn cried, "Oh, I must explore all of it before we leave for Nuruzambora!"

Hogg turned in his seat and gave her a stern, measuring look. He was a chunky little Scotsman in his late forties, with a broad seamed face like cracked leather and tiny bearlike eyes that Olwyn found somehow intimidating. He had bristling gray whiskers —there were even tufts of hair sprouting from his ears and nose, she observed—and a general air of authority and prosperity about him.

"Don't be daft, lad," he told her, putting paid to her desire to see all of Cape Town. "There are places where white people are well advised not to go hereabouts, at least *decent* white people." Olwyn could tell from the look he gave her that Hogg had yet to decide just how "decent" *she* was. Did the man sense something strange about her? she wondered uncomfortably. He had such sharp, piercing little eyes, and she felt he wasn't the type, unlike James, to accept anyone at face value.

Their host proudly pointed out the stately government buildings. As they climbed into the hills, the residences became larger, grander, the grounds around them more spacious, most of them barely glimpsed behind the trees and high, protective walls surrounding the properties.

Hogg's place turned out to be equally pretentious. The tall gabled house, he said, had once belonged to a Dutch sea captain, but through the years since his ownership had been added to extensively, with wings running off on either side, one of them for the servants. Olwyn was to be shunted to a tiny chamber in this section, apart from the rest of the family—the merchant and his wife were the types to keep people in their place—though she didn't know it then.

Mrs. Hogg, a stout, snobbish little woman, immediately treated them, especially Hannah, in a patronizing manner. Through her many contacts in Scotland, especially in the Church, Nan Hogg was well aware of the standing of the Scobbies at the time they left Scotland. Though she also knew that Hannah was from money, she still made it clear in a none too subtle way which of them was in the stronger position now.

"My dear Mrs. Scobbie, you do look dreadfully weary after your long journey," she greeted the missionary's wife, her eyes sweeping over Hannah's best gown, made by herself from a length of flawed and faded silk she had purchased cheap at the mill, its workmanship and quality strikingly inferior to the shimmering gold satin gown worn by their hostess, complimented by the flashing topaz necklace she was wearing about her plump neck. She clucked on, pretending distress, "Oh, dear, I'm afraid the sea air has quite taken the color out of your frock! But I'm sure one of the servants would be happy enough to have it."

Hannah had worn the dress for the first time that day.

Olwyn took an immediate dislike to the couple. For all their pious ways, they were far from charitable. It angered her to see poor Hannah's embarrassment; she was tired, too, of being made to feel inadequate, her worth measured by monetary standards, yes, even here in Africa! That depressed Olwyn for a moment. She had thought it would be different here, but if she could judge by Cape Town, in reality a small dot on the fringe of civilization, then it must be the same the world over, she mused with a sigh. One day, Olwyn told herself, people would not look down on her. She was suddenly very determined about that; to best them at their own game. No wonder Maury Howell had been so anxious to make good! she thought irritably. She decided then that when her time was up working for Mr. Scobbie, she would very seriously cast about and seek out a good opportunity for herself.

After refreshments, many kinds of cold drink, dainty sandwiches and frosted cakes that had the boys' eyes popping wide—"just a little snack to tide you over until supper," said their hostess—they were finally shown to their rooms, about ready to collapse by this time.

Olwyn smiled thinly when a black servant led her away from the others to the servants' quarters—but at least she had a room all to herself. If the Hoggs could only know it, Olwyn thought to herself, her accommodations were far better than anything she had ever lived in at home.

The tiny room she was shown into by Lobule, the maid, was starkly plain by comparison with the rest of the house, which in Olwyn's eyes had been ostentatious and even vulgar. Here she had a narrow bed, an old oak chest and an oil lamp. The only picture on the wall was that of the crucifixion. The rather chilling painting was given a prominent spot directly opposite the bed, the first thing to be seen upon rising in the morning.

Lobule left her for a few minutes, then returned with a washbowl and a pitcher full of warm water for her toilet, towels, and a cloth over her arm.

"Thank you," Olwyn said when the maid made her way back to the door.

Lobule turned in surprise, obviously not used to being thanked for her services. A wide white smile flashed across her face. "Thank you," she echoed, then shyly darted from the room.

Left blissfully alone at last, Olwyn began unpacking her few belongings. The only things of value she owned were her medical books, and those she lined up neatly against the back of the chest. Her medical bag and contents were certainly worth something, too, but in effect they belonged to James Scobbie since he had bought and paid for them.

Then there was something else . . .

Carefully wrapped in a piece of gauze torn from her bandages and hidden away inside a pocket in her medical bag was the tiny piece of graphite. Once she had bathed and changed her clothes, Olwyn fished it out of her bag and lay down across her bed to examine it. The sight of the pebble brought back a flood of memories that made her blush, and filled her with a confusing mixture of excitement and anger. Not an hour went by when she didn't think of Justin Wentworth. And she didn't *want* to think of him, or what he had done to her! He had taken her virginity—yet in the end had cared more about his silly graphite, worthless stuff where her virtue had been beyond price.

*I really ought to throw it away*, Olwyn thought, examining the stone as it lay in the palm of her hand, here and there twinkling like a tiny fallen star, rather pretty in its way. *If I get rid of it, then I might not be reminded of him so often*, she told herself. *Especially of what happened between us.*

It made Olwyn hot and agitated just to recall it.

Wentworth had caused her another worry. What if her monthly flow didn't come as usual? Dear God, how would she handle *that* disaster?

No, no, Olwyn told herself quickly, she wouldn't go looking for trouble. Enough of it managed to seek her out. But the thought of them traveling to Nuruzambora in Wentworth's company made her insides churn. In reality there was no point in tossing away the stone since he would soon be with them in person, far more of a trial than memories could ever be.

To think he had accused her of being a thief! He was no better than Devlin Sproat, who had tried to make serious trouble for her, using the ploy that she had robbed him! Well, Olwyn thought grimly, Sproat hadn't succeeded either, nor would Wentworth. She was a little surprised—very surprised—that he hadn't complained about her to Scobbie, especially that he hadn't divulged the shocking truth about her to her employer. And that's where Wentworth differed from Sproat. Olwyn jumped up then and paced about nervously. He different from Sproat in other ways, too, but she didn't want to dwell on that!

Standing at the window that faced a courtyard, Olwyn gazed down at the little stone in her hand and was suddenly struck by how much it flashed in the sunlight streaming in. Even if it had no real value, she reflected, it was still quite a pretty thing and would make a very interesting necklace, if somehow a chain or cord could be bored through to make a hole.

An idea sprang into her mind. It was only nine days to Christmas, and if she could only find someone to put a chain through it, the graphite would make a nice gift for Hannah. Mrs. Scobbie had been so kind to her; she had taken the trouble to make her the new clothes.

And she could always buy sweets for James and the boys.

At that Olwyn ran to her bag to fish out her money. She had only a little over a pound left, but perhaps it would be enough. Pleased with her idea, she made up her mind to sneak into Cape Town at the first opportunity and find a jeweler, then surprise Hannah and family with the gifts at Christmas.

It was easier to steal away than she'd thought. In spite of all the supplies James had brought with him from Scotland for the mission station, he still needed to make immediate arrangements for wagons, oxen, men, and other equipment to be waiting for them at Algoa Bay, the spot from where they would finally strike out for the interior of the country. Wentworth's experience was a great help to James, and he was able to advise him about exactly what he would need. Olwyn knew that Scobbie had met with the trader twice during their first few days in Cape Town as they couldn't afford any delay. Also, Walter Hogg helped by introducing James to people who might add to the knowledge he was gathering about the area they were going to.

Through Harold, Olwyn learned that his father was taking instructions on the use and handling of firearms from a retired big game hunter in the area.

"Mama doesn't like guns," the boy said, "but Papa explained that they were necessary—and they are! Think of all the dangerous beasts we might run into; elephants, lions, and the like." His eyes sparkled with relish. "We've got to be prepared to defend ourselves."

For once Harold was in his father's corner.

Mrs. Hogg kept poor exhausted Hannah running to luncheons, teas, and jaunts into town to do their Christmas shopping, though Hannah had scant money to spend and found these shopping trips embarrassing under the circumstances.

Olwyn was left largely on her own, which suited her fine. She bided her time and noticed that the servants had their own cart for driving into town to fetch supplies, which they did almost every morning. On Thursday, four days after they landed, Olwyn begged the driver, Manelo, for a ride into town. He was a grizzled Hottentot in his fifties who seemed surprised that she would want to travel in the servants' cart. "Why you want to go der?" he asked her, gazing down from his high perch behind the rump of an ox. "Why you want go in dees cart? Peoples here"—he jerked a thumb at the house—"not go in dis one."

"Oh, that's all right," Olwyn told him with a smile. "I don't mind."

"Why you go?" He was obviously unhappy about the idea.

Olwyn tried to be casual, even as her fingers closed over the little package in her pocket where the stone snuggled in its wad of gauze.

"Oh," she said, smiling, "I would just like to take a stroll about town."

His dark eyes rolled around the sun-dappled courtyard with its acacia shade trees that made Olwyn think of a lady's parasol, and banks of bright orange flowering aloes and fluffy-looking blood lilies, until they finally came back to her upturned face. "Who you go wis?"

"Myself." Olwyn took a deep breath, nervous and impatient and anxious to get away before anyone else saw her. She decided to take a tip from the Hoggs and became more authoritarian. "Is there room for me to sit beside you or must I ride in the back?"

When Manelo seemed inclined to ponder this Olwyn simply climbed up onto the wagon and forced him to move over a little, and finally they set off down the long driveway, the driver shaking his head and muttering under his breath, "No good, no good you go alone," then continued in the same vein in his own language.

Down the hill they lumbered into town, and as soon as they reached an area of respectable shops, Olwyn had Manelo stop the cart, thinking that she could easily have walked down on her own and been spared the scolding and constant frowns of disapproval that the driver sent her way. She thanked him and would have hurried away when he called to her, "I get you back?"

"No! I'll find my own way back."

"No good, no good . . ."

Olwyn didn't wait to hear more. She disappeared into the nearest store and stayed there until Manelo got tired of waiting and moved off down the street still grumbling to himself about the vagaries of white people, particularly *young* white people.

Since she had very limited funds Olwyn decided against the first two jewelers' shops she came to and decided to try the third, which gave the appearance of being more modest. It seemed very dark inside after the brilliant sunshine, and she had to blink her eyes a moment or two to accustom them to the gloom. Once they did adjust Olwyn encountered the smiling face of a very young man behind the counter. He was Dutch, the son of the owner, and at first greeted her in his own tongue, quickly switching to English when Olwyn confessed that she didn't understand him.

She was lucky that his father wasn't in the shop and had stepped out to partake of his morning coffee only moments before, temporarily leaving the teenage boy in charge.

The youngster carefully examined the stone that Olwyn passed over to him and then announced that it definitely wasn't graphite. "No, no." He laughed at her suggestion and, jabbing at it with the tip of a letter opener and not making as much as a dent, added, "It much too hard."

Olwyn was taken aback, remembering what Wentworth had said. "Are you sure?"

He nodded, now peering at it through a funny-looking glass as he held it up to the window.

"What is it, then?"

There was a silence. The boy was sixteen years old, fresh from school and new to the business and still had everything to learn, but he did know that the small stone he held in his hand was certainly not graphite. He had a suggestion for Olwyn: that she take her pebble to a mineralogist to try to find out what it was before deciding what to do with it, which he felt was the correct advice. Then he directed her to the office of Knute Bleur.

Back out on the street, dazzled by the strong sunlight and steadily rising temperature, though it was still only ten o'clock in the morning, Olwyn set out to find Bleur's establishment several blocks away. Soon her throat stung and her eyes teared in the dusty air, and her senses reeled at the strange sights and sounds all around her. There was great activity in town and great variety in the people, who seemed to have converged on the Colony from every corner of the globe—the somber black dress and manner of the Boers with their rumbling ox wagons taking their farm produce to market, the white robes and knotted headdresses of the Arabs, their beautiful copper trays and inlaid tables and ornaments displayed all about the exterior of their shops, tempting Olwyn to pause and take a look, even if she couldn't afford to buy anything. And the natives, many dressed in their own colorful kiltlike garments or loose-flowing wraps, but sometimes in a weird combination of European and native clothing that made Olwyn smile in surprise and amusement.

She saw dusky women with hoops through their noses and ears, and with untold numbers of bracelets jingling on their arms, and gasped in astonishment and some horror at a man with a stick thrust through his lip, causing it to jut out at an alarming degree, and yet others with hideous mutilations done to their faces, as if some fiend had scored them with the tip of a knife, like a demented artist wreaking havoc on his canvas.

The pleasant scents of coffee and spices hung in the air, as well as others of a much less salubrious nature. Once or twice, passing an alley, Olwyn was so overcome with the stench that she had to hold her nose, at the same time fighting the urge to gag. Everywhere there was noise. "Kengwe!" cried a man with a tray of watermelons, while another stood outside his lean-to shop yelling "Boyalwa!" and urging the pedestrians to try a cup of his beer.

Before she had gone very far Olwyn was streaming sweat and had to cough to dislodge the dust from her throat. She noticed that the closer she got to Bleur's premises—or where it was supposed to be—the dingier grew her surroundings.

Finally, just when she thought she was lost, Olwyn found it. It was down a narrow side street, and an unpretentious little office it was, with the owner's name written in faded lettering above the door and the word MINERALOGIST painted across the window in the shape of an arch.

Though there was a lamp burning inside, the interior seemed very dim to Olwyn after the street outside, and it was a moment or two before she noticed the squat little sallow-skinned man hunched over a desk in the corner, working on a stack of papers piled up in front of him. A younger man stood motionless by his side, his eyes also on the papers. Though the latter was also dressed in European clothing he was quite dark, Olwyn noted once she could see better. He was either an African, the girl thought, or more likely an Arab.

The younger man drifted away through a curtain into a back room a moment after she entered.

"I—I'm looking for Mr. Bleur," Olwyn told the man who remained seated.

"I'm Bleur," he replied shortly.

His eyes were moist and heavy-lidded and disconcertingly far apart, lending him an unfortunate reptilian appearance.

"Well," he said, seeming bored, "what can I do for you, young fellow?"

Olwyn took out the stone and set it on his desk. "I would like to know exactly what that is," she said and, as he stared, added "I'm Oliver Moore."

Bleur heaved a sigh, pushing aside his papers with the air of a man resigned to be patient regardless of how much he was put-upon. "Very well. My fee is one pound sterling."

Olwyn gaped at him as he set about lighting more lamps and lifting several objects from his desk drawer, one of which looked like a mallet and another like the sawn-off top of a dark bottle. His fee seemed to her exorbitant, and if he didn't already have her stone and hadn't seated himself again to examine it, she would have dropped it back in her pocket and walked out.

"Sit down, boy," he ordered in the same work-weary voice without raising his head, and she glanced around and spotted a chair, one of several lined up against the wall at the opposite side of the room.

Once seated Olwyn gazed balefully at the top of Bleur's bent head, which she could barely see above the clutter on his desktop. His bald pate, encircled with a ring of bushy black hair, made her think of an egg snuggled in a nest of dirty straw. She glanced about the dingy little room, one ear cocked to the rustling, tinkling, and to her surprise, hammering going on behind the ledgers stacked on the desk. This was followed by a jarring screech like a nail makes when drawn across a piece of glass.

Her head swiveled to the desk, there to find two froglike eyes staring at her over the books. Further, Bleur's smooth, hairless pate was now beaded with sweat that glistened in the light of the lamps. He looked excited, the girl thought, or perhaps in shock. She started to rise when he called out in a high-pitched squeak, "It's a diamond, for the love of Christ! Get in here, Mahmet!"

The lean, dark man glided silently back into the room, almost colliding with Olwyn as she rushed up to the desk, her senses reeling. "Is it *really* a diamond, Mr. Bleur?" she cried.

The dark man asked in a heavily accented voice, "How beeg?"

The mineralogist laughed gleefully. "About twenty-two carats. Uncut."

Both men turned to look at her. Something changed in Bleur's eyes. It was as if the shutters had been lowered on a window, giving him a cunning, secretive look. "It's not a very good stone," he told her, turning it over in his thick fingers. "It's badly flawed. But . . ." he raised his head and gave her an ingratiating smile, "I'm a generous man and prepared to give you fifty pounds for it?"

Olwyn couldn't think. She was stunned. Even now she felt sure there had to be some mistake. Wentworth had told her it was graphite. Worthless! Yet now that she thought about it, hadn't he gone to some trouble to find the stones when they were tossed about his stateroom in the storm, practically ignoring her in spite of the fact that they'd just made love!

He knew! Aye, her mind rushed on, suddenly making a connection, and it was the stone—now in Bleur's hands—that he'd accused her of stealing! A stone that wasn't worthless after all.

The mineralogist was staring at her fixedly and, thinking she was holding out for more money, blurted, "Very well, boy, I'll give you one hundred pounds for this very poor diamond. Take it or leave it!"

The girl blinked, her mind dragged back to the present at this astounding offer, a veritable fortune to someone in her position. She noticed that Bleur was trickling sweat now and that his hands were shaking, and suddenly Olwyn knew that the diamond was worth *much* more than he proposed to give her for it.

"Five hundred!" he cried, his excitement and greed boiling over. "*Provided* you also tell us where it came from?"

Olwyn could see that he meant to have it at all cost—only it wasn't hers to sell! When she still hesitated the two men exchanged a look and the one called Mahmet sidled between her and the door.

# 9

A menacing aura had infiltrated the dingy little office.

"Cat got your tongue, young sir?" the mineralogist queried impatiently. With a negligent flick of his fingers, as if he had made her the offer against his better judgment, he dropped the stone on his desk and shook his head. "It's not worth a fraction of the sum I'm prepared to give you, but if you tell me where you got it—"

Olwyn pounced on the gem and in a flash thrust it into her pocket.

"It's not for sale," she told him breathlessly, beginning to get really nervous now. "It . . . it really belongs to a friend of mine, and—and I shall have to consult him before we decide what to do with it." She pulled her last pound out of her pocket and laid it before Bleur. "I believe that is your fee."

She wheeled around to leave when she saw the man called Mahmet lounging with his back against the door, barring her exit. He straightened instantly at her approach and tensed, as if he meant to grab her, at the same time rattling off something to the mineralogist in a language Olwyn couldn't understand. Bleur interrupted the flow curtly and shook his head, and Mahmet nimbly stepped aside to let her pass, though Olwyn could tell from the anger in the black eyes that he would have preferred to detain her.

She ran from the office, banging the door behind her.

Bleur crooked a finger at his assistant, bidding him come closer. The older man instructed quickly, "Follow, but don't apprehend him. Take note of where he leads you. I have a hunch that that boy will lead us to a strike."

Mahmet nodded and vanished out the door.

Bleur, the son of a Dutch mother and French father, sat where he was, drumming his fingers on the desk, the sweat drying on his forehead. He dearly hoped that his instincts, usually quite reliable, would prove to be correct. It seemed to him that there was only one way such a young lad could have an *uncut* diamond in his possession. The chances were good that he worked for some up-country prospector who had just made a strike!

Bleur, in the course of conducting his business, knew many of these prospectors, men who roamed the hinterlands of Africa in the wild hope of unearthing a fortune. Most of them were loners, rough, independent types who distrusted the motives of others and were usually very secretive about their own affairs and movements. If one such had gotten lucky and decided to have his stones valued, it was natural that he would send an underling in his place to avoid being recognized and bombarded with awkward questions, thought Bleur.

For years there had been vague talk of gold and precious gems in Africa. The mineralogist was aware that a small amount of gold had actually been found here and there, though not enough to make large-scale mining a viable proposition. Many garnets and even a few diamonds had also been discovered, but again not in any great quantity nor enough to stir real interest. Bleur recalled that the last man to find a diamond had been murdered on his way to town to have the stone appraised, and that very few of the people who actually made the discoveries lived long enough to benefit from them.

Olwyn became lost in the back streets of Cape Town on her way to the Hoggs' place, but eventually arrived home safely, dust-streaked, sweating, and exhausted, desperate to plunge into a nice cooling bath.

Olwyn's experience with Knute Bleur had sobered even as it enlightened her. She still found it hard to believe that the funny little stone was a precious gem—one she was anxious to return to its true owner as soon as possible. The stone fairly burned her fingers now when she touched it, even though she hadn't stolen it. Olwyn sensed that it wasn't going to be easy to convince Justin Wentworth of that. Not now.

The trader had a home in Cape Town, she had heard, so the first step was to find out his address. That evening when she saw James Scobbie she brought up the subject casually, as if merely curious about what Wentworth's house looked like.

"Oh, it's a mansion," said James somewhat dryly. "My, my, it's truly astounding what the likes of beeswax, indigo, and bird feathers must bring. We can only hope that Mr. Wentworth apportions some of his wealth to the Church," he went on a bit dourly, "or to the many beggars in this town. Do you know, I even saw some lepers today, Oliver. Hideous!" he finished with a shudder.

James wasn't precisely sure how to reach Wentworth's house. Cape Town seemed like a confusing maze to the missionary. Both times he'd visited the trader it had been in a coach and he'd paid more attention to the sights than the route they traveled. But being James, he never cared to admit to being ignorant about anything and in answer to Olwyn's question about where Wentworth lived, he tossed off a few directions in his usual positive manner, never dreaming, of course, that his young assistant meant to go there.

A picnic had been arranged for the family the next day—Friday—and once they left, Olwyn set off down the hill toward the town. Even by ten o'clock in the morning the heat was already fierce, promising to be the hottest day she would experience yet. Bad as it was in the hills, it became that much worse as she descended into the valley, puffs of fine reddish-brown dust swirling up about her with every step she took, tickling her nose and bringing on fits of sneezing and coughing. Wild, aggressive foliage threatened to choke off the road in places, and strange flowers in bright orange, scarlet, purple, and white filled the slumberous air with a heavy, exotic perfume that was almost too sweet. Bees and other insects buzzed and droned and numerous lizards, some quite large, skittered across her path and vanished into the undergrowth. As she reached the native shanties on the fringe of Cape Town proper, Olwyn noted that the unpleasant smells had triumphed over the pleasant ones that morning.

Her nervousness at the thought of confronting Justin Wentworth increased. There was the diamond, of course, now carefully rolled up in its protective wadding in her pocket—would he believe her story about that? Then there was the other . . . thing between them. Olwyn's heart fluttered madly at the memory. She had made up her mind to be brisk and brief when she met him, to get their awkward business over and done with as quickly as possible . . . but suddenly she wasn't ready to face him quite yet. Just thinking about his penetrating blue eyes and lazy smile made her faint and light-headed.

She procrastinated instead of making directly for his house, wandering about the shops examining the interesting goods she saw displayed there, one twisting street leading into another until she came to a colorful bazaar where the noise and bustle made her head spin. In a detached way, her mind still on Wentworth, Olwyn noticed vaguely that this area was quite dirty, if intriguing, and that there were fewer Europeans about here. She pushed her way past stalls piled high with weird fruits and vegetables and sacks of grain, others where beads and bangles, brass and copper goods were on display. She spied crudely made bamboo cages housing pigs, fowl, monkeys, and songbirds, all of whom added their voices to the general pandemonium. Hawkers screamed and gestured at her, trying to induce her to buy something, and some made rude gestures when Olwyn shook her head and continued walking. She saw many of the beggars Scobbie had mentioned the previous evening, and when one of them brushed very close to her Olwyn put her hand in the pocket of her breeches, judiciously covering the package holding the diamond.

Early afternoon found her still meandering, still unable to dredge up the courage to face Justin Wentworth. In fact, the more time passed the worse she got, much to her disgust. Finally Olwyn decided to stop off somewhere for a much-needed cup of coffee—she could not afford to buy anything to eat—then, she promised herself, she would definitely make straight for Wentworth's house.

The café Olwyn selected was not far from the bazaar and seemed deliciously cool and dim after the broiling glare of the sun outside. She smelled the rich odor of the very dark coffee favored in Africa as well as the pleasant aroma of highly spiced food. It took a moment for her eyes to adjust to the gloom, and she heard the low murmur of voices before she actually saw the customers seated at the tables; then they materialized out of the shadows.

There were no Europeans in the café at all.

A black-eyed servitor led her to a table, made of brass and very low, and Olwyn sat down self-consciously and gave him her order. He seemed to understand for he scurried off at once, disappearing through a beaded curtain into the kitchen area, leaving her to look about. Two Africans—wealthy men by the look of the numerous gold chains about their necks and the fine silk of their wraps—eyed her gravely from the next table as they delicately sipped their afternoon coffee from tiny brass cups. Beyond them she saw others in robes of various kinds, some she felt must be Arabs and others of indeterminate origin. All gazed at her with interest, as if surprised to find her among them.

Her coffee was brought to the table—black, thick, sickeningly sweet. Nevertheless Olwyn gulped it quickly, her haste raising the eyebrows of the other patrons, since coffee was a treat to be savored, quickly paid for it, and left the café, almost colliding with a figure in robes loitering about outside.

Within ten minutes of leaving the café Olwyn knew she was hopelessly lost. At first she wasn't worried; she'd become lost the day before and had eventually managed to get her bearings, but when an hour passed and she found no familiar landmarks she began to get a little uneasy. Somehow or other, she had wandered away from the shopping district into an area of crumbling old buildings and narrow dirt streets no wider than eight or ten feet across, shadowed and rubble-strewn streets, hemmed in by the structures rising on either side and the high walls between them. Gazing about, Olwyn glanced over her shoulder and saw two robed figures turn into the street behind her. One of them shouted something to the other, then both broke into a run, swiftly closing the distance between them and her.

She felt first a start of surprise, then came a surge of terror. Olwyn had always been quick on her feet and dashed away, her heart pounding, but within a minute or two they caught up with her, sending her tottering with a blow to the back of her head. It was as if some invisible hand had switched off the sun and she plunged into darkness.

*   *   *

Two hours later Olwyn revived in a fetid little cell in a waterfront brothel, the only light in the room a stubby candle flickering inside a stone jar. She was completely naked, bound hand and foot to the wooden frame of the pallet she lay on, the mattress a thin layer of reeking straw. As her still-dazed eyes roved the room and her mind began to absorb the horror of her situation, Olwyn's attention was drawn to a faint hissing sound close by.

There was a narrow ledge above the foot of the bed, and on the ledge rested a cage that was too big to be secure on its perch. Behind the flimsy bars of this cage rose a large black serpent, his prison swaying precariously with each whiplike movement of his body. Olwyn's eyes widened as she visualized the cage toppling over at any second, landing on the bed.

She screamed hysterically, the sound reverberating off the surrounding stucco walls, and the snake hissed and whipped himself into more of a frenzy, his prison rocking wildly now and moving ever closer to the edge of the shelf.

A door opened and Mahmet glided silently into the room, much like a snake himself. He glanced at the reptile then down at Olwyn and laughed aloud.

"Eee make good watch-dog, yes? Eee tell us when you wake."

"Cut me loose!" Olwyn shrieked, struggling to free herself and get away from the ledge. "That cage is about to fall—"

"Not fall," Mahmet assured her, now seating himself on the edge of her pallet. "Be silent and snake settle down. Not like noisy woman . . . or man who turn into woman."

His liquid black eyes greedily roamed her naked body, stretched out like a banquet before his eyes—and suddenly Olwyn was shrinking away from *him*! She had no doubt at all that Knute Bleur was behind her abduction. Bleur had wanted the diamond and when she refused to sell it to him had decided to take it however he could. Mahmet was simply following his master's orders. Well, she thought, her heart plummeting, now they had the stone—so why were they keeping her here like this? What else did they want from her?

Olwyn gasped in revulsion and started away, tugging frantically at her bonds as Mahmet's brown hands closed over her breasts, squeezing them into cones and rubbing the tips vigorously with his thumbs until they hardened. He bent his dark head, his tongue flicking out.

Olwyn's breath choked in a scream and her flesh cringed in disgust as Bleur's accomplice boldly invaded her body until not an inch of it escaped his hands, lips, and tongue, then he stood up and ripped off his clothes and cut her hands free. "Now," he grinned, "you do to me."

"Never!" Olwyn spat at him. "Never! You—you're vile and disgusting." She grabbed up handfuls of the filthy straw and tried to cover her body, hiding it from his eyes. Mahmet turned and lifted a hooked stick from the ledge where the snake's cage rested, and with a smug glance at her, slid the hooked part under the latch of the cage door.

"What are you doing?" she shrieked at him, her face blanching.

He paused but didn't take the hook away. "Maybe you like eem loving you better?" he purred, then chuckled thickly, his eyes sliding down over her body to her thighs. "Snake know how. Eem make you behave—"

"Oh God!" Olwyn moaned, twisting her head back and forth helplessly. "Why are you doing this to me? You've got the diamond; what more do you want?"

"Ah . . . yes, you almost make me forget." Mahmet's lean face sobered.

Quite abruptly his manner changed. He unhooked his stick and tossed it back on the ledge, the snake rewarding him with a loud hiss and darting motion of its tongue, the sinewy body striking the bars of its cage and tipping it alarmingly. Mahmet took a moment to glance behind the contraption to where an oily piece of rope stretched from the cage to a ring in the wall, fixed in such a way that it was concealed from whoever might be occupying the bed, then satisfied that it was still secure, he sat down on the bed once more.

Bleur had given his assistant very specific instructions and as Mahmet well knew, the mineralogist could be merciless when his orders weren't carried out to the letter. Once the decision had been made to kidnap the youth and the place for his interrogation chosen, Bleur had said, "Do whatever you must to get the information we seek but if possible do not mark him. He is most comely, I noticed, and could fetch a handsome price at the auctions, provided he gets there basically intact. And Mahmet . . ." Here he had gazed at the young Arab balefully, his cold reptilian eyes making his servant quail. ". . . I know how you can be with pretty young boys as well as women, but that must not happen with this one. Pure flesh brings the highest prices."

In his amazement at discovering Olwyn to be a woman, his master's instructions had flown right out of Mahmet's head . . . almost. Now, as he sat on the side of her bed admiring her tempting beauty, the young man was thankful that he hadn't lost his head completely and taken her, as even now he craved to do but didn't dare.

"Where you get the diamond?" he asked Olwyn abruptly, as he'd been commanded to do. "I must know."

She turned her head away and kept silent.

Mahmet had a hot temper made hotter at being denied what he yearned for, and he seized her by the jaw and whipped her face back around to his, snarling, "You tell me truth! We make sure it *is* truth before we let you go, so not lie." At that he threw back his head and shouted something in his own tongue, and a moment later Olwyn heard somebody shuffling to the door, then a strange and horrible apparition entered the room, one that scarcely looked human at all.

Mahmet waved this creature over to the lighted area by the pallet, and the light fell on his face, or what had once been a face.

He was a leper.

Olwyn jerked away and struck the wall by the bed, too terrified to utter a sound, while Mahmet grabbed his shirt and held it over his nose and mouth. She had only encountered one of these poor unfortunate creatures before, while working for Dr. Gibb in Glasgow. The man, who had been a seaman, had fallen ill of the disease while overseas and come home to die. He had lived in isolation on the outskirts of Glasgow, and except for taking him food and medicine, which he left at the garden gate, even Gibb hadn't been brave enough to go near him. Olwyn had only seen the sailor once, when he'd come to the door of his shack to wave his thanks at them—this was just before he mercifully died—and she'd been aghast at the sight of him. She remembered Gibb saying sadly, "There's nothing we can do for him except try to make him as comfortable as possible. There's no cure for leprosy and it's a long, agonizing death. We must pray this poor fellow has not long to wait now for release."

Mahmet, behind the protection of his shirt, laughed at Olwyn's terrified expression. To her horror the leper laughed, too, exposing toothless gums, and sidled a little closer. Olwyn had no way of protecting herself, naked as she was and with nothing at hand to hold over her face. When the poor creature extended a wasted hand on which most of the fingers were gone, as if he meant to stroke her cheek, Olwyn cried, "Dear God . . . don't!" holding an arm up before her as a shield.

Mahmet seized the arm and pulled it away.

"Where you get the diamond?" he suddenly

shouted, nervous himself at the creature hovering so close. "You tell now or I give you to eem. Eee like women and have none for long time."

Olwyn's golden eyes started out of her head as the leper chuckled again and bent over her so that she could smell him now, the sickeningly sweet and revolting reek of decay. "It came from Teragno," she almost screamed. "Please, *please* make him get back from me—"

"Who you get it from?" Mahmet interrupted relentlessly.

She only hesitated a fraction of a second, long enough to reason that her life was worth more than a diamond—and surely Justin Wentworth would think the same.

"From a man who owns a trading post there," Olwyn blurted.

"Ees name?"

"Justin Wentworth," she moaned, nausea welling up in her so that she began to retch uncontrollably, clammy sweat breaking out all over her body.

"Wentworth?" Mahmet considered the name, recognizing it immediately. Though he traveled about the country extensively, Wentworth was a well-known figure in Cape Town; well respected, too, for what he'd accomplished in such a short time. Now it was obvious how he had managed such a feat.

The Arab felt a wild spurt of elation and excitement. He could hardly wait to tell Bleur his wonderful news, aware that he'd be generously rewarded for the information—as well he should be!

Mahmet finally waved the leper away with a backward snap of his hand, but Olwyn's ordeal wasn't over. Pretending sudden concern at her near-hysterical state, Mahmet fetched her a kind of tea and ordered her to drink it, lying, "It make you feel strong again."

The brew did just the opposite. After two sips Olwyn's head reeled and a great feeling of lethargy washed over her, but the Arab prodded her to dress and bundled her into a cart waiting in the alley at the side of the building.

It was late afternoon, the time the British flocked to their favorite clubs and taverns for what they called sundowners, the hour when they met with friends for pre-dinner drinks and conversation. As the cart rumbled through the streets with Olwyn huddled in a near-stupor under a pile of rags, her countrymen flocked into these places in droves, anxious to relax with their friends. Big Ben's was one such place, for all that it was on the harbor. Ben Barkley, the owner, was a jolly giant of a man, originally from London, and he gave his establishment a welcoming conviviality and color. Barkley was a retired sea captain who still liked to live within sight of the ocean. He kept his customers entranced with tales of his many adventures while traveling to different countries, stories that appealed to Maury Howell in particular.

Howell and his friends were regulars in Big Ben's. Anyone anxious to contact Maury knew they could always find him there on Fridays—though he frequented the tavern at other times too. Big Ben's was a kind of unofficial business address for the young engineer, who usually had what he called "many irons in the fire" over and above his government job.

That late Friday afternoon as the sun sank into the west, turning the sky a burnished orange, many ships bobbed at anchor out in the bay, including an Arab dhow some distance apart from the others. These vessels had a dubious reputation and, rightly or wrongly, their owners were accused of trafficking in opium and slaves, which was not always the case as blockades had been set up to stamp out this scourge and any found carrying such cargo were severely penalized. But as Howell had once remarked to a friend, "There are more ways than one to skin a cat." The vile trafficking still went on, since it was well-nigh impossible to patrol and keep a close watch on every one of the countless little lagoons and inlets all up and down this stretch of the African coastline; so those

willing to take the risk often escaped detection—and
for the successful the rewards were great.

Up to five o'clock in the afternoon Mahmet had
handled his assignment well. Bleur would have been
proud of his assistant. Then the overeager young Arab
made a mistake. In his impatience to get back to the
mineralogist with his exciting information, Mahmet
wanted the girl off his hands and safely installed
aboard ship as soon as possible, a ship bound for the
slave auctions of Zanzibar, most of its cargo to be
picked up at a secret place farther up the coast.

Had he waited an hour Mahmet would have been in
the clear. The sun was going down and in an hour it
would have been dark, but the overzealous Mahmet
couldn't wait, in a positive frenzy to get back to Bleur
as he was. Besides, he told himself as the cart turned
into the harbor, he only had this one passenger to get
aboard rather than the usual complement consisting
of hundreds of roped, struggling and, without exception, reluctant passengers. One, he reasoned, would
certainly not be noticed, especially drugged and doc-
ile as she was, though not so drugged that she might
attract attention.

There he made his second mistake. Olwyn, even
through the fog swirling in her head, sensed that she
was in terrible danger by the very fact that the Arab
hadn't released her once he had her information.
When Mahmet pulled her out from under the filthy
blanket he had tossed over her and tried to lead her to
a rowboat tied up at the quay, she suddenly raised her
hand and clawed at his face, and as he howled and
jerked away, Olwyn staggered blindly to the edge of
the landing and toppled over into the water.

Maury Howell heard the shouts of excitement as he
sat enjoying a glass of gin in his favorite tavern. He ran
outside with some others, as curious as the rest to see
what was happening, and they reached the quay in
time to see an angry Mahmet hoisting Olwyn from the
water.

"I know that lad!" Howell cried with a jolt of

surprise. He wheeled on the Arab, demanding, "What's going on here? What are you doing with that boy?"

Seeing the way the wind was blowing, the black driver of the cart suddenly whipped up the horse and sped away, leaving Mahmet stranded. As Maury made a threatening move toward him Mahmet backed off and let Olwyn slump to the ground, then spun around and dove into the water, swimming like a seal in the direction of the dhow anchored several hundred yards off-shore.

"Filthy slaver!" Howell hurled after him, surmising what his intention had been. "I hope the sharks make a meal of you; that is, if they aren't too particular about what they eat."

Maury glanced down in consternation at the dripping figure sprawled at his feet, now being examined by one of his friends. "He's unconscious but alive," the fellow announced after a moment. He turned Olwyn over onto her stomach and began kneading and slapping her back, and after a moment she began to splutter and cough, water trickling from her mouth.

Howell frowned, his former distaste coming back as he remembered Wentworth's dinner party on the *Randolph*. He had no idea at all where James Scobbie was staying while in Cape Town but one thing was certain: he had no intention of being lumbered with the lad! That only left one other person who might be induced to take the boy off his hands.

Within minutes Olwyn was lying inside a carriage on her way to Justin Wentworth's house at last.

—◇— **10** —◇—

Olwyn started to revive as she was being carried into a very grand house that looked rose-white in the setting sun, a house with graceful pillars across a wide, shaded portico, set amid verdant gardens where the slumberous air was heavy with the perfume of flowers.

With a start she saw she was being supported between Justin Wentworth and Maury Howell—and knew then that she was dreaming. She felt totally befuddled, her limbs leaden and useless, her mouth dry, but nagging behind the mist swirling inside her head came a blurred memory of a recent and terrible fear. Whimpering, she buried her head against Wentworth's chest.

Once the two men deposited her on a sofa inside the house Howell gave the owner a brief account of how he had come to find her, then bid Justin a speedy good-bye before he could change his mind and refuse to take on the burden. Howell breathed a sigh of relief as he jumped back into the rented coach and directed the driver back to Big Ben's, there to play the part of the hero in rescuing the lad from the clutches of slavers.

"In trouble again, *Master* Moore?"

Justin bent over the wet, bedraggled girl on the sofa, then recoiled at the smell of engine oil and putrid harbor water emanating from her clothes. He considered a minute, then decided against having his housekeeper arrange a bath for the girl and someone to clean her up. Like servants everywhere, his gossiped as enthusiastically as the rest. Most British people in Cape Town knew each other at least slightly, and their servants knew each other, too, and liked nothing better than to exchange the latest tidbits about their masters, the spicier the better. He didn't care for himself, but for Olwyn's sake thought it best to be prudent.

Justin picked her up easily and carried her upstairs to the new bathing room he'd had installed the previous year, a room with pink marble tiles on the walls and floor, a pedestal-type hand basin in the shape of a shell, and a sunken tub at one corner of the chamber. Huge fluffy towels, soaps, and a razor and shaving brush sat neatly on a shelf under a mirror, and there was even a sofa and chair, where one could sit down to remove one's boots or lie down for a relaxing nap after the pleasant ritual of the bath.

Bathing rooms were the very latest thing, imported from Turkey, where it was said the Sultans set great store in the rejuvenating properties of the bath—not just a quick splash and scrub to get clean, but a long, warm soak in scented water where the stresses and strains of the day could be eased and both mind and body refreshed.

Justin kept Olwyn in the small dressing chamber until the servants filled the tub with water, tested it as they always did to make sure the water was exactly the right temperature, then sprinkled in a few drops of the expensive spice-scented oil from France—a scent tailored to suit a man rather than a woman.

Once they all departed, no doubt to gossip madly in

the kitchen, thought Justin, aware that his gardener had seen Olwyn carted into the house, he pulled off her filthy, wet clothes and carried her naked to the bath and carefully lowered her body into the foaming warm water.

Clouds of perfumed steam tickled Olwyn's nose and she sneezed and opened her eyes with difficulty, so heavy did the lids feel. Everything about her was blurred and dreamlike, the frothy blanket of iridescent bubbles covering her body, light and soft as thistledown. The shining pink marble of the nearby wall, and Wentworth's face so close to hers as he leaned over the side of the bath, an arm about her to prevent her from sliding under the water.

Olwyn gave a great start at the sight of him. "Where . . . what?"

"You've been drugged," he said, gazing at the pupils of the golden eyes fixed on his with alarm, adding dryly, "But you are safe enough now, even if you find that hard to believe. It's time you kept better company, Miss Moore. The day will come when nobody will be around to rescue you."

With that he thrust a huge honeycombed sponge into her limp hand, urging, "Wash yourself; you smell like a sewer rat. Top to toe, now!" he went on like a drill sergeant. "Nothing missed."

"But—"

"You'd prefer *me* to do it?"

"No . . . no—"

Then hurry! The quicker that muck is off you the better for both of us."

Olwyn tried, but it was hopeless. She had no energy whatsoever. It was night now, and she'd had nothing to eat but some fruit and coffee for breakfast, and that one cup of hideous coffee in town; that plus the ordeal later—it began to come back to her in snatches—had left her completely worn out.

Justin watched her ineffectual efforts for a moment or two, then took the sponge away, rubbed soap on it, and proceeded to wash her himself, growling when

Olwyn protested, "I'm particular who sleeps in my bed," and laughing when she glared at him.

He cleaned her very thoroughly, too, firmly pushing her hands away when Olwyn tried to stop him, his large tanned hand so dark against her skin and the frothing white bubbles, sliding over her wet breasts and stomach and between her legs, making her squirm and cry, "You—you have no right—"

"Be still!" Wentworth commanded. "I have the right to do whatever pleases me in my own house, and there's nothing I detest more than a dirty woman."

Olwyn gasped, protesting. "You—you think I'm a slut, don't you? You treat me as such." Her voice cracked and tears filled her eyes as she went on. "Yes, even though you know I've had no other man except—except . . ."

"Me."

Justin looked at her from under his brows. Her face was shining clean now, slightly flushed from the steam, and there were daubs of soap suds on her nose and chin. Suddenly she looked startlingly young and pure to his eyes, tears sparkling on her lashes, her lips soft and trembling and at that moment touchingly vulnerable.

He felt something unexpected then, like a blow in the region of the heart and, disconcerted, quickly lowered his head and got on with the task of bathing her, muttering, "Now the hair. Be patient; your ordeal will be over in a moment."

Olwyn bit her lip, furious at herself for breaking down. It was just that she felt so weak, so helpless, and confused by everything that was happening to her, especially her chaotic feelings about him.

She gave him a sidelong glance to find him frowning, as if concentrating on his task, his strong features betraying no emotion whatsoever, adept as he was at hiding his feelings. Finally he rose and fetched one of the large fluffy towels from the shelf, wrapped her inside it, and carried her through the dressing room into his enormous bedroom beyond, where he pulled back the covers and set her down, still snugly bundled in the towel, then pulled up the coverlet and tucked it under her chin.

"I—I can't stay here!" Olwyn cried, even though it felt warm and pleasant in his bed and more than anything in the world she longed to close her eyes and lose herself in sleep—if only to stop the alarming memories now surging back into her mind. "I *must* get back to the Hoggs'! Mr. Scobbie will be so worried."

Justin stared down at her; he looked very serious.

"I'll send him a message," he said. "I'll say that you've had a slight accident but are basically all right, and will return in the morning—"

"I can't stay here with you!" Over the top of the blue silk cover Olwyn's eyes were enormous.

"I can't, I can't," he mocked, and suddenly sat down on the side of the bed, grabbing her by the shoulder when she started to move to the other side of the bed. Justin thrust his face very close to hers, and there was a gleam in his eyes now, one that set her heart clamoring like a trapped bird in a cage. "It seems that we can't avoid each other," he told her gruffly, his gaze moving slowly over each flawless feature of her face. "On the other occasion you were dumped at my door. On this occasion Maury Howell delivered you here, and very glad to be rid of you he was, though . . ." His eyes moved down the slender column of her throat and over the cover to where it rose in twin peaks. "Neither of us sought the other out," he continued after a slight pause, in the deep, hypnotic way Olwyn remembered so well. "But here we are anyway. Together. For better or for worse," he added with a strange little smile.

Olwyn tore her eyes from his, turned over and buried her face in the pillow.

A moment later she heard him leave the room.

Then she lowered the cover and turned her head to the door, which was closed now. "Dear God!" she whispered, and slumped back against the pillows, her eyes fixed worriedly on the ceiling.

"For better or for worse," he'd said, little realizing that it was going to be the latter, Olwyn fretted. She had lost his diamond! Aye, and she had been forced to give his name to Mahmet as well as the location of where the stone had been found. What would the Arab do with the information?

Teragno was very far away, Olwyn told herself soothingly. It was in the remote hinterland of Africa and, no doubt, very difficult to find for those not familiar with the area. The chances were good that Mahmet would either forget the strange-sounding name of Wentworth's trading post or, because it was so far away, decide not to do anything about it.

Oh, how she wished now that she'd returned the acursed little gem while she was still on the ship—but of course she had thought it was worthless then. Justin had told her so himself!

He had lied to her about that. Olwyn couldn't believe that he didn't know the value of what he had, but of course that was his own business and in a way she couldn't blame him for keeping it to himself. Besides, hadn't she lied to *him*? If only things could have been aboveboard and simple!

She sighed, rubbing her hot cheek against the pillow, trying not to think too much about that episode in the bath. Maury Howell hadn't wanted anything to do with her once he discovered the identity of the victim he'd rescued—but Wentworth had taken her in, which had to mean something. How he would regret that kindness once he found out the truth about his diamond!

# 11

Justin let her sleep for close to six hours, then sure she must be ravenous, prepared a tray for her himself —tissue-thin roast beef, sweet yams from his garden, and fruit and wine.

They had a sort of indoor picnic in her room at midnight.

Once Olwyn ascertained that he had sent the message to Scobbie she needed no urging to eat; she was famished.

"I like a woman with robust appetites," Justin remarked, laughing as she attacked the food with relish. "I'm beginning to see you do most things with enthusiasm."

Olwyn's eyes flickered to his face and she flushed, aware of the other appetites he was alluding to. They sat on the bed with the tray between them and tonight, she noticed, he was dressed casually in a crisp white shirt open at the neck, and snug-fitting twill breeches. The burnished dark copper of his skin glowed in the lamplight, always such a striking contrast against his hair and the vivid blue of his eyes, eyes that gleamed a little as they smiled into hers. There was also something decidedly wolfish about that flashing white smile, Olwyn thought uneasily, and decided that it was best to ignore it. "It was kind of you to allow me to come here," she said, stiffly polite.

Wentworth laughed. "I had no choice; Maury dropped you and ran. You seem to have a chilling effect on Howell, but then he doesn't know you quite as intimately as I do . . ." At that his eyes, very bright and bold, went to the spot where Olwyn had the cover drawn primly across her chest and tucked firmly under her arms. ". . . Or his response wouldn't be quite so cold. How did the slaver come to get his hands on you?" he asked abruptly, taking her by surprise. "And what were you doing in Cape Town alone?"

Olwyn's appetite promptly vanished, yet she knew she owed him some sort of an explanation considering the trouble she had put him to. Now was the time to tell him the truth about his diamond, to explain that it had been taken from her by force—but would he believe her? On the ship he had accused her of stealing the stone. Now, were she to reveal that she'd taken it to a mineralogist there was every chance that he would think that she had gone there with the intention of selling it, and been robbed of it instead!

"I—I was anxious to see Cape Town before we moved on," Olwyn began, her eyes on her plate, and hastily made up a tale about being attacked and drugged while wandering in the bazaar. She thought it prudent not to mention the diamond at all unless he specifically brought it up; then, she'd have no option but to tell him what really happened.

He was angry at her anyway. "This isn't Glasgow! You don't go roaming about on your own here. That's like begging for trouble."

"I didn't know that!" Olwyn snapped, her temper flaring in the tense atmosphere that had suddenly fallen between them. "I'm sorry that Maury Howell brought me here, so if you'll kindly fetch my clothes I'll leave at once and spare you anymore trouble."

Justin pushed her back against the pillows. "Your clothes have been washed and at this moment are drying—"

"Then I'll go as I am," Olwyn choked, grabbing the towel about her and standing up. "I won't stay where I'm not wanted."

She had only taken a few steps when suddenly the towel—which she'd decided to turn into a wrap, native-style—was whipped away from her and Wentworth drawled, "I believe this belongs to me."

"Knave!" Olwyn gasped, frantically trying to cover her nakedness as bold, mocking eyes roved over her body. "You—you are despicable, Justin Wentworth, and don't imagine—"

He sprang up and seized her in his arms and silenced her with a savage kiss, then tumbled her back on the bed, where Olwyn's struggles were swiftly subdued. Leaning over her, Justin caught her by the chin and looked deep in her eyes. "I'll tell you what I imagine. I imagine that you really want to stay here—"

"Never! I—I hate you!"

Slowly, maddeningly, he shook his head and went on as if she hadn't interrupted. "I also imagine—I know!—that I *want* you to stay."

"And I know why!"

"Oh?" His brows rose in that sardonic way that Olwyn found so infuriating. "Then we must think alike. That's a good start to our friendship."

Enraged at his audacity, at the sheer arrogance of the man, Olwyn again made a futile attempt to throw him off, but Justin simply let his weight rest a little more heavily on her and put his lips to her ear and whispered, "For a recent virgin you certainly know how to arouse a man, Olwyn Moore."

It was then she became aware of the hardness of him against her and lay perfectly still.

He kissed her again, this time more gently, linger-ingly, the persistent pressure of his lips forcing hers to part. Lying rigid beneath him, Olwyn held her breath and willed herself to feel nothing as his tongue leisure-ly explored the delicate curve of her mouth, even as his warm hand explored the curves of her body, seeking and finding those special parts of her that he alone had awakened and stirred to tingling awareness.

Then he took her by surprise as his lips began to follow the path his hand had taken moments before, his tongue igniting a spark that rapidly turned into a raging inferno, burning away her resistance so that instead of pulling away from him, Olwyn arched her body closer, shuddering as wave after wave of ecstasy pulsed through her.

Justin held her for a moment until the storm began to subside, then rose and swiftly threw off his clothes. He lay down beside her and pulled her hungrily into his arms, and Olwyn thought she heard him murmur, "Sweet love," as he buried his face in her hair. His need was obvious, yet he entered her carefully, as if anxious not to hurt her, and though Olwyn could feel the tension in him mount, Justin moved above her slowly, almost leisurely, and kept up the erotic pace until he felt her stiffen as tingling fire fanned over her flesh. Then his rhythm changed. In seconds he drove her to the brink of that plateau that Olwyn had come to associate with these moments in his arms, and as she plunged over the edge she kissed him with real feeling, with all the passion surging through her body, and for the first time spoke his name softly, and with warmth.

Justin kissed her very tenderly afterward and cud-dled her close in his arms, and Olwyn felt again that special warmth, the comfort and sweet security that she remembered from the last time, and now realized, with a pang, that she'd yearned for ever since. It made something hard and cold melt inside her. It filled up a void. She opened her eyes for a moment and gazed at the strong, brown, protective arm wrapped tight about her and suddenly she began to cry. "There's something you should know," she sobbed, the words gushing out of her. "I—I must tell you. I'm sorry, but . . . I lied."

Justin turned his head and their eyes met, hers flooding over.

"Trust me, darling," he murmured, touched, aware all along that she'd been hiding something, and since his experience with Christina evasiveness was a quality that had never endeared him to a woman.

Shattered as she was from the stress and trauma of the day she had just lived through, Olwyn still hesitated. The instinct for self-preservation, honed to a keen edge during her years of growing up in the slums of Glasgow, warned her to remain silent, especially about how she had come to lose his diamond.

Justin leaned forward, taking her hand. "Olwyn, trust me!" he repeated. "It's time we were open and honest with each other, or . . ." He shrugged.

"I—I'd better start at the beginning."

"Yes," he nodded, smiling encouragement, at the same time a little concerned about the agitation he could sense seething inside her. Her hand resting in his was unnaturally cool, considering the warmth of the room, and her cheeks had lost all their rosy color. The beautiful eyes fixed on his so earnestly—and that melted him—were feverishly bright.

"As you already know, I grew up in the Gallowgate," she began, her voice slightly hoarse. Slowly, painfully, Olwyn took him back to her past, her life with her father, the way he had driven her to achieve something so that she could one day leave the slums behind. Justin listened without interruption while she told him about working for Dr. Gibb, and her plans to go to nursing school, then the shock of her father's death. He felt her begin to tremble when she reached the part about Anderson's College and Enid MacCutcheon, who had frozen her tentative overtures of friendship, then she paused, her throat working, and blurted, "There was this medical student, Devlin Sproat . . ."

Again she broke off, all the horror of that betrayal flooding back, and her terror and desperation when she realized the predicament she was in, the need to leave Glasgow no matter how she had to do it.

Justin saw that her face had gone stark white. Hastily he took his hand away from hers, poured her a fresh glass of wine, and held it to her lips, but Olwyn pushed it away and blurted, "Sproat tried to rape me! Then . . . then he twisted things around to make it seem that I had tried to rob him, and attacked him when he caught me doing it. He vowed to have me put in prison, and he had the power to do it too! I knew then that I had to leave, get away from Glasgow any way I could."

Wentworth stared at her strained face in silence. He already knew that she was a very bright girl, with all her wits about her, and for an instant it occurred to him that this could be another clever acting job; a bid for his approval and sympathy, as another woman had once done in much the same way, only to stab him in the back once his defenses were down.

He had sworn never to be taken in in this way again.

"You do believe me, don't you?" Olwyn asked anxiously, her eyes searching his face.

He nodded, chiding himself for being so distrustful. "And this time you're telling the truth?"

"Yes!" She was close to tears.

"You must tell James Scobbie—"

Her eyes widened in horror. "I can't do that! He trusts me, and"—she swallowed convulsively, looking away—"I'd die rather than have to admit that I—"

"Deceived him." A hard edge had crept into his voice and a sternness to his eyes. "He'll find out soon enough," he went on. "You won't be able to keep up this ridiculous masquerade in Nuruzambora, and by putting it off you'll only make things worse. I'd advise you to own up immediately and take your licks. The most he can do is sack you."

Sack her! And send her back to Scotland on the next ship?

"Tell him tomorrow," Justin urged, thinking that if Scobbie did let her go, then he would be there to help her—but of course Olwyn couldn't read his mind.

She looked at him and saw a rich man surrounded by affluence and security; a man who had never gone without anything in his life, she was certain. How could she expect him to appreciate what it was like to be poor and destitute, to live in a world where only the fittest, the most courageous, could survive? Aye, and where one was often compelled to do things and make choices that the wealthy never encountered at all.

"Here, drink this," Justin ordered, his voice brooking no refusal as he raised the glass to her lips once more. "You look exhausted."

When Olwyn had taken a few sips he set the glass on a table, took her in his arms and kissed her. They lay down in bed and Justin pulled the coverlet snugly up around her shoulders. "Better?" he asked her softly.

She took a deep breath. "Justin, there's something else."

"Not now, darling. We've lots of time."

He drew her closer until she felt the heat of his body brush the coolness of her skin, and kissed her again more deeply, and the moment passed. It was the last time they were to be so completely alone together for many weeks to come.

Shortly after a Christmas that didn't seem like Christmas, sweltering as they were in hundred-degree temperatures, the Scobbie party bid farewell to the Hoggs and left Cape Town to sail on to Algoa Bay, where they would finally leave the coast behind for the long trek into the interior.

The massive bulk of their equipment and supplies

had already been shipped on there ahead of them, and Wentworth's foreman and guide, Tondo, had everything organized and under control; the ox wagons, oxen, porters, food, and everything else they would need. Tondo, a huge, strapping man in his late thirties, had been with Justin from the beginning. He was a Griqua, of mixed Kaffir, Bushman, and Dutch blood, and his skin was the color of coffee mixed liberally with cream. Tondo, much traveled, had previously worked for an English trader and big-game hunter who had been killed during a buffalo hunt. He spoke fairly good English, was intelligent and very capable, and above all understood the habits and peculiarities of this race he had tied his fortunes to. Above all he understood Justin Wentworth, who had been fairer and kinder to him than his previous master, and Tondo was prepared to defend him with his life, if necessary.

As was the custom when two caravans journeyed together, Scobbie, too, had his foreman and guide, a man found for him by Walter Hogg. This was Mikololo, whom James promptly nicknamed Mick. Mick, a lean, yellow-skinned little Hottentot with a sprinkling of Portuguese blood in his veins, always traveled with his fat wife, Floekele, a lady who was to become the main cook. Her name was immediately shortened to Flo. Altogether, including the porters, there were almost two hundred people in their party, each of the huge, lumbering wagons pulled by twelve oxen. Plus there were surplus oxen, for food or bartering purposes along the way, and a few mangy dogs who had attached themselves to the large group.

The caravan left Algoa Bay just before dawn on January the sixteenth while the temperature was still cool, and by the time they pitched camp that night had traveled twelve miles, which was pretty good for the terrain. When they halted some of the natives immediately set about cutting poles and gathering grasses and fronds for impromptu shelters, while others went in search of wood for the fires. By twilight these were all blazing cheerily and the delicious aroma of roasting meat filled the air, soon to be wolfed down with great gusto, the leftovers, such as they were, tossed to their faithful followers, the dogs. Then, seated around the camp fires, the natives began to sing, their exuberant voices rising into the clean, still air, and several even sprang up to dance, leaping and throwing themselves about to the great delight of the children, who watched everything that went on with the keenest interest.

Quite soon the camp grew quiet and the entire company, or most of it, retired to bed, since they had to be up again before dawn in the morning. Hannah, James, and the boys were to sleep inside one wagon, which, unlike the two others, was not too cluttered with supplies. Tondo, Mick and his wife, and all of the natives, slept in the huts. Nobody thought anything odd about Wentworth and Oliver bedding down in one of the other wagons.

They still had no real privacy, and didn't dare curl up together, but had to sleep a distance apart in the large conveyance for appearance's sake. The Watch, as Justin called the four men who were always on patrol at night, circled the area inside the hastily erected thorn fence continuously, and there were scores of people in flimsy huts—some preferring to sleep on the bare ground—just outside their shelter. And sound carried a long way in the stillness.

Olwyn's pallet was at the rear of the wagon, spread on top of a stack of wooden packing cases containing such items as tea, coffee, sugar, and other foodstuffs. Through a chink in the heavy canvas side she looked out on the ring of smoldering fires, the little grass-topped huts, the cattle huddled together well within sight of the fires, which, Justin had told her, brought them comfort, as wild beasts hated fire. To Olwyn the scene had a primitive, timeless quality that she found charming. Moonlight silvered everything about them, contrasting with the velvety darkness beneath the trees, and the sky was ablaze with stars.

Olwyn snuggled deeper under her covers in the night-time coolness, finding her wagon shelter surprisingly comfortable for all that she shared it with boxes and sacks and other supplies. She felt secure and happy and filled with a childlike excitement, reflecting that she could take to this gypsy life quite readily.

Wentworth had still not appeared.

An hour went by and Olwyn again peeked through the chink in the canvas. She spied one of the Watch, a tall, rangy fellow proudly patrolling with the rifle assigned to him in his hand. One of the curled figures sleeping on the bare ground, as many of them liked to do, sat up and spoke to him, and their voices carried to her quite clearly, though they were more than a hundred feet away.

Olwyn lowered herself back on the pallet, too restless and excited by the novelty of her situation to sleep. She waited, listening to the silence, and heard the small sounds she had missed before, the low humming of the insects, the cry of a hunting owl somewhere in the vicinity, and the snores and grunts and occasional cough of the people and animals that made up their camp.

Wentworth appeared quite suddenly in the opening at the front of the wagon. Olwyn sat up with a gasp; she hadn't heard as much as a footstep. She was soon to discover that the Wentworth of the town was quite different from the Wentworth of the bushveld; that he had developed the ability to move about with great stealth, an ability that had saved his life more than once.

"Hullo, Oliver," he greeted her gruffly, at the same time warning her by the use of her assumed name that someone else was very close. Justin had made no comment when she had arrived in Algoa Bay still wearing her breeches but he'd given her a long, hard look before turning away. They hadn't been alone together from that time on and still weren't alone now, not with two hundred other people ranged about beyond the canvas walls and roof of their wagon.

One of the Watch came up and exchanged a few words with Justin in Bantu.

"What did he say?" Olwyn inquired, eager to start a conversation once the man had moved off.

"He said that the night is bright and peaceful, that the moon is our friend. In other words, no problems."

Olwyn laughed softly. "The natives have a pretty way of putting things. What happens when there's no moon?"

He chuckled dryly. "That's when we keep the fires blazing until dawn and pay closer attention to the fences. The big cats never hunt in the moonlight."

She shivered, and the trek suddenly lost some of its fairy-tale-like quality.

Standing at the opening of the cart, outlined against the glow of the main kgotla fire, Justin quickly pulled off his clothes, stood for a moment looking out—while she looked at him and the muscular body revealed to her in silhouette—then stretched and lay down on his own bed at the front of the wagon.

"Good night, Oliver," he said.

For a moment Olwyn didn't answer. She felt indescribably hurt at his terseness, a certain distance and coolness in his manner, as if that passionate night in his Cape Town house had never taken place. As for today, he had made no attempt to come near her, had hardly looked at her, and wouldn't have spoken to her at all, she was suddenly certain, if she hadn't approached him while he was examining an ox with a thorn in its foot and asked him a few questions about these enormous animals who were of such value in Africa.

Earlier she had excused his brusqueness, telling herself that he was very busy, that he had so much to attend to, and also that they had to be very careful with each other since there were so many people around. Well, she fumed as she tossed and turned in her bed, no longer quite so comfortable, the people were still around—but not so close that he couldn't have at least whispered a few friendly words to her!

He was punishing her, Olwyn suspected, because she hadn't told Scobbie the truth about herself. What he couldn't seem to understand was that it wasn't quite so easy as he seemed to think. James liked her and had come to depend on her. He felt comfortable having her with him in case his family became ill— but he'd be forced to let her go if he discovered that she had lied to him. Scobbie's rules, Olwyn had already observed, tended to be strict and inflexible.

She glared in the direction of his pallet, thinking that it was easy for him to tell her what to do. He had never known what it was like to be deprived of anything, certainly not the necessities of life like food, shelter, or the warmth and companionship of others!

"Good night!" Olwyn finally snapped.

There was no answer.

Only a brief year later Olwyn looked back on that time and marveled at her recklessness and daring in taking yet another step away from civilization and deeper into the unknown. Cape Town had taught her very little about Africa; it was a case apart and no indication about what the rest of the country was going to be like. The Cape was a small coastal pocket originally established as a stopping-off and supply point for ships in the long journey to India and the East, and it was remarkably civilized by comparison with the rest of the country and had the largest European population in southern Africa.

At the time they left Algoa Bay, Olwyn knew next to nothing about the country as a whole—but then neither did the rest of the world. It remained much as it had always been, a land shrouded in mystery and obscurity, a place largely ignored by foreign governments since it seemed to have so little to offer.

The few scouts sent out to explore and report on its potential returned—if they returned at all!—with gloomy tales of heat and drought, strange diseases usually fatal to the white man, and savage beasts and even more savage tribes who had scarcely advanced culturally since the Stone Age. Commerce on any decent scale at all was quickly discovered to be impossible since none of its great rivers could be navigated because of cataracts and rapids and the sudden fluctuations in the water table, flooding one moment and dry the next. In light of this the outside world lost interest in Africa.

Some adventurous souls remained—Dutch, Portuguese, British, and French—and of course Arabs. The latter had discovered some potential in Africa over a thousand years before, namely slaves. Except for the Arabs, the majority stayed around the only towns of any size, Cape Town and Port Elizabeth. The Dutch farmers, known as Boers, also decided to branch out in a bid to escape the restrictive British Government at Cape Colony.

The British were in control of Cape Colony—a vast area with Cape Town on the coast at one end, and Nuruzambora at the outer reaches on the other—but even they displayed only tepid interest in Africa, mainly as a port of call for their ships on their way to richer and more lucrative lands.

Long afterward, Olwyn was to remember that journey from Algoa Bay to Nuruzambora as a time of bitter-sweet magic, but magic, indeed, considering what was to come.

# 12

At first everything in the caravan was harmonious in spite of the coolness between Olwyn and Wentworth. They had much to catch their interest during the first week or two: the variety of the scenery, quite verdant and lush when they started out from Algoa Bay. The hot summer had passed its peak and some rain had fallen to fill up the dry rivers and bring moisture to the parched earth, and plants and flowers burst to life in an explosion of color and form that seemed incredibly beautiful and interesting to Olwyn. Near the water graceful ferns and fronds vied for moisture with elegant pink and purple orchids, and in the wooded areas delicate lilies and pale lilac balsam flowers thrived. Pokerlike aloes flamed red, orange, and yellow, and in a grove the mopane trees hazed the air with blushing pink. All this brought cries of delight from both Olwyn and Hannah.

Olwyn suspected that Hannah was not in the least sorry at leaving the Hoggs, though she had spent her time there in comfort and even luxury. Hannah liked to chat and sorely missed her mother and sisters in Scotland, with whom she'd enjoyed many a good gossip, much to the irritation of her husband. James was not a man for small-talk and since there was really no one else in the party she could relate to, his wife turned increasingly to Olwyn—which almost landed the girl in trouble. Coming upon them chatting one day, James scolded his wife. "For goodness sake wheesht, woman! Oliver isn't one of your 'sweetie wives,' so don't subject him to this infernal nattering." And at her hurt look he added with a grin, "You'll be giving our wee doctor a sair heid."

Hannah protested. "Oliver doesn't mind. He enjoys a blether now and then, don't you, lad?"

"Lads have better things to do," said James before Olwyn could answer.

From then on Olwyn made a note to herself to be more careful, but in a way she was sorry she couldn't spend more time with Mrs. Scobbie and thereby get to know her better. Hannah, too, she sensed, was lonely in her own way.

The farther north they got the sparser and more rugged the terrain became, making things much more difficult for the ox wagons, not to mention the porters and the rest of them. It became hotter, dryer, barer, the scenery around them more grimly dramatic as they encountered their first mountain range and then a limitless vista of barren rock, sand, and leafless dwarf bushes, an area that Justin called the Karroo. Here the rivers were all dry and water became a problem, especially for the oxen who, staunch and long-suffering in other ways, refused to proceed without it.

In a strange way Olwyn found the Karroo to be hauntingly beautiful, a stretch of land like no other she had ever seen, in places flat and blistering under the merciless sun and in others broken up by the kopjes, stunted hills with their peaks sliced off and odd terraced sides, as if sculpted by a giant hand long ago. At first glance this territory seemed lifeless and barren, but Olwyn soon discovered that this was not the case at all. Life thrived, she saw, even in this hell on earth, a testimony to its endurance. Hannah screamed at her first sight of an enormous centipede peeping out from inside the boot she was about to put on, but he was not the only inhabitant of the Karroo. There were lizards by the thousands, hyraxes, scorpions, snakes, gazelles, rhinoceroses, and it was here that they heard their first lions roaring in the night.

The heat was savage and thirst constant—just when water was so scarce! Problems soon developed with the wagons as they creaked and bumped over the hard, boulder-strewn ground, and this caused delays that were very time-consuming, not to mention irritating for all concerned, especially with water at such a low point. It was very rough-going and by the time they fell into bed at night they were exhausted. These days about the most Justin said to Olwyn was "good morning" and "good night" and—if she was lucky—a few brief comments in the course of the day, all of them impersonal. As they continued north they began to encounter some small tribal villages. Most of the people were friendly, after gaping at them and exclaiming over Wentworth's hair, which had lightened in the sun, even as his skin had darkened, and pointing out anything they found astonishing or intriguing. To these people Justin made a gift of beads or small knives, mirrors or other trinkets, and they in turn would respond with clay pots of honey, gourds of butter, millet beer, or meal. Sometimes they offered meat, usually putrid, a delicacy to them if not to the Europeans. Naturally, Wentworth accepted all this, including the meat, most graciously.

But one day six weeks into their journey, in a lightly forested area, they happened upon a tribe not so friendly. A member of the Watch alerted them in the middle of the night, rushing up to warn Wentworth, who lay at the front of the wagon as usual, his Enfield rifle at his side. The man babbled softly but excitedly, and the moment he left, Olwyn scrambled from her bed and scurried down the vehicle to where Wentworth was sitting up, his back against a sack of grain.

"What did he say?" she whispered nervously, standing before him in her knee-length white nightshirt, the fullness of her unbound breasts provocatively apparent through the thin material, her hair charmingly rumpled around her face.

Justin looked up at her lazily, his own hair tousled, the strong plains and bone structure of his face sculpted reddish-brown in the light from the kgotla fire directly outside the wagon. "He said we can expect company in the morning," he drawled.

"Company?"

He turned his head and glanced out into the night, narrowing his eyes a little. There was no moon and only a few stars dotted here and there; both inside and outside the protective thorn fence around their camp everything was still, except, of course, for the low humming of the insects.

After a minute, when he seemed to be listening, he said in the deep, low voice that had begun to stir a throbbing excitement in Olwyn's blood, "There's a band of Zulus nearby, a splinter group broken away from the main body of their people farther east. This bunch"—he rubbed at his jaw and yawned—"you might say are renegades, though they've been gathering strength over the past two years and have established a good-size village. Their chief is Tchamoko, a wily villain and robber." He chuckled and went on. "I imagine he'll be here to pay his respects in the morning, or more likely send one of his henchmen, and he'll demand toll before he allows us to move through his territory."

Olwyn was too frightened by this news to appreciate that Wentworth had said more to her tonight than at any time since the beginning of the trip. She stepped up to the rim of the wagon and peered out, seeing nothing unusual. Nor could she hear anything out of the ordinary.

Justin watched her, especially the way the firelight

filtered through the threadbare fabric of her shirt, the luscious shape of her outlined in silhouette. During the course of the day she trussed herself up flat as a boy. Then it was easier to forget that she wasn't a boy, and she proved to be much less distracting.

Olwyn glanced down at him and whispered, "I don't see anything. Perhaps your watchman was mistaken."

He shook his head.

"Then—you don't seem very worried."

"It's pointless to worry."

"But what if they attack us? Perhaps now, while everyone is asleep."

"I'm not asleep, nor is Tondo."

Again she stepped up to the opening, her eyes going to the area of the main fire where the big Griqua always slept, right outside the wagon of his master. The spot was empty.

Wentworth chuckled low in his throat. "You see . . ."

He looked very relaxed as he leaned against the sack of meal, his powerful torso bare, a faint mocking smile on his lips as if her anxiety amused him. His seeming indolence in the face of danger shocked and angered Olwyn. Instead of lounging about with his head tilted back making fun of her, he should be out rousing the entire camp and warning everyone to prepare to defend themselves, she thought.

"Go back to bed, *Oliver*," he purred.

"Do you really expect me to sleep now?" Olwyn hissed, scowling down at him as Justin made himself more comfortable and casually folded his arms behind his head. With every movement the muscles rippled across his shoulders and chest, she noticed, and his eyes, gazing up at her, glinted in the firelight, taunting her—or so she thought—with all that had passed between them.

"What are you staring at?" Olwyn demanded angrily, sparks from the fire flaring in her eyes, his complacency after what he'd done to her—infecting her with a kind of fever that kept her tossing and turning through the long hot nights—finally boiling over. "Instead of gaping at me you ought to be out there"— she flung an arm out the opening—"rousing the camp and warning them to prepare to defend themselves."

Justin laughed softly at her wrath. He had never seen a woman so appealing and desirable when furious.

"You may sleep in peace," he assured her, his eyes never leaving her burning face. "They never attack at night—"

"Peace!" Olwyn spat the word. "There has been no peace in my life from the moment you came into it, Justin Wentworth!"

So saying, she wheeled about, almost falling over a packing case, and made to flounce back to bed. Suddenly he sprang up behind her, so swift and silent that she gasped in fright. Hands like vises clamped down on her shoulders and he hurled her ahead of him to the back of the wagon and threw her across her bed; then he made as if to turn away. The next minute, with a kind of groan, he seized her again and crushed her against his chest, his kiss savage.

For one fleeting instant Olwyn tried to push him away but his hungry mouth stirred a raging thirst within herself, and she felt as if her bones were melting and her limbs had lost all power to fight back as Justin fell onto the blankets on top of her.

There was no tenderness in his lovemaking that night but starved as she was, Olwyn didn't crave tenderness. Instead she craved the burning, bruising kisses and caresses that instantly set her aflame as his hands and lips brought her sweet ecstasy. She was ready, more than ready, when Justin mounted her— but it wasn't really *her,* she told herself. Some other ravenous creature had taken over her body; a voluptuous being who loved him back with the same heated abandon as he displayed, her tongue seeking and exploring his, her lips hot and devouring, her trembling, sweating hands caressing the tense, corded

muscles of his shoulders, his back, the smooth taut-
ness of his hips. Every pulse in her body throbbed
with anticipation. A kind of dark and frantic drum-
beat pounded in her head, her senses, her blood.
Nothing on earth could have halted what they had
begun; neither the savages watching and waiting in the
forest, Scobbie coming upon them, not even Satan
himself.

He drove himself inside her and claimed her lips in
a brutal kiss to stop her crying out, not with pain—he
could tell that from her eager movements beneath
him—but with joy. They moved with a rhythm
perfectly attuned to each other and again Justin kissed
her as he felt her begin to shudder, then suddenly arch
high against him. "My love . . ." he breathed, seized
with the turbulence of his own release. "Sweet, beautiful Olwyn, I—"

Whatever he had been about to say never materialized.

A figure appeared at the opening at the front of the
wagon, only the upper portion of the tall, powerful
body in view above the raised bed of the cart. It had
come upon them suddenly, silently, and now stood
patiently waiting.

Olwyn's first indication that they were no longer
alone was felt through the jolt of surprise in Justin's
body. He lifted his head from her, groaning, "Christ!"

It was Tondo.

Naked, Wentworth rose from the tangled covers of
her bed and went forward to speak to his foreman.
Olwyn plunged her head into the blankets, almost sick
with shame. She could well imagine how awkward
Justin felt at that moment. Tondo, after all, thought
she was a boy!

*Please, please don't let him have seen!* Olwyn found
herself praying.

She soothed herself by thinking that it was very
dark in the wagon; that there was no possible way that
Tondo could have seen. The next minute her heart
sank. He might not have *seen* them—but he would

have heard the sounds, much as they'd tried to muffle them, and besides, these people had an instinct, far more acute, Olwyn had noticed, than most Europeans.

Tondo would have guessed the truth, and wonder . . .

Justin pulled on his breeches and picked up his rifle and left with the black man without a word to Olwyn. He was gone about half an hour.

"What's happening?" Olwyn whispered when he returned.

Justin had been on the point of setting down his rifle. He straightened and peered down the wagon. "Are you still awake?" Before she could answer he said harshly, "There's nothing happening, so for God's sake get to sleep!"

Olwyn recoiled at his tone of voice but she had to ask, "Did you tell Tondo about me?"

This time Justin set aside his rifle and pulled off his breeches before he responded. "I suppose you would prefer him to think I'd been making love to another man?" he inquired cynically.

Olwyn bit her lip. "No, of course not, but—"

"Your secret is safe," Justin broke in curtly, then as he lay down he added with some heat, "I hope you appreciate what your lies have cost me?"

"I'm sorry, Justin." And she was. She felt very troubled and ashamed. Again, rather meekly, she sought to explain, "Please try to understand—"

"Good night!"

"Justin?"

But he didn't answer.

I'll make a clean breast of it to Mr. Scobbie in the morning! Olwyn promised herself in a rush of contrition and bravado.

They appeared out of the dawn mist early the following morning, weird, hideously painted and tattooed creatures with plumed headdresses, bow and arrows and spears, hundreds of them completely circling their camp.

Hannah took one look at them and screamed hysterically, then promptly swooned. James, too, looked badly frightened, as did the porters at this show of strength from the Zulu renegades. Only Justin and Tondo made a good show of being unconcerned as they went out to meet the spokesman, a fearsome fellow, almost naked like the rest, with a flap of beaded cloth covering his muscular loins. When he shouted something at Justin Olwyn caught a glimpse of his teeth; strong, white teeth filed down to sharp points. She shuddered as she knelt over Hannah, nervously fanning her as the men parleyed in what seemed to her shockingly loud, aggressive voices. *If I die now,* she thought, *it will be as Oliver Moore.* The disturbing thought kept coming back to her.

Chief Tchamoko, as befitted his station, had not deigned to come himself but had sent a spokesman in his place. The result of the shouted discussion was that all the porters and underlings should stay where they were in the camp, guarded by the Zulus, of course, while the "chief"—Justin—and the rest of the white people should be brought to account to Tchamoko.

Wentworth made it clear that this did not suit him. As the chief of his own tribe, he pointed out, he had a right to bring with him at least a small guard. After ten more minutes of tense negotiations he was permitted to take Tondo and ten of his best shots with him, together with a small chest containing bartering goods —beads, cloth, salt, and the like.

Once this was settled, they were briskly marched five rough miles to Chief Tchamoko's kraal, which turned out to be far bigger than even Wentworth had suspected. They spied sentries in the trees and atop boulders long before they reached the village. With chilling, high-pitched cries, these sentries sent their exact location back to Tchamoko, thus keeping him apprised of their progress. Finally the first of the huts appeared and, at a fence outside a huge kgotla, a clearing where meetings took place, the Zulu halted them. The spokesman turned to Tondo, who spoke their language much better than Justin, and barked something that Olwyn couldn't understand.

Tondo, drawing himself up to his full height, which was about six feet and four inches, cupped his hands to his mouth and shouted something in a loud, proud voice. Later, in questioning Justin, Olwyn learned what it was. "The great white god comes among you! He comes in peace, with pleasant gifts. All he desires in return is leave to go forward."

Tondo, as was the custom when entering a village, had acted the part of a herald.

On a high, wooden dais at one end of the clearing sat Chief Tchamoko, very splendid, indeed, in a fine leopard-skin wrap, a fearsome-looking sword, or assegai, across his knees. Somehow Olwyn had been expecting a huge man much like Tondo, but Tchamoko was only of medium height and with a wiry rather than a heavily muscled frame. She noticed something odd about this chief; he had the smooth body of a young man and the wrinkled, wily face of an ancient. It was impossible to guess his age.

With a haughty flick of his brown hand, the chief bade them come forward to squat on the grass mats provided for them. By this time poor Hannah was reduced to a whimpering, quivering mass of terror, and clung to her husband like a leech. Olwyn cuddled little Jamie close—he was also weeping—with Harold practically welded to her on the other side.

There were hundreds of armed warriors forming an outer circle, and no sign of any women or children at all, which Olwyn later came to understand was ominous.

As their herald or spokesman, Tondo was required to inform the chief of their plans; their reasons for wanting a pass. Once this was dispensed with, the cunning leader of the village pointed to their guns, and some of his men came forward to take them away, but at that point Wentworth jumped to his feet and angrily resisted. He told Tondo to inform the chief that their guns were few and the spears of his warriors many, and that a spear could be thrown much faster than a gun could be loaded; therefore, their weapons were of no threat to him and only kept for show.

Tchamoko, not used to being refused anything, glared down at the big white man with the flowing mane of a lion, and his hand was suddenly tight around the hilt of his sword, but Justin didn't flinch and continued to gaze back at him steadily, his jaw clenched, eyes like flint.

Suddenly the chief threw back his head and roared with laughter. A few titters rippled through the ranks of his men, then they burst out in loud guffaws that shattered the tension in the clearing.

The haggling began then. Justin presented Tchamoko with a fine red jacket trimmed with gold braid, and beads and trinkets for his many wives. The chief accepted them graciously enough but said through Tondo, "I am childlike in my curiosity and would see what else the white god has in his chest."

The result was that Justin also presented him with a bolt of red cotton, red being a favorite color with the natives. This too was accepted politely but it still wasn't enough. When Wentworth firmly banged the lid on the chest and refused to give more, since they still had some distance to go and other petty chiefs and their demands to satisfy, this particular chief was most displeased and screamed threats at Justin and the trembling little group huddled together behind him.

"Give him anything he wants," James burst out.

"I know this man," Wentworth growled back. "No matter what he gets, he won't be satisfied. It's time to take a stand."

"Give it to him!" Scobbie shouted, losing his head, and when Justin made no move to comply James scrambled to his feet, grabbed the chest with the rest of its contents, and staggered forward to within ten feet of the dais, where he set it on the dusty ground.

Tchamoko smiled down at him, exposing his pointed teeth, and nodded. Then with a laugh he made a sidelong remark to a headman seated nearby. As James scurried backward and slumped down, panting, on the mat, the chief now boldly asked for an ox.

Hannah let out an anguished wail and Scobbie cried, "Let him have the blasted beast! I won't have my wife and children slaughtered because of an ox." Justin, his face grimer than Olwyn had ever seen it, glanced back over his shoulder at Hannah Scobbie, now near collapse, and nodded stiffly to this greedy request, though against his better judgment.

Tchamoko heaved a great sigh and once more communicated with them through Tondo. "I am a man of great kindness and compassion. How it wounds me to eat good flesh while the rest of my people go hungry. As you can see, my people are many and one ox is not enough to feed them all. Two more would at least give them all a small taste."

"I refuse!" Justin roared, and there was no need this time for his foreman to interpret. From the look of fury on the white "god's" face, Tchamoko understood exactly what he was saying.

At a signal from their chief, four painted and tattooed warriors burst into the clearing with spears raised and quivering on their shoulders, but at almost exactly the same moment Wentworth lifted his rifle and coolly aimed it at Tchamoko's chest. Again no explanation was needed. Savage he might be, primitive and in the eyes of the civilized world, ignorant, but the chief recognized immediately that before his warriors had killed the prisoners he himself would be dead.

Again he roared with laughter, and gestured for the spearmen to leave. It was just a joke, he assured them. He wouldn't dream of harming these worthy ambassadors from beyond the vast waters.

Tondo took this opportunity to inform the chief that if the white people were to perish at his hands, then a great battalion of their own warriors, at that very moment not too far away, would descend on them and wreck a terrible vengeance.

Whether he believed them or not was hard to say but Tchamoko suddenly waxed benevolent. Reminding them again that he was a kind, compassionate man, he grandly presented them with gifts of his own, a honeycomb, some tobacco, which the natives liked to pulverize into snuff, and a chunk of maggoty elephant meat that could be smelled a hundred feet away.

"You see the kind of man I am?" said the chief, spreading his arms wide and smiling broadly. "You must pay no attention to my little jokes. You may pass through my land and continue safely on your way."

The moment they returned to camp Justin prepared to leave immediately. He still looked grim, Olwyn noticed as the men got everything ready, and spoke only to the carriers and Tondo, and once to Harold, who had attached himself to Wentworth from the start of the trip, following him about like a shadow.

It was obvious that he was angry at James for interfering in the negotiations with the Zulu chief; reasonable enough, Olwyn supposed, when Scobbie had no experience in dealing with such things. Lack of experience never stopped James. He was the type of man who plunged right in, as Olwyn well knew, even where he wasn't needed or wanted. Only a few days before he had meddled, objecting to the form of discipline Wentworth doled out to two of his men who had been engaged in a fight, and more than once he had disagreed with the way Justin was handling things.

By now Olwyn knew her employer fairly well. He was a good man and basically kind and fair, and he had a dry sense of humor that could be very amusing, but James was also obstinate, opinionated, and not one to bend when he felt strongly about something—

and since Wentworth was just as strong-willed and assertive, she supposed it was inevitable that the two men would clash. The question wasn't if it would happen but when.

They had more important things to worry about at that time. No one could relax or feel really safe until they were well away from Tchamoko's territory, and that day they traveled farther than usual and didn't make camp until dusk had already fallen. Then it was a frantic rush to set up the fence and gather wood for the fires, though there was no chance of erecting the little lean-to huts that many of the men felt safer sleeping in. Most bunked in the open that night, none, including Justin, sleeping very well, but neither was he in the mood for conversation.

Olwyn tried, asking softly, "Do you think the Zulus have followed us?"

"Doubtful, but hard to be sure."

"Have you met Tchamoko before?"

"Not personally, but I'd heard of him."

She glanced down the wagon and saw him sitting up against the sacks, smoking one of the cigars he indulged in occasionally, a habit that had earned him a scolding from James, not that Justin had paid the slightest attention. His face was turned away from her as he gazed out into the clearing, flickering orange tongues from the fire beyond playing over his body. Olwyn tore her eyes away and made one last attempt to be convivial. "Why is it that the lions are always noisiest on the very dark nights?"

"Their habit."

Disgusted, she threw herself down on the bed and tried to get to sleep.

It wasn't easy, for various reasons, nature itself a contributing factor. They were camped near a pool in a lightly wooded area, a shallow valley below a broad, open plain. By now Olwyn was convinced that the whole of Africa was built in a series of terraces, like mammoth steps up the side of a colossal pyramid. It was always noisier close to woods, where countless nocturnal creatures conducted their business with scant regard for those who chose that time to sleep, and of course the pool, or any source of water, was always a great attraction.

Through a chink in the flap that closed over the back of the wagon, Olwyn lay awake listening to the evening symphony, though hardly enjoying it—the rustling, humming, scurrying, and now and then a sudden, piercing cry, as from some animal fallen a foul of a predator. From the plain above their valley the lions continued to roar, the deep, rumbling sound bouncing and echoing off the kopjes and spreading across the wooded area below like thunder.

Once or twice she rose slightly and looked down the cart; he was still sitting there, his head back and resting against the sacks. Olwyn was not sure whether he was awake or asleep and she thought it best not to inquire.

Her first flash of anger at this taciturn mood that had fallen over him gradually waned as the night wore on, and she found herself making excuses for his behavior. Ultimately, she supposed, the safety of them all rested on his shoulders, and he'd had much aggravation to contend with from problems with the oxen and wagons, scarcity of water in places, to outbreaks of jealousy and hostility among the men. Then, of course, there was James.

It occurred to Olwyn that, from his point of view, she, too, had added to his burden, but that, of course, was a matter of opinion.

Again she thought of how Tondo had come upon them the previous night and wondered how she would be able to look the big Griqua in the eye, not that she'd had to worry about it today with all the upheaval. But tomorrow?

How had Justin explained himself to his foreman? Or had he bothered to explain at all?

As these thoughts were running through her mind,

Olwyn suddenly noticed that everything about them had quietened quite abruptly. The noisiest of the lot, the lions, had finally shut up and the other residents of the bush seemed to have taken their cue from the so-called kings of the jungle. Even the insects had broken off their monotonous droning.

An eerie hush settled over the camp.

# 13

Now, just when she should have been able to sleep, she couldn't. Maddeningly, she felt the need to go out.

Earlier, when they'd come upon the pool they had all consumed copious amounts of water, and Olwyn knew there would be no peace for her that night if she didn't first pay a visit to the bushes.

Here there was a problem. She couldn't simply avail herself of the facilities of the camp itself lest one of the Watch come upon her behaving in a most unmanly way. It meant a brief trip outside the fence itself.

Fortunately, their wagon was near the back of the site and not more than fifty feet from the barrier. Once she reached it she could follow it, staying well in its shadow, all the way around to the gate. There were plenty of trees to help conceal her, though that was hardly necessary since the night itself was so dark, and the fires little more than smoldering piles in the ground since they'd had little time to collect wood before dark.

To avoid disturbing Justin, Olwyn quietly untied the flap at the back of the wagon, climbed over the side, and dropped lightly to the ground. In a moment or two she had reached the fence, also hastily erected that evening and much lower than usual. She followed it for a little way once her eyes began to adjust to the gloom, then drew herself into its deep shadow and stopped when one of the sentries appeared, lingered by one of the fires for a few minutes where he turned to toast his rump, then continued with his rounds of the campsite.

Olwyn let out her breath. She listened for a second or two, and cautiously picked her way down the side of the fence. When she reached the gate she again paused, thinking of the Zulus, but by then nature's call had become urgent. Fumbling with the rope that secured the gate, she decided that there was little risk involved if she only ventured out a few feet, just far enough to duck behind the fence where none of the Watch could possibly see her.

She stepped outside into long, dew-laden grass, ice cold against her warm flesh. The shock of it made her gasp and almost cry out, so numbing cold did it feel. It caused the skin all over her body to prickle and shrink and her teeth to chatter uncontrollably. It was so dark here that she couldn't see at all; it was like looking into a pit.

The stillness was thick and oppressive; then, barely discernible, Olwyn heard the long grass stirring—though there was no breeze—and caught a whiff of the stink.

A vaulting, choking clutch of fear cut off her breathing.

Wentworth woke up with a start, much as he had done off and on all night. Neither the camp nor the moonless night was to his liking. Though no one could be blamed, everything had been too hastily arranged, and the two negatives combined made him restless.

They were in lion country, obvious from the din all evening. He knew from experience that the beasts restricted their hunting to the darkest nights unless lack of food over several nights drove them to take risks. And he also knew that the creatures could be amazingly cunning and stealthy. During a buffalo hunt two years before, one of his bearers had been plucked right out of his tent well inside a stout fence, carried back to it in the powerful jaws of a lioness, and there she had leaped over with her helpless victim to vanish into the darkness. They had come upon his bones two days later.

Each time he woke that night Justin's hand had automatically dropped to his gun even as his eyes carefully scanned the clearing, his ears straining for the slightest sound, then he had always glanced to the back of the wagon, more out of curiosity than anything else, interested to see if she was as restless as he was. It was very dark back there. Curled among the tangle of blankets he couldn't actually see her if she were lying down—but he could clearly hear her breathing. After five years roaming the wilds his hearing had become very acute; sometimes his life had depended on it.

This time when he glanced back he heard nothing. More ominous still, the flap of the canvas in the rear wall gaped open.

"Tondo!" he bellowed, springing to his feet with the gun in his hand. "Rouse the men!"

The silence in the camp exploded in pandemonium. Justin hadn't been the only one worried about the lions that night, and when he shouted that Moore was missing everybody feared the worst.

One of the methods employed in chasing away predators was to make as much noise as possible, and Justin's men went to it with a vengeance, shrieking, roaring, yelling at the top of their lungs. At the same time they tossed anything that would burn into the fires, including boxes containing some of their provisions. First one and then a dozen rifles cracked in short spurts of flame, their muzzles pointing skyward rather than through the thorn fence, afraid as they were to strike Olwyn rather than the beast, if, indeed, one was prowling. Scobbie's droll Hottentot foreman saw little sense in this. As he remarked to a porter, "Better to die quick than have leeuw munch slowly."

Justin and Tondo snatched chunks of the flaming packing cases from the kgotla fire and raced for the gate in the fence, which they saw was open. A dozen or so others were hot on their heels but many followed more reluctantly, terrified of having to confront an animal known to be the supreme hunter in the dark.

Inside their own wagon, Hannah Scobbie screamed hysterically once more and mercifully swooned. "Stay with her!" James ordered his oldest son, and jumped from the cart with his shirttails flapping. He was half way across the site when a great savage roar like thunder caused the ground to tremble beneath him. The lioness had finally decided to make her presence known.

Then they heard the woman shriek.

Olwyn never saw the lion at all until the camp burst to life but she sensed and smelled it. Hesitating in the dark with that peculiar rank odor strong in her nostrils and a visceral numbing fear swelling inside her, she suddenly knew that her last moment had come. Then, like the curtain going up on a dark stage and the lights coming on, she found herself face to face with her killer.

The beast was crouching in the tall yellow grass not fifteen feet away, her quivering body blending perfectly with her hiding place. She was tense, her tufted chin jutting forward, primed and ready to spring. As light from the torches flared up behind her, bathing the glade in a weird orange light, Olwyn's eyes locked with those of the predator.

Such eyes they were! Demonic orbs of flaming

yellow, soulless and indescribably cruel. For just a second, as she launched herself with a mighty roar that struck Olwyn's ears like a blow, those merciless eyes flickered to the source of the light behind them.

The lioness was in the air when the rifles exploded —Olwyn could actually *feel* the strenuous effort behind that spring as a vibration in her own body—but at the crack of gunshot and the shouts of the approaching men, the beast instantly altered course in mid-air. Instead of landing on top of her intended prey, she crashed to the ground about three feet away but behind the fence, where the light still hadn't penetrated. Then, as is their habit when disturbed at a hunt, the lion paused only long enough to maim her victim with the intention of slipping back later to finish her off.

One swipe of a massive paw knocked Olwyn off her feet, the razor-sharp claws opening her leg from knee to ankle. With a last ear-splitting roar, the creature wheeled about, vaulted up the embankment, and vanished into the darkness.

Olwyn shrieked in agony at the searing pain. She clamped both hands to her leg and screamed again as she felt her own hot blood bubbling through her fingers, so warm by comparison with the dew-drenched grass . . . and the chill numbness that was swiftly spreading through her body and all the way up to her brain. Then she was silent, immobile.

When Justin came upon her Olwyn was sprawled on the grass, the bottom of her white shirt and most of her legs drenched in blood.

"My God!" Wentworth threw aside the torch and stooped and gathered her up in his arms, running with her back into the clearing and yelling at Tondo to fetch his first-aid kit and light the lamps in the wagon. Once at the cart he laid her tenderly in his own makeshift bed at the front and piled blankets over her, only leaving the badly lacerated leg exposed, then stuffed pillows and whatever else came to hand under her head, to raise it high above the level of her body.

Frightened at her pallor and the clammy coldness of her flesh, Justin took her face between his hands and showered it with frantic kisses, crooning, "Hold on, my darling, hold on! Olwyn, love . . ."

"Master," Tondo broke in heavily, standing over the pair with the medical kit in his hand. The brown face of the Griqua registered no expression whatsoever at this startling outburst of emotion from one man to another, but as Justin seized the kit, his foreman gave a nod in the direction of the clearing, where nearly two hundred men stood in awed silence watching, including the missionary, James Scobbie.

Justin paid them no attention. He had only minutes before his sweet love bled to death before his very eyes, and the sensibilities of the onlookers meant absolutely nothing to him at that moment.

"Thread the needle, Tondo!" he yelled, his own fingers slippery with blood. "And bring that damned lamp closer! And hurry, in the name of Christ!"

While his foreman hastened to do his bidding, Wentworth tried to staunch the flow of blood as best he could by making a pad of one of his shirts and pressing down on her ankle, just stopping short of breaking it.

Scobbie, once he'd recovered a little from his own shock, made his way up to the crude "operating room," where he stood for several minutes in silence, watching Justin carefully rejoining the torn flesh, much as Hannah stitched together the separate parts of a garment, taking every bit as great care in the process.

James cast a sidelong glance at the trader's face and saw that the big man was sweating profusely, though the night had become quite cool. The dark face was harsh and intense, the flesh clamped so tight over the strong bones that they shone through quite clearly. A pulse throbbed with great agitation at the side of his mouth, and never had Scobbie witnessed a man under a greater strain, or seen such raw emotion in the eyes fixed on his patient.

Scobbie's own wits were suddenly in chaos once more.

"Is . . . is he going to be all right?" he asked Justin hoarsely, his normally strong voice weak and unsteady. "He's a fine lad and . . . goodness me!" Scobbie was at a loss to describe exactly what he was feeling and wondering at that moment.

Justin gestured impatiently to his foreman. "Gauze, Tondo! Lots of it. And fetch the laudanum."

He hadn't even heard what James said to him.

Harold was suddenly beside his father, eyes huge as he rose on tiptoe to get a better look into the cart and saw that the area around the bed resembled a slaughterhouse with all the blood. It blasted the message he'd brought his father right out of his head and kept him staring in morbid fascination for all that it made him feel a little sick.

Harold wouldn't have admitted it to anyone, but he'd been terrified at the thought of lions invading the camp; more than all the other predators he was especially afraid of these beasts because they were always so stealthy or, as Mr. Wentworth had once put it, the perfect instruments of death. Much as he had grown to love hunting, even when dangerous animals were involved, Harold was quite certain he would never want to hunt lions. They were the type of quarry, as Wentworth had said, perfectly capable of turning the tables and becoming the pursuer instead of the pursued.

Watching the proceedings with great interest, Harold was suddenly struck by something he hadn't noticed before—how much like a girl Oliver looked in his nightshirt, especially with his hair tumbled loose about his face. Yes, and his legs were girlish too. No muscles there! And not even any hair!

James, silent and thoughtful for some time, now came to a decision. He wanted Oliver out of this wagon! Aye, and he wanted Hannah, rather than

Wentworth, to look after the lad, who from his fluttering eyelids and faint moans thankfully showed signs of reviving.

With mixed emotions, Scobbie watched a big grin of relief spread over Wentworth's face. Tondo laughed, too, and bellowed out to the silent crowd, "He be fine! He live!"

A cheer went up from the men that was ear-splitting.

When it died down James turned to his son. "Where is your mother?"

Harold gave a guilty start. "Oh! Mama's very sick; she's vomiting a lot—"

"What?" Scobbie gripped his son's shoulder angrily. "Why didn't you tell me this before instead of standing here gaping like a dough-heid?"

Before he hurried back to his wife the missionary spoke to Justin.

"I'll be over in the morning but send a message if there's any untoward change in the lad's condition. We must make proper arrangements for Oliver's convalescence."

# 14

Hannah Scobbie was in a state of nervous collapse. As a gently bred young lady growing up in the genteel area of Bearsden in Glasgow, nothing in her formative years had prepared her for anything like this. She was quite overcome, in a state of shock, and of course it had affected her stomach, which had always been rather delicate. Now it was more delicate than ever, and for a very good reason. She was pregnant.

James had no idea; she had simply never found the right time to tell him. Nor was she sure how he would take the news, another reason she had kept it to herself.

In the early hours of that morning when he returned to his wagon with Harold, Scobbie found his wife pale and sick and distraught. "Did they find the lad?" she cried, clutching her husband's hand. "Oh, please tell me that he's all right?"

James hastened to assure her that Oliver had been

found and, though wounded, there seemed a good chance that he would recover. *At least physically* he thought to himself, his mind still alive and reeling from the dark thing he'd discovered. *Though I'm not so confident about his moral health.*

Naturally, he said nothing about this to Hannah. He and his wife never discussed such matters.

"I want to go back to Scotland," Hannah suddenly announced, and burst into anguished weeping.

In the bed at the back of the wagon the two boys exchanged a look, and Harold muttered under his breath, "Bugger it!"

Jamie's eyes went wide as they always did when Harold swore, and he was swearing quite a lot lately. Now the smaller boy wasn't sure whether his brother was dismayed that they might, indeed, return home, or whether he was angry at their father taking their mother away in the first place.

The two children, peeking over their pile of blankets, watched and listened to everything that was going on at the front part of the cart, but soon lost interest when, after calming Hannah down, James launched into a long, rambling prayer in which he beseeched the Lord to give his wife and helpmeet strength and fortitude to carry her through this difficult mission He had entrusted them with. "Forgive her her faintness of heart," he droned on, "and teach her not to question the plans You have in store for us, but to accept them with a willing heart as a good Christian should."

By the time the prayer ended the boys were asleep and Hannah thoroughly ashamed of her weakness.

In the pre-dawn stillness she softly told her husband the joyous news.

Scobbie was appalled. "Oh, surely not?" he burst out before he could stop himself, his first thought that the wilds of Africa was no place for a tiny baby. The second that Hannah had already suffered five miscarriages and each time had been quite ill afterward—

and here they lacked a qualified doctor to look after her.

"It will be all right this time, dear," she assured him, taking his hand, guessing at his fears. "Just think of it, James, what if we have a bonny wee girl!" Hannah had yearned for a bonny wee girl for years, even though she loved her sons dearly. James, for his part, had never felt the lack of more females in the house; he'd been plagued with enough of them via his wife's bossy mother and gossipy sisters in Glasgow! Women . . . women were a bother, he reflected, there was no doubt about that. They were such fragile, twittery, empty-headed creatures, always on about such silly things like cooking recipes, clothes, what this person said, or what another person did—and of course they nattered incessantly about babies! A girl child in Africa would bring even greater problems. For instance, his mind ran on, where would she eventually find a decent chap to marry; an honorable, God-fearing chap?

The lack of wholesome partners of the opposite sex was indeed a grave problem . . . and again his mind turned to Wentworth and his innocent little Oliver. Cold fury bit deep inside Scobbie. Aye, and disgust too. And to think that he had admired the trader! He'd even been prepared to overlook the opinionated, know-it-all tendencies he'd noticed in the man throughout the course of this trip, yes, even when it went against the grain. He had actively sought Wentworth's friendship. And never, never would he have guessed that he would turn out to be depraved, or go so far as to corrupt poor, naïve wee Oliver! The boy must be got out of his clutches in the morning!

"James?"

Scobbie dragged his attention back to his wife. "Yes, my dear?"

"You *are* pleased about the baby?"

James clenched his jaw, then relaxed it. "Delighted," he fibbed, hoping God would forgive him since he'd lied to spare Hannah further grief. "Absolutely overjoyed."

She patted his hand, quite satisfied.

He was glad, for once, that women were so gullible.

For a day Olwyn was conscious of almost nothing but pain, though Justin administered careful doses of the precious painkiller and sedative, laudanum, which dulled the worst of it and at least made her sleep for long stretches at a time. Each time she awoke, though dazed and in agony, Olwyn was conscious of Wentworth being with her, stroking her hair, sponging her sweating face, kissing her with such tenderness that it penetrated the fog clogging her mind, filling her with a wild, sweet happiness for all that she was in such discomfort.

Then she would feel for his hand and when his strong brown fingers closed over hers, shut her eyes and sigh, thinking that if she died now, then at least she wouldn't be alone. She had someone—someone wonderful.

Wentworth kept the caravan in the valley for the next three days, afraid that the bumping and swaying over the rough ground would start up the bleeding again. Since many of the men were superstitious and grumbled about the lions—which continued to roar nightly—being evil spirits, supernatural beings, he allowed them to spend time reinforcing the fence and making it three times as high as necessary, and passed out more guns to the natives, which pleased them enormously.

Fresh meat was shot every day, the best cuts lightly cooked and coaxed on Olwyn. "It will help you get back your strength." Justin smiled.

She wrinkled up her nose. "But it's still bloody!"

"Eat it, darling; it's better for you that way."

So she ate it to please him. She also drank the broth, rich and meaty, that he had Flo cook for her, and she tried not to fuss or cry out when Justin changed her bandages and gently but thoroughly cleaned the wound, which looked disfiguring and hideous to Olwyn.

Again Justin reassured her. "Ah . . . but it's a straight cut, from here to here." His brown finger traced the route with a feather-light touch, making her shiver, though not with pain. "It's a neat, thin slash, and assuming I'm up to my usual high standards with the needle," he grinned, "then it should heal leaving only the faintest white scar."

"I'm jealous." Olwyn pretended to pout. "I'm beginning to suspect that you know more about doctoring than I do." She glanced down at the long row of stitches and livid-looking wound. "Have you done much of this kind of thing before?"

Justin laughed, thinking of some of the frightful injuries he'd had to contend with during his five years in Africa, including stitching up wounds far worse than hers. "Yes," he nodded, "but I've never had a more beautiful patient to work on." His eyes roamed the length of her long, slender leg and he added, "Or one who proved more distracting."

Olwyn was swaddled in one of his shirts, now carelessly open to the thigh. She closed the flaps, blushing, and stammered, "You . . . I think you are a very good doctor, and I've something to confess. I wasn't so drugged yesterday that . . . well, that I couldn't tell you were taking very . . . that you have a lovely bedside manner."

Wentworth stared at her as she sat with her eyes on her hands, the pink flushed cheeks fragile as rose petals, smooth as porcelain against the tumbled mass of jet-black curls. At that moment her manner was uncertain and achingly sweet, he was thinking, like a little girl asking for a special favor and not sure she would get it. But then her eyes lifted to his face, long, luminous, and incredibly provocative, and in that instant everything changed and any illusion of a little girl vanished. The power of those eyes immediately stirred his senses and a thought flickered through his mind that she was aware of her ability to attract; what woman, even a young one, wouldn't be?

Justin moved away a little. "I want you to promise me something?"

She nodded quickly.

"Never leave the campsite alone again, even in the daytime."

There was the faintest look of surprise on her face, as if she'd been expecting him to say something else.

"I won't," Olwyn replied a bit snappishly.

"Won't promise?" His brows rose, and Justin felt the peculiar tension that always crackled between them come creeping back.

"Won't leave," she said, and closed her eyes.

Scobbie paid her several visits over the next two days, once alone, but usually accompanied by Hannah or the boys. He could see Olwyn was foggy with the laudanum and in pain, and Wentworth busy looking after her and at the same time keeping an eye on the men. There was no opportunity to have a serious talk with either of them, at least for the time being.

He'd already felt Hannah out, without disclosing his reason, of course.

"Oliver might be more comfortable traveling in the supply wagon for the remainder of the trip."

"Why?"

"Well . . . his injury will naturally make him restless, and with all he has to attend to, Wentworth needs his sleep."

"Has Mr. Wentworth complained?"

"Nooo . . . not exactly."

"Then why should you fuss?"

James threw up his hands in exasperation. "I'm not fussing, woman; it was just a suggestion."

His wife sighed. "Simmer down, James." Then she indulged in a Scottish expression that he himself was so fond of. "You have been looking a bit torn-faced lately. Do cheer up."

Hannah never resorted to broad Scots slang, and it proved to be disarming. Scobbie threw back his head and howled with laughter.

By the third day after the attack Olwyn felt a little better. Her wound was still painful and badly inflamed, and she still felt weak from loss of blood, but she'd stopped taking laudanum and at least her head was clear. When he inspected the laceration that morning Justin announced that they'd be able to leave the next. "It's knitting together nicely," he said. "And it's unsafe to tarry in one spot for too long."

"Are you discharging me as a patient?" Olwyn said it teasingly to cover the pang she felt at the thought of losing his almost undivided attention, for during most of this time Justin had delegated a lot of his work about the camp and authority to Tondo and Scobbie's foreman, Mick. She would miss that.

Justin gave her a quick—too quick—kiss on the lips.

"Not quite. I'll still keep a close eye on you."

Late that afternoon when Wentworth went out to supervise preparations for leaving just before dawn the following morning, James appeared and climbed into the wagon. "How do you feel?" he asked a bit abruptly.

"Better, thank you." Looking up at him from her bed, Olwyn thought he had a funny expression on his face; she could tell he was displeased about something and wondered if he'd had another difference of opinion with Justin.

James glanced out of the cart, then back at her. "Get your things, lad. I'm taking you out of here."

"What? But . . . where am I going?" Olwyn was completely befuddled.

He quickly explained that for tonight she would sleep in their wagon and in the morning a bed would be made for her in the supply cart.

"I simply cannot countenance this situation another minute!" he burst out obscurely, and after that refused to answer any more of her questions and kept urging her to hurry as she searched about for her breeches and boots. Scobbie knew as well as she did that she wasn't supposed to walk or even put pressure on her injured leg but he voiced his intention of assisting her, saying, "I'll support most of your weight, never fear. You can sort of hop a bit on your other foot."

In this way, with Scobbie's arm about her waist, they were on their way across the clearing while the men were working with the animals and loading the supply wagon near the gate, when Mick, Scobbie's own man, turned and spotted them. He nudged Tondo and pointed, and Tondo called sharply to his master.

"What in Christ's name are you doing, Scobbie?" the trader yelled across the campground.

James ignored him and kept going.

Justin was livid when he caught up with them. Even Olwyn shrank from the cold fury she saw blazing in his eyes, and for a horrible second she thought he meant to strike James. Instead, he wrenched her out of his grasp, swung her up in his arms and stalked back with her to their own wagon while Scobbie, just as angry, stalked after them.

The resentment steadily building between these two strong-willed men erupted inside the cart. While Justin carefully settled Olwyn back in bed and stooped to have a look at her leg—fresh blood could be seen seeping through the gauze—Scobbie coldly stated that in all good conscience he could not allow the "vile association" to continue and demanded that Olwyn be removed at once to the wagon he shared with his wife. "And I trust God will have mercy on you for the woeful sin you have perpetrated against this innocent boy," he finished darkly in the tone of one who felt such a grievous sin should *not* be forgiven.

Wentworth shot to his feet and towered over the smaller man, and Olwyn cried out, expecting to see James hurled from the cart. "Scobbie," Justin began in a voice that was deadly patient, "never preach to me again. And don't interfere with my running of this caravan—or my life!" he finished in a shout that made Olwyn jump.

James, too, flinched, but Scobbie was the kind of man who had to be battered into submission. "It's my duty to preach!" he shouted back, chin thrust out pugnaciously. "What kind of minister would I be if I closed my eyes to the abomination taking place in this wagon—"

"Abomination?" Wentworth gave a chilling laugh. "Then prepare yourself to wrestle with much worse," he warned, thinking of the situation at Nuruzambora.

"What do you mean?" When Justin remained silent he cried, pointing to Olwyn, "That boy is my responsibility; he works for me, and I want him removed from this cart immediately. I demand it!"

Wentworth loomed over the missionary, the muscles bulging in his back and shoulders, a dark flush on his face. As he raised his hands Olwyn screamed, "Stop! Dear God, stop this!" Then, gulping to clear the sudden tightness at her throat, "I—I have something to tell you, Mr. Scobbie."

Both men turned to look at her.

# ◇ 15 ◇

My name is really *Olwyn* Moore."

Scobbie just stared at her, uncomprehending, his mind unable to take it in.

"I . . . I'm a woman, Mr. Scobbie."

James's stony face came alive at that. He started to frown, then suddenly the corners of his wide mouth shot upward and he burst out laughing.

"Dinna be daft, laddie! What rubbish is this?" He turned a suspicious eye on Justin, who stood beside him in silence, his expression unreadable, and accused, "Is this another of your dastardly tricks to get me to—"

"No!" the girl broke in, clenching her hands to stop them from shaking, though nothing could stop her heart from pounding or her mind from screaming at her that she was making a terrible mistake; that she had just destroyed what little security she had. "No, I'm telling you the truth."

"Nonsense!"

Olwyn opened her shirt, unpinned the bandages,

and as they came away and James caught a glimpse of her breasts he sucked in his breath, stumbled, and sat down on one of the sacks. He looked shattered, stunned, his face blasted as he gazed straight ahead of him out of the wagon and across the campsite. For one of the few times in his life he could find nothing to say.

Olwyn blurted out the tale of how it had all come about, not even sure James was listening. He seemed to be in shock.

"I'm not trying to excuse what I did," she finished, "but I was desperate. I could have spent years in prison for something I didn't do. There was just no possibility of someone like me, from the Gallowgate, standing up to these people."

That much Scobbie understood!

"I'll work hard for you, sir!" Olwyn rushed on when he remained wooden and silent. "And I didn't lie to you about the medical part; I have trained under a doctor. Oh, Mr. Scobbie, I'm sorry, but—"

"Enough, Olwyn!" Justin interrupted grimly, and with a nod to James, "He's not listening."

The minister stood up abruptly, jumped down from the wagon, and walked rapidly away. Olwyn put her face in her hands and wept. Aside from what it could mean for her future, she was so sorry that she'd had to do this to James, who had been good to her and, even if unwittingly, had helped her out of a ghastly situation. Aside from that, Olwyn felt that Scobbie had been genuinely fond of her, and that had brought her great comfort. It was all ruined now . . .

Justin put a hand on her head, then he knelt down beside her bed until his face was on a level with her own, and tilting up her chin he kissed her tear-streaked face, then told her softly, "Don't fret, darling, I'll help you." He glanced back over his shoulder and his face hardened. "He's a self-righteous, sanctimonious, pedantic—"

"Don't, Justin." Olwyn buried her face in his neck. "Can't you see he's had a terrible shock? Think how you felt when you found out the truth about me—"

"Oh, I was delighted!"

Olwyn looked up quickly, anxiously searching his face. He was grinning, and there was a hedonistic glint in his eyes.

"Just the same, you were still angry," she said. "Admit it?"

Justin sobered. It was true. Under his surface surprise and pleasure he had felt a sharp disappointment, a cynicism, akin to being presented with what looked to be a flawless diamond, only to find out it was a fake.

"I was a little annoyed," he confessed. "Nobody likes to be duped."

"Justin—" she caught him by the shoulders, determined to get something else off her chest, weary of having it always lying between them like some sort of trap that could spring and—

"I suspect you have something else to tell me."

Both Olwyn and Justin looked around to see Scobbie's head and shoulders over the opening at the front of the wagon. He hoisted himself inside and plunked himself down on a grain sack. As he'd stamped around the clearing trying to digest the very unpalatable news about his assistant—and even yet it hadn't sunk in!—something else Wentworth had hurled at him had sifted back into his mind; a disturbing comment he'd made about Nuruzambora. At that a fresh surge of irritation and alarm had swept over him. James was direct; he had to know what it was immediately.

While Justin and Olwyn exchanged a look, he barked, "Well, what is it I'm supposed to prepare myself to wrestle with at the mission station? Out with it, Wentworth!"

Justin leaned against the side of the wagon and thrust his hands in his pockets. He hated having to be the bearer of bad tidings, but more than that he disliked giving the appearance of scandalmongering. Just the same, he was still angry at Scobbie and felt less inclined to spare his feelings. There was the thought, too, that it might be best to warn him in advance; that way the shock would be lessened.

"There has been constant trouble at the mission station from the start," Justin began. "And you can blame that on Sloan and Erskine." He glanced at Scobbie from under his brows. "Do you know much about these men?"

"Very little," James admitted.

Basically, Wentworth went on, the problem lay in the fact that the men were very different types and even under the best of conditions would have had trouble agreeing on just about anything. Add remoteness, isolation, and extreme hardship, frustration, and often danger, and it brought out the worst in them in very short order.

First, Wentworth continued, they disagreed about how the mission station should be set up, then on how they should handle the local tribe. "Erskine takes a hard line with the natives, and he's impatient for results. He wants to convert them to Christianity all at once, and with that in mind preaches hell fire and brim"—here he threw Scobbie a pointed look—"and attempts to frighten them into accepting his religion. Sloan is just the opposite; he's too soft with the locals and they haven't been slow to take advantage."

Justin paused, then he said, "I think I should warn you that Robert Sloan has gone native."

Both Scobbie and Olwyn stared at him in confusion. They had absolutely no idea what he meant.

Wentworth groaned inwardly at the blank looks on their faces and ploughed on. "He's become so enamored with their customs, their habits and so forth, that for the past year he's spent more time in the village than at the mission station . . . and he hasn't preached Christianity for a very long time now."

James looked flabbergasted.

"And he's taken a native mistress."

Scobbie groaned loudly and put his face in his hands.

Justin lit a cigar and went on philosophically, "Africa has a peculiar effect on many Europeans. Blame it on the climate, the isolation—"

James tore his hands away from his face and broke in furiously, "That's no excuse, man! It's like saying a murderer was provoked by his victim, therefore he was quite justified in killing him. Oh no!"—he shook his head emphatically—"that won't cut the mustard at all. Sloan is—is contemptible, and I tremble for him on the Day of Judgment when he must account for his sins to the Lord."

"He might not have to wait so long," Wentworth said dryly. "The natives don't think too well of him either. Believe it or not, they have their own code of ethics and despise an outsider using one of their women. Old Seconda, the chief who died recently, was surprisingly tolerant, but his son M'Buru tends to view things differently."

James again bolted to his feet and stumbled out of the wagon.

Olwyn sighed, looking after him. "Poor Mr. Scobbie, what a day this has been for him."

"Well," Justin shrugged, "now he knows."

By morning the whole camp knew, at least about her, thanks to that infallible device, the bush telegraph. They stared but said nothing.

Just before dawn the caravan moved out of the valley and the oxen, well rested now, readily pulled the wagons uphill onto an immense, dry plain where in spite of the scarcity of vegetation large herds of buffalo, blue wildebeest, and impala roamed. Following them, as usual, came the predators, the hyenas, and bush dogs, and though they could rarely be glimpsed in the broad light of day, lions. They were there, though, in thickets or basking in the tall grass or under trees, their tawny hides merging marvelously with their environment.

Mick, James's foreman, pointed out a pride to her—a sight she would have missed—all sprawled under a giant baobab, trees that always made Olwyn think of arthritic old men, tortuously twisted and gnarled as they were. Olwyn felt a chill at the sight of them, her own terrifying experience so fresh in her mind. Mick seemed to understand and patted his rifle. "No get you," he comforted at the look on her face. "No hunt now; too hot."

Not only did Mick know that, but the other prey animals seemed to understand it, too, because to Olwyn's horror they grazed all around the lions' den while a few of the predators, those not asleep, watched them lazily, now and then opening their lethal mouths in a yawn, displaying teeth that were awesome. The graceful dik-diks and gazelles, tails flicking while they fed, astonishingly didn't seem very impressed and did no more than glance at the pride now and then with no outward show of fear. The lions, for their part, looked haughty and bored.

Mick chuckled. "Leeuw think, eat well and grow fat. Make better feast tonight."

Olwyn hugged herself. "Then there's no danger during the day?"

The Hottentot carefully considered her question, his yellow face wrinkled up in thought. "Not say never," he finally replied. "Most often not, but leeuw in certain circum . . . circum—"

"Circumstances?"

He nodded. "Sometimes he kill in daytime. It depend."

Later that afternoon, as misty blue shadows lengthened across the plain and the sun had moved into the west, Olwyn noticed a change in the grazing animals. They became more active and restless, as if smitten with a kind of nervous confusion, milling about here and there in groups, noses up sniffing the air, then in dusty clouds scudding away from the tall grasses and scrub into the bare, open veld where there was less of a chance of them being ambushed.

Just before dusk they witnessed a kill that had Olwyn weeping and beseeching the men to shoot the predators, in this case bush dogs. A pack of the scruffy little creatures, about the size of the average domestic dog, had been within sight of the caravan all afternoon, while the dogs had been within sight of a herd of wildebeest. The patchy little canines hadn't seemed particularly interested. They stopped to take frequent rest in the shade, to yap with each other and to frolic with their pups. Olwyn found them quite amusing to watch. But suddenly, as twilight approached, their easy-going manner changed. The two largest dogs stood stiff and tense, noses in the air, then started loping in the direction of the wildebeest, the others following. Then they speeded up, streaking across the dusty earth at an amazing speed for their size, scattering in all directions to mingle with the wildebeest, but united in their quest to find a likely victim. They found her, a young female with an injured hind leg.

Immediately they surrounded her, separating her from the rest of the herd, who paused in their own flight to gaze back in helpless terror. The bush dogs moved in on the much larger creature with jaws snapping. One seized her already injured leg and bit deep while another raced around to her head, leaped up and sank its teeth into the wildebeest's throat and hung on while she frantically tossed her head, trying to dislodge him. True to habit, the other dogs dove into her from behind, quickly crawling underneath to her soft belly, yelping and slavering ecstatically as they ripped her open, her intestines spilling out on the dusty earth in gleaming red coils. Doomed and in agony, the wildebeest continued to stand there for a moment, her stricken eyes facing the caravan, then she slumped down with the dogs swarming all over her.

"Why didn't you shoot?" Olwyn screamed at the men. "Oh, this is a horrible, blood-thirsty land and I—I hate it!"

Mick picked his teeth with the point of his knife until her weeping subsided, then said, "Dogs must eat too." He glanced at her tear-streaked face and inquired gently, "You not eat cow?"

Olwyn sat silent and somber around the camp fire that night, unable to eat anything. It had been a dreadful day all the way around and now her old feeling of loneliness and isolation had come back for all that there were nearly two hundred people in the camp. Justin had been too busy to spend time with her all day, except to quickly change her dressings, and hampered as she was with the injured leg she'd been restricted to the wagon—there to do nothing but think!

Mostly the others had left her alone. James hadn't come near, nor had Hannah or the boys. The porters, if they looked at her at all, did so in quick, furtive glances, a kind of superstitious dread in their eyes. Only Tondo seemed pleased by the astounding metamorphosis that had taken place under their noses, his high estimation of his master fully restored.

It was now known by one and all that the lad they had started the trip with had astoundingly changed into a girl.

Olwyn slept in the supply wagon that night, even more hemmed in by boxes and equipment, and here she was to sleep for the remainder of the journey, now nearing its end. What would happen to her once they reached Nuruzambora? Olwyn brooded, gazing out through the canvas flap at a sky sprayed with stars. Would James send her back to Cape Town in the next caravan, and from there home to Scotland? He hadn't said anything about that, but then he'd been too upset the previous day to come to any decision about her, especially once Justin revealed what was happening with Sloan and Erskine. In a way that had distracted Scobbie; she wasn't his only problem.

Olwyn felt very sorry for James and bitterly ashamed of herself.

Justin paid her a visit at midnight, long after the camp was asleep, and found Olwyn gloomy and fretful.

"You shouldn't have come!" she hissed when he appeared out of the darkness, though deep inside she

was very glad to see him. "I'm in terrible trouble as it
is."

When he made to kiss her Olwyn pushed him away.

His strong white teeth flashed in the gloom, and he
shrugged. "Darling, you've been in trouble from the
day I met you—"

"Yes, and you've caused at least half of it!" she
interrupted peevishly. "It's thanks to you that James
found out!" Even as she said it, Olwyn knew she was
being a little unfair, but she was in no mood to shave
hairs or analyze the exact nature of their relationship,
particularly her own side of it.

Leaning in the opening, his elbow resting on a crate
containing tea, coffee, and sugar, Wentworth gave her
a long, appraising look in the light from the nearby
fire, and asked, "Then you wouldn't have told Scobbie
otherwise?"

"Oh . . . eventually, but I'd have chosen a better
time." Frowning, she turned her face away from him,
uncomfortable at the way he was looking at her, yet
annoyed too. Everything was so easy for him! she
fumed inwardly. What did he have to lose? He was a
man, and a wealthy one at that! Hard as things were
for a woman in her position in Britain, they were a
hundred times more uncertain here in the wilds of
this cruel wilderness. Oh yes, it was easy for him to
criticize!

"You'd better go before someone sees you," she
said, even though she didn't really want him to leave,
angry or not. His company, she thought, was better
than none at all.

"Good night," Justin responded shortly, and turned
away at once.

Olwyn slumped down on the pillow and bit her lip
to stop herself from calling him back. Her mind said,
*Good! Let him go. You don't need him.* But her
emotions rose up in clamoring protest, crying, *You do!
You do!*

It occurred to Olwyn, staring out at the velvet,
star-studded night, that it would be grand to be so

cool, self-sufficient, and yes, secure, that she had no need of anyone. She could always get a pet to shower her affections on, when and if she could ever achieve that exulted state of mind. Pets were rarely much trouble and had the advantage of never talking back —or criticizing!

Justin, too, lay gazing out at the night. He estimated they were about a week away from Nuruzambora, where he would thankfully break off from Scobbie's part of the caravan and depart for Teragno.

"Thank God!" he muttered.

Shifting restlessly, he pounded his pillow to reshape it and lay back down with his arms behind his head, completely naked under the mosquito net. In the distance, very faintly, the throb of drumbeats drifted to him in the night, the pulsing sound echoing in his blood, dark and insistent, giving him no respite. He imagined her, too, naked and lying beside him, her satiny skin dewy with sweat, burning against his, her soft lips parted and their tongues probing hungrily and his hand, then his mouth at her breast, her thighs . . .

Justin sat up abruptly and lit a cigar. He cherished his freedom and with a pang of dismay he realized that it was draining slowly away, replaced by an urge to cherish her instead!

She was still in many ways an enigma, and that bothered him. By turns she became a warm, passionate, infinitely desirable woman—then a sweetly uncertain little girl. She veered from being earnestly candid and open to mysteriously elusive, like quicksilver. And her stories, true or false?

For a woman, Olwyn Moore was too proud, too daring and independent—yet in reality Justin admired all those qualities, yes, even when they exasperated him. And of course she was always, always so beautiful; he yearned to dress her as she should have been, in silks and satins, and drench her in diamonds, white fire entwined through the shining ebony ripples

of her hair, at her throat and wrists. He pictured her in
an elegant white gown studded with diamonds, radiant, ravishing, and not at all impossible if his plans
worked out. He—

He was a fool! Justin shook his head, chuckling a
little at this fanciful turn his mind had taken when
only a moment before he'd told himself he'd be glad to
get rid of Olwyn and the entire party at
Nuruzambora! They would reach the mission station
in no more than a week, Justin estimated.

Moodily, he flicked ash from his cigar out into the
night and listened to the muffled beat of the drums, no
doubt pounding out a message to the next village they
encountered that strangers were on the way, white
gods among them, he thought with a sigh. Thus
alerted, the next chief would be waiting with a welcoming committee to greet them, hoping to receive
many fine gifts, and when they were not forthcoming,
immediately demanding toll.

These people were astonishingly quick to learn,
Justin reflected, and like the rest of the world, could be
exceedingly greedy. Unlike the rest of the world, who
knew better, these people fully believed that the white
man's pot of gold was self-filling, and never ran out.
Like Tchamoko they could be dangerous when denied, especially if they sensed they had the upper
hand.

One more week and he would be free to pursue his
own affairs. He had already spoken with his lawyers
while in Cape Town and they were prepared. The next
step was to buy all the land he could surrounding the
spot where he had found the diamonds, then set his
men at Teragno to digging furiously.

Justin had learned something interesting while in
Cape Town—a Boer farmer had found a large diamond on the Orange River almost three years before!
At the time it was considered to be a freak occurrence
since no more were discovered. Similiar solitary diamonds had popped up now and then in other parts of

the world, but more than one discovery was necessary to arouse widespread interest.

Justin had found twelve in all!

Four had been sold off in London, leaving him with the original eight, but one of those eight was missing.

Again his mind returned to Olwyn, then he shrugged. Would she have been likely to bury herself in a remote mission station if she'd found a diamond? Hardly likely! He frowned at the glowing tip of his cigar, castigating himself for accusing her of stealing it, done in the heat of the moment, he recalled, but striking him as being disgustingly unfeeling and crass now.

Afterward they had never discussed it.

He had an idea: When everything was settled at Teragno he would invite her over for dinner and there present her with the best gem of the seven he had left, and tell her—no, show her!—how sorry he was.

Justin was able to sleep then.

They arrived at Nuruzambora on March seventeenth, the beginning of autumn in southern Africa. Even as close as a mile from the village no one appeared to meet their caravan, neither the local tribe—and this was unheard of—or the missionaries.

Justin knew then that something was wrong.

An eerie silence hung over the valley, that was really only a slight dip in this vast upland plateau. They were now over three thousand feet above sea level and while the days were still hot, the nights were chillingly cold, so cold that heavy blankets were required and all the flaps of the wagons closed tight to keep out the lonely wind blowing across a wilderness that had changed hardly at all from the beginning of time.

Justin had timed it so that they would reach Nuruzambora before dark. It was now after four o'clock and in an hour dusk would fall, perhaps sooner, thought Olwyn, in this indented, wooded area. A tributary of the Orange River flowed through the valley, a catch-basin for rain—when it remembered to fall!—and there were date trees, the umbrellalike acacias or thorn trees, mopani and dense groves of intertwined papyrus.

The caravan halted on the rim of this shallow valley, and as if at a signal, everyone seemed to be listening. Beneath them a mauve haze hung over the trees and the light had a strange, shimmering quality, so that the branches seemed to sway and the tall grasses stir and bend, as if someone, or something, had passed below. But no one appeared.

Justin knew M'Buru and had permission to enter the village of Nuruzambora at will, but since he had strangers with him custom dictated that they wait outside until given leave to enter; normally there was no waiting involved. The tribal spokesman, the chief's right hand man, was invariably there to meet them, together with the elders in the council. Even unfriendly tribes followed this procedure, if only to warn the strangers away; in this case, as well as the elders, they always had their fiercest warriors along.

There was no doubt that M'Buru knew they were coming. All of them had heard the drums in the night. Justin and Tondo exchanged a look, the same thought in both their minds. The only time a tribe never appeared at all was when they had ambush in mind; when for some reason they fully intended to kill the newcomers, or when they themselves had been cut down by an enemy tribe or through disease. M'Buru could be unpredictable, as Justin well knew, but he was certain the chief would have sent people to greet them, out of curiosity and greed if for no other reason. He decided to wait a little while, and signaled for the porters to lay down their burdens. When they did so a few hunkered on the grass but the majority milled about uneasily, constantly peering into the trees. Normally they were a garrulous lot and jabbered incessantly but now they merely stared at each other, communicating in silence, the whites of their eyes gleaming large and eloquent in the gathering dusk.

Half an hour passed and still a dreamlike hush filled the valley, the only moving things the shadows, deep purple, gliding down the sides of the squat hills, or kopjes, higher up and toward the northeast.

The porters began a muffled dialogue that sounded like a low droning of bees when something threatening approaches their hive, and Justin heard the dread name Imba mentioned. The Imba were an offshoot of the Bantu, who lived in the gloomy darkness of a forested area to the east, beyond the range of hills, and among their many vices was a taste for human flesh. The more well traveled of the carriers knew of their habit of striking at dusk or at dawn, when the ash they covered their bodies with afforded them excellent cover.

The men were growing rapidly more agitated, in a mood to bolt.

Justin motioned his foreman over. They would go on to the mission station and risk slighting M'Buru by not paying him a visit first, and once they knew what was happening with the missionaries, then look in at the village.

The mission station—the piece of ground bought from Seconda, M'Buru's father—was about a mile from Nuruzambora proper, and lay to the east. The three dozen men allowed to handle guns now primed and loaded their weapons and they set off around the lips of the valley in tense silence, skirting the village.

$$\diamond\quad 16 \quad\diamond$$

When they reached a point where a dirt trail meandered downhill into the ravine Justin left most of the armed men to guard the wagons, Tondo in charge, and went forward with twenty others, including Scobbie, who insisted on going along.

Olwyn and Hannah watched them disappear from view, swallowed up by the trees, and the older woman suddenly clutched Olwyn's hand. "Pray, lad . . . I mean, lass! Pray they return to us safely." She began to weep, her whole body shaking. "Oh, why did I ever allow James to bring me to this place?"

Olwyn put an arm around her, finding no answer to that, and together they stood waiting, taking comfort from the heat of each other's bodies in the sudden chill that overtook the warmth of the day, snuffing it out.

It was darker among the trees and slightly moist from the pre-winter rains that had fallen over the past few weeks. As the reconnoitering party moved swiftly and silently through the trees a clammy-cold mist rose from the ground, pungent with the strong odor of dark earth and vegetation, some of it rotting and quite rank. Soon the mist had cut off their feet, then their legs, until they seemed to be floating ghostlike above the ground. Even the woodland creatures remained mute and watchful, making no sound unless outright disturbed. James started and sucked in his breath when a great African owl fluttered from the trees over his head, with a loud and angry flapping of its strong wings. The tiny saucer-eyed galago or bush-baby it had been about to make a meal of scurried away to rejoin its careless mother. Sporadic outbursts of scolding rained down on them from the vervet monkeys who were on the point of settling themselves for the night, and somewhere deeper in the woods a nightjar sang a sweet, haunting lullaby for all the little creatures snuggling down to sleep.

There was no sign of humans at all.

The trees thinned out and before them Justin and his men saw a large clearing. There were several dilapidated huts, a fenced kitchen-garden area, a well covered over with stone, and what looked like a pen for animals, all eerily still and forlorn in the fading light and obviously deserted.

Scobbie's head swiveled to Wentworth and he gasped, "Is this . . . is this the mission?"

When Justin nodded the missionary looked crushed for a moment, then burst out, "But where are Erskine and Sloan? The place looks abandoned."

A quick search of the huts showed this to be true. Further, Justin felt that it hadn't been lived in for some time, at least several weeks.

By this time the men were very agitated. Now, as well as well as the Imba, they whispered about evil spirits, the barimo who swooped out of nowhere and stole people away and carried them to the land of the dead, never to be seen or heard of again. Then, just when the porters seemed ready to desert in terror, they all smelled smoke and saw a flare coming from the direction of the village.

Out of the trees burst no less than M'Buru himself with a detachment of his elders and of course his guard, fifty near-naked warriors armed with broad swords and spears and carrying blazing torches over their heads, the flickering orange light dancing over muscular bodies weirdly painted and faces that looked ferocious rather than friendly. M'Buru himself, a handsome man of about thirty, stood tall and proud in his scarlet loincloth, which was lavishly decorated with multicolored beads, shells, and edged with feathers. He stood silent and aloof while Justin, and the others taking their cue from him, rubbed their arms and faces with dust and bowed their heads to the earth before him; then and only then did he deign to greet them.

Though they'd heard nothing, Justin knew the natives must have been hiding nearby in the woods all along, watching to see their reaction once they came upon the deserted mission station. When they felt they had been kept in suspense long enough they had lit their torches and finally made an appearance.

"What happened here?" Justin asked the chief, waving around the mission.

M'Buru, primitive or not, was a highly intelligent man and quick to learn. Through close contact with the missionaries and occasional visits from Justin, he had learned to speak English quite well—and liked to demonstrate his ability in front of strangers. He answered Justin in that language.

"Imba come and take all cattle and food; steal some of they men. Sloan and Erskine has bad fight together after and say they not stay here no more. They go home 'cross water. I's many sorry, White Lion."

James was flabbergasted. "They went home!"

At a warning glance from Justin, Scobbie, for once, abruptly closed his mouth. Justin next asked the chief why he hadn't come out to meet them, as was the custom. At this M'Buru heaved a loud sigh and struck his forehead several times with the palm of his hand, a sign of deep upset or sorrow.

"I no want tell you evil news. Much sad brothers go." When Justin asked when they left he thought a moment and sighed, "Some week. Many."

Then some of the chief's elders came forward with jars of mead and beer to quench their thirst and also to show friendliness, and once they drank—with James having to force himself to consume the dubious-looking beverage—M'Buru next invited them all to spend the night in his kraal. Since by then it was too dark to continue on to Teragno—and only a foolish man turned down an invitation from a chief— Justin accepted.

The wagons and the rest of the caravan were brought down from the ridge, and they all proceeded to M'Buru's large and impressive main village. Scobbie was taken aback at the size of it and the hundreds of thatched-roof huts, huge pens for cattle, and what seemed like thousands of people milling about to gape at the strangers. It had been an honor for M'Buru to come himself to welcome them, even if belatedly, and the chief treated them royally that night, furnishing Justin and the Scobbies with huts already built and reserved for important visitors, and providing Justin's men with material to make their own shelters with the assistance of some of the villagers.

The cooking fires roared and food, too, was generously lavished upon them—buffalo and elephant meat, maize paste, which they scooped out of the bowl with their fingers, honey, and berries. Once the white man's gifts had been presented, three pounds of colored beads, salt, calico cloth, a rifle for the chief, and some gunpowder, the Scobbies and Olwyn were formally introduced to M'Buru and, to show goodwill, he sat down to eat with them.

M'Buru went into more detail about the departure of Sloan and Erskine, who, as they all knew, had been at loggerheads from the inception of the mission. The Imbas attack had brought everything to a head, it seemed, and without waiting to inform the directors of the Free Missionary Society, both men packed up and left. M'Buru wasn't certain if Sloan meant to return home to Scotland. "He say he might bide"—a Scottish word he had picked up from the missionaries —"in big kraal on water"—Cape Town—"but he brother want go home to his people, he say. I give some men and food for travel," the chief stressed. "Imba take all they has. No has nothing."

James was perplexed. "I'm surprised that we didn't pass them on the way."

Wentworth didn't find this in the least surprising. Though they had used the most direct route up from the Cape, there were many others, and something might have caused the missionaries to detour or stop off at one of the villages along the way. It was easy to miss other travelers in such rugged territory.

Yet Justin, too, felt troubled. Sloan and Erskine would have been poorly equipped for the nearly six-hundred-mile journey back to Cape Town, and it would have been most unlikely for M'Buru's men to stay with them for much more than a third of the way. There was always the chance, though, Justin reasoned, that they had met up with another caravan along the way and gone the rest of the trip with them.

As M'Buru's people clustered curiously around the perimeter of the royal lodge, vastly larger than the other huts in the village, Wentworth scanned the female faces searching for Ngara, the native girl that Sloan had been involved with, and the daughter of one of the chief's more junior elders. Not only was there no sign of the girl but her father, too, was nowhere in sight. There could have been countless reasons to explain their absence—and it wasn't the sort of question he could ask the chief—but still it bothered Wentworth. He decided to bide his time and make inquiries about them in due course, but certainly not that evening, with them all so dependent on M'Buru's hospitality.

During the meal the chief leaned toward him and queried, "This brother Scobbie like they other?"

Justin chuckled. "He's a missionary, a man of God, but he's not like the other two. He's a . . . a very good man; he has great honor. I hope you will offer him the same generous help you gave his brothers?" In point of fact, M'Buru had frequently thrown obstacles in the path of Sloan and Erskine, or conversely showered them with more "help" than they wanted, depending on his mood; and M'Buru's moods fluctuated wildly.

The chief considered this for a while as he sat absently chewing his elephant meat, his face in the firelight cast in a bronzelike glow, his expressive eyes, an odd shade of dark hazel, narrowed consideringly. He turned to Justin once more. "This brother buy me mission land also?"

Justin stared at him, annoyed but concealing it. "Sloan and Erskine already paid you for the mission."

"They go. This one come."

Exasperated, Justin tried to explain. "Scobbie is part of the same organization; the same council. And the council has already bought the land and paid for it. It belongs to them."

M'Buru negligently tossed a bone in the direction of a pack of mangy dogs sniffing around, and turned to Wentworth haughtily and in his turn explained, "This land"—he lifted a brawny arm and waved around—"come from my father. He get it from he father. Now it me. This brothers only use, never belong. Scobbie buy."

With that the chief gave the signal for the dancing to begin. The discussion was over. No one ever argued with a chief. Certainly not a chief with M'Buru's mercurial nature.

For the next two hours the night pulsed with the pounding of drums. The weary caravan stoically sat through war dances, singing, and native plays acted out energetically and melodramatically, and when Justin and party felt about ready to drop, M'Buru suddenly stood up and clapped his hands. The evening's entertainment was over. "Go now and sleep," said the chief in paternal fashion, as he might have spoken to one of his many children. "The Eagle he guard you well. No harm come."

Justin thanked him for his gracious hospitality and they all, at last, retired to their huts.

Justin settled himself for the night with his rifle in his hand. He would rest, he knew, but not sleep.

Scobbie sneaked in to see him about an hour later once silence had descended on the kraal. James was very upset at the defection of his fellow-missionaries, whom he called traitors, but staunchly declared himself ready to take up the banner that they had so spinelessly cast down. When Justin asked him to reconsider Scobbie brushed it aside. He would not go back on his word to the Free Missionary Society, he said firmly. Aye, and he would succeed where the other two had failed.

"M'Buru seems fair enough," he remarked to Wentworth. "I'm highly impressed. And he speaks English too!" James had been having serious difficulty in trying to learn Bantu, the dialect changing from district to district as it did. The fact that he spoke English greatly elevated M'Buru in his eyes, as did the chief's kind treatment of them. He wasn't even much put off when Wentworth informed him that he'd have to purchase the mission land all over again.

"Well," he responded with a shrug, "that must be the custom. They obviously think of it as rent, rather than an outright purchase."

Justin then warned him about M'Buru's changeable temperament.

Scobbie laughed. "I've dealt with worse in the Church at home!"

Wentworth gave up then, but he insisted that Scobbie and party go on with him to Teragno, at least for the time being, thinking privately that it would give him a chance to make subtle inquiries about the native woman, Ngara, Sloan's erstwhile mistress. When James showed signs of balking he said irritably, "The mission is in a shambles and the huts need repair. You'd ask your wife to live in them as they are?"

Finally the stubborn James agreed but reluctantly.

They continued north in the morning and reached Teragno in the early afternoon. A man on horseback could have done it much quicker—even an unhampered man on foot—but there was no possibility of the cumbersome wagons, loaded heavily as they were and traveling over the roughest terrain, accomplishing it much sooner.

Wentworth owned nearly two thousand acres along the banks of the Orange River. Though he wasn't a farmer as such, he had fifty head of cattle, goats, chickens, and some crops, mainly maize and corn, as well as an extensive garden that produced cabbages, onions and peas, and other vegetables. They grew pineapple, oranges and date palms, and nut trees of various kinds, and since they could shoot all the meat they wanted, the trading post at Teragno was entirely self-sufficient, thanks to good farm management and careful forethought.

The main homestead and outbuildings were built in the shape of a horseshoe, with the homestead in the center facing down to the river. Behind were the dozens of thatched-roofed houses of the men, with the pens and enclosures for the smaller animals in the rear. The main buildings were all of stucco painted white, and overall there was such an impression of neatness and cleanliness and order, the gardens in front of the courtyard blazing with color after the recent rains, that the Scobbies and Olwyn all gasped in astonishment. "Well!" said James. "I never thought to find anything like *this* here! It's like being back in civilization again."

"I can't take all the credit," said Justin modestly. "It belonged to an English trader before me, and a Dutchman before that."

Tondo snorted. "It mess then. You make it good."

Thankfully they all trooped inside into blessed

coolness and tranquility, to spacious rooms that were tastefully furnished but uncluttered, with low-slung sofas and chairs, native pottery both massive and tiny, and carefully selected examples of African art placed here and there for the most dramatic effect.

Once inside they were introduced to Kelly, Justin's farm manager, who liked to boast that he ran Teragno like a sergeant-major. A small, trim little man with the lingering hint of an Irish brogue, though he had been away from his homeland for over twenty years, Kelly had a brisk manner and a face the color and texture of a cracked brick. "You'll be wanting refreshments," he said after a brief chat when his sharp blue eyes had taken their measure. "I'll just away and alert that woman, ah, Talla."

"That woman," as Kelly called her, was Justin's housekeeper. Tall, lean, and silver-haired, Talla was in her fifties, and every bit as trim and spick-and-span as the Irishman. Justin had inherited her from the former owner and at the time she'd been timid, slovenly, and seemingly incapable of taking instructions, all due to maltreatment. "Leave it to me," said Kelly at the time. "Patience and kindness is the answer—but of course you still have to be firm."

Kelly's instructions had worked all too well. Now the pair were in constant competition, trying to prove which of them was the most efficient. Talla had found her tongue, too, and the little Irishman often felt the rough edge of it, but underneath their constant bickering the pair adored each other—though neither would have admitted it for the world.

Hannah Scobbie settled herself comfortably in her easy chair and glanced around, her battered and bruised body grateful for the repose. Aside from that, her morning sickness forgot to depart in the early hours and plagued her on and off throughout the day. Her nerves were shattered, her spirits at a low ebb, and she felt she had reached the stage where she could take no more.

"Oh, I'm so glad you decided to bring us on here,

James, dear," she burst out during a pause in the conversation. "Teragno is just the—the oasis I needed. Mr. Wentworth"—she smiled at Justin wearily—"you might find it hard to get rid of us, so I shouldn't make us *too* comfortable if I were you."

"Stay as long as you wish," Justin replied, not looking at Scobbie. "And it's time to stop being so formal with each other. You must call me by my first name from now on."

"And you must call me Hannah!"

He made her a polite little bow.

That night, bathed, well fed, and in a real bed in a proper room for the first time in weeks, Olwyn stretched out atop the coverlet and let the stress of the journey seep out of her body. Like Hannah, she, too, could have remained at Teragno quite readily, and dreaded the time when they would have to return to the mission.

Her future was still undecided. James Scobbie had hardly spoken to her since the day of the revelation but sometimes Olwyn had turned to find him regarding her soberly; perhaps, she thought, trying to decide what to do about her. Hannah, she felt, could be persuaded to accept her for what she was. Even the boys, though suddenly awkward and shy, had made tentative overtures at establishing a new relationship. A few days before Harold had blurted, "I knew all the while that you weren't a *real* boy!" then had darted away before Olwyn could respond. Little Jamie had been more to the point. "Why do you still wear breeches?"

"Because I have no other clothes to wear," Olwyn told him with a smile.

He nodded. "Mama might make you a gown. I heard Papa say that he hates to see a woman in breeches."

Did this mean, Olwyn wondered now, that there was some possibility of James letting her stay? Had he discussed it with his wife? Was it possible—

Oh, it was pointless to speculate, Olwyn thought

with a sigh. As usual her life was in a state of uncertainty, and she supposed she should be used to it by now. She wasn't; and she was no more certain of Justin Wentworth than the others. He, too, had hardly spoken to her over the past week.

When she announced that she felt stronger and fitter and could change her own dressing he had let her.

Olwyn was examining the wound when the door opened softly and the man himself stepped inside. He strolled casually to the bed and gazed down at her injury. "It seems to be coming along nicely," he remarked.

"Yes, doesn't it? The swelling has gone down too."

"So I see. That's a good sign. There's always the fear of infection with wounds like that."

Without their eyes meeting once since Justin had entered the room, they kept up this polite conversation for some while, Olwyn fixing her attention on the clean bandage she was winding about her leg, even as her heart raced and every nerve in her body felt stretched to the snapping point.

"You have a very nice home here," she told him, knotting the gauze securely, then because she was anxious, in trouble already, saying "Did . . . did anyone see you come into my room?"

"I don't give a damn!"

Olwyn raised her head and their eyes met. Bending, he caught her face between his hands and kissed her soft mouth, then with a groan took her in his arms and kissed her more deeply, at the same time pushing aside the opening at the neck of her nightshirt, and slipped his warm hand inside. A jolt raced through her body as Justin cupped her breast and his thumb lightly stroked her nipple, causing that delicious tingling warmth to seep out over her flesh, melting her very bones. For a moment or two Olwyn succumbed. She was tempted to forget that James and Hannah were just down the hall and the two boys in the next room; tempted to forget how wrong this was and that she'd promised herself it would never happen again. She had been luckier than she deserved so far. Her last monthly flow had arrived on schedule, but—

"You mustn't!" Olwyn pushed him away, even as she longed to draw him closer. "The Scobbies . . . if James were to guess . . ."

"James Scobbie may go to hell!" Justin caught her again, his face flushed and determined, but again Olwyn pushed him back, this time more firmly.

"*You* might not care," she said with some heat, "but I can't afford to be so reckless. And besides, this is wrong. It can't happen again."

Justin smiled at her, and that lazy, mocking smile maddened Olwyn.

"I mean exactly what I say!" she snapped, her golden eyes flashing. "Do you think you can come to me whenever you wish and that I will—will be forced into intimacy against my will, not once but many times? No!" She shook her head emphatically, getting angrier and more indignant with every word she said, working herself up to a grand show of outrage. "No!" she repeated. "Never, ever again!"

Justin gazed at her in amusement, admiring her clean, smooth skin, the soft shine of her newly washed hair, the beauty of her tawny, feline eyes when she was angry, and his frustration melted into tenderness. He took her hand and raised it to his lips, suddenly the courtly gentleman that she seemed to want at that moment, and murmured, "Then I wish you a pleasant good night."

He stood up and quietly left the room.

Olwyn stared after him, her mouth sagging open. She'd expected him to argue, to coax, and if all else failed, to ignore her resistance and continue making love to her until she responded—which had happened in the past. This unexpected behavior was most unsatisfactory. It left her feeling cheated in more ways than one. She'd wanted to force him to admit—

That he loved her? Needed her? Wanted her with him always?

Olwyn fell back on the bed and stared hard at the ceiling. She tried to laugh at her silly thoughts and couldn't. She tried to tell herself that she didn't care in the least how he felt about her, but suddenly knew it wasn't true. Then she tried not to think at all, yet her mind rushed on anyway, forming the question that had her heart thudding madly in her breast.

Did she love Justin Wentworth? Did she need him? And did she want him with her always?

Yes! Passionately! Desperately!

Olwyn turned over and ground her hot face into the pillow.

Hannah came to her the next morning with the gown over her arm. Afterward Olwyn was to mark that day as the happiest she was to have for a very long time to come. Laying it on her bed, Mrs. Scobbie said, "It was always too tight for me, and if you just wind this sash at the waist and draw it snug, well . . . I think it will do you nicely for the time being."

Olwyn gazed at her in surprise, then at the mauve muslin dress sprigged with violets. A dozen questions occurred to her at once, all tumbling over each other in her mind, and out of this chaos came nothing. She was silent.

"Mr. Scobbie doesn't like to see you in breeches, dear," Hannah explained, thinking that she might be too proud to take the gown, or resent the idea of accepting castoffs. "I'll make you something of your own when time permits; you could think of it as a sort of uniform for the job—"

"Does this mean that Mr. Scobbie wants me to stay?" Olwyn burst out then, her heart fluttering.

Hannah blinked at her. "Stay?"

In all the huffing and puffing James had done after learning the truth about his assistant, never once had he broached the subject of the girl being sent back. Indeed, how could she be sent back? They were nearly six hundred miles from Cape Town and another six thousand from Britain! And whether Olwyn was male or female didn't alter the fact that James needed a medical assistant. "Look here," Hannah had interrupted while he ranted and raved about deceit, untrustworthiness, and so forth, "we need her more than ever now. Have you forgotten my condition? I can tell you this, James, I'd much rather have a woman attend to me when the time comes than a callow lad! Besides, where's your compassion? The poor lass was driven to do what she did. The same type of people who drove her out of Scotland drove you into leaving the Church there!"

James said no more after that.

Now Hannah smiled at Olwyn and cried, "Of course you are staying! My dear, where else would you go?"

Olwyn threw her arms around the older woman, weak with relief, and there was nothing for it then but for Olwyn to try on the gown, and Hannah to fuss and measure and tuck, and within the hour the dress almost looked as if it had been made for her, if one didn't look too closely. Olwyn's thick, shoulder-length hair was then pulled free of the string that secured it at the back of her neck, and the glistening black curls brushed out by Hannah and twined with a length of white satin ribbon. Then the missionary's wife stood back and critically examined her handiwork.

Hannah was at a loss for words as she stared at the girl. The change in her was stunning. There she stood, tall and radiantly beautiful, the delicate shade of the dress strongly emphasizing her exotic coloring, the firm white breasts that had been hidden so long now rising proudly above the bodice of the gown.

"Is . . . is everything all right?" Olwyn queried anxiously when Hannah just stood there staring.

"Oh!" The older woman clasped her hands together and nodded vigorously. "You look absolutely ravishing! On you that simple dress looks like a ball gown." Then a tiny frown puckered her forehead and she stepped forward and drew the bodice of the frock a little higher before James saw the girl, well aware of how he would disapprove of such a tempting sight. Hannah was virtually quivering to find out exactly what was going on between this lovely girl and Justin Wentworth—and she knew *something* was going on —but of course one shouldn't seem to pry, and she still didn't know the lass very well. Forced to swallow down her avid curiosity, difficult for one who enjoyed nothing more than the excitement of romance, even when it concerned other people, she still felt it her duty to caution the young beauty. "Many men will find you . . . shall we say, desirable, but Olwyn, you must always conduct yourself as a lady and not give Mr. Scobbie reason to—to—" She floundered, embarrassed.

"I understand," the girl broke in quickly, and blushed to the roots of her hair, wondering how the Scobbies would react if they knew just how far it had gone with Justin Wentworth, and more determined than ever not to allow him to take advantage of her again.

She saw nothing of Wentworth all day. Together with James and some of the men, he had ridden back to Nuruzambora to assess the damage to the mission station in the broad light of day and see what would be involved in restoring the mission to some semblance of order. They would also parley with M'Buru to find out how much he wanted for the ground this time around.

Talla, the housekeeper, liked to keep everybody as busy as herself, and late that afternoon she stuck a basket in Olwyn's hand and said in her forthright way, "You go pick flower for house. Just 'fore twilight best time. Not good to do in heat of day. Flower, she wilt then."

A languorous air hung over the garden amid the steady low droning of bees. All about Olwyn was a haze of color, pink and purple cinerarias washing into the scarlet and yellow poinsettias, blurring beautifully to the ranunculus and anemones and fuchsias in almond-drop shades of lilac, sugar-pink, and palest peach. Around a dark pool, lacy ferns and mist-soft lichens flourished, and of course the elegant orchid in stately white, rich purple, and cream.

The perfume was heavy and mesmerizing in the stillness of late afternoon, and as she carefully snipped her blooms, Olwyn had a sudden urge to lie down and dream in this enchanted garden, perhaps curling up under a giant creeper straggling over a low wall, its tiny bell-like pink flowers spilling forth like bubbles blown from the pipes of Pan.

She almost missed the snake. Its brindled skin blended perfectly against its bed of speckled lilies. Reaching forward to pluck one of the flowers she first saw the prey—a hapless mouse—then the serpent.

She screamed.

"Lady go get flower," Talla informed her master when Justin emerged from his room freshly bathed and dressed in clean clothes after his dusty trip to Nuruzambora. His housekeeper, normally terse, added with a twinkle in her eyes, "Now she *look* like lady." When he eyed her quizzically Talla waved to the window. "You see. Go, go!"

As he turned down the path to the flower garden a figure flew toward him in a flurry of billowing mauve and streaming ebony curls. Justin felt a start of surprise and delight to see her in a frock but it was quickly doused at the look of raw terror on her face. He caught her up in his arms, gazed into her white face, then over her head at the bluish mist now hanging over the garden.

"What's wrong, darling?" His voice was harsh with concern. "What frightened you?"

"A snake! Oh," Olwyn shuddered, "it was horrible! The creature was eating a mouse!"

He laughed and hugged her fiercely, and as one of his men had come running, Justin despatched him for a gun. Amused as he was at her distress over the plight of a mouse, he realized, too, that the unfortunate little creature had probably spared Olwyn's life, or at least saved her from a very painful injury.

With his arm about her Justin led her to a nearby garden bench and there turned to face her, with the intention of giving her a stern warning about flower-picking in a tropical garden where many dangers could lurk beneath the surface beauty. He also made up his mind to castigate Talla for sending her out; his housekeeper knew what to look for and was careful, but Olwyn lacked her knowledge and experience. But when he turned to the girl all the scolding words died in his throat. Instead, his eyes went over her gown, lingering on the creamy fullness of velvety flesh at the bodice, rising slowly to her face and hair, to the beautiful amber eyes fixed on his with such appeal, and Justin felt himself floundering under the on-slaught of an emotion that momentarily rendered him mute.

"Are . . . are you angry with me?" Olwyn asked him nervously, so sober and intense did he look.

He wanted her all to himself! He longed to clear everyone out of the house, or spirit her away some-where where they could be completely alone; where he could speak to her seriously, freely, without interrup-tion, and where he could make glorious, passionate love to this vibrantly beautiful woman through the long, dark tropical night, the drums beating in tune with their blood.

He could do none of those things. Courtesy dictated that he stay and play the considerate host to the Scobbies. Propriety dictated that he not be alone with Olwyn again. And the plans he had mapped out for his fledgling diamond industry dictated that he not allow himself to be sidetracked, that every minute he de-layed going into operation was a minute when some-one else could discover diamonds and beat him to the punch. Only that day, riding back from Nuruzambora, they'd met a small Portuguese trading caravan who imparted what they thought was an astounding piece of news—there truly *were* diamonds in Africa! Yes, they gushed, the vague speculation that had circulated for years had proved to be correct after all.

According to the Portuguese, a shepherd who lived some forty miles northeast of Teragno had recently found a big stone, definitely a diamond, and now the little settlement of Hopetown was crackling with excitement, the news flashing like a bushfire to other areas and inevitably bound to reach Cape Town.

"There's been many strangers on the veld of late," one of the traders told Justin in his own tongue. "And they have the smell of diggers about them. The lust for treasure is unmistakable in their eyes."

Wentworth found that very ominous.

He knew he could afford no distractions or delays; too much was at stake. Yet—

He looked at Olwyn and teased, "What a woman you are! I don't dare let you out of my sight. Every time I turn my back you get into trouble, so obviously I'm going to have to do something about that." His smile faded and he became suddenly serious. When he reached for her hand Olwyn's heart gave a mighty leap and she almost stopped breathing. "At the moment I'm involved in a new business venture," Justin admitted, "but soon, *soon,* my love," he went on urgently, leaning closer, "you and I—"

A blast of gunfire shattered the stillness in the garden.

"He dead!" yelled the native excitedly. "He all dead now!"

Everybody poured out of the house to see what was happening, and the lovers drew hastily apart and stood up.

Later Olwyn couldn't shake off the superstition that that snake was an omen, a warning of things to come.

That night she waited for Justin to come to her room, almost sick with nervousness but determined to tell him what had happened to his diamond, anxious that there should be no more secrets between them.

He didn't appear.

While Olwyn fretted and restlessly paced her own room, Justin stood at the window of his smoking in the darkness, his eyes on the moonlit veld beyond his own property, wild territory that seemed to stretch on forever without end, habitat to vastly more animals than people.

He restrained the strong urge to go to her. Appearances mattered not in the least to him but for a woman it was different, and he would no longer compromise her reputation to satisfy his own craving. Somehow he would find the patience to wait for her sake.

Bemused, Justin realized that she had tamed something hard and ruthless inside him. She had gentled him, stirred protective instincts he hadn't known he possessed, and somehow or other, in her unique, bewitching way, made the past fade into irrelevance.

He had found love in a pair of golden eyes, in a sweet, seductive smile, in a soft touch that melted his soul and brought him joy. Soon neither the walls of rooms, other people, or anything else would keep them apart. He would ask her to marry him and bring her to live at Teragno, and sometimes at Cape Town, and he would do everything in his power to make her happy.

Her betrothal ring would be made from one of his original eight diamonds, fashioned in the shape of a star, the cut that reflected the most fire. Justin smiled, certain she would understand the significance.

# 17

The prospectors arrived at Teragno just after ten o'clock in the morning. They were five white men led by Knute Bleur and his son, Fabien, and thirty black retainers, all heavily armed. Leaving their one wagon outside, the five prospectors walked boldly across the courtyard to the house, ignoring the startled stares of the farm workers then in the area, and banged loudly on the thick teakwood door. When it was opened by Talla, Bleur politely doffed his dusty, wide-brimmed hat and said, "Greetings! We come from Cape Town and have business with your master, Mr. Wentworth."

Talla asked them to wait.

Neither the Scobbies nor Olwyn was in the house at the time. Once breakfast was over Justin had suggested that Tondo take them for a picnic to the beautiful waterfall about eight miles upriver, a place so stunning and ethereal that he was sure Olwyn especially would be enchanted. While they were gone he could get on with pressing business that demanded his immediate attention, work that had piled up while he was away.

Justin was surprised to receive visitors all the way from the Cape, but he asked Talla to invite them into the house and give them refreshments, saying he would join them shortly. When he did he found five total strangers waiting for him, and his first question to Bleur was, "How do you know my name?"

Instead of answering the question, the mineralogist came straight to the point. "I understand diamonds have been found in this area?"

Justin felt an inward jolt of dismay, which he tried hard to conceal. He shook his head and laughed. "You must be thinking of the shepherd who found a stone up near Zandfontein—"

"No," Fabien Bleur broke in impatiently, "we know stones have been discovered here at Teragno, so please don't waste our time by lying, sir! We have come too far and endured too much to return home empty-handed."

"Yes," purred his father, but more subtly than his son, "what we wish is to purchase claims, for ourselves and on behalf of other interested parties at the Cape. Name your price—"

"Who told you this nonsense?" Justin interrupted angrily.

Then it all came out, and as he listened, Justin flinched as his plans for himself and Olwyn cracked and crumbled to dust at his feet.

Never dreaming that she was right there at Teragno and could refute his version of the story, Knute Bleur told how a young lad named Oliver Moore had one day walked into his office with an uncut diamond that he was anxious to sell. "It was a very good stone," the mineralogist admitted, and then lapsed into falsehood once more, "and being an honest man with a reputation to uphold, I offered the lad five hundred pounds for it, and he readily accepted. I was satisfied and thought that was an end to it, but the enterprising young rascal then offered to provide me with the location of where it had been found if I paid him another five hundred." He chuckled, adding, "Moore assured me that the river beds hereabouts were studded with the gems."

Justin was crushed. He had wakened that morning with the warmth of love in his heart, and would lie down that night nursing the coldness of hate, a stark reminder of what a fool he had been—again!

"There are no diamonds at Teragno," he told them stonily. "You have come for nothing."

Then he ordered them out of his house and off his land.

With many furtive glances among themselves, the five men seemed about to comply and turned away as if to leave but at the door the hot-headed Fabien Bleur spun around with his revolver in his hand—and the fighting began.

It was vicious while it lasted but it didn't last long. When the first shot was fired the rest of Bleur's men rushed in through the courtyard to support their employer but Justin's men, too, had heard the shot, and thirty-five men are no match for nearly a hundred —those of Wentworth's crew in the vicinity at the time. With fortune-hunting fever strong upon them, Bleur and his desperate gang battled furiously all the way out to the courtyard and beyond, even though a third of their number fell to litter the path along the way. Finally forced to concede defeat, Fabien and two of the younger men fired into the thatched roof of a large storage barn, setting it ablaze then, leaving their wagon and twelve oxen behind, they sped for the nearest dip in the land and disappeared from view.

Justin would have gone after them and hunted them down but his barn was on fire, the sparks carried on the breeze to the roofs of nearby buildings, and he immediately had another battle on his hands. By the time they finally had it under control the barn and another building had been burned to the ground,

equipment and food for the animals destroyed in the
blaze. But worse was to come; his herdsman had been
killed and ten of his men wounded, two seriously.

In a towering rage Justin waited for Tondo and
party to return from their day's outing to the waterfall.

Tondo first smelled the smoke when they were still a
full mile away from Teragno, and he cracked the whip
over the backs of the four oxen pulling their cart, a
smaller version of the wagons that had brought them
up from Cape Town.

They had just enjoyed an idyllic day amid the most
glorious scenery that Olwyn had yet viewed in Africa,
made more enjoyable still by the lightness and happiness in her heart. It swelled and bubbled like a
fountain, making her laugh at the slightest thing, and
hug Jamie or Hannah in sheer exuberance until James
looked at his wife and cocked a questioning brow.
Hannah just smiled back and said nothing, keeping
her thoughts to herself, thoughts she wouldn't have
dared share with her straitlaced husband. He would
have been shocked.

The sight of the burned buildings at Teragno instantly sobered them. Men came running to meet
them to inform them that there had been a fight with
hostile strangers, white men among them, but none of
the natives knew the exact details or what had caused
it.

Both Olwyn and the Scobbies were shocked to learn
that one man had been killed and others wounded.
Olwyn immediately ran to get her medical bag but
Talla intercepted her in the hall, saying that the master
would like to see her in his study. At once.

Olwyn burst into the room totally unsuspecting. He
was standing at the window, his back to her, and he
had watched them arrive. Then he turned and Olwyn
saw his face—hard as granite—and the bottom
dropped out of her bright new world.

"Knute Bleur was here today," he said.

Her legs wobbled beneath her.

"He came to collect what you sold him."

Olwyn felt the blood drain from her face, and suddenly felt sick.

Justin inhaled, and then she saw the struggle he was having trying to control his fury, and thought that if she'd been a man he might have killed her there and then—without hearing her version of the story! He had tried and condemned her on the strength of what Bleur, a total stranger, had told him, and this was the man who had promised that soon—

"I want you out of my sight as soon as possible," the deadly voice cut into her thoughts. "Now, go!"

Olwyn's first dismay turned to a cold, biting anger. So . . . she thought, he expected her to skulk away with her tail between her legs, which only proved how little he knew about Olwyn Moore!

Having dismissed her, Justin had his back to her again. Olwyn stared at that broad, rigid back and wondered how she had ever imagined herself to be in love with this man.

"You sold out to Knute Bleur yourself!" she hurled at him icily. "None of this would have happened if you hadn't lied to me about the stone in the first place."

"*I* lied!" Justin swung around to face her and his harsh, sardonic laugh was like a blow to her ears. "Save your tricks; they won't work anymore."

"Did you or did you not tell me that stone was graphite?"

Something flickered in the cold eyes but he didn't answer.

"And did you or did you not say it was worthless?"

He still didn't answer.

He hadn't asked for her version of the story but Olwyn was determined that he would get it anyway. She began by explaining how, after she returned to her own cabin following the storm on the *Randolph*, she had found his stone among her clothes, but since he'd assured her it wasn't of any value she hadn't bothered to return it to him. Hannah Scobbie had been good to her, Olwyn went on, and she longed to show her appreciation with a little gift at Christmas, so she decided to have the graphite—Olwyn's voice dripped with sarcasm at the word—made up into a pendant for her, and innocently took the stone to a jeweler in Cape Town. The jeweler in turn sent her to Knute Bleur.

"Stop, for God's sake!" Justin interrupted at this point. "I'm not interested in your fairy tales."

"You will listen!" Olwyn suddenly shouted, trembling from head to foot. "At least have the decency to hear me out, as you clearly did with Knute Bleur."

While Justin leaned against the wall in an attitude of disinterest and boredom Olwyn continued relentlessly, telling of her chilling experience at the hands of the mineralogist—her abduction to the brothel, the leper, how Mahmet forced the information out of her about Teragno, then Howell and his friends coming upon the scene when she was about to be taken aboard the slave ship. "And Howell can attest to the truth of that!" she finished triumphantly.

Justin merely shrugged. "Howell knows nothing beyond finding you at the harbor." He smiled bitterly and shook his head. "What an imagination you have! But surely you don't think I'm quite that gullible—"

"Wait!" Olwyn interrupted desperately, her mind grappling for a way to convince him she spoke the truth. "Think of this; if Bleur had paid me for the stone and the information about Teragno, do you think I'd be here now, working for nothing at a remote mission station?"

Justin chuckled grimly. "Probably not, but then Bleur doesn't strike me as being the kind of man to let anyone walk away with so much of his money, and certainly not a strange young lad, which he thought you were. No, once he had what he wanted from you his next step would be to get his money back—and make a little profit at the same time, by putting you on a ship to Zanzibar."

Again he shook his head, saying, "Sorry, but it won't work, Olwyn. I've heard too many outrageous tales from you to swallow this one." His brows went down and he added, "You lied to me, and you lied to James Scobbie, a minister, which I suppose is even more despicable. Now go, and stop wasting my time."

Olwyn didn't move. She wanted to tell him how sorry she, too, was about all that had happened here today, and could readily understand why he was so upset. One of his men had been killed and others wounded, and part of his trading post had burned down. Then he'd lost a valuable diamond worth a great deal of money. In a way she could even understand why he had difficulty believing her story after the deception she had perpetrated on James Scobbie —but on the other hand it would have been nice to get a little understanding from him!

Olwyn was driven to try again.

"Please, Justin, can we not—"

"Get out!" he snarled, and waved at the door.

All her feelings of injustice and anger came surging back.

"What about the graphite?" she challenged.

"What the stones are or are not is my business."

"Really?" she sneered. "Then my reasons for passing myself off as a man are mine!"

Olwyn swept out of the room then and banged the door shut behind her.

For the next week Olwyn, Hannah, and Talla nursed the injured men, all of whom mercifully began to recover. The burned buildings were rebuilt, all signs of destruction cleared away, and everything put back in order. By then James was showing definite restlessness, anxious to get on with his own work at Nuruzambora, and returned there with some of his men to repair the dwellings, for a start, in preparation for them moving in, reasoning that all they needed in the beginning was a place to live.

Scobbie had brought a hundred men of his own up

from Cape Town but it was understood all along that half of them would go back. What James didn't anticipate was that twenty of the crew he had left would desert in the middle of the night. Since the day they'd arrived these men had whispered about bad medicine in Nuruzambora, so he supposed he should have been warned, but the loss of nearly half his crew made things much more difficult.

M'Buru turned out to be very helpful. He had some of his own people chop down trees for the mission buildings and stockades and even provided Scobbie with laborers. James was heartened and delighted with the generous response from the chief, who even stopped by to see how work was progressing in person. Pointing to the sky, which was cloudless, M'Buru said, "Rains come soon. Hurry, hurry little brother. Not want you sleep with water. Get drookit."

Startled at hearing Scottish slang come out of the mouth of a black savage six thousand miles from his homeland, James burst out laughing.

"Why you laugh?" The chief didn't look very amused.

It took Scobbie some time to explain, but when he finally understood M'Buru's own booming laughter rang out. He slapped Scobbie on the back so hard it almost knocked James off the log he'd been sitting on. The bigger man turned and gazed into his face, his smile warm and benevolent, the burnt-sugar eyes glittering with mirth. Still smiling he whipped out a dagger, and James froze but restrained the impulse to jerk back as the chief slid the tip of the weapon between his lips; lips suddenly gone bloodless and rubbery.

"Man who laugh at Great Eagle not keep tongue," said M'Buru, his strange eyes fixed on Scobbie's mouth. Then they rose to his and the missionary willed himself not to look away. For a fraction of a second the tension was excruciating as both men regarded each other in silence. M'Buru removed the blade, relaxing with a laugh. "You brave little brother.

You like"—he drew back from James a little and examined him keenly, consideringly, then nodded— "you like badger. Great Eagle call you Badger now. No like Schoobie."

"Scobbie."

"You Badger," the chief repeated firmly, and again slapped James on the back, roaring with amusement at the look of consternation on the white man's face.

James returned to Teragno that evening to apprise them of his new name.

Olwyn saw very little of Justin during that time. Either he was out supervising the repairs to his property, attending to the business of the trading post itself, or away from Teragno altogether, she knew not where. Once he was gone overnight.

At the first opportunity Justin paid a visit to Hopetown to make inquiries about the fate of Erskine and Sloan. He was aware that James had already written a long and no doubt vitriolic letter to the Free Missionary Society about the conduct of these men, and how they'd abandoned the mission station at Nuruzambora. This dispatch had been given to a passing peddler to carry to Cape Town, and from there sent by ship to Britain. Scobbie, as far as Wentworth could see, had accepted M'Buru's account of their disappearance verbatim. He himself wasn't so sure.

Hopetown, the largest settlement in the area, was no bigger than a small village, and a poor one at that. A straggle of rickety buildings with corrugated iron or thatched roofs stood incongruously on either side of the unpaved main street, a tiny pocket of civilization flung up defiantly amid the untamed veld. Karl Goetz was the man to see in Hopetown. As the owner of the grandly named Imperial Hotel—a two-story, dilapidated flea trap—and the equally impressive-sounding General Emporium and Agricultural Supply Depot, Karl knew everyone for hundreds of miles around as they all had to come to him eventually, and while there the lonely colonists lingered to chat. Not a shred of gossip missed Karl's large, bat-shaped ears, and the stocky Dutchman added his link to the bush-telegraph by enthusiastically passing the word. The minute he spied Justin he wanted to know all about the trouble at Teragno, which he had somehow heard about already. Then he had an exciting tidbit of his own to pass along.

"You've heard of course about the diamond find at Zandfontein?"

Wentworth nodded noncommittally.

Well, said Goetz, he happened to know that hundreds, perhaps thousands of prospectors were rushing to the area that very moment. In light of that he had ordered a massive shipment of picks, shovels, sifting pans, and other paraphernalia a digger would need, asking it to be sent express from the Cape. "I like to be prepared," he said, practically rubbing his hands with glee as he anticipated all the sales he would make.

"These prospectors . . . they are on their way to Zandfontein?"

Karl pushed back the few strands of flaxen hair he had left, and gave out one of his disconcerting high-pitched giggles. "Oh no, not just there! Word has it that diamonds have also been found along the river, up by your place, Wentworth. You must have heard about that!" When Justin reminded him that he'd been away the Dutchman giggled again. "But back just in time to strike it rich, eh?" And ever the salesman: "How many picks and shovels can I sell you today?"

"Twenty of each," Justin replied promptly. "I, too, like to be prepared."

Then he inquired about Sloan and Erskine but he could see that Karl found this subject small potatoes when compared to talk about diamonds. He sighed and blew out his lips. "Those two, the saviors of mankind. Ha! A fine pair to convert others!"

The last he had seen of Erskine had been in early February when he had come in to purchase provisions —quite a lot of them. "I asked him if he was making a journey and he said yes, he was going home, but I took little stock of it because he had often said that before." Karl stopped wiping his counter and paused to reflect. "He did seem more determined that time, now that I think of it, and confessed that he was tired of the struggle and heartily sick of his partner, the natives, the country itself. He seemed dejected . . . beaten. I actually felt a bit sorry for him, though he was always a taciturn, dour sort of man. Anyway, I wished him better luck at home."

"And Sloan?"

"Him! That one went to the Devil a long time ago!"

Karl could not confirm that either man had definitely left Nuruzambora in February but Justin tracked down a native driver through a stock-dealer he knew, and this man said that Erskine at least had left for Cape Town. Some of the driver's friends had joined the caravan. As for Sloan, he was less sure about him, but he'd heard at the time Erskine pulled out that his partner was making preparations to leave for Port Elizabeth almost immediately.

Justin looked at him in surprise. "Port Elizabeth?"

"That what I hear."

"And you are positive he left?"

The driver scratched his head, looking perplexed. "You say you'self he not at Nuruzambora, so he go." He eyed Justin as if he were stupid.

Justin nodded. "Right!"

He had to be content with that, at least as far as the missionaries were concerned. As for the native woman, Sloan's mistress, that might be even more difficult as he certainly couldn't start questioning M'Buru, but he could visit the chief's kraal and keep his eyes and ears open. Justin knew he wouldn't rest easy until he discovered Ngara's fate, preferably before Scobbie and party left for Nuruzambora.

The day after he visited Hopetown Justin went to talk business with Jonos van Klerk, one of the Boer farmers in the territory, with the hope of purchasing a few hundred morgens of his land, at the very least, though his intention was to try to talk van Klerk into selling him a few thousand. His own land bordered the Boer's on the west and that of a minor Bantu chief in the northeast but it was near van Klerk's property that he had found the diamonds.

Justin was destined to be disappointed. The Boer was adamant. He would not sell his land, poor and bare as most of it was; land so worthless that it took fifteen acres to feed a single cow!

And Justin had offered him very good money for the dusty rubble.

"No, never!" said the sober Dutchman, speaking the Taal, the common bastardized version of his own language mixed in with some English, French, and German, with a few Bantu words tossed in just to make things even more confusing.

Thwarted, but sensing that he would never get van Klerk to change his mind, Wentworth gazed in amazement at the hovel the farmer lived in with his overworked wife and six children, five of them girls, at his primitive and largely self-made farm equipment, the scrawny chickens scratching vainly for sustenance in the barren yard, then out at his modest herd of cattle, and he felt a burst of anger. With the money he had offered the Boer could have improved his lot considerably and made things easier for his wife and family, but Justin knew better than to argue with a Boer. He saved his breath.

He had better luck with the Bantu chief, a poorer version in every way of M'Buru. Justin came away with two thousand more acres in exchange for four pounds of beads, ten of salt, two oxen and a revolver —which he knew the chief would never use but would keep for show, since a spear could be thrown faster than a gun could be loaded. The old man, however, was overjoyed. In native terms he had struck it rich. Justin hoped to do the same with the land he had purchased, not too put out about van Klerk's refusal since by now it was obvious that diamonds could be found over a wide region and not just along the river banks.

Only one thing remained to be done, then he could turn his attention to business.


"He die." M'Buru struck his forehead several times with the palm of his hand, a demonstration of sorrow. "He now go join his before-fathers. Wound of rhino kilt him in the end."

They were discussing Surelele, one of his late elders, whom only that moment Justin had learned had died. And it was true that Surelele, father of Ngara, had been gored during a rhinoceros hunt two years before, and had suffered on and off from the wound ever since.

"That's a great pity; a great loss," Justin murmured, and slapped his own forehead to show respect. "His poor daughter Ngara must be very sad—"

"Woman made much sad for father when he live!" the chief interrupted harshly, his nostrils flaring as they always did when he was aggrieved. "Make much —much embarrass for Great Eagle! She go too," he added, and nodded.

"She's dead?" Justin widened his eyes in a show of surprise.

The chief looked at him, and the people M'Buru looked at closely had the feeling that they were being taken apart, each cell and organ examined minutely under his strange, penetrating eyes. He had a habit of moving very close to the people he was speaking to, especially if he wanted to impress or intimidate. As the two men sat smoking—the chief had taken readily to a pipe and grew his own tobacco, which was also pulverized to make snuff—he turned so that his head was within a foot of Wentworth's, and said, "Why you think woman die?"

Justin was used to his tactics and didn't move back, though he was close enough to see the pores of M'Buru's dark golden skin, and the cobweb-fine veins in the white's of his eyes. Justin was strong-willed and determined and, as M'Buru himself had witnessed, courageous, much as he knew himself to be, and the two men had a wary respect for each other.

"You said she went too," Justin replied. "I assumed you meant the same route as her father."

"Route?"

"In the same direction." He was sure M'Buru was being deliberately obtuse, perhaps trying to rattle him, so he added bluntly, "To the grave."

The tiny red points in the black man's eyes seemed to flare, to seep into the surrounding brown until there was no brown there. He stared at Wentworth with a thunderous frown on his face, nostrils wide, full lips drawn taut over his teeth, in a kind of hooded snarl. Justin gazed back at him calmly, at the same time wondering if he could draw his loaded revolver faster than M'Buru could pull his knife.

Suddenly the clearing rang with booming laughter that sent the monkeys scattering in the acacias surrounding the Great Eagle's lodge, and M'Buru's face cleared as if he had just understood Justin's meaning that minute.

"Woman not at grave!" he chuckled, shaking his head as if it was a ridiculous notion. "Not know what make you think so, White Lion; why you think that?"

Wentworth shrugged.

"She marry and go live far away in other kraal." Then he said more softly, with a sidelong flick of his eyes to the white man's face, "No, no, she not die . . . and slavers not catch her."

Justin's face hardened as the seed of doubt was dropped into his mind. He wouldn't have put it past M'Buru to sell the girl into slavery, and perhaps her father with her. It was highly unlikely that he would ever know for certain as none of the chief's people dared give their leader away; if they did and were caught, M'Buru had a way of making their death last a week, every second of that time fiendish agony.

Justin called Scobbie into his office when he returned to Teragno that evening, and this time he didn't mince words. "It appears that Erskine is on his way to Cape Town," he said, "but the fate of Sloan is much less certain, also that of his native mistress."

At mention of this affair James's lip curled in disgust and he burst out wrathfully, "Sloan deserves whatever he got! Assuming, of course, that M'Buru did anything at all. The chief likes to tease, I've noticed." He thought of the incident with the knife. "But still, he strikes me as being too intelligent a man to go so far as to harm a subject of Her Britannic Majesty. Think, man! He'd have the Garrison down about his head in short order."

Justin pointed out that the Garrison was very far away, and in these parts M'Buru was a law unto himself.

But Scobbie was resolute. "Well," he said, "I don't anticipate any trouble. I'm not a Sloan and neither am I an Erskine. The chief will have no reason to take umbrage at me." He frowned at Wentworth irritably. "Surely you don't think I'm the type to give up even before I've begun my work here?"

That was exactly what Justin was afraid of but he realized that there was nothing he could say or do to get Scobbie to change his mind. The only thing left to him was to try to keep a close watch on the little mission station at Nuruzambora, not easy when he had so much on his own plate and was already pressed for time.

At dawn on the Saturday of that week James Scobbie and his team left Teragno for Nuruzambora. The lovers parted with the coolest of nods. As Scobbie's heavily loaded wagon rumbled across the courtyard of the trading post to the wide iron gates, Olwyn kept her eyes fixed stoically ahead, resisting the temptation to look back.

*It's finished,* she thought dully, *and I'll just have to get on with it.*

She vowed then never to pin her hopes and trust on

another human being again. From now on she would
look to herself and no other; that way she would avoid
the bitter disappointments and heartache laying in
wait to trip her up and plunge her whole being into the
darkest depression, almost past bearing.

*Think of something else!* she told herself bitterly.
*Brooding about it will only invite even more pain.*

She raised her head to the clean blue morning sky,
eternally fresh and unsullied, and turned her eyes to
the waving golden grasslands bending before the
caress of the wind. Out on the tractless plain a herd of
gazelle sped joyously into the sunrise, celebrating the
new day. Monkeys chattered; birds swooped and
soared. The flash of kingfishers wings flared again and
again over the river valley, bright in the silvery mist
rising from the water.

Below the rim of the plateau they were following a
naked black figure, spear upraised, stood poised and
motionless on the banks of the Orange—as his kind
had done since time immemorial—waiting to catch
his breakfast.

The silence was sweet, the air aromatic with acacias, wild jasmine, and scented gums.

Olwyn marveled at the variety to be found in
Africa; the dusty plains now erupting in lush gold as
far as the eye could see, thanks to the recent rains. The
strangely shaped granite kopjes, the color of an elephant's hide; the low blunted hills, and here and there
in the shallow valleys, humid forests dripping with
mystery, some near-impenetrable except to the natives who lived there.

James had likened Africa to a great and glorious
banquet where nature had forgotten to invite the
guests. At the dinner table at Teragno he had frequently bemoaned the fact that no real interest was shown
in Africa by the foreign powers with the means to
develop the forgotten continent. True, the British
were in control of Cape Colony and the Dutch the
Transvaal and the Orange Free State, but these far-
away powers had never displayed more than the most

tepid interest nor given more than the most grudging support to their brave subjects who had blazed a trail into the wilderness. As far as Britain and Holland were concerned it was enough that they—rather than one of their rivals in Europe—had possession of these places, but neither had any desire to properly colonize or develop the desperately poor and backward areas they laid claim to. They were even unconcerned about where the boundaries of one sphere of interest ended and the other began. Neither Britain nor Holland saw any point in fighting over territory that was essentially worthless, though each lent token support to their Colony on the one hand, and obscure Republics on the other, when now and then grievances and disputes flared up between them.

All this Olwyn learned while sitting around the dinner table at Teragno but now as she gazed over the land she had a sudden hope that Africa would continue to stay as it was and never change, an Eden ignored, sanctuary to the birds, beasts, and the dark peoples who had inhabited it since before the time of the Stone Age. How lovely, she thought, to follow the meandering passage of the Orange River to the blue horizon, the lone fisherman the only human in sight. Though he was a quarter of a mile away they saw the glint of his spear flash downward in the sun and heard his whoop of delight. He had his fish for breakfast, and he was happy.

# The Blazing
# Stones

# ──◇── 18 ──◇──

*Griqualand,*
*April, 1869*

It's a diamond!" Justin gave a great whoop of triumph and held the small stone up to the sunlight.

His crew dropped their tools and rushed up from the river bank to converge on the sorting table under the shade of a thorn tree, pushing and shoving each other to get a glimpse of the reason for all their hard toil.

Most of the natives looked disappointed as they beheld the reason for all the excitement. To them it was much like any other pebble. The color of watered-down milk, rough and dull except in spots where the surface had been rubbed or abraded. At these spots it gave off a shower of sparks in the sunlight.

A few of the men remembered playing with such stones as children, kicking them around in the dust, little realizing that they were kicking away a fortune. They were still very skeptical of their worth, and privately felt that Wentworth had lost his wits. A man who owned many head of cattle had wealth in their eyes. A man who owned his own farm had substance.

A man rich enough to afford many wives was the envy of his fellows. But a man with shiny pebbles that could be bartered for nothing was clearly deluding himself if he imagined they would make him rich.

Justin saw the doubts in the dark faces around him; he saw the embarrassment, how they pitied him, and knew that by that evening they would be whispering that witch spirits had invaded his mind and made him sick.

Justin knew it was imperative that the men take the new business seriously, and he thought he knew of a way to help convince them of the value of the gems.

"This," he said, holding up the stone, "can be turned into cash that in turn can buy cattle—perhaps many head of cattle, depending on the quality of the stone—or sheep, or even wives," he added with a grin. Then when they still looked skeptical he threw out an inducement. "The next man to bring up a bucket of shingle containing a diamond, no matter how insignificant or poor the stone, will get an ox and a sheep for his diligence."

The natives gaped at him, then turned astonished eyes on each other, but when his offer had sunk in they all gave a mighty shout of glee—and raced each other back to the river bank to resume digging frantically. An ox or a sheep! They couldn't believe it. To own even one of these creatures gave a native man a certain status in the eyes of his peers. They didn't raise their heads from the plot they were working on for the rest of the day, except for the times they raced back to the sorting table with their loads of sand and gravel.

Finding that one diamond came after three weeks of back-breaking work under the hot sun. Though it was the beginning of winter the sun was still fierce, and coolness came only when the great golden orb sank below the horizon; then, suddenly and shockingly, the temperature dropped. From sweltering heat the night would be freezing.

Their method of diamond recovery was the same as had been used in other diggings around the world, most recently in India and Brazil. Since most gems to that date had been alluvial-type diamonds, found near water, Justin's crew restricted their digging to the banks of the Orange River. Shingle was carted from there to a sorting table where it was washed in river water, then the clean material was spread out thinly across the table, and closely inspected by Justin himself, the only one guaranteed to recognize a diamond, or by his manager, Kelly. The little Irishman was none too sure himself but brought any likely stone to his employer's attention.

Tons of shingle had been picked through during those first three weeks and dumped with no success. That's when the doubts had begun eating into Justin's mind. Perhaps the original gems he had found had been a freak occurrence, his mind ran on; the same thing had happened in other parts of the world, never to be repeated. The first batch had been discovered right next to Jonus van Klerk's land, and they were digging a little farther back from that spot now, so perhaps that was the problem. There wasn't much he could do about it, Justin fretted. Van Klerk would never part with as much as one morgen of his land— nor cared a hoot about searching for diamonds himself. Diamonds, if they existed at all—and the Boer certainly didn't think so nor would he waste his precious time searching for them—were flashy, worldly things of the type that painted women wore and men fought over, sometimes to the death. There was no market for anything like that on the wild African veld, and certainly no rich people to buy them, with the possible exception of Wentworth himself. Van Klerk was a simple man, a religious man who had trekked to Griqualand to find peace and tranquility, much as the other Boers had done who lived in the same region, and they scorned the idea of hunting for silly baubles, but even more they despised the greedy, grasping men who came in search of them, men sure to destroy the very thing they held most dear— solitude and the right to farm their land as they saw fit.

Justin knew it was useless to return to van Klerk with a better offer, and as time passed with no results he grew desperate and increasingly frustrated. He had suspended his trading operation and staked all on this new venture, and already, with every passing day, it was costing him a small fortune—the equipment, loss of the revenue from his former business, all his men to pay and the expenses relating to the running of his farm, the legal costs of purchasing more land and setting up the new business, Teragno Minerals.

All this weighed heavily on his mind as he stood over the sorting table in the stifling heat, the muscles in his back and shoulders aching as they washed and lifted tons of gravel then spread it out across the table, and found nothing but one small garnet. Logic told him then that he had made a mistake, that it might be better to cut his losses and return to his former business with all speed, before he was too much out of pocket. Justin decided to give himself till the end of April.

At ten on the morning of April twenty-second they found the diamond.

Justin's wild shout of glee and relief brought his men running, and once he had made them his offer, their cries of jubilation echoed his. They were most definitely in business. Teragno Minerals was alive and kicking.

Downriver an elephant pricked up its ears at the commotion. Standing in the shadows of a mopani grove, it might have been carved from ancient stone. On a ledge above, a cheetah sprawled in the dark entrance to a shallow cave, her spotted coat well camouflaged in the dappled sunlight slanting down through the trees. She had been lucky, too, that morning and had quickly made a kill, dawn and early dusk being the cheetah's slot for hunting. Darkness brought out the larger predators like the lion and leopard, creatures with eyes more suited to hunting in the dark.

Before the voice of man destroyed the silence both

the elephant and the cat knew he was there, his unpleasant sweet scent drifting to them on the breeze. Both had learned to tolerate man in small doses, but the sound of him that day was disturbingly loud and more annoying than usual. Finally, though, the yelling and shouting faded and silence again prevailed. The cheetah yawned and settled herself to sleep with her head on her paws, and the elephant resumed stripping the bark off the mopani trees, both oblivious to the fact that their peaceful environment was about to change radically, and not for the better.

Justin made all his men examine that first diamond very thoroughly so that they would know what to look for in future. The day after his first find was unsuccessful but the day after that they found four, and the following day, five. By then they were all in a fever of excitement, immune to the searing heat or the sudden chill as they trudged home in the early evening, almost too exhausted to eat before collapsing into bed.

At the end of the month the first eager prospectors arrived.

The newcomers camped on the other side of the river, on tribal land. Justin counted four men in the party, all equipped with picks, shovels, and sifting pans. They had come prepared.

He gazed at them across the water and felt a vicious pang of bitterness that brought Olwyn Moore back into his mind. By all intents and purposes this team should have been part of the lengthy caravan at that moment beating a frantic path to Zandfontein some sixty miles to the northeast, where the latest large diamond had been found by the Griqua shepherd, a find that was now general knowledge all over the southern part of Africa. Justin had heard from a passing trader about these caravans, and they seemed to be coming from everywhere—even some from overseas, including Britain, Australia, and America. Though many were inexperienced fortune-hunters some of these teams knew what they were about, he had heard, having been involved in diggings in India and Brazil. From all across the land they were streaming up to Zandfontein or the Vaal River, territory that seemed to offer the best potential for reward.

There was only one reason this team had come here, practically camping on his doorstep. Justin glared at them across the river and it seemed to him, though he couldn't be positive, that one of these men might have been attached to the party that Knute Bleur had brought to Teragno, though Bleur himself certainly wasn't among them, which didn't mean that they weren't working for him. Bleur, Justin thought grimly, would have known better than to show his face himself.

There was nothing that Justin could do. He didn't own the land across the river and could hardly order them to leave. Angrily he watched them set up tents, then pass a bottle around—perhaps as a toast to their future success, Justin thought balefully, and after that they proceeded to dig at a spot directly opposite his own crew.

One of them yelled across, "Any luck, mates?"

"Nothing," Kelly shouted back. "Where are you men from?"

"Cape Town," the fellow responded promptly, which didn't necessarily mean anything. He went on, "Most on their way up here are headed for the Vaal River, but we got a good tip that this could be the best place to look. We'll soon find out, I reckon."

Kelly glanced at Justin and growled, "If they are the only ones we have to worry about it won't be so bad, I suppose. D'you still think they're connected to Bleur?"

Wentworth shrugged; there was just no way to be sure but somebody had certainly directed them to the Orange River. He wondered how much these men had had to pay for the information.

The very next day three more wagonloads of prospectors arrived and set up camp beside the others, and the day after that six more. Soon there were a hundred men furiously digging on the other side of the Orange

—then a thousand. Daily more and more arrived until a long untidy camp straggled farther and farther along the bank of the river, blighting the lonely beauty of the landscape and destroying the tranquility with their raucous and often drunken laughter, their shouting and swearing, and the frequent noisy fights that broke out among them. Soon the area was littered with refuse, and in the heat of the day the smells from the camp were pungent. Some of the newcomers didn't care whose land they were on, and several times Justin had to chase them off his property. He was also compelled to leave an armed guard at his own site at night, once he had proof that some of the prospectors had rowed over to nose around once his own crew had left.

Jonus van Klerk also had trouble with trespassers, and this enraged the Boer farmer, who valued his privacy and solitude beyond anything else. This was the reason he had trekked so far out into the hinterland in the first place. One morning a furious van Klerk arrived at the river bank with some of his own men, all heavily armed, and nailed up wooden boards all along his own side of the Orange, threatening to shoot on sight anyone trespassing on his land.

The Boer was surprised and then incensed to find Wentworth's crew digging as assiduously as the others, and immediately knew the reason the former trader had been so anxious to buy some of his land—even before the prospectors arrived on the scene. He immediately assumed that Justin Wentworth had started the rush in the first place, and at that moment Justin made a powerful enemy in Jonus van Klerk, and to make an enemy of one Boer meant that all of them were against you.

Van Klerk was a tall, stocky man of forty with a head of thinning sandy hair and a sober, introspective demeanor, a difficult fellow to get to know at the best of times, let alone make friends with. His father had first trekked out of Cape Town to avoid the restrictions of the British Government, and when he grew up van Klerk had trekked farther. From the day he was born the Dutchman had known nothing but struggle and hardship, not to mention deprivation, first as a boy wrestling alongside his father in trying to clear the virgin land for their farm, at the same time fighting off unfriendly tribes and defending themselves against dangerous animals, battling disease, drought, and the devastation of their crops by locusts. The sum total of his life had hardened him to the point where he could be callous and even brutal, and his strong Calvinistic views on religion did nothing to soften his nature.

Justin had observed during visits to his farm that van Klerk was also strict and quite harsh with his wife and children, all except for his only son, Pieter, a thirteen-year-old boy with a shy smile and great artistic ability; an amazingly sweet, gentle lad considering the background he had sprung from. Van Klerk doted on the child. The sun rose and set on Pieter, who was like a shadow and followed his father everywhere. Otherwise van Klerk was not a man to tangle with.

"You will pay for bringing this riff-raff here," he told Justin that day, with a scornful glance at the pile of discarded gravel rapidly reaching the height of a small mountain. "You throw away the peaceful life for this! These stones, the diamonds, will cut your heart out. You will soon find out that the riches you had were better by far."

Regularly now there were wild outbursts of joy from both sides of the river as new stones were found, and it was the same on the banks on the Vaal, at Klipdrift and other sites wherever men had gone to dig. By this time it dawned on Justin, and others, too, that they were working atop perhaps the biggest treasure trove of riches that the world had ever seen; that great fortunes were in the making—not just for one man but for many.

The incredible news whisked around Africa like a bush fire, leaped across the oceans of the world, and set fire to imaginations all around the globe.

The first batch of foreign prospectors pulled in, quickly followed by others, some with experience and many with only the raw and desperate instinct to dig. The numbers of newcomers swelled from five to ten thousand and grew by the day, flooding into the desolation of Griqualand to an area that could barely support the few people it had had.

The face of the tranquil landscape was radically changed. Along the rivers sprawled a vast chaotic camp of ten thousand or more men, some living in tents or shacks with corrugated iron roofs, or hovels made of saplings with thatched roofs. Many slept even rougher, on the bare ground. Griqualand was nearly four thousand feet above sea level and at first the weather was cold, especially at night; then the torrential rains began and the entire site was flooded. This was followed by searing heat, with flies and, inevitably, disease and death, but the men kept on digging.

Many couldn't afford to stay. As they soon discovered it cost a fortune to live like pigs. Every single aspect of life was exorbitantly expensive on the veld since almost everything had to be brought up from Cape Town, more than six hundred miles away over the roughest, most dangerous territory imaginable. Those determined to stay were often compelled to sell fine stones for a few pounds just to enable them to keep on digging, lured on by the hope of bigger and better strikes. When Justin observed this practice he started buying these stones himself, and in this way increased his growing fortune, but he wasn't the only dealer. Before very long there were hundreds scurrying about from site to site, all eager to purchase gems from those forced to sell just to stay alive and working, and many of these dealers were dishonest, only paying the diggers a fraction of what their stones were worth, then selling them at the Cape for enormous profits.

Storekeepers arrived and threw up tin-roofed shops selling food, clothing, and equipment of the type prospectors would need. There were taverns and a rickety bug-infested hotel, a one-room casino—where the men, with little other stimulation available to them, often gambled away their profits. The dealers, who made money and generally knew how to keep it, conducted their business in shanties.

Sixty miles up and down the river banks were heaving with frantic men digging furiously, racing against time, for time cost a fortune on the diamond field. The dealers, or kopje wallopers, plied their trade. Almost none of them knew anything about diamonds but they did know how to make crafty deals and they, far more than the common digger, ended up growing rich. Into this congested field still more prospectors arrived—only to find that there was no room for them; that every single yard of space had been taken. The newcomers pleaded with the Boers and with Justin to let them buy claims on their land and offered to pay good money in advance.

Justin immediately saw the sense in this. As he told Kelly, "Short of taking on a thousand extra hands there's no way we can prospect all the area ourselves, so why not let others do it for us and pay us handsomely for the privilege?"

The claims he offered were gobbled up in one day, even though he also charged a royalty for any diamonds discovered. Observing how he was prospering, some of the Boers also gave in, thinking of all the livestock and modern equipment they could purchase with the money. A man would be a fool, the more forward-thinking among them remarked to each other, to pass up this chance—perhaps the only one they would ever get in their lifetime. A few even became infected with the now rampant fortune-hunting fever themselves and joined the other prospectors.

Jonus van Klerk and the other elders watched all this sadly. "Wentworth is responsible for contaminating our youth," van Klerk cried. "He brought all this rabble to our peaceful land and turned it into a circus of greedy ruffians, and he must be stopped before it's too late!"

The others looked at each other uneasily, well aware of what he had in mind and not quite ready to take such a drastic step, especially as they still felt the diamonds would soon run out. Certainly they couldn't last forever.

It seemed for a while that these sober men would get their wish.

Within weeks of selling claims Kelly came to Justin to report that no new gems had been found for a week; that it looked as if their field was running dry following all the frenetic activity. "Most of the outsiders are moving off in search of better prospects," the Irishman went on anxiously. "Some are even trying their luck farther inland, away from the rivers."

"Then they are fools!" Justin replied with a shrug. "Most of the world's diamonds have been found near water, in India, Brazil, and elsewhere."

"But . . . this is bad for us," the little man pointed out. "We've sunk a fortune into the operation." He hesitated, then made a suggestion. "Perhaps we should go prospecting for new strikes ourselves. This" —he waved to the river—"can't be the only diamondiferous soil around."

"Let me consider it," was the only answer Justin would give him.

Kelly stood his ground, feeling as strongly as he did, surprised, too, that Wentworth couldn't see the sense in it. But the Irishman had already observed that his employer hadn't been himself lately. Even when they found a large stone, definitely something to celebrate, his reaction had lacked his initial enthusiasm. It was as if all the excitement had gone out of it for him; that something else, or *someone* else, was claiming more and more of his attention. Kelly had a very good idea of who that someone was.

He felt compelled to try again. "We shouldn't tarry. It could be ruinous." Then he ventured, "It isn't like you to procrastinate—"

"Leave it for now," Justin snapped, and turned on his heel and walked away.

It proved to be a dreadful mistake.

Within two weeks most of the outside prospectors had vanished from the river bank and most of the remainder were preparing to follow suit, yet Justin still refused to take action. Kelly couldn't understand it, and he was beside himself with worry, but he also recognized the futility of approaching Wentworth now. Justin rarely appeared at the diggings anymore and when he did his mood was distant and grim, his mind quite obviously elsewhere. The day came when Kelly finally lost his temper and shouted, "Go to the bloody woman and get it over with! Do you want to see everything you've worked for slipping away—her included?"

That hit the mark. Yet Justin's pride, the monster he'd wrestled with for many a month, still searched for another excuse for visiting Nuruzambora. He found one quite easily. A few months before Hannah Scobbie had had her baby. He would take the child a gift, something he'd been meaning to do since it was born.

Instantly his lethargy vanished. He hurried home to bathe and dress and have his horse saddled, feeling more alive and full of energy and purpose than he had for months.

Riding through the countryside, Justin passed yet another caravan of would-be prospectors on their way up to the diamond fields. Normally he would have tarried to chat with them and answer all their many questions—and they were always foaming at the mouth with eager inquiries—but not that day. With a jaunty wave he rode by, scarcely paying them any attention. Nor did Maury Howell, seated at the front of the first wagon with a book on his lap, bother to look up. Maury was avidly reading yet another book about diamond-mining. He had quit his job with the government and was in the process of preparing himself to make a fortune, or, as he saw it, confront his destiny.

# 19

A ghost!" little Jamie cried, pointing into the woods. "I see a ghost!"

He flew to his mother and buried his face in her lap, and the group around the camp fire immediately lapsed into silence, the natives peering into the trees, then at each other, their evening meal forgotten.

It was their first day at the mission station at Nuruzambora, most of it taken up with putting the finishing touches to the house and erecting the huts where the men would sleep, these made with saplings and reeds and topped with a circular thatched roof. During the time they were at Teragno James and his crew had come back to the mission and done their best to repair and extend what would be their residence, a rickety building first constructed by Sloan and Erskine. It sat up on stilts as a precaution against serpents, rodents, and other unwelcome pests common in the area, and consisted of a narrow veranda along the front, this leading into a modest living area with three small bedchambers directly off this front room. James and Hannah had the bedroom to the right, with the children in the middle, and Olwyn on the far side.

The entire house was devoid of furniture. Whatever the previous occupants had had was gone now. To make things more homey Olwyn suggested they bring in trunks and packing cases from the wagon and drape a colorful plaid blanket from Scotland on the wall, but in spite of these efforts the house retained its dank, abandoned air, an aura that hung over the entire mission station like a pall, all the worse when contrasted against the warmth and comfort of Teragno.

The drums began at dusk, about the time they lit the fires and began preparing their evening meal. To the children, Harold in particular, it was all a big adventure. The boy had been no trouble at all from the time they landed in Cape Town, with so much to see and do, and that day he'd worked as hard as any of the men setting up what he called their camp in the bush. Jamie, while the evening meal was being prepared, darted about among the trees surrounding the clearing, clapping his hands and trying to catch the twinkling flies that came out at that time of night, intending to put them in a jar that he would use as a lantern.

Hannah had just called him to come for his meal when his cry of "Ghost!" rang out, and the chattering and laughter around the fire instantly stopped.

James and his men, most of them very reluctant, grabbed their guns and went off to check the area around the mission station, leaving Mick and a dozen natives to guard the women and childrne. Pointing to his departing comrades, the Hottentot foreman said, "They not want go. Fear Imba. They not like here."

His plump wife Flo nodded agreement and hugged herself, the whites of her eyes large as she glanced nervously about the clearing. "Ja, bad spirit here in this place." She looked at Olwyn and Hannah. "You not feel?"

"Nonsense!" Hannah said, to her credit, smoothing

Jamie's hair as he lay cuddling close in her lap. "This is a good place, a Godly place, so we must have no more silly talk about evil spirits. Mr. Scobbie wouldn't like it."

Flo said no more in English but she muttered to herself in the Afrikaans she spoke most of the time, a sort of communal language in the southern part of Africa, spoken by whites and natives alike, especially the white Dutch settlers. Little Jamie began to blubber as they waited anxiously for the others to come back. "He . . . *its* face was all white . . . and its eyes were like coal. It was over there in the trees"—he waved vaguely without raising his head from the security of his mother's breast—"and it was watching us, just waiting for it to get really dark—"

"You made it up!" Harold interrupted angrily, not wanting to hear anymore, and secretly scared himself. "You ought to get a whipping for trying to frighten the ladies. Just don't talk about it anymore."

Jamie burst into tears. "Oh, what if Papa and the lads don't come back? What if it gets them, just like it did with the other missionaries—"

"Jamie, hush!" Hannah's brittle courage cracked and she, too, looked apprehensive.

James and the men returned shaking their heads. They had seen nothing more worrysome than a hyena bitch with her half-grown cub, but the pair had bounded away the second they spotted them and, cowardly as they were, James announced that they had nothing to fear from them.

He instructed the men to keep the fires blazing that night and put on an extra guard and, very subdued, the rest of them made tracks for bed, curling up tight under their quilts and blankets to ward off the evening chill, not very successfully as drafts whistled in everywhere through cracks in the wooden structure. Their home, not much better than a shack, had openings for windows, but there was no glass to cover them with, nothing but fine screening to keep out the insects. James had promised to make shutters that could be closed over these openings when he had time but for the moment Olwyn couldn't help feeling uneasy and vulnerable as she lay awake in her bare little room, her bed a mattress on the floor, listening to the branches of a nearby tree scraping back and forth across the screen in the night breeze.

The drums from the village pounded long into the night and now and then from the forest a hyena—perhaps the one James had seen—let out sudden fits of shrieking and giggling that had her starting up in alarm at the suddenness of it, like a lunatic screeching in a vast, echoing room. Flo had said, "You not feel?" and neither Hannah nor herself had answered her question—but Olwyn did feel something disturbing at Nuruzambora, an atmosphere of foreboding hanging over the mission station, and she wished heartily that James had chosen somewhere else to bring Christianity to the heathen.

That was their first night at Nuruzambora, a sleepless one for most of them. The next day their true work began, heavy, often frustrating work that rendered them too fatigued to think of anything at all when their heads finally touched their pillows at night.

The men immediately plunged into activities like clearing the watercourses already there and digging extra ones, as a precaution against the dry season. They also built a small dam, prepared a large garden for planting vegetables, and readied the field behind the mission for crops. With only thirty men—and Harold—to help him, James found this hard going until M'Buru generously supplied two dozen men of his own to help with the task. The villagers often came down to observe what was happening, and Scobbie took full advantage of these visits to preach the gospel, first struggling along in the native tongue but quickly lapsing into a jumbled combination of Afrikaans—which most understood—and English, which many of them also understood through contact with Sloan and Erskine.

Though James certainly didn't neglect the Lord's

work, he was forced to spend much of his time with mundane tasks like repairing broken wagon wheels, making hoes and other necessary garden tools, constantly sharpening the blades of their makeshift plough when it became blunted on the rough ground, and very important, hunting for fresh meat to feed his team. This meant keeping the guns in fine working order, and when the villagers saw how adept he was at this—James had a natural aptitude for anything mechanical or technical—they brought their own often ancient weapons for him to repair. This, more than all his preaching, elevated him in their eyes. Now, suddenly, the Badger, as the chief called him, had real status in their eyes and became an important member of the community. By this time most of the tribes in the area at least had some guns but very few knew how to repair them. To possess such modern weapons, and to have someone capable of fixing them, gave a tribe a great advantage over its enemies.

"You good brother!" M'Buru praised as he watched James mend an elderly short-barreled Remington rifle that the chief had bought off a peddler, a weapon that had never worked from the day he got it. When James finally handed it to him and M'Buru aimed at a chicken in the yard and promptly blew its head off, the black man was overjoyed, even if the gunsmith and chicken were not.

That afternoon M'Buru sent down a gift of a dozen hens in prime laying condition, and that evening the decapitated cousin was added to the pot for dinner.

For the first three months of their stay in Nuruzambora Chief M'Buru was generally benevolent and supportive and keenly interested in what they were doing, other than preaching, though Scobbie tried to get around this antipathy by talking about God in a conversational manner while repairing a gun or agricultural implement. Sometimes the chief listened and asked questions, and James would feel a rush of hope, thinking he was truly interested. But at other times M'Buru would counter impatiently,

"Who dare tell Great Eagle what he do? Great Eagle not give up he wives and only has one. He like many woman; he important chief."

While James struggled to put Christianity across and at the same time improve conditions at the mission station, Hannah and Olwyn were also busy from dawn till dusk. Daily there were mountains of laundry, which the boys helped them carry to the stream, and once it was dry there were always torn clothes to be mended. They sewed, helped Flo with the huge amount of cooking, cleaned, and tried to improve the appearance of the house with bright foliage and berries from the woods, patchwork cushions and wall-hangings sewn from snippets of Hannah's leftover fabric, which she always kept. They even made small pieces of furniture such as stools, an open cupboard, and their biggest achievement of all, a rough plank table where the family could dine regally on the veranda!

Within days of arriving at the mission station Olwyn's skills as a medical woman were required when Harold was carried home from the woods with a huge thorn in his toe. The boy was pale and sweating and obviously in great pain, the wound itself already red and swollen and so tender that he winced and then screamed when Olwyn attempted to remove it. "We hold him down," said Mick matter-of-factly, and gestured for some of the other men to help him, though James, pale himself, quickly shook his head and cast beseeching eyes on his medical assistant.

"Let him go," Olwyn ordered the foreman. "I have a better way."

She administered a strong dose of laudanum to Hal and talked quietly to the boy until it took effect, asking him how it had happened. When his voice began to slur she pushed him gently back on his bed, took a pair of pincers from her medical bag, and carefully removed the thorn—but the point broke off and remained embedded in the wound. Her eyes met the foreman's in dismay. Both knew the seriousness of leaving even a tiny fragment of these poisonous thorns in the flesh. As Justin had told Olwyn on the way up from Algoa Bay when she'd watched him remove a similar thorn from one of his own men, "Many a man has lost his toe or even his foot after stepping on one of these things. They have to be cut out if necessary and the wound poulticed to draw out any lingering poison."

"Burn heem out," Mick suggested. "Fire clean wound."

Hannah, at the head of the bed with her son's head in her lap, choked and then whispered that she was going to be sick, or faint, or both.

"Take her outside," Olwyn ordered Mick grimly.

Temporarily alone except for the anxious black faces peering in the door behind her, Olwyn felt a rush of dread and terror and a crippling doubt when she considered her own inexperience in light of what she was about to do, but she was the only one with any real medical knowledge and if she didn't help Harold who would?

Grinding her teeth, Olwyn dipped into her medical bag and brought out a small surgical knife, gauze, and a ready-made solution of chloride of lime. Mick watched with interest as she disinfected the knife with the latter solution, instead of putting it to fire as he would have done, then inhaling deeply, the girl bent over the cause of the trouble. Quickly she cut into the area where the thorn had been before she could lose her nerve altogether. There was one chilling moment of horror as Harold moaned loudly and blood gushed up out of the cut, then as she soaked up the flow with a pad of gauze and Mick hurried to the head of the bed in readiness to restrain the boy if he should begin struggling, a curious calm settled over Olwyn, the awareness that she had been brought here for this job and she would do it to the best of her ability.

It took several minutes of poking about with the tip of the knife before the head of the thorn came free and floated out of the wound in a fresh gush of blood.

Olwyn studied it well to make sure she had it all, then cleaned the wound thoroughly with chloride of lime, packed it, and finished by bandaging the injured toe. For the next week she applied poultices made from linseed, starch, and powdered charcoal, changing them three times a day, and by the end of that time Harold, cranky by then and exceedingly restless, was in less pain from the injury and showing definite improvement. But no sooner did Olwyn have the boy off her hands than one of the crew, in the act of chopping down a tree with an ax, missed and chopped his leg instead, and she had her second patient at Nuruzambora.

About this time Hero, the chief's private doctor, made a dramatic appearance, dashing into the mission about the time the fires were being lit at twilight, timing his entrance to perfection.

The sight of him threw everyone into a great state of commotion.

Hero looked like a giant red bird, though in fact he wasn't a tall man at all. The waving ostrich plumes rising from his head only made him look that way. His entire body was painted with red ocher. On top of this weird and frightening pictures and symbols had been picked out in white, his face made to look like a hawk or some other bird of prey. His scarlet apron was trimmed with the skulls of tiny animals and he had bracelets of bones jingling at his ankles and wrists. Dangling from his necklet was a huge tooth, perhaps from a crocodile, shells and ivory ornaments, and various charms. He swept into the clearing with his staff of office raised high, topped with a human skull. Behind him came his silent disciples, four men entirely dressed in black, but with the same hideous birdlike masks and feather patterns picked out on their faces and bodies in white, an eerie spectacle in the dusk.

Hannah screamed and flew into the house with Jamie, and most of their natives dove into the woods to hide. Olwyn had to admire James at that moment. He simply stood up from the fire with his rifle in his hand and quietly waited for the newcomer to introduce himself. This took a little time. First Hero pranced around the clearing making a shrill, high-pitched howling noise, at the same time gesturing with his staff at their house and other buildings, then at the mission people themselves, the few that remained cringing at the fire.

The howling stopped abruptly. There was a moment of great tension as the witch doctor stood facing Scobbie in the light of the fire. Then he smiled, displaying teeth that had been filed to sharp points, making his grin chillingly evil-looking. "You see before you Hero, greatest medical man of Griqua," he announced.

To Olwyn's utter amazement this barbaric creature spoke very good English!

When James introduced himself Hero continued in the same immodest vein. "You see before you man who talk to spirit; who make rain come and sun grow crop; who slay enemy with witch medicine; who help make M'Buru strong."

For fully five minutes while they all sat transfixed they listened to a long recital of Hero's powers and achievements, then with a sweep of his staff around the clearing the native doctor said darkly, "Bad medicine in this place. You want I make it go? Only cost two ox."

Olwyn saw James's shoulders relax. The weird creature before them was all too human after all. Scobbie thanked him politely and tried to explain that he trusted in his own God to take care of them. "I hear of you God but no see him!" Hero interrupted with a scornful laugh. "Why you trust God you no see? How you know he there?"

Again James sought to explain, and again the witch doctor broke in, switching abruptly to a new topic. "Where you medicine woman?"

When Olwyn was presented the chief's doctor broke into hysterical laughter. "She too young!" he scoffed, peering into her face. "She no got staff, no got charm." He rubbed his cheek, still looking at her closely, then glanced at the few men standing around before turning back to her to inquire, "You got husband?"

"No," Olwyn whispered.

More pealing laughter rang out, and this time Hero's disciples joined him.

"You no got nothing," the witch doctor said, and with a final scathing look at all of them, swept out as abruptly as he had come.

"Obnoxious fellow," James grumbled as he resumed sitting at the fire.

Mick looked after the departing retinue thoughtfully. "Maybe you should have give him the ox."

That night it rained and continued for a solid week, torrential rain such as Olwyn had never seen before, gushing from the leaden skies to turn the clearing into a muddy lake crawling with leeches. No matter how good the thatching, it still found a way into the house, soaking their food supplies, their clothing, their bedding. Overnight green mold formed on everything they ate, wore, and touched, and gave off an odor like rotting vegetation.

Yet for every drawback there was something to compensate. The winter rains washed the dust from the land and trees. Protea and aloes burst forth in a riotous profusion of pink and yellow. Riverbeds filled and crystalline waterfalls cascaded from ridges and hills, falling like sheets of silver into dark green pools floating with waterlilies. Though the nights were cold the sun rose triumphantly almost every morning to bathe the steaming land in pleasant warmth, burning off the veil-like mist and shining through gigantic spiders webs draped from the trees, showing them up in great and exquisite detail for a brief space of time, like fragile strands of minute pearls in the sunrise.

In the stillness of early morning cattle lowing in the meadow had a melodious sound. They stood feeding in grasses undulating before the wind like a silvery sea, dew-laden and sparkling. The air was joyous with the songs of larks, laughing doves, thrush, and the vibrant sunbird. Sunset was an orange inferno, offset with the lacy black of ferns and acacia trees.

There was no tsetse fly in the area, that scourge to oxen, horses, and dogs, but the wet weather encouraged the mosquitoes. Hordes of them came out every evening the moment the sun went down, buzzing and stinging and passing on the fever, though at the time the blame was laid on the humors rising from the swampy ground, rather than from the insects themselves.

Dr. Gibb had always preached that prevention was better than cure so, taking a tip from her mentor, Olwyn had begun dosing her people with quinine while they were still on the ship. They slept under nets at night and Mick urged them to smear themselves with mud before dark, as he and the natives did to ward off the pests. Harold and Jamie were delighted to comply but the Scobbies and Olwyn shuddered at the thought of the slimy stuff hardening to an uncomfortable cake all over their bodies. The next time Hero breezed into the mission at dusk, as usual, and saw them madly swatting the pests, he laughed and offered to supply some of his special oil that was guaranteed to repel the insects. "I give you for a sack of millet," he said.

James was about to refuse but Olwyn, covered in bites by this time and almost driven out of her mind with the itch, as was poor Hannah, begged him to accept the deal. The meal was duly handed over and Hero sent one of his disciples back to the village for his oil.

The witch doctor had come to invite them to attend M'Buru's court, which was held quarterly. At such times grievances were aired and disputes settled and those guilty of any crimes punished. "Great Eagle say you must come," he added firmly when James again started to shake his head.

Olwyn knew she would never forget that court session to her dying day. The village of Nuruzambora was usually a bustling place, a kind of thatched-roofed city on the veld. Women swept, cleaned, washed their clothes, and gracefully swayed back and forth with water jugs balanced on their heads, small infants clinging to their legs, while the men tended the animals, worked the fields, scraped and cured hides and, of course, hunted for meat. The air about the village was bright with the sounds of soft native voices, of laughter, and the playful shouts of the children. Late every afternoon the citizens could be found sitting under a massive black baobab tree happily exchanging the latest gossip and drinking their mead or beer. Often, too, they smoked mutakwane, a weed that made them even drunker and considerably more excited than did the brew.

The day of M'Buru's Court the atmosphere had radically changed. When the Scobbies and Olwyn arrived, as they had been ordered to do, they found the whole place in silence, though more than a thousand people ringed the huge central clearing before the chief's lodge. About thirty feet from where M'Buru sat with his counselors, witch doctor, and guests, a platform had been erected for those who had business with the chief, whether of a pleasant or unpleasant nature. On either side of this fairly large platform two crosses loomed dark against the clear blue sky, and under each a heaping pile of wood and dry branches had been placed. There was also a huge stump from a baobab, an ax beside it.

Hannah clutched her husband's arm at the sight of the crosses.

"Oh, I don't like this, James," she whispered as they made their way to their seats beside the chief. "Why is it necessary for us to be here?"

"Because M'Buru wants us to witness how he dispenses justice," Scobbie replied grimly.

The chief greeted them with a nod; he seemed unusually grave that day, as if he had the weight of the world on his shoulders. But under his surface gravity Olwyn sensed that he was excited. He stamped the ground below where he sat restlessly, as a bull will the moment before it charges. He shifted about in his seat, scratched his head, now and then jabbed or waved his judicial sword about, a vicious-looking weapon with the head of an eagle at the hilt. A tall, muscular, handsome man in the very prime of life, M'Buru had a leopard-skin cape about his powerful shoulders today. As he turned in her direction to speak to his witch doctor, Olwyn saw that his eyes were bloodshot; she smelled the sweetish odor of mutakwane heavy in the air.

It began with the blast of a horn and ended with the screams of the doomed and the smell of blood and fire and charred flesh.

M'Buru quickly dispensed with the grievances and squabbles of his flock with a rigorous hand. A man accused of stealing a chicken from another was ordered to give the plaintiff his entire flock. A woman who had started a malicious rumor about another was banished from the village for a month, with the warning that if the offense were to be repeated her tongue would be cut out. Fines were imposed for bartering sour mead, and the suspicion of putting witchcraft into food given to another. A boy received a lashing for fighting with his father, another for drinking while on duty guarding his herd. One young mother, not more than fifteen, was brought forward with her infant and the child taken off her and given to his grandmother to raise. The charge? Neglect.

Then the blood began to flow.

A young warrior charged with treason, passing information to an enemy tribe, was marched up to the baobab block and decapitated with one swipe of the burly executioner's massive assegai, his head bouncing along the ground with the eyes still blinking.

Hannah screamed and swooned against her husband. Olwyn had to stuff her fist into her mouth to stop herself from being sick. But it was only the beginning. They were forced to watch ears being chopped off for eavesdropping on the chief's business, and a tongue being cut out for repeatedly telling lies. A man was castrated for "interfering" with another's wife and a woman speared in the heart for drowning her newborn baby.

When a horrified Scobbie tried to intervene M'Buru thundered, "Be silence! These people do evil thing. Now they punish." He glared down the bench at James. "They my people so punish quick. Outsider . . ." he let the meaning sink in for a moment, ". . . outsider linger."

They saw an ample demonstration of this when two wretches from an enemy tribe, both accused of witchcraft, were burned alive on the crosses, their shrieks of agony and the reek of burning flesh rising in the still, clean air, and a third captive, a woman, had both eyes knocked out for spying, and enticing away one of their best young warriors.

Olwyn had to stop several times on the way home to be sick, and Hannah was in a state of collapse, wailing that she wanted to return to Scotland immediately. "I will not have my child born in this terrible place!"

Mick, though, shrugged philosophically. "That their way. Not know any other—"

"Then they must be taught!" James broke in harshly. "Somehow or other a way must be found to bring Christ and His mercy to these barbarians. This carnage cannot go on!"

"But they not want taught," his foreman said impatiently. "They never believe in God they no see." He glanced at James's stony face and went on more quietly. "Be careful, master . . ."

Scobbie brushed off his advice. "I refuse to bend before heathens! I came here for a purpose and I will see it through." He ran fingers through his hair and cried in a broken voice, "Those poor, suffering people!"

Turning a deaf ear to Hannah's entreaties, to Mick, Olwyn, and even his sons, James set out determinedly for the village a few days later and started preaching to the usual crowd always hanging about under the baobab tree late in the afternoon, a kind of desperate bravado in his attitude. M'Buru and his witch doctor soon joined the others, and for a few minutes they all stood listening to him, their eyes following his every gesture—and James used a lot of body language that day—then nudging each other as he knelt down before them to pray. Kneeling in the dust was a sign of subservience to these people. They had no way of knowing that Scobbie wasn't bowing to them but to God.

M'Buru's booming laugh rang out, drowning out the missionary's prayer. Then the whole assembly began to shriek with laughter, some even going so far as to imitate Scobbie, waving their arms about and crouching in the dirt. When James, undaunted, tried to talk to them M'Buru and others interrupted, shouting over and over "Where this God you say? Why he no show face?"

Hero sneered, "White man try to frighten Great Eagle with this God; want take away he power like Waterboer." (Chief Waterboer, another Griqua chief, was generally despised as a weakling for allowing himself to be seduced into adopting European ways, even going so far as to wear white men's clothing on occasion.)

M'Buru pointed to Scobbie sternly. "Badger go. Not come back till I's tell he. Go!" he roared, when James showed no sign of leaping to obey his command.

The missionary trudged home in near-despair, finally appreciating exactly what Erskine and Sloan had been up against. Nothing had been heard of either man since they left Nuruzambora, and after what he had witnessed three days before James felt deeply worried. He had never expected it to be easy in Africa and he wasn't a man to give up but if there was a chance that the chief had had these two men murdered . . .

Scobbie was silent and withdrawn that night at supper, in one of his dour moods as he thought things over, wondering what he would do if he did return home in defeat. There was nothing for him in the Church in Scotland, and preaching was all he could do. Depressed, he asked himself if he could be expecting too much from the natives in too short a time. As for Sloan and Erskine, well . . . he had no proof that M'Buru had harmed them. His court, after all, had no jurisdiction over Europeans.

At the end of that week a passing trader—who frequently acted as postman—brought several welcome letters from home, including one from the Free Missionary Society. James gave a shout of relief when he read that Basil Erskine had arrived back in Scotland safely, resigned from missionary work, and was about to return to his former occupation of engineering. The Directors wrote that they'd had no word from Robert Sloan, whom they soundly condemned for the behavior Erskine had reported. But they also expressed concern for Sloan and asked that Scobbie use every means at his disposal to make inquiries and try to discover his present whereabouts.

Olwyn had not seen or heard from Justin from the day they left Teragno and did her best to block him out of her mind. It helped that she was constantly busy and generally fell asleep the moment she lay down in bed at night. Fifteen of their men were very sick with fever; Hannah, too, was ill, but then Hannah had been in delicate health through her pregnancy and was now big with child and very uncomfortable. Olwyn worried about her swollen hands and feet and frequent dizziness, and made her rest as often as possible. This meant that she, Olwyn, had Hannah's work to do as well as her own, plus a small hospital of patients who were either shivering violently with chills or prostrate and sweating profusely as their fever mounted. All suffered from violent headaches, vomiting, bowel disturbances, and extreme weakness. They could do almost nothing for themselves. Olwyn had to do it for them.

She grew reed-thin and gaunt but somehow this only emphasized the exquisite bone structure of her face and gave her an ethereal, haunting loveliness. Her black hair had grown rapidly and billowed in a mass of unruly curls about her face and over her shoulders, and her white skin had given way to a burnished golden tan. As she flew about the clearing, busy with her tasks, her usual garb was a long black or gray skirt—cut down from two of Hannah's oldest gowns —and either a white or yellow blouse, also made for her by Hannah.

One day in August as she was gathering flowers in the woods to freshen Hannah's room Olwyn suddenly came upon M'Buru. He was alone, leaning casually against a tree, and Olwyn sensed that he had been watching her for some time. She had been stooping to pick wild orchids from around a pool and, hearing a slight sound, raised her face into the sunshine, the light falling across her tawny eyes, the rest of her face streaked in light and shadow from the branches above her head.

"You like leopard, woman," the chief commented, his strong voice quite low. "What you do out here alone?"

Olwyn held up her basket of flowers; she was suddenly apprehensive under the stare of his glowing dark eyes that always reminded her of the color of burnt sugar.

"Imba might catch you," he said, and smiled. He looked at her yellow blouse where the fullness of her young breasts peaked the material, then at her silky hair, and inquired in the same low tone that Olwyn had never heard him use before, "Why you no has husband?"

"I—well, I—"

"Brother Sloan take one of my women," M'Buru cut in unexpectedly, and without taking his eyes from her face flicked a fly off his leg with the whip he was carrying. "He take my woman and no ask, no pay. He owe me for that woman."

A dreadful fear held Olwyn rigid and froze her tongue.

"He owe one woman," the chief repeated, watching her closely.

A terrible hush seemed to fall over the woodland.

"What you say, leopard-woman? You no speak?" He smiled slightly, sensing her fear. "Badger speak much. He women say nothing." He twitched the whip against his powerful thigh and looked her up and down, then shook his head, still smiling. "Badger no feed he woman. You too thin. No meat."

With that he strode right up to her and plucked an orchid from her basket and pushed it into her hair, and for a moment the chief's eyes met Olwyn's and she felt his potency, his savage power. She couldn't breathe.

But after an excruciating few seconds that seemed to last a lifetime, M'Buru said, "Go now, but not forget what I say."

He stepped back to let her pass, and Olwyn heard him chuckling as he watched her hurrying away into the trees. When she arrived at the mission she couldn't bring herself to tell anyone about her encounter with M'Buru, but when the drums began that evening at dusk they seemed to carry a special message to her from the chief.

Lying uneasily in her bed that night Olwyn seriously contemplated the idea of leaving Nuruzambora when her time with James was up, which it would be shortly. James had said nothing about paying her to stay on, and Olwyn seriously doubted he would ever be able to afford to. But far more than money came into it now! She loved these people; they were her family.

Olwyn shivered, cocking an ear to the screened window, where other furtive sounds could be heard now that the drums had finally ceased. She was deathly afraid, yet even if she'd wanted to go—even if she'd been willing to leave the Scobbies—she had no money or a destination to go to. Besides, with the birth of her child imminent, Hannah needed her, and she would rather die than leave her good, dear friend in the lurch. She was in a kind of trap. To try to avoid M'Buru was the only solution that she could think of.

Isobel Margaret Scobbie arrived on August fifth, more than two weeks before she should have. It had been a long and difficult birth and by the time it was over both Hannah and Olwyn were exhausted, though overjoyed at the appearance of the longed-for baby girl, tiny and feeble as she was. Olwyn first felt a chill of foreboding when the infant had to be coaxed to eat, then promptly brought her nourishment back up again. Little Isobel almost never cried; she scarcely moved in the rough wooden cradle her father had made for her.

"She's a good wee lass, isn't she?" James said proudly. "Not the noisy, greedy rogue her brothers were."

How Olwyn longed to hear a lusty cry as she hovered over Isobel's cradle day and night, trying to will some life into the infant while Hannah, still very weak, watched her anxiously from the bed, too ill to care for the child herself.

"Will she be all right?" Hannah asked over and over again, and the strain of forcing a cheery smile became increasingly more difficult for Olwyn as the weeks and months passed and tiny Isobel barely made any gain in spite of round-the-clock attention. When the van Klerks paid a visit in mid-October, as they often did while on their way back and forth to market in Hopetown, Helga van Klerk took Olwyn aside and stated bluntly, "She will not live to see in the New Year. In fact, she would have been dead already but for your care, but in the end it will be all for nothing. God wants this little flower home to take her place with the angels."

She was right. The baby closed her eyes for the last time on October twenty-fourth as Olwyn rocked her gently, singing a lullaby.

# 20

Justin came back to her at the worst possible moment. Had it been months earlier, or later, Olwyn told herself afterward, she would have been able to keep that promise she had made to herself the day she left Teragno. Upset as she had been that day after their fight over Knute Bleur, she had still been strong. Her very anger had given her added determination.

How different things were the day he finally returned to her!

Baby Isobel had been dead for a week and the mission station in deepest mourning. Hannah Scobbie lay prostrate in her darkened room, silent and withdrawn, refusing to eat or speak to anyone, including her husband. James, distraught himself, wandered the countryside like a drunk man, staggering about with no thought to where he was going or what danger might lurk around the next bend. When Olwyn tried to speak to him he merely grunted, not seeming to hear. She couldn't tell whether he held her responsible for the tragedy or not but his silence and Hannah's was an added twist of the knife in her heart. Even the men, she felt, avoided her.

Finally, unable to stand it another minute, Olwyn stole away from the mission in the sweltering heat of the early afternoon when both humans and animals alike curled up in the shade to escape the worst of the heat of early summer. Picking wild flowers as she went, Olwyn reached the spot where the baby had been buried, a simple wooden cross marking the grave on a ridge above a small dark pool. Kneeling to place her bouquet beside the others already piled there, Olwyn thought of the infant she had adored and cared for from the moment of her birth, thinking that she had been the first to look on the tiny face and the last before Isobel died. A choking surge of grief swelled inside her, yet still the tears would not come. They lay, an ocean of them, like a block of black ice in her breast, even as the dark thoughts clogged her mind, the sorrow, regret, and guilt. How she had wanted that little girl to live! Yet for all that she had tried mightily, using all the skill she possessed, Isobel had slipped away from them. Could someone more qualified, more experienced, have saved her? That was the question that threatened to drive Olwyn mad.

After carefully arranging the pile of flowers around the cross Olwyn stumbled downhill to the pool and sat there dismally in the tall, lush grass by the water. It was cool and shady in the narrow ravine, and strangely peaceful, though there was no peace in her heart. But at least here she escaped the many eyes at the mission station, eyes that she sometimes felt were accusing, though no one had uttered one word of blame.

As Olwyn sat absently tossing flower petals into the water, she heard the sound of a rider approaching in the stillness—and a stab of irritation pierced the heavy melancholy cloud that hung over her.

No one at the mission station wanted visitors!

Hannah refused to leave her room. James was off on one of his aimless walks. And she—she certainly wasn't up to entertaining anyone!

Olwyn dragged herself up the slope to the dirt road and stood waiting to intercept the rider, determined to turn him back after explaining the situation at the mission. It was open here and the ferocious sun beat down on her mercilessly, the glare making her dizzy so that she swayed a little, the ground tilting in front of her. She was weary to the bone. After three months of nursing the baby and Hannah, who had been slow to recover from the birth, and tending to those of their men who had fever—and a few always seemed to be suffering from the recurrent scourge of malaria, and refused to touch the bitter medicine, quinine—Olwyn felt she would drop where she stood from utter exhaustion. Then the rider came into view and she almost did.

Justin reined in his horse abruptly when he spied the figure blocking the track ahead. He didn't recognize her at first. Olwyn looked like a wild thing at that moment; she might have been a woodland nymph, or a trick of the light. Wraith-thin, her beautiful face honed to the delicate bones, her thick hair a wild mass of unruly curls, far longer than when he had last seen her, Olwyn looked nothing like the woman who had left Teragno eight months before.

Recognition came to Justin in a powerful surge of emotion that smote him to the core. This skeletal, ragged creature was the same woman he had accused of selling his diamond, and doubling the money by supplying the information about Teragno to Knute Bleur! Justin was hardly aware of leaping from the saddle to rush across the space that separated them, there to enfold her tenderly, contritely in his arms, so thoroughly disgusted with himself that for a moment he couldn't speak. Finally he said: "My God, what has happened to you?" His eyes raked her wan, upturned face. "Olwyn . . . my love! I—I'm so sorry . . ."

Olwyn could see plainly just how sorry he was. He

looked shattered at the sight of her, his eyes, normally such a bright, vivid blue, looked bleak, stricken. Some of the ice around her heart began to crack and melt away. And more than anything in the world Olwyn needed love and support at that moment.

She pointed across the ravine and choked, "The baby died a week ago. We buried her over there . . ."

Justin thought of the gift he'd brought, but too late, and again berated himself fiercely. Why hadn't he come sooner? God knew he'd wanted to!

"What happened, darling?" he asked her gently, aching to kiss her so much that he trembled. "Was it the fever?"

Olwyn shook her head, and without thinking rested it against his broad chest and closed her eyes, struggling to stave off the faintness that kept coming over her in waves. "She was very tiny and feeble," she began in such a weak voice that Justin had to bend his head to hear. "No matter what I did, she . . . she just couldn't seem to get a firm grip on life. Sometimes"— Olwyn sucked in a breath, her voice cracking as she went on—"sometimes she seemed stronger . . . but she always slipped back." Then it came out. "Perhaps someone else, someone who knew more about medicine, might have saved her. Oh God, how I wish now that I'd never taken on this job!"

Justin felt a shudder go through her, as if something were breaking up inside, then Olwyn began to weep, rough, harsh, anguished weeping that frightened him, even as he knew that it was a release that would help her once it was over.

It was grueling standing under the hot sun. Glancing about over her bent head, Justin spied the ravine. He swept her up into his arms and carried her down into shade and coolness after the glare up above. Very gently he set Olwyn down in the lush grass surrounding the water, the tall fronds forming a kind of screen around them. There he took her into his arms and held her against his heart, and when the sobbing finally subsided he gently raised her wet face to his and kissed her. There was such feeling in that kiss, such deep tenderness and caring, that Olwyn felt as if a powerful ray of light had sliced through the murky darkness of her soul, unlocking it from a gravelike cold. It breathed new life into her. She felt as if she had been plucked from a pit into vibrant sunshine. There was one tepid instant of resistance when she remembered that day in his office at Teragno, then it no longer seemed important. If he let her go, Olwyn was convinced, then she would perish.

Justin made love to her then as if he meant to cherish every inch of her body, sweetly ravishing her mouth, her cheeks and ears, throat and breasts with lingering tenderness, checking his own pounding need out of love and respect for her. At first Olwyn's body was limp and unresponsive under his hands and lips, then he felt a faint quiver go through her, and to Justin that first tiny response was more precious, more exciting, than anything he had ever experienced in the diamond fields.

Olwyn felt a quickening, a sharpening of her dulled senses as his firm, warm lips whispered upward from her ankle to her knee, then from her knee to her thigh, his fingers making a path for his lips to follow. She arched against him suddenly, the lassitude that had gripped her giving way to a feeling of expectancy, then urgency, as her tired flesh came tinglingly alive, the long battle of the last three months flying out of her head.

"Oh, why did you stay away so long!" she cried, at the same time plunging her fingers into his shining fair hair and bringing his face close to hers. Then before he could answer she kissed him passionately, her hands cupping the bulging muscles of his shoulders, his chest, her fingers sliding sensuously down the smooth bronzed flesh of his back, moving inward to his thigh, her heart leaping as she felt how powerfully he needed her, reassurance that at least that hadn't changed.

Justin's control slipped under her teasing fingers.

"I came here today to see you!" he admitted in a fierce, low whisper. "Not a day has passed since you left Teragno that I haven't longed to hold you, to kiss you, to be close like this with my dearest love."

"Love?" Olwyn's luminous golden eyes searched his, now dark and hot with passion. "Love, Justin?"

"Do you doubt it?" he said, and hungrily covered her lips with his own, sweat bursting out on his skin as he strove to enter her gently, to curb eight months of pent-up desire, afraid he would hurt her. But he needn't have worried. Within seconds her need blazed to match his own. The moment before she reached the brink of rapture Olwyn clutched him fiercely and cried, "I love you too! Oh, God, I love you! Love you . . ."

The first words Justin said to her afterward were, "I'm taking you back to Teragno." And when Olwyn looked at him questioningly, "Now! Today!" He held her away from him a little, his expression hardening as he shook his head. "And not a minute too soon. A week from now there would be nothing left of you. Scobbie had no right to work you so hard—"

Olwyn covered his lips with her hand but she was smiling, warm and contented as a kitten, her skin and eyes aglow. "It's my job—"

Justin caught her hand and kissed the palm. "From now on your job is to stay within arms' length of me, where I can make sure you get all the care you need, and all the love you need too," he added with a grin. Then he sobered. "You've been with Scobbie a year now. Your time is up. Now it's our time, Olwyn. I need you much more than he does."

Olwyn wanted to say yes, that she'd go with him immediately; that she yearned more than anything to stay by his side and never leave it again, but it wasn't that simple. The question of Knute Bleur couldn't just be swept aside, only to rear up again at a future date. And of course there was Hannah Scobbie; she couldn't desert Hannah while she was ill.

262 ◇ Catherine Linden

It was difficult to bring up the subject of Bleur and risk spoiling the new closeness between them. Wondering how to do it with the least risk to their happiness, Olwyn turned away and plucked a handful of grass and tossed it aimlessly into the pool while Justin sat watching her profile. He knew her so well, he sensed what was on her mind. "Hopefully," he said, "we've both matured over the last eight months and now realize what's most important to us." He picked up her hand and lightly stroked it with his thumb as he continued in the same serious vein, "I do, at least. I came here today determined to make things right between us." He sighed and smiled ruefully. "And to tell you how sorry I am about that day in my office at Teragno."

Olwyn turned her head and met his eyes. "Then you *do* believe me about your diamond?" She had to know; had to hear it from his own lips.

"Yes," Justin nodded, "I believe you, darling."

It disgusted him now to recall the vile suspicions he had once harbored about her, but since then he'd had ample time to sort out his priorities, to realize that diamonds weren't everything. It seemed incredible, on looking back, that he had once considered the possibility of Olwyn being in cahoots with Knute Bleur, making up her wild story about Bleur just to make it seem that they were enemies when in fact they were working together, she as a kind of scout near the diamond fields. This notion would have been ludicrous if it had involved any other woman but by then Justin had had ample opportunity to note that Olwyn was a very special woman, more spirited and daring than other females who had crossed his path. With her, he thought, anything was possible.

Well, any lingering doubts he might have had had been dispelled today, he thought as he gazed at her fondly. No one connected with the diamond industry would have needed to subject themselves to eight miserable months on a mission station, almost killing themselves in the process. There were less painful ways of lying low, if that had been her intention—which of course it hadn't.

He leaned forward and kissed her, then said softly, "I'm going to make you the happiest woman in Africa. You are already the most beautiful. Once back at Teragno—"

"I can't go back with you today, Justin, much as I long to."

Olwyn explained about Hannah Scobbie. Justin understood and sympathized—but it was hard to curb his impatience. He had craved Olwyn every minute for the past eight months. Further delay threatened to drive him out of his mind.

He made a suggestion then. "We can move Hannah to Teragno and she can convalesace in comfort there . . ."

Olwyn was already shaking her head. Hannah wouldn't leave James and James wouldn't leave Nuruzambora, especially as some of the natives were showing signs of interest in Christianity at last. Daily a handful would trickle down to listen to him preach. To James it seemed incidental that they usually brought their broken farm implements and guns with them, and these he would repair while telling them about God. "I don't think they are truly interested," Olwyn said with a sigh, "but no one can convince Mr. Scobbie. He feels he's making progress."

In the end it was decided that Olwyn would remain at Nuruzambora for one more month—but not a day longer.

"It will be the longest month of my life," Justin groaned.

"Mine too." Olwyn smiled at him.

They embraced fiercely, and Justin promised to return the next day with a very special gift for her. "Meet me here at this same time tomorrow," he said. "I want you all to myself for at least a little while, then we'll go together and tell Scobbie our plans."

Olwyn looked up at him earnestly as he sat astride his horse.

"You will come?"

"If you doubt it, I'll sweep you up and take you with me now."

Olwyn relaxed then and waved him off with a smile. Left alone in the glade she looked about her and felt a great sense of wonder at the change she felt in herself, from deepest gloom to radiant joy. Quite suddenly she began to laugh, then to twirl around on feet that suddenly felt light as thistledown. *I'm in love,* she thought, then she said it aloud, just to listen to the sound of it.

In the trees above her head the monkeys paused to listen, and somewhere in the woods a hyena shrieked with laughter, as if mocking her.

# 21

Justin was within two miles of Teragno when the shot rang out.

For perhaps the first time since he'd arrived in Africa he had been careless, riding along blind to everything but the future, his mind spilling over with glorious plans, seeing nothing but her, thinking of nothing but her, completely oblivious to his surroundings and with his instincts atuned to love rather than danger.

The bullet struck him between the shoulder blades, just grazing the top of his right lung, the impact sending him lurching forward in the saddle over the strong neck of his horse. He never saw the would-be assassin, nor attempted to twist around to look back. He could feel the warm blood gushing from the wound and knew, as he felt the weakness begin to take hold of him, that he would need every ounce of strength and will he possessed just to hang on. MacBeth, his horse, knew the way home, and if he could just stay in the saddle . . .

Olwyn arrived at the pool well before the appointed time the following day. As usual, she placed a huge fresh bouquet of wild flowers on the baby's grave and threw all the withered blooms away, at the same time feeling a little guilty for being so wondrously, deliriously happy in such a sad place.

Then Olwyn sat down to wait, but almost at once was up again, too restless to contain herself. She listened; she ran up the slope to the track and peered eagerly into the trees. Back at the pool, she decided to play a trick on Justin. She would hide in the bushes and watch him arrive and begin to look for her, and she'd keep him waiting just a tiny bit—if she could restrain herself—then she would spring out and throw herself into his arms and shower his face with kisses.

Laughing merrily, Olwyn crept into the shadows of a thicket above the pool where she would have a better view of the track. She hunched down and separated the branches slightly in front of her, her heart beating as excitedly as a mischievous child's. It was the quiet, hot time of day and everything was still, except for the occasional scolding cry of a monkey in the trees overhead when one of its own kind moved and disturbed its rest. A warm, earthy smell rose from the ground and mingled with the heavy scent of flowers releasing their perfume in the heat, and tiny sounds, not normally heard, came to her quite clearly; the low hum of bees gathering nectar, the cool-sounding splash of a frog leaping into the pool, a bird fluttering its wings to cool itself with a soft whirring of feathers.

A few minutes passed and Olwyn's legs began to ache and she changed her position. She stuck her head through the opening in the bush and listened. Not a sound.

Justin was a little late. Ten minutes passed and Olwyn left her hiding place—it no longer seemed like such fun—and returned to sit by the pool. An hour later she was still there, waiting. Something must have detained him, she told herself; something important. He would never have kept her hanging about like this otherwise. But he was a very busy man, her mind ran on, and these things happened. No, she wouldn't start to worry! He would come as he'd promised, though . . . perhaps not today.

An hour later Olwyn returned to the mission but she was back again at the pool the following day, and the day after that. Dropping handfuls of grass into the water, staring at her now sober face in the glassy surface, Olwyn told herself over and over that Justin did love her; had she not seen it for herself in his eyes? Something must have happened at Teragno. He would not have willingly stayed away . . .

Had he not already stayed away for eight long months! Was that the action of a man supposedly madly in love? she asked herself—and with that the sickening doubts flooded her mind. She remembered how Justin had made passionate love to her on the ship, then changed abruptly when he couldn't find his diamond. Then at Teragno he had accused her of selling him out to Knute Bleur. "You lied to me," he said in that hard voice that chilled her blood, "and you lied to James Scobbie. Go now, and stop wasting my time."

As he had wasted her time for the last few days! Could this be his revenge for what he imagined she had done to him? Olwyn fretted.

On the seventh day she threw herself down on the tall grass, near the spot where he had made such tender love to her, and wept until she had no tears left; until her eyes burned and her throat was stinging raw. A fierce physical pain doubled her over and Olwyn crouched on the grass and the world seemed to grow dark around her. What a gullible fool she had been! Justin had never truly loved her; all along he had loved his precious diamonds more. He was cruel and heartless, cold to the bone, in his way no different from Devlin Sproat!

Anguish suddenly gave way to fury. Frantically she scooped up water from the pool and dashed it against her face, hot and blotched with tears, the cool water sending a chill through her that was never really to leave her for a very long time to come. Something soft and warm and tender congealed and died inside Olwyn at that moment. When she walked up the slope for the last time, her face set and hard, she was a different person.

Later that day she sat down and wrote Justin a letter. It was brief, and perhaps it stretched the truth a little but she no longer cared. Surely her pride was worth something, too, she told herself grimly.

"I hope you didn't keep our tryst at the pool on November second," she wrote. "After seeing you on the first I went home and did some serious thinking and I'm afraid I concluded that we have nothing whatsoever in common. In light of that, I have no desire to see you again. I hope you will respect my wishes." She signed it simply, "Olwyn Moore."

She sent it to Teragno a few days later with a traveling peddler, and once it was away Olwyn felt a little better, thinking that at least Wentworth would never know that she'd lowered herself by waiting all these days at the pool; waited in vain.

Oddly enough, it was Maury Howell who brought laughter to the mission station at Nuruzambora again. Howell had quickly established himself at Klipdrift and started digging with his usual energy and exuberance, and within a week had found his first diamond —and a decent stone too! The following week he uncovered three more, not as good, but the kopje walloper who bought them found himself paying out more money than he normally did; Maury was a persuasive bargainer. Besides, he had made a study of diamonds and couldn't be fooled as so many of the other diggers were.

By the end of the month Howell felt on top of the

world, convinced he had found his niche at last. The promise of prosperity and increasing riches made him benevolent and expansive. Soon he was advising the other young hopefuls at the new Klipdrift strike, and it gave him an added sense of importance and power to be in a position where others looked to him for direction, where at the Cape he had been little more than a lowly serf at the bottom of the great government machine, one that ground far too slowly and sluggishly for a man of his obvious ability. Nobody had taken him seriously there, he knew that, and it had always irked him. If only those same friends could see him now!

It was during a vicious fight at one of the rickety taverns dotting the diamond field that Howell's mind was jolted to recall young Oliver Moore.

"What we need up here is a church!" one of the overseers shouted as he booted the culprits out of the tavern. "What we don't need is any more bars."

Howell, seated at a table surrounded by a crowd of his young protégés, suddenly thought of James Scobbie and the mission station at Nuruzambora, a place he had once promised to visit. Of course that had been before he knew what Oliver Moore was like. Still, his curious mind was intrigued to know how they had fared at Nuruzambora and the temptation to go there and brag a little was too much for him to resist.

Maury called the overseer over and said importantly, "I might have a preacher for you. Just give me a few more days to look him up."

At the end of the month he mounted a borrowed horse and set off to find the spot where young Moore had buried himself, at the same time thinking that the lad was a fool.

Maury, when he finally located the mission, was in for a shock. For one of the few times in his life he was speechless when James Scobbie led Oliver out of the house and onto the veranda and the pair of them stood there looking down to where he waited in the clearing below. "Behold, Oliver Moore!" said James, and with a flourish indicated his assistant.

Howell's mouth sagged open. His agile mind reeled as he gazed up at the beautiful girl who stood there with an amused smile on her face. So comical did Maury look at that moment that Scobbie burst out laughing and continued to laugh so uproariously that Hannah finally dragged herself out of bed to see what all the hilarity was about—and ended up smiling too.

"Tarnation!" Howell cried, torn between anger and mirth. "What in the love of God is going on here?" He ran up the stairs and stared hard into the girl's face, then looked at James. "She's his twin, isn't she? I mean to say—"

"No." Olwyn shook her head. "I'm the same person you met on the boat." She glanced at Scobbie, then added quietly, diffidently, "I passed myself off as a man to get the job with Mr. Scobbie."

"What!" Again a turbulent mixture of emotions crossed Maury's face, but he ended up beaming, delighted with his surprise. "I knew it!" He laughed, slapping his thighs. "I knew it all along! In here"—he tapped his head—"I figured out that no man on earth could be so delicate and beautiful. It stands to reason . . ." Again words failed him.

Howell was persuaded to stay for supper, then overnight. He agreed so readily that James winked at Hannah, who, for the first time since Isobel had died, stayed up to dine with them. It was a cheery meal. Howell, when he could tear his eyes away from Olwyn, fairly bubbled over with excitement about his new life on the diamond field. He bragged a little about how successful he had been, how he had carefully made a study of the gems so that now other diggers came to him for guidance. He told them funny stories, then hair-raising tales that had Jamie and Harold hanging onto his every word, as stimulated and interested as the adults. The children were overjoyed when Maury promised to take them to see the fields for themselves, then he turned to James and added, "You must come, too, sir. They need you desperately at Klipdrift. I think you'll find the men there worse than the savages at Nuruzambora." And carried away with himself, he said, "I will personally guarantee you a large congregation—even if I have to drag them in by the hair of their heads!"

James perked up at once. "Well, well," he said, "that's certainly something worth considering. I'm not a man to turn down an opportunity to preach the gospel, wherever it may be. We must talk about this again, Mr. Howell—"

"Oh, please call me Maury," the young man gushed, his green eyes bright in the light from the fire, especially when they turned to Olwyn. "I dare to hope that we shall all be good friends and see a lot of each other. I so enjoyed meeting you on the ship coming over, and I made up my mind then that I would look you up at the first opportunity."

James nodded, smiling dryly. Howell had barely said two words to him on the *Randolph* but he supposed that was beside the point. The young fellow was engaging and entertaining. His coming had swept the gloom from the mission and lured his wife out of bed at last. And Olwyn . . . Scobbie eyed his assistant consideringly, trying to gauge how she felt about their unexpected visitor, and failed. The girl looked pleasant, interested, but reserved. Perhaps a little skeptical, he thought. It suddenly occurred to James that she had been unusually quiet and distant lately, but of course like the rest of them she had been devastated when wee Isobel died. Poor lass, she had almost killed herself trying to save the baby. James made a note to himself then to speak to her about that, to tell her how much he appreciated it. Until now he hadn't had the heart to mention their loss.

When he left the next day Maury promised to visit them again in a week. He returned three days later, his

arms loaded with gifts—boxes of sweets for Hannah
and the boys, coffee and salt for James, since he'd
mentioned being short of these items, and a length of
pale lemon muslin for Olwyn so that she could make
herself a pretty dress.

Howell came for Christmas with more presents,
then again at New Year. He galloped into the mission
regularly like a breath of fresh spring air, full of
laughter and stories and crackling energy, and if at the
same time he boasted a lot and seemed a bit con-
ceited, they forgave him. The boys admired Maury
and Hannah wanted to mother him. James suspected
he was a rascal but still found him amusing and
likeable.

Olwyn . . . Olwyn continued to be cool, distant,
and reserved, little realizing that her very remoteness
was an irresistible challenge to a man of Howell's
nature. He had fallen instantly in love with her from
the moment she had appeared on Scobbie's veranda,
and Maury yearned to tell her so in his own flowery
way, while at the same time showering her with
presents. But he had been well brought up for all that
he had turned out to be the black sheep of his family,
and he made up his mind to court her properly, as a
gentleman should, anxious that he should stand tall in
her eyes. Besides, instinct warned him that any impetuous move on his part would immediately put her off,
a thought too deflating to contemplate.

He had already made up his mind to marry Olwyn.

At Teragno, Justin was fighting for his life. A
surgeon had been brought all the way up from
Grahamstown to remove the bullet and treat the
severe infection that had set in. On top of that he was
very weak from loss of blood.

For the entire month of November he lay in a fever
of delirium hovering on the brink of death, but by
mid-December he had rallied a little, though he was
still far from able to attend to business or even glance

at the mail awaiting his attention in his office. It was the beginning of January before Kelly finally gave in and brought the mail into his bedroom. Among it Justin found the letter from Olwyn, telling him that she hadn't kept their appointment after all, nor wanted anything more to do with him.

That same day Tondo informed his master that James Scobbie and family had visited the diamond fields, where they had been shown around by a young man called Maury Howell. "He new here," said Tondo, grinning, "but everybody know him already." The black man made snapping motions with his fingers to indicate a fast talker. "Howell think he chief," Tondo went on with a scornful laugh. "He strut about and show off to that girl . . ." Uncertain as to how it was between his master and "that girl," the Griqua broke off suddenly, rubbing his ears with his knuckles as he always did when he was nervous.

"Olwyn Moore?" Justin inquired mildly, none of his inner turmoil showing on his face.

Tondo nodded.

"I think they'd be good for each other," Justin said bitterly.

Again Tondo nodded, but he sensed he had made a mistake.

The man who shot Justin was never found or punished, but his own conscience punished him enough. The instant he pulled the trigger, Jonus van Klerk was appalled at himself. He knew then that a demon had taken root in his head and that God had deserted him.

It had been a spur-of-the-moment thing. He had just come from chasing yet another wagonload of rowdy prospectors off his land, and this time they had killed and cooked one of his oxen. Further, they had laughed and jeered at him and threatened to drive the rest of his herd off the edge of a cliff. Only his towering rage and his warning that he would shoot them all on the spot finally got rid of them. Then, on his way home, he had spotted Wentworth in the distance, his golden head and huge black stallion unmistakable.

Wentworth had been whistling jauntily, the sound of a happy man at peace with the world but pure mockery to the ears of the Boer listening to him. Without knowing what he was about to do, only that his spirit was black with anger, van Klerk melted into the trees. Wentworth had passed with a smile on his face. Watching him, something exploded inside van Klerk's head. The next thing he knew he had rushed out behind him, raised his rifle, and squeezed the trigger. The instant he did Jonus knew that he, as much as Wentworth, was doomed; that he would pay dearly for his sin. No matter how much the man had wronged him, van Klerk knew he had no right to judge, let alone condemn, another human being.

From then on the Boer lived in dread.

In March, the beginning of autumn, they had a great deal of rain, always a welcome sight to farmers on the dry veld. Riding home from market in Hopetown, van Klerk and his son were caught in the downpour and quickly drenched to the skin. "Good growing weather, ja, Pieter?" the Boer remarked with a glance at the teeming sky. "And good day at market too." He slapped his saddle bag, adding, "Soon we'll have enough money to build a fine new barn."

The youth nodded. "I'll paint a sign for it with the oils you bought me. It will say, Jonus van Klerk and Son."

His father laughed and looked at him fondly as they rode along. His heart swelled with such love and pride in his only son that he sometimes felt it would burst. His Pieter had been born to paint pictures—and he had no choice but to make a farmer out of him. Yet not one word of complaint had ever passed the lad's lips. He had the sweet nature of an angel—

As the thought crossed his mind Jonus felt a fleeting chill.

"We should hasten," he said, spurring up his horse.

"And pull up the hood of your cloak, Pieter. Next time we go to market I'll buy you a proper cape and hat. You are a man now and shouldn't wear children's garments."

The boy threw him a smile that pierced his father's heart.

# 22

I love you, surely you must realize that?" Maury Howell cried in an impassioned voice, seizing her hand and covering it with avid kisses. "I'm out of my mind with love for you, my sweetest, darling Olwyn, and you won't as much as grant me one single kiss!"

Olwyn gazed at him cynically. She was completely unmoved. Love no longer interested her. So often it was merely a pretty word to mask a baser emotion—lust.

Maury's outburst had spoiled a perfectly delightful picnic, she was thinking. They had ridden out into the hills on his horse—Howell owned one of his own now—and had found a pretty spot overlooking the valley where they spread out their blanket, then they'd settled down to devour the delicious basket of food he had brought and afterward enjoyed yet another of their long, interesting talks.

Then he had to ruin things by kneeling in front of her, gazing into her eyes with earnest persuasion. "I can offer you a good life," he went on. "Certainly vastly better than the one you have now at the mission station. And later," he sucked in an excited breath, "and I don't mean *much* later, I'll be able to offer you much more. You see, I own many claims at Klipdrift now and most of them are producing nicely. Soon I'll be a man of means, Olwyn, and—and I want you to marry me!" he burst out.

Olwyn still regarded him coolly but with slightly more interest. Marriage? Well, this put an entirely different slant on things. Assuming that he meant it, of course. As Olwyn well knew, men would say anything to get their way, though Justin Wentworth had stopped short of mentioning the word marriage. Perhaps he'd felt that he didn't have to go that far. A man like Wentworth, worldly, experienced, had other ways of making a girl do what he wanted—

"We'll set the wedding for September," Maury gushed on, breaking into her thoughts. "James Scobbie can conduct the service—"

"I didn't say I would marry you," Olwyn snapped, determined not to be pushed into anything ever again.

"Oh, but you will!" Maury beseeched, his green eyes imploring her, his smile coaxing, his very manner filling Olwyn with a delicious sense of power—power she had never been able to exert over Justin Wentworth! "I'm going to shower you with everything your heart desires," Howell promised. "Beautiful clothes, jewels, fine homes—"

At that Olwyn broke down and laughed. "Maury, dear, you aren't a rich man yet!"

The word dear emboldened him and he leaned forward and kissed her mouth, and though Olwyn stiffened and instantly pulled back, the touch of her soft lips, after months of hopeless yearning, set the blood pounding through Howell's veins. There she sat so tantalizingly close to him in her pale lemon-yellow gown made from the muslin he had given her, the delicate color and gauzy material against her dark beauty turning her into an exotic butterfly—one that he felt might fly away from him at any second.

With a loud groan he grabbed her and greedily, frantically ravished her mouth with his, kissing her gluttonously like a starving man seeking nourishment, his lips moving to her cheeks, her eyes, her ears—then dropping suddenly to the creamy swell of her breasts rising proudly from the rounded neckline of her gown.

At that he completely lost his head. It had been many months since he'd had a woman, and never had he enjoyed a woman remotely as beautiful as this. "My sweet darling!" he chocked, bending her back on the blanket. "I can scarcely wait to marry you. Oh, Olwyn, dearest . . ." He crushed his mouth to hers, at the same time leaning over her so that she could plainly feel his need—but it left her ice cold.

Her mind was sharp and clear, no longer dulled by her emotions. Olwyn reminded herself that for several weeks now she'd been plagued by a vague worry, one she hadn't allowed herself to dwell on. She also reminded herself that she genuinely liked Maury Howell and enjoyed his company. Further, she supposed he was a very good catch, and few eligible men appeared at the mission station.

All these things she coldly considered—as she meant to consider everything from now on, always with her own best interests in mind—at last! If it meant hardening her heart, then so be it, Olwyn told herself. What had a soft heart brought her but anguish!

When she felt Maury's hand slide up under her gown, Olwyn cuffed him smartly on the ear. "Stop that this instant! How dare you treat me like a common slut!"

Howell was immediately contrite and stammered out an apology, saying her radiant beauty had turned his head and promising it wouldn't happen again.

He caught both her hands in his. "Say you'll marry me and I'll be the happiest man in all Africa," he begged.

Olwyn studied him in a detached way, his rumpled black curls, bright green eyes, the flush on his face, and felt how much he desired her, a powerful emotion she herself had once felt for another man.

"I'll think about it," she replied.

A week later Harold Scobbie came across Olwyn being sick behind the henhouse.

"What's the matter, Olwyn?" he asked, concern in his voice. "You've been sick a lot since New Year. You are just like Mama was when she was having the baby."

Olwyn finally had to confront it—she was pregnant! No longer could she convince herself that her monthly flow always stopped when she was under stress, as it had at the time her father had died, then after Devlin Sproat had attacked her and, more recently, during the last terrible month when she had struggled to save baby Isobel's life.

She was going to have his baby! It was the very worst thing that could have happened to her. Bad enough that he had loved and left her. Now she was being made to pay, to suffer the shame, disgrace, the stigma of having an illegitimate child, and left to raise that child alone. Olwyn knew she couldn't hide it from the Scobbies but she made up her mind then that they would never know the father's name, not even if James tried to beat it out of her.

Half an hour later, after she had told the Scobbies the truth, he almost did. "I demand to know who the father is!" James roared, his face livid with anger. "It's Howell, isn't it? Well, he shall marry you at once!"

Hannah stared at her in horror, wailing, "Oh, how could you? Think of the scandal, the disgrace. How could you do this to us, to yourself?"

Olwyn bowed her head and suffered their abuse in silence, her teeth clenched, lips tight, fuming inwardly when she thought of the man who was responsible and who had walked away scotfree, leaving her to bear the brunt of it. James was raving about Maury Howell but Maury would never marry her now, even if she wanted him to. She was trapped, with no way to turn.

How would she ever raise a child on her own? Olwyn asked herself. She was penniless, isolated on a remote mission station, forced to live with people who detested her now that she'd brought shame to their door.

After ranting on about fallen women and Jezebels and the sin of fornication Scobbie ended by announcing that he would ride out and pay Maury Howell a visit.

"He will make a respectable woman of you!" James shouted. "Or as respectable as you can be at this late date."

Olwyn lifted her head then and looked at him steadily.

"Go then," she said dully, "but I won't be here when you get back. I'm not marrying Maury Howell!" she suddenly screamed, her nerves snapping. "I'll kill myself first."

Everything went silent as the Scobbies gaped at her, then Hannah, recovering herself first, took her husband's arm firmly and led him outside onto the veranda. She was pale and shaken herself but struggled to control her shock and horror at the situation she found herself in, the stuff nightmares were made of to a woman of Hannah Scobbie's refined upbringing. All she could think of was, *Thank the merciful Lord we aren't in Glasgow now!*

"All right, James, all right," she began, and took a deep breath and continued in an undertone, "We must try to calm ourselves and not be too hasty. It's horrendous, of course, but . . . we owe the girl a great deal and must never forget that." She looked into his furious face and added softly, "Remember how good she was with Isobel? She fought to save the baby to the end."

Their eyes met and Scobbie's tense shoulders slumped. "Yes . . . it's true, and all along she has worked for nothing. That has always bothered me, Hannah."

She patted his arm. "We'll manage somehow. At

least we are off the beaten track here. But I wonder why she is so against marrying Maury Howell; I thought she liked him. Perhaps not as much as she liked Mr. Wentworth—" Hannah broke off then, her eyes wide. "You don't think—"

"Impossible!" said James, shaking his head. "It's Howell, all right. Olwyn hasn't seen Justin Wentworth for a year."

There was a heavy, oppressive atmosphere in the clearing that night as they all sat around the huge camp fire. As always happened, their men were quick to pick up the mood of the family, though they weren't exactly sure at that point what was wrong. They'd had a thunderstorm late that afternoon, and as dusk fell a thick mist rose steaming from the ground and swirled about the trees surrounding the camp, adding a ghostly quality to the gloom.

Mick kept getting up to check this or that, and Olwyn heard him mutter to one of the natives, "It's too quiet. There's a strange feeling . . ."

The other man nodded in their direction to where the family always sat together, as if to say they were the cause of it. Olwyn dropped her eyes and stared at the food on her tin plate—and suddenly her stomach gave a sickening lurch that caused her to drop her dish and rush headlong for the hen house. It was set back from the house at the outer rim of the clearing and the light from the fire barely penetrated the darkness. As she stumbled around to the rear of the building she happened to raise her head—and saw white faces staring at her from the trees. Even as she blinked, startled, they vanished like phantoms.

Olwyn stood stock still, her heart squeezed tight with terror, a kind of icy paralysis freezing her limbs. Had she really seen them? she asked herself. A moment ago she had felt faint and sick, her head spinning as a spasm of nausea washed over her. Might that have been the cause of her weird vision? After the uproar earlier today she dreaded to make a fuss.

Olwyn slowly backed away and edged around to the

front of the hen house, her eyes fixed on the woods. Suddenly a ghostly white naked figure burst from the misty darkness not twenty feet behind her, and in a moment of shocking clarity Olwyn saw him clearly in the light from the fire. His entire body was covered with some sort of ashy substance. Only the sockets of his eyes were black. Transfixed, she saw his lips draw back in a snarl to expose jagged, pointed teeth, then he raised his bow and inserted his poisoned arrow.

Olwyn shrieked at the top of her lungs and collapsed, and the arrow struck the hen house with a dull thunk, only inches above her head. In a flash the clearing was surrounded, the apparitions emerging out of the dark woods. Before James and Mick and the other men could reach for their guns four of the crew lay dead. The quiet of the mission erupted in frantic gunfire.

Olwyn lay where she had fallen, oblivious to the gruesome figure creeping out of the woods toward her. In a second he crouched above her, his breath excited and fast, his eyes devouring. The Imba seized her roughly and started to toss her over his shoulder when a shot exploded behind him. For a second he froze, the girl tumbling out of his arms, then he sprawled face down in the dust.

Harold Scobbie, now a strapping six-footer nearing his fifteenth birthday, raced across the clearing, now blazing with gunfire, and hastily picked Olwyn up and deposited her in the hen house with three dozen squawking chickens, all fluttering madly on their perches, furious at the disturbance. Then Harold ran back to join the others, leaping over several ashen bodies as he went, but in minutes it was all over. A hush descended on the mission again. The Imba had vanished as suddenly as they had appeared.

The next morning at dawn, as they were burying the dead, Hal commented to his father, "If Olwyn hadn't gotten sick and gone to the hen house we would all have been dead before we knew what was happening

—or taken back to their kraal as captives for their feast. It was her cry that saved us."

James glanced at his son and realized that he was growing up, and like most men he had observed, had become enamored with the girl, but all he said was, "God works in mysterious ways, Harold. He does indeed."

Harold plucked up the courage to mention something that had been on his mind. "Papa, I don't care for the way M'Buru looks at Olwyn. I've noticed she always hurries into the house when he comes to visit, and he's been paying us a lot of visits lately." Hal went on worriedly, slightly angry. "But he always asks to see leopard woman and she's forced to come out. I don't like it, Papa," the boy repeated, his hands tightening to fists. "I'd shoot him if he tried to hurt her."

James heaved a loud sigh that was more like a groan.

Harold grabbed his arm. "Can't we go away from here?" His blue eyes were pleading. "Poor Mama, I swear she's about to have a nervous breakdown after all the things that have happened—"

"But the Society won't pay me if I quit the mission!" Scobbie burst out in a despairing tone. "And we need money to survive, lad. Where would I go? What else can I do?" James looked away, admitting, "There's nothing left for me in Scotland, so it would be pointless to return there."

Hal sucked in a deep breath, steeling himself against the outburst that he felt certain would follow his announcement. "I want to work in the diamond fields! I'm old enough," he rushed on when James turned to stare at him, frowning. "Maury said there's lots of boys younger than me at Klipdrift." The strong young hand tightened eagerly, persuasively on his father's arm, "Please let me try, Papa? Please! I know I could do well and earn money for the family."

In utter horror Harold watched his father break down in tears.

"It seems I'm useless," James choked.

Scobbie jumped to his feet and hurried, almost ran, off into the woods. Hal sat by the grave they'd been digging, staring after him, wishing heartily that his father had shouted and roared at him, or even hit him, rather than what he had just done. He was still sitting there gloomily when an agitated Jonus van Klerk galloped into the mission, yelling that he needed the doctor immediately. His son Pieter was gravely ill.

Olwyn spent five harrowing days at the van Klerk farm battling to save the teenager's life. Once she'd examined him and reviewed the symptoms—the severe headache, chills, high temperature, and the rapid, shallow breathing and steady pain in the chest— Olwyn knew that Pieter had pneumonia, one of the great killers at that time. When he coughed up a rusty, blood-flecked sputum and his pulse, instead of being strong and pounding, was feeble and excessively rapid, Olwyn's first fear was that Pieter van Klerk was on the verge of going into heart failure.

His mother, thinking she was doing the right thing, had put the boy to bed in a tiny dark room with the window tightly closed and a gigantic fire blazing. Further, she had a veritable mountain of blankets piled on top of her son to keep him warm. The room was stifling and airless, the covers stacked on top of the patient too heavy, making it all the harder for him to breathe.

Olwyn first had him moved to a bigger, better-ventilated room, and placed his bed in such a position that the sunlight coming in the window fell across the patient. Since he'd been having cold sweats for the past two days, Olwyn stripped him off—much to his mother's horror, terrified as Helga was that he would catch more cold—and gave him a sponge down with tepid water, then slipped a clean nightshirt over his head. She discarded the pile of heavy quilts in favor of two warm woolen blankets. Next she dosed Pieter with sal volatile to stimulate his flagging heart and gave him nine grains of quinine to bring down his raging temperature.

In spite of round-the-clock care the patient trembled on the brink of death for the next two days. In the other room Olwyn could hear his five adoring sisters wailing and lamenting, and in Pieter's room Helga and Jonus constantly got in her way, hovering over their son, questioning her treatment, even going so far as to ask her if she knew what she was doing. "If he dies," the white-faced father cried at one point, "then I'll shoot myself. This is all my fault. I've been an evil, wicked man and this is God's way of punishing me, the worst way He could have chosen." He began to sob harshly then, his thick shoulders heaving, his eyes bleak. He looked at Olwyn and suddenly burst out, "Save him, girl, and everything I own is yours! I have to atone, you see . . . I must, I must . . ."

Olwyn glanced up at van Klerk in surprise, startled at how this normally tough, unemotional man had crumbled. It was perfectly natural that he would be dreadfully upset but knowing van Klerk, Olwyn would have expected him to hide it. Not so. He was nearly hysterical, babbling about sin and wickedness when he was the most religious of men and lived strictly by the Book. Olwyn had no idea what he could be referring to but patiently explained, "I don't want anything, Mr. van Klerk. Like you, I only want Pieter to get well."

Exhausted as she was, Olwyn knew she didn't dare doze off to sleep. Death could come so suddenly in such cases; she was terrified it might steal up on Pieter if she as much as closed her eyes. As it was, each time his tired heart flagged she dosed him with digitalis, forced to increase the amount each time. Helga van Klerk, unlike her husband, who kept up his pacing and muttering about sin—and the patient's five devoted sisters in the next room whom she could hear weeping and lamenting—sat quietly now watching Olwyn battling to save her son, gratitude and trust in the washed-out blue eyes. At one point she touched Olwyn's hand and said gently, "You rest now. You've done everything humanly possible. Pieter is now in God's hands."

But Olwyn couldn't rest. "I'll make him a poultice," she said, "for the pain in his chest. It might help."

They struggled against death all that night and into the third day.

That afternoon the crisis came. Pieter's ashen face flushed bright red and he began to perspire copiously. He stopped panting for breath and began to breathe more normally and his pulse slowed considerably. Leaning over him, Olwyn saw that he was now sleeping much more peacefully, and her heart gave a leap of hope and relief.

At ten o'clock that evening the boy was able to take a little beef broth and a few spoonfuls of milk pudding. By morning Olwyn felt fairly confident that he was on the mend, though he would still have to be watched carefully and allowed a long time to convalesce, every care taken to prevent a relapse.

She explained all this to his mother, also advising her on the type of nourishing food to feed the patient, who was still very weak, but had finally managed to give them one of his slow, shy smiles.

Jonus van Klerk's joy was touching to watch. He laughed, he sobbed, he kissed his son, Olwyn, his wife, and each of his daughters. For the first time since she had known him, Olwyn saw softness, radiance in that sober, craggy face. Van Klerk was like a man reborn, and his wife and daughters, who had often borne the brunt of his harsh nature, regarded him in wonder, astounded at the change in him, a change that was to last.

Olwyn left the farm on the fifth day with a gold ring that had belonged to Helga's mother. "You must take it," Helga pressed, her eyes brimming. "You must. You have given me back my son."

The girls came to Olwyn shyly and thrust home-made gifts into her hands, pieces of sewing they had labored over, a length of satin ribbon, a pretty shell. Like their mother, they insisted she accept these small offerings, all they had to give. It was their way of showing their deep gratitude, and rather than offend them Olwyn accepted—though that first sweet smile from Pieter had been thanks enough.

In the yard of the farm van Klerk, too, had a gift—a donkey.

At Olwyn's look of astonishment he said, "He's not young but he's sound. And remember, the tsetse fly cannot hurt this creature, as it does the horse, so he can take you anywhere you want to go." He smiled at her, adding, "Now get in the saddle. There's something else I wish to show you."

They detoured before they returned to the mission station and rode up into the veld near the Orange River quite close to Teragno property. This stretch of van Klerk's land was the part Wentworth had been interested in purchasing, though Olwyn had no way of knowing that.

They stopped and Jonus waved around him. "This fifty-acre parcel of land is now yours," he announced. "Today I will ride into Hopetown and make everything legal. It's not good land, unfortunately," he went on with a sigh. "Little of the land is good here. But you could graze a few head of cattle or even some sheep and with work it would produce a few crops." He smiled, adding, "Do with it as you wish, and with my blessing." He screwed up his eyes and glanced upriver to where, in the far distance, they could just make out the hillocks and rubble and white tents of the prospectors' camp, where about two thousand diggers were still avidly working Teragno land.

Van Klerk hunched his shoulders, then let them sag. "You know, there was a time when the sight of that camp enraged me," he told the girl quietly. "Now . . . what does it matter? Perhaps it was meant to be," he continued, as if thinking aloud. "Who am I to judge? It might be His way of bringing prosperity to the area . . ."

Olwyn was flabbergasted with the gift. For a Boer to part with his land was akin to parting with his life's blood, regardless of how poor that land might be. She thanked van Klerk warmly and started to refuse to accept it, but Jonus wouldn't hear of it. "It is yours," he repeated firmly, and with a wave to the donkey, "and he will bring you here whenever you wish to visit, for land without a way to reach it is useless."

Impulsively, Olwyn hugged him fiercely. "Oh, Mr. van Klerk, I—I don't know what to say—"

"Say nothing," he interrupted, hugging her back. "I will pray it brings you happiness and prosperity."

Olwyn's eyes sparkled as they rode around her land. It seemed to her the most beautiful land on earth. Every tree, blade of grass, even a turquoise length of the Orange River—all hers! At one point she jumped from the donkey, bent down, and scooped up huge handfuls of the earth, laughing as she let it trickle through her fingers. "Some day I will build a house here!" she burst out, her mind soaring. "Some day there will be cattle, horses, and sheep. Yes, and crops, and . . ."

Jonus sat his horse, smiling, pleased that she shared his deep reverence for the land, though experienced as he was, he knew a miracle would have to take place before she could do all the things she talked of doing. Still, the girl was happy and he let her dream. Sometimes dreams were all he'd had to sustain him through the years. When they finally left the property and started down the track for the long ride back to the mission station Jonus van Klerk was satisfied that he'd done what he could to make restitution for his crime, even if in a roundabout way. And Justin Wentworth, he had heard, had recovered. Perhaps, he mused, God hadn't forsaken him after all.

James Scobbie faced Howell grimly. "You are no longer welcome here. Olwyn doesn't wish to see you, let alone marry you."

Maury's face flushed a deep red. He recalled the last time he had seen Olwyn on the day of their picnic, and how angry she had been when he had lost his head. Still, she had seemed to forgive him and agreed that they could remain friends.

Howell stood his ground at the mission station and faced up to Scobbie. "Where is she? I would like to hear this from her own lips."

James's face tightened. "She has gone to visit friends—"

"Friends?" Maury looked puzzled. "What friends? Olwyn never mentioned—"

"That's no concern of yours," the missionary interrupted coldly, his eyes hard when he thought of how they had welcomed this man to the mission station— and how Maury had repaid their hospitality. James was convinced now that Howell was the father of Olwyn's child, and had this been Scotland she would have been forced to marry him, like it or not! Once he had recovered from his first shock at hearing the news, Scobbie reasoned that Wentworth couldn't possibly be the man. To the best of his knowledge Olwyn hadn't seen Wentworth since the day they left Teragno, and that was a year ago now.

When Olwyn returned from the van Klerk farm James prudently kept silent about Maury Howell's visit, thinking that if she wasn't going to marry him then the young reprobate was best forgotten. Certainly he wanted nothing more to do with him. Just the sight of Howell made his blood boil, and it was all he could do to restrain himself from taking a whip to the rogue—which he would if he dared come near the mission again.

Olwyn had exciting news to tell them; first that Pieter had recovered, then about her gifts from the van Klerks. Both Hannah and James were amazed to hear that the Boer had parted with some of his precious land; that certainly didn't sound like Jonus van Klerk, Scobbie found himself thinking.

"Does this mean that you will be leaving us?" James inquired somewhat diffidently, with a sidelong glance at his wife.

"Oh . . . no, of course not." Olwyn looked at them and suddenly wondered if they wanted her to go now that she'd turned out to be an embarrassment to them. After an awkward silence she ventured, "That is—I mean, if you'd rather that I leave?"

"You must suit yourself," Scobbie replied. He didn't want her to go but since he still couldn't afford to pay her, felt that it wasn't his decision to make.

For the next week things went on as usual at Nuruzambora, with James conducting his late-afternoon church in the clearing, reading the gospel and singing hymns with his modest congregation of Griquas who filtered down from the village, most of them bringing something to barter for beads and cloth, others with articles to be repaired. Olwyn noticed that many of the natives chattered away to each other during the service. Some even laughed at James when he occasionally got carried away with the power of the scriptures, raising his voice, stamping up and down, and shaking his fist at them in frustration.

The Griquas found these times highly entertaining.

Olwyn knew then that Scobbie was wasting his time. These people much preferred their own more flamboyant forms of worship, their witch doctor and pagan rituals to the dull, rigid rules and self-sacrifice demanded by the white man's God. Sometimes she wondered if they had a right to try to convert the natives at all. From what she had observed they seemed perfectly happy with their life; they even accepted the harsh form of justice doled out by M'Buru. There was very little crime in Nuruzambora Village—M'Buru's Court saw to that!

While James struggled to get his message across, Olwyn worked with the women and took care of anyone who happened to be sick, and there was always someone ailing or recovering from an injury at

Nuruzambora. She also helped Flo and Hannah with the cooking, washing, and cleaning. They had their times for making soap and candles, for drying and smoking meat, for mending and sewing.

The warm relationship Olwyn had established with Hannah was now strained. The older woman never mentioned her pregnancy. Olwyn could see that the thought of it embarrassed and offended Hannah's delicate sensibilities, the prospect of an illegitimate baby shocking and abhorrent to one raised in the Victorian strictness of upper-class Glasgow. Again Olwyn was left feeling ostracized, shut out, lonely, even though Hannah was unfailingly kind and considerate. More than anything Olwyn yearned for somebody to talk to but Hannah couldn't bring herself to discuss the matter that filled both their thoughts.

When Olwyn first broached the idea of visiting her land the Scobbies tried to dissuade her, but seeing she wouldn't be put off, they ordered Mick to accompany her. Olwyn supposed it was better than not going at all, though she really wanted to be alone to think, something impossible to do with the chatty Hottentot by her side.

Her depressed spirits immediately rose when she reached her own land. The vast sun-scorched plain was always cracked and dusty-dry in summer, but now, after the heavy rain at the beginning of March, it had been magically transformed. A sea of waving green grass and golden wild flowers swept away to a blue horizon, with here and there a gnarled baobab tree black against the sky. The river had begun to fill with sparkling water that gurgled merrily over its gravel bed, a pleasant sound in the stillness. Delicate antelopes grazed; birds sang.

"Oh, is it not beautiful?" the girl cried, turning to Mick. Then she had a burst of inspiration. "I'm going to call it Moorelands!"

The Hottentot was not impressed. He continued to suck on a blade of grass for a moment, then spat it out.

"This land"—he waved his arm—"is bitter and dry. Soon all this grass wither and die and everything bake as before. It no use—"

"Stop!" Olwyn clapped hands over her ears. "It's my land and I love it. With a lot of work it can produce . . . something."

"Ja, ja, something," the little man repeated cynically. "But what?"

To Olwyn's annoyance he then turned in the saddle and squinted in the direction of the prospectors' camp about a quarter of a mile away, a sight much more interesting to Mick than the boring veld she wanted him to admire. He placed two fingers to his lips and emitted a piercing whistle, then waved his arms to attract attention.

Angrily Olwyn grabbed one of those arms and scolded, "Stop that this instant! What on earth are you doing?"

"We go see them," Mick suggested hopefully. He licked his parched lips. "I's thirsty and they has beer in camp—"

"No, indeed we will not!" Olwyn snapped, her expression grim. "We will ride over my land and then return home, and if you are thirsty, then drink the water in your canteen. We are not going near that camp, I assure you!"

Standing in the open veld as they were, they were easily seen, even from a distance away. The diggers at Teragno yelled, waved, and whistled at them, but Olwyn ignored them, even as Mick looked back longingly, thinking of the beer. For the remainder of their time at Moorelands the Hottentot muttered and complained under his breath, quite spoiling Olwyn's visit to her property. She made up her mind then never to bring him back again.

But the land drew her. The urge to return there was strong, insistent, finally overpowering. A week later she grabbed a gun and slipped away by herself during siesta, leaving a note behind so the Scobbies wouldn't worry. The closer she got to Moorelands the more her spirits rose, but she had barely prodded Amos up the kopje to the plain when she heard another rider galloping toward her from the direction of the camp at Teragno.

There was one instant when Olwyn refused to turn her head and look; one second when she closed her eyes against the dizzy surge of hope that overwhelmed her, knocking the breath from her lungs. Then her hands tightened on the reins until the knuckles gleamed as white as the dried bones littering the veld, and the hot fury poured through her blood like liquid fire.

## 23

Justin reined in his horse about ten feet away and in a moment of vivid clarity Olwyn saw them as an artist would, the powerful black stallion and his tall, blond rider, as if cast in bronze against a sea of waving gold.

She felt something leap and expand inside her as his eyes met hers and the silence was suddenly full of chaos: her clamoring heart, harried breathing, the blood pulsing in her ears. The brittle calm shattered and Olwyn felt herself trembling in agitation under his keen, probing gaze, those eyes that always saw far more than she wanted to reveal.

"Why did you write that letter?" Justin asked her without preamble.

"It explained itself well enough—"

"Why did you write it?" he repeated, a hard, accusing ring to his voice, in sharp contrast to the expression in his eyes that mirrored quite a different emotion, one that tugged at her strongly, insistently, beginning to exert the familiar hold over her. Olwyn hastily turned her head away and at the same time dug her heels into Amos, pointing his nose in the direction of the river. "I asked you to respect my wishes." She spoke without looking at him as she started to move away. "Please leave. I came up here to be alone."

She rode away and left him in the open, and once at the river dismounted and led Amos down the embankment into the coolness of the trees, secured him, and stooped at the water's edge and splashed some over her burning face, telling herself, willing herself, not to give in. This was the man who had used her, Olwyn reminded herself desperately. He had failed her in the worst possible way. He came to her when he felt like it and left when he had what he wanted. Justin Wentworth had manipulated her for the last time!

She heard the stallion snort to a halt on the high bank above the river, then the sound of Justin's boots on the boulders and rough shingle of the embankment. He seized her by the arms, hauled her to her feet, and spun her around to face him, his muscular chest grazing her breasts, his breath in her hair, arms pinning her close to him. "The men told me you came here a week ago," he said. "Every day since then I've watched for you—"

"Just as every day since I left Teragno you longed to hold me?" Olwyn mocked, and she raised her head then, her tawny eyes flaring into his. "Longed to kiss me, to be close to your dearest love? No, Justin"—she shook her head and, echoing something he had once said to her, added, "Your tricks won't work anymore. Now go, and stop wasting my time."

He flinched, then Olwyn saw a fierce determination come into his face.

"Enough, Olwyn! We will hash this out here and now. I know . . . I think you want that as much as I do." His eyes searched her face, as if for confirmation, and his arms tightened around her. "Do you know why I didn't turn up as I promised—"

"How *would* I know?" she broke in quickly, heat flooding her face. "I didn't go either. And—and I'm not interested in listening to your excuses, so save your breath. Go back to your precious diamonds!" she spat at him, all her hurt and anger surging back as she remembered that desolate time of waiting day after day at the pool. "They are all you really care about. Diamonds come first! I—I want a man who will put *me* first—"

"Surely you can't be referring to Maury Howell?" Justin sneered.

The scorn on his face infuriated Olwyn. She wrenched away from him, sparks flashing from her eyes. "Maury Howell is a gentleman!" she informed him haughtily. "He's a man of his word. And—and he loves me and wants to marry me!" Olwyn finished wildly, desperate to wound him as he had wounded her. "You . . . you are nothing but empty promises!"

Justin's reaction was not what she had expected. He threw back his head and laughed. "Howell," he grated, "is an opportunist and a fool! If you want to spend your life chasing rainbows, then marry him, but you know, even as you stand there ready to deny it, that he can never make you happy, never fulfill you, and never love you as I can," he told her, his deep voice very low, almost mesmeric, sapping her will. "You know that, Olwyn."

In two long strides Justin had her in his arms, his hungry mouth claiming hers, his strong body overwhelming her in a way she knew so well and felt so helpless to resist. Olwyn's head spun as he lowered her to the grassy bank of the river, the gurgling water merging with the blood singing in her ears, the endearments he was whispering to her. "I do love you, never doubt that again! Diamonds are my business, it's true, but you, my love, are my life! Always you come first to me . . . always . . ."

Justin covered her lips, face, throat with lingering kisses that melted her bones and filled her with a sweet, honeyed weakness. Impatiently he tugged down the bodice of her gown, ripping it slightly to free her breasts, fuller now, ripe and exquisitely sensitive to the moist heat of the mouth that teased and then covered an already turgid nipple. She felt the thrusting hardness of his manhood against her thighs, urgent and compelling. Olwyn closed her eyes then, wailing inwardly, *Oh, why can't it be like this with Maury! Why—why—*

She felt her gown being raised, heard him say, "Come back to Teragno with me now! Today!"

These words shook her, blasting her out of the languorous trance she had fallen into. They stung her, like a handful of ice thrown in her face, and awakened a painful memory of the same words being spoken at another time.

It was all happening again! Olwyn thought in horror. Nothing had really changed. Love, he'd said, love—but no mention of marriage!

Olwyn fought him off like a wild creature and jumped to her feet, her naked breasts heaving, a livid flush on her cheeks. "I hate you!" she screamed and, backing away, "Leave me alone! Get away"—she gestured vaguely in the direction of Teragno—"get away and leave me in peace. I don't want you, don't need you . . . I despise you, Justin Wentworth!"

He stared at her, flabbergasted.

"Go!" Olwyn repeated, her voice shrill, her eyes filled with cold fury.

Justin looked her up and down, and never had she looked more beautiful with her shining black hair in wild disarray, golden eyes flashing like molten honey, her breasts—he suddenly noticed how they bloomed, riper, fuller than he remembered. She was determined to punish him, he thought. There was a hardness, a ruthlessness in her that he had never seen before.

Justin smiled knowingly. "Why have you been coming down here recently?"

"That is my business."

He glanced upriver in the direction of the camp— and Olwyn guessed then what he was thinking, that she had come to Moorelands with the sole purpose in mind of attracting his attention, hoping to lure him back to her!

Olwyn's eyes narrowed and without realizing it she took a step toward him.

"You are trespassing on my land," she said.

Justin stared at her and warned himself to be patient. "Olwyn, stop this—"

"Get off my land!"

"Don't be ridiculous. This land belongs to Jonus van Klerk."

"No!" she shook her head. "It belongs to me now. You may ask Mr. van Klerk if you don't believe me."

For a moment Justin frowned, then his face cleared and he chuckled. "Van Klerk would sooner sell his wife and children than a single morgen of his land." He recalled his own futile efforts to buy this very parcel, offering the Boer far more than it was worth as farmland, only to meet with a curt refusal.

"He gave it to me," Olwyn informed him sweetly.

"Gave?"

She nodded. "I have the papers at home to prove it."

Olwyn had the satisfaction of watching the self-assurance wiped off his face and doubt set in. "Why in God's name would van Klerk give his land to you?"

"I rendered him a service, and he was grateful. And I would be grateful if you would leave now, as I asked you to, and never set foot on this land again."

Justin's face was now like stone. He felt he was looking at a stranger. Or perhaps, he thought bitterly, this was just another of the many roles she assumed, depending on which one best suited her purpose at any given time. Had he ever really known her? he asked himself grimly. Who was the real Olwyn Moore? He turned away without a word, thinking that he had fallen in love with a fantasy, a woman who didn't exist.

* * *

Olwyn's satisfaction was short-lived, her pride in the way she had handled the situation all too fleeting. Hardly had the sound of the stallion's hoofbeats died away on the veld than a numbing pall of bleakness settled over her, the silence pressing in until she wanted to scream—or weep.

Angry at herself, Olwyn got up and wandered along the river bank, gazing at the shining water, the lush ferns and trees lining its bank, the ocean of yellow wild flowers like a carpet on the plain, acres upon acres of it—all hers. As she tried to take comfort and pleasure in the sight of gazelle and wildebeest grazing, an eagle, scarcely moving, glided overhead with outstretched wings, impaled against an azure sky, Olwyn tried to convince herself that she owned treasure far beyond price even as a cynical voice—Mick's—forced its way into her mind. "This land," he'd said, "is bitter and dry. Soon all this grass wither and die and everything bake as before. It no use."

No *practical* use, Olwyn thought. And he was right! What could a single, penniless woman—a pregnant woman!—do to make the land produce? Nothing. It would neither put food on her table or a roof over her head nor provide a morsel of sustenance for the child she would have in less than five months' time! What was she going to do? Olwyn asked herself as she walked along with bent head, kicking the gravel lining the riverbank in a sudden paroxysm of despair and frustration. She was in love with a man who was not prepared to marry her. She worked for a missionary fighting a lost cause. And how could she find work to support herself and the baby in the middle of a wilderness?

She was trapped, Olwyn thought, venting her desperation on a pile of loose shingle. Trapped . . .

She stopped, distracted by a bright pebble twinkling in the sunshine. It lay among the gravel she had just dislodged, only a yard from her feet. Curious, Olwyn walked over and knelt down to pluck it from its duller cousins, turned it over in her hand, and held it up to the sunlight. The thought crossed her mind that it was very similiar to the one stolen from her in Cape Town—and her heart was suddenly fluttering, her mouth dry.

Sparks flew from the stone, hard and flashing with promise, reflecting in her eyes, driving out the hopelessness of moments before. She sat very still, turning it slowly in her fingers, scarcely daring to breathe or give credence to the incredible thought that leaped into her mind.

It was a diamond! Olwyn was sure of it. It was almost the same, though perhaps slightly larger, as the one Justin Wentworth had accused her of stealing. And it was hers!

Laughing, sobbing, Olwyn doubled over until her forehead touched the ground, her entire body trembling with the shock of her discovery, the diamond clutched tight in her hand. Hers, she thought feverishly, to do with as she wanted! This stone could finance her way out of Africa and beyond the reach of a man who was beginning to drive her mad. She could go anywhere, set herself up in a new town, support her child, be independent!

But . . . why *should* she go? Surely slinking away would be a very defeatist way of handling her problems, Olwyn mused. She sat up and looked about her land, then down at the stone in her hand, the product of that land, the fruit of it, in a way, and suddenly a much grander idea came to her. With this foundation stone she could stay in Africa and build something fine; a life that would bring her respect and a sense of achievement—and keep her much too busy to brood about Justin Wentworth.

Busy was far too tepid a word to describe Olwyn over the next few weeks, driven as she was to accomplish as much as possible before her advancing pregnancy slowed her down. Her first step was to visit Jonus van Klerk, when Olwyn told him about the diamond and outlined her plans. "Do you have any objections?" she asked him. Jonus thought a minute, then gave her a rueful smile, reflecting that this was God's way of humbling him, of showing him whose will would prevail. "No," he finally replied. "It was meant to be. I have no objections whatsoever." Nor would he accept any part of her new-found wealth. "I'm a rich man already," he smiled. "I have Pieter; my family."

Hannah and James proved more difficult. When Olwyn announced that instead of selling the gem and contenting herself with the money, as they fully expected, she planned to go into business and start digging at Moorelands herself, they gaped at her, speechless, the more so when Olwyn added that it was all going to be set in motion before the baby was born!

For a moment the Scobbies were dumbstruck, then Hannah gasped. "You—you can't be serious? What an idea! You, a woman . . . and pregnant . . . it simply isn't done."

James soothed, "She's hysterical. The excitement has gone to her head. Just give her a little time and she'll come back to her senses presently—"

"I intend to do it," Olwyn interrupted firmly.

They gaped at her, realizing by the look in her eyes that she meant it.

Young Harold thought it was a wonderful idea and immediately offered his help, which Olwyn accepted, saying, "Provided your father has no objections?"

James had a hundred objections as he regarded the youthful pair watching him so intently while they awaited his answer, but not one of them passed his lips. What could he tell his son? Stay in Nuruzambora and molder? Bury yourself here with me and listen to my sermons fall on deaf ears? Watch me destroy myself? No! Harold was a strapping youth with energy and ambition. He longed for challenge and stimulation, and had the right, James supposed, to go his own way and hopefully learn from his experiences, good and bad. No, no, he could not stop him, either of them. He could only hope they would always come back.

James nodded, not trusting himself to speak.

The very next morning Hal and Olwyn set off to visit a lawyer in Hopetown, and the day after that they rode to the big, sprawling camp at Klipdrift, an impermanent city of tents, shacks, the offices of the diamond dealers little more than corrugated-iron shanties with dirt floors, flimsy shops set up to supply the diggers, taverns and hotels, equally sordid, the latter virtually seething with vermin and lice. The stench as they neared the camp was overpowering, and Olwyn felt her stomach heave in protest, but when Hal looked at her questioningly she clenched her teeth and shook her head, indicating that they would proceed.

Klipdrift, she saw, was much, much worse than when Maury Howell had brought her here for a visit with the Scobbies less than three short months ago, and there were far more people—thousands more—of every shape, size, and color, only united in one thing: determination to find diamonds.

The camp made Olwyn think of a vast, festering sore on the veld. It hummed with activity and reeked with appalling odors under the hot sun, yet the diggers and their laborers seemed like a gay, happy lot as they went about their business, soon to be her business too. The unexpected novelty of a beautiful white woman riding into camp almost caused pandemonium. The men gaped, whistled, shouted, and clapped their hands as Harold helped Olwyn dismount from the donkey, gathering up her skirts to avoid contamination from the filth of the open sewer ditches running down each side of the makeshift roads.

Harold took her arm. "We shouldn't waste time," he said with an uneasy glance at the leering onlookers. One or two or even three Hal felt confident of handling, but not hundreds. "We should go straight off to Maury," he suggested.

Olwyn shook her head. "We'll visit the other diamond dealers first," she said cannily, "and Maury last."

It proved to be a wise decision.

The first dealer offered her fifty pounds for her stone, the second ten. Olwyn thanked them politely and moved on. The next man took longer to inspect the uncut diamond and finally said, "Not a bad stone. I'll give you a hundred pounds sterling."

Harold, standing behind Olwyn, sucked in his breath. One hundred pounds sterling! His blue eyes bulged. A man could buy two farms for that amount of money! He could travel in style back to Britain and still have enough cash left to purchase a house! He could—

"Take it!" Harold blurted, giving her a little nudge.

Instead, Olwyn took her stone to yet another of the many dealers littering the encampment, and kept on going until she found a German dealer, somewhat more professional-seeming than the rest, and this man, after a careful examination of her gem, said, "Three hundred pounds," and when Olwyn hesitated, "Well, what sum were you thinking of, Frau . . . eh?"

"Olwyn Moore."

"And your price?"

"Five hundred pounds," Olwyn told him coolly.

He started to smile and shake his head, then looked at her more closely, and finally back to the stone. "I accept," he replied with a sigh.

The dealer was angry when Olwyn told him that she would first have to consult another party. "I may not offer you as much later," he warned when she made for the door.

She glanced at him over her shoulder. "That, of course, is your decision," she said, and swept out of his office, Harold stumbling after her, certain she had lost her mind.

Maury was amazed and overjoyed to see them when they entered his tiny business premises, every bit as crammed and seedy as all the others they had been in.

Questions fairly bubbled from his lips. What on earth were they doing here? Had they come especially to see him? And on and on. Over coffee Olwyn explained about her gift of the land and finding the diamond, her plans to hire a crew and start digging herself, and sell claims to other prospectors. Maury was thunderstruck and reeled back in his chair. He started to speak and laughed instead. "Olwyn, Olwyn my sweet, what a jester you are! Why, I almost believed your fairy tale for a moment."

She took the stone out of her purse and plunked it on his desk.

"How much will you give me for it?" Olwyn asked crisply. Thinking of Justin's diamond and remembering Knute Bleur's assessment, she added, "I would say it's at least twenty-two carats. Uncut."

A sudden silence fell over the trio. Howell had been bending over the stone but at her last remark he lifted his eyes and gazed at her soberly from under his brows. Olwyn met his green stare with the utmost composure. Maury felt he was seeing her for the first time, or at least a part of her that he had never known existed, and from her manner he sensed that this was no mere social visit. It was business.

He felt something strange then, something that made him feel uncomfortable, at a disadvantage, almost as if she were in control of the situation and he had come to her with his hat in his hand, rather than it being the other way about. He shook his head, trying to throw off the unpleasant sensation. "Olwyn, dear," he said, sighing, "the stone isn't nearly that big— though for your sake I wish it were, naturally. But no . . ." He lowered his eyes and pretended to give the gem another appraisal, though from the first he knew that it was a far better than average stone. "I'd say, well, I could probably stretch to a hundred pounds, but only because it belongs to you, dear," he added craftily, flashing his dimpled smile. "There you are! You are now a woman of means."

Olwyn snatched the diamond off his desk and stood

up. Her eyes were cold. "You are a conniving scoundrel," she told him icily, "a liar and a cheat. Good day to you, Mr. Howell!"

Maury sat frozen at his desk, his mouth sagging open, and watched her sweep out of his office followed by an embarrassed Harold Scobbie. After a moment he passed a shaking hand over his face and blinked rapidly, as if to clear his eyes of a most disturbing vision. Could this hard, arrogant woman possibly be the same sweet Olwyn Moore he had visited at Nuruzambora? Howell asked himself in wonder. No! A hundred times, no! Some dreadful transmutation had taken place in her, he thought gloomily, and beautiful as she still was, her nature had undergone a drastic change—and not for the better.

The things she had called him! Lud, he fumed indignantly, had she been a man he would have taken a stick and whipped an apology out of her. And to insult him in front of a third party, why, it was reprehensible!

Of course, he *had* fibbed a bit about her diamond— but that was business! Let her go to some of the other dealers, he thought huffily, and she'd fare much worse. A hundred pounds was an awful lot of money, especially to a woman like her. In his mind Maury no longer thought of Olwyn as a girl, nor at that moment even noticed the change in the way he viewed her now. Other more important things crowded into his mind and chief among them was the fact that Olwyn Moore owned the land where her diamond had been found! Further, it was adjacent to the lucrative Teragno diggings, soil that had produced many fine gems and made Justin Wentworth a millionaire.

Horrified, Maury was struck by the thought that he had ruined a wonderful opportunity, by far the best that had come his way so far—perhaps the best that would ever come his way! Olwyn was a single woman. She had no one to help or advise her, certainly no one with his knowledge of diamonds and business in general. Oh, dear God! he thought, springing up and reaching for his hat. Dear Christ in heaven, what had he done?

Ever the optimist, Maury dared to hope that it still wasn't too late to undo the damage. He flung open the door and bolted out of his office.

By the time Olwyn and Harold started back home to Nuruzambora many things had been settled to Olwyn's satisfaction. She now had a manager, an overseer, and fifty Kaffir laborers, not bad for a start, though four more overseers would be required and another fifty laborers. Production was scheduled to begin at Moorelands in two weeks' time.

Maury had been hired as her manager only because she needed him and, as Olwyn reasoned philosophically, better a devil you know than one you don't. She had given him a stern lecture and a warning, and naturally she would find a way to keep her eye on him at all times. Harold, young as he was, would be her head overseer. He was a strong, smart, quick-witted boy, and Maury had been instructed to teach him all he knew about diamonds. Before production began at Moorelands Harold would spend a week working with Howell at Klipdrift.

The Kaffirs . . . ? The Kaffirs were desperate for work. Like many tribesmen they had been lured from their tribal land in the hope of making enough money to buy wives, cattle, guns, and fancy trinkets, all the things that made them wealthy and important in the eyes of their peers. From Maury she had heard how brutally some of these native laborers were treated by their prospector employers, and she was determined that nothing of the like would happen at Moorelands. Nor would the diggings be allowed to turn into a filthy slum in the wilderness.

Olwyn went to bed that night exhausted but at the same time she was intoxicated, bubbling over with the certainty that she was achieving something at last. Already her life had changed dramatically with the discovery of the diamond—but that was just the beginning, she thought, feverish with excitement, even bolder and more lofty ideas swelling in her mind. Nothing and nobody would be allowed to stop her or hold her up, Olwyn decided firmly. At the age of twenty she was finally in control of her own destiny; her own life.

It was hard to sleep that night, but just as she finally began to doze off Olwyn felt a curious fluttering sensation in her stomach. Immediately she was wide awake, both hands clamped to her abdomen. She held her breath and waited and after a moment or two it came again, this time stronger. A great burst of joy and wonder swept over Olwyn. Laughing, though with tears in her eyes, she sat up in bed and almost shouted aloud that her child was alive and had finally made his presence felt; she was desperate to share this joyous moment but had no one to share it with. No doting husband, of course; Justin Wentworth wasn't interested in marriage. Nor even an interested friend; Hannah and James almost never mentioned her pregnancy; they tried to pretend it didn't exist. Alone in her bare, mean little room, Olwyn began to weep. This should be a moment to celebrate, she reflected dolefully; it was one of the truly great moments in a woman's life—and she was alone!

In a curious way she felt the baby had been cheated, and of course he had. He had no father!

"I'll make it up to you, my darling," Olwyn whispered fiercely, holding her stomach. "Mama will see you have everything you need. You'll . . . you'll hardly miss a father."

Tears flowed down her cheeks. Olwyn lay back and buried her face in the pillow.

# 24

Production began at Moorelands in April, and for two weeks the diggers found nothing. With so many men to pay and equipment to buy ruin stared Olwyn in the face and kept her awake tossing and turning for most of the night. Then one of their Kaffir laborer's dug up a large diamond, almost fifty carats, and again Olwyn's fortunes changed overnight.

News of finding a big stone always caused avid excitement among the prospectors; these stones were worth far more than many smaller ones totaling the same weight. Diggers arrived at Moorelands in droves desperate to buy claims. The going rate at the time was ten shillings a month; Olwyn charged one pound, twice that amount, and the claims were snapped up so fast that on the very first day of selling they ended up with a tin box virtually overflowing with money.

"We're rich!" yelled Maury and, unaware that she was pregnant, he danced Olwyn wildly up and down the riverbank until Harold angrily caught him by the shoulder, bringing him to an abrupt stop.

"Don't be so rough!" the boy told him, scowling. "She's not a sack of potatoes to be tossed around."

Howell's laughing face instantly sobered. His green eyes narrowed as he stared up at the youth who was several inches taller than he was. "She's not made of glass. For God's sake don't be such a wet blanket, Scobbie!" Maury wrenched himself out of Hal's grasp, adding, "And don't put your hand on me like that again. The last man who did has a twisted nose to show for it."

Harold laughed. "You couldn't reach that far, Howell—"

Maury hit him then, a hard blow to the stomach that took the boy by surprise, but Hal recovered himself quickly and put into practice the boxing lessons his grandfather had taught him before he left Scotland, including a few tricks Ramsay had picked up while working in the coal mines.

"Stop it!" Olwyn screamed, and started to rush between them, then remembered the baby. "Over here!" she waved and yelled to some of their laborers. "Hurry!" But before they could drop their tools and run to intervene, Maury Howell lay flat on his back. The look of surprise on his face was almost comical; the hot-tempered Maury had rarely come out worst in a fight—and never to a lad of fifteen! Now he lay defeated with a bloody nose and rapidly blackening eye in full view of their work force, many of whom were grinning and nudging each other, highly amused.

Black fury almost choked Howell when he gazed up at the circle of snickering faces surrounding him. He was stunned and mortified, his ego flattened. Nor did it ease matters when Olwyn treated both himself and Harold to a stern lecture, warning them that it had better never happen again. "Now shake hands with each other!" she commanded, and when they stood unmoving, "Go on, I insist! I won't have bad feeling in this camp."

Grudgingly, the men shook hands, but from that moment on Maury and Harold hated each other.

Within a week or two a thousand, then five thousand prospectors were frenetically digging at Moorelands and reaping glittering rewards, none quite as glittering as Olwyn Moore, the owner. Her own work force had expanded to five hundred men, plus she had the cash from the claims she sold and royalties on every single diamond found. The scores of overseers she employed kept a sharp eye on each stage of the process—the shingle was dug up and taken to be washed and screened in something the prospectors called cradles, a kind of rocking sieve, then the residue was carefully spread out on the sorting tables and any diamond found carefully recorded. Her overseers also recorded any gems found by the other prospectors.

Each prospector who bought a claim either dug for himself or in turn employed native laborers to do it for him while he stood on guard to make sure his men worked as they were supposed to and, even more importantly, didn't steal. Many gems recovered from the soil mysteriously disappeared en route to the washing process or the sorting tables, later to be sold privately on the black market flourishing at every diamond site at that time.

Most newly arrived prospectors could not afford to employ native labor and dug for themselves, or in groups made up of their friends, and soon hundreds of these various teams stretched along both sides of Olwyn's land on the Orange River. Farther back was the camp, the waggons, tents, huts, and thatched-roof grass houses where white men lived as well as the natives. Then stacked all around were their equipment and supplies, everything kept in reasonable order at Olwyn's insistence, though she soon saw that she couldn't be too demanding in such a frantic atmosphere, where men worked nonstop from dawn to dusk.

Like predators following the game they fed on, the dealers, traders, and shopkeepers followed the prospectors to Moorelands. Many of these businessmen howled in outrage when they learned how much they would have to pay the owner for the privilege of setting up shop at Moorelands but it was a case of take it or leave it. Most accepted the terms offered.

At first most of the prospectors seemed to imagine that Maury Howell owned Moorelands. When they found out that the owner was a woman—the same woman they saw at camp almost every day talking to Howell or the overseers—they were stunned. Their assumption that Olwyn was Maury's sister, wife, or girlfriend was quickly dispelled the first time Olwyn gathered them all together for one of her Camp Meetings, which thereafter she held once a month.

Her ownership caused a sensation. Olwyn herself caused a sensation. But young and beautiful as she was, these tough, adventurous men were soon made to realize that she was no mere empty-headed girl or a puppet manipulated by Maury Howell. The day Olwyn climbed up on the flatbed of a wagon to apprise them of the rules governing the site, the prospectors lost any preconceived notions they might have been harboring about her.

Olwyn was inwardly very nervous that day and far from sure of herself. Outwardly she forced herself to stand up confidently and speak in a clear, firm voice. She wore her hair, long now, piled high on her head and wore the yellow dress made from the fabric Maury had given her; a dress that was shabby now and had been let out twice by Hannah to compensate for her added weight. The minute she started to speak the whistling and cat-calling died and a hush fell over the camp, and by the time she finished the beginning of respect dawned in the prospectors' eyes, a respect that was soon to become absolute. In time Olwyn was to make bitter enemies; she was to encounter men who were jealous and resentful of her position—and women who were jealous of her beauty and acclaim and success with the opposite sex—but even these people, however grudgingly, respected her.

That first camp meeting was Olwyn's initial step into the limelight.

One day Harold came to her and said many new diggers had moved from Teragno to Moorelands. "They say Teragno is pretty much dug out," he said.

Maury added, "The feeling is that there's still plenty of stones over there but they are getting much harder to find, and time costs money."

The Teragno diggings were less than a quarter of a mile from Olwyn's camp. Twice before her confinement she spotted Justin Wentworth riding down the perimeter of his land atop MacBeth, and each time she turned her head away and forced her mind to other things, refusing to allow her mind to dwell on him for more than a second, but even that second dampened her spirits for the rest of the day.

Justin was the president of the official Diggers Committee and every new claim had to be registered with this group. In this instance, Olwyn was quite willing to allow her manager, Howell, to conduct any business they had with the Committee. She could force herself to do many things, but coming face to face with Justin wasn't one of them.

During the first weeks of production at Moorelands Olwyn insisted on riding to the camp every day, a distance of eight miles. She and Harold left Nuruzambora at dawn and returned just before dusk. She had a fairly comfortable wagon placed on the site for her convenience, a place where she could shelter from the hot mid-day sun and the occasional torrential rain that sometimes bucketed down over the winter months. There were days when it was cold, too, especially late in the afternoon or when it was overcast; by the time she and Hal rode home it was often freezing. Griqualand was almost four thousand feet above sea level.

Finally Hannah could contain herself no longer. Reticent as she was about alluding to Olwyn's condition, she burst out one day at the beginning of June when the girl returned from the diggings pale with fatigue. "This cannot go on! If you care nothing for your own health—and it's clear you don't!—give a thought to the child you carry. For its sake you must take care of yourself!"

It was because of her child that Olwyn was driving herself so hard, determined as she was to ensure that he had the security she herself had never known, until recently. And even now . . . even now she didn't dare slacken and sit back complacently. She was making good money it was true but her expenses were exorbitant, and only the really big diamonds brought good money. The big diamonds were few and far between. Sometimes . . . sometimes Olwyn felt they should be getting more for their gems. It was something she meant to look into seriously once she'd had the baby and the first mad flurry of activity settled down. Just getting started had taken every ounce of energy and concentration she possessed since there were so many new aspects of the business to learn.

Maury had been a great help. He had made a study of the diamond trade and was the one with the necessary contacts in Cape Town. Unlike most of the prospectors, Olwyn didn't sell her stones to the many dealers hanging like vultures over the diamonds fields. Her gems were sent by courier to Cape Town, to a company called Fabien Precious Gems, Ltd., a firm Maury assured her was one of the most reputable on the coast. They in turn sold the diamonds to Europe and the rest of the world.

One day in early June Olwyn had a question about this company. They had recently shipped them a batch of better than average stones and received what she felt was a very poor price for them. When she explained her feelings to Howell he said, "You don't understand. The price of diamonds fluctuates wildly on the world market. Fabien can only pay us accordingly, regardless of the quality of the stones. If they get a poor deal, then so do we."

Olwyn looked stubborn and thoughtful. After a minute she said, "What we really ought to do is to cut out this middle-man and make our own contacts in Europe—"

"Don't be ridiculous!" Maury replied heatedly. "Do you realize how much time that would take; time neither of us can spare, as you well know?" His green eyes glittered and he looked exasperated and angry. "Accept the bloody price you get and just concentrate on building up the business. It's not as if we aren't doing well."

"I want to do even better," Olwyn informed him bluntly. "And besides," her eyes moved over his flushed face, "why are you so annoyed? It was only a suggestion."

Howell made an obvious effort to relax, and his infectious grin replaced the scowl on his face. "I'm not annoyed, love"—he took her hand and squeezed it—"but it hurts me when you seem dissatisfied with the effort I've put into the business. I'm doing my very best, Olwyn; I'm on the field from dawn to dusk. As for Fabien, well, it's the best company I know—"

"Oh, Maury dear, I'm sorry!" Olwyn told him feelingly, ashamed of herself. Impulsively she leaned forward and gave him a quick kiss on the cheek. "I'm not dissatisfied with you! Please never think that. It's just, well . . . I think we should examine all the possibilities open to us and not fall into a rut—"

"A rut!" He broke into a loud guffaw, his eyes twinkling with amusement. "Olwyn, my dear, sweet, lovely girl, we've only just started in the business! We're still at the stage of cutting our teeth." To demonstrate Maury snatched up a diamond from the many on the table between them inside their wagon office, placed it between his teeth, and bit down on it hard. This was something he always did when one of the more desperate prospector's brought him his gems, anxious for a quick sale to pay pressing debts and expenses. At such times Maury went through an elaborate routine calculated to impress; to show that he was giving serious consideration to the quality of their stone, and of course to make sure it really *was* a diamond. First, he would bite down on the uncut gem, then he would scratch his name with it on a piece of glass he kept handy for such times. He would even strike it with a mallet! The drama always ended with Howell offering a rock-bottom price.

"What a clown you are!" Olwyn laughed, pulling his hand—and the stone—away from his mouth. She scolded, "You'll ruin your teeth if you keep doing that. And just take care you don't choke if it slips down your throat."

Howell rolled his eyes. "What a way to pass on! I can't think of a better—"

"Stop it!" Olwyn slapped his hand. She sighed. "Anyway, I suppose you are right about exploring other possibilities. We've enough on our plate at the moment." She smiled at him, adding, "We'll take it one step at a time, as you so wisely suggested, sir!"

"Marry me!" Howell seized her arms and bent forward swifly to kiss her on the lips. "Please, please marry me, you enchanting, bewitching woman, before I go out of my mind." His eyes hotly, yearningly roved her face as they sat with the narrow table between them. "Do you know," he went on when she sat smiling at his antics, "I believe business is good for you. You are positively blooming! But seriously, when are you going to do me the great honor of becoming my wife, Olwyn Moore?"

She turned away from the entreaty in his eyes. Maury rushed on persuasively. "We have so much in common, Olwyn. We are both enthusiastic and ambitious, dedicated to the same business, and we even like each other and enjoy each other's company—which is more than most married couples can say! Oh, Olwyn, my dearest, can't you see that we were meant for each other? If two people were ever destined to marry, it's us!"

In a way Olwyn supposed it was true. They had more reason to unite in matrimony than most young couples and would probably make a go of it—except that she was carrying another man's child! Further, she wasn't in love with Maury Howell, much as she tried to be.

Struggling to hang on to the lightness of a moment before, Olwyn took a deep breath and turned back to Maury with a grin. "As you so wisely told me only a minute ago, we have quite enough on our plates at the moment—"

"But soon!" he cut in urgently. "Soon!" He laughed, adding, "Before I pine away altogether out of unrequieted love for you."

Olwyn playfully cuffed him on the ear. "You look perfectly hale and hearty to me, you rascal. I've also noticed that you have an appetite like a horse. So much for pining away!"

Olwyn had noticed Flo giving her some speculative looks just lately. That early evening when she and Harold returned to Nuruzambora the mission cook, who hadn't been informed of her condition, remarked, "You once skinny. Now you get fat." Before Olwyn could anticipate what she meant to do, Flo reached out to pat her stomach, which was now swollen and tight and bulging more by the day, it seemed to Olwyn. So much so that no matter how Hannah added material to her gowns it could no longer be concealed. Even Maury had commented that she was blooming.

The cook sucked in a sharp breath when she encountered that tell-tale bulge and her black eyes snapped up to meet Olwyn's. "You got baby in there."

It wasn't a question. It was a statement.

Olwyn's face blazed with embarrassed color. She didn't know what to say. She could hardly deny it, obvious as it was.

"You marry Mr. Howell," Flo advised in her direct way. "You do it quick." She clucked and shook her head admonishingly. "You wait, baby not have father name. Very bad, very bad . . ."

Olwyn hurried to her room and sank miserably down on her bed and wept.

Then something happened that brought things to a

head. Two days later as Olwyn and Harold were returning to the mission from the diamond fields they were intercepted by M'Buru, Hero, and some of the chief's elders, all returning from hunting, carcasses of impala and kudu strung out on poles carried between them. It had been a very successful hunt and M'Buru was in an expansive mood. He invited, and that meant insisted, that leopard woman and little "brother" return with him to his kraal for a refreshing drink of beer.

When Olwyn and Harold dismounted outside the chief's lodge M'Buru's glowing dark eyes, eyes that always watched her closely, went immediately to Olwyn's stomach. His hand, big and brown, immediately followed, closing over her belly above the voluminous folds of her gown. "What you got here?" he growled, gazing angrily at her from under his brows. "What you got, woman?" he demanded harshly when Olwyn went pale and tongue-tied, paralyzed with terror.

"You not got husband!" he shouted, the sound rumbling across the clearing and scattering the villagers who had started to build the cooking fires. "Who give you this thing? Who go inside you?"

For a second there wasn't a sound. Hero and the other elders froze. They gazed across the clearing into space, bracing themselves for the dreadful wrath they knew must come. Harold stood white-faced and rigid beside Olwyn, his hand on his gun, gazing transfixed at the chief who was angrier, more incensed than the boy had ever seen him, and he had often witnessed M'Buru in one of his towering rages. Even the normally courageous, confident Harold was badly frightened at that moment, thinking that even if he shot M'Buru, he would have the chief's well-trained warriors to contend with.

The enraged man stepped right up to Olwyn until their bodies were no more than an inch or two apart. A massive brown hand clamped down on her shoulder and M'Buru glared down into her eyes. "Speak!" he roared into her ashen face. "Tell me he name?" Then, his voice suddenly dropping to an eerie rasping whisper, he told her, "I kill he! I find he and cut he. He no do this evil again."

Harold blurted then, "She—she's getting married—"

M'Buru, eyes bloodshot, lips frothing, swung on the boy. "What you say? Who she marry? Speak! Speak!"

Harold flung a helpless, apologetic glance at Olwyn and replied, "Mr. Maury Howell. You—you've met him—"

"Why he wait? Why he not marry her yet?" M'Buru looked angrier than ever.

"Because . . ." Hal thought quickly, ". . . because he hasn't had time. He's been kept very busy working for the British Government"—and Harold stressed these last two words, hoping they would have a restraining effect on the chief, since he'd noticed that M'Buru had a healthy respect for British authority— "and he—"

"That man work at diamond field," M'Buru snarled, taking Hal aback. "You think I no hear?" He took a step toward the lad, head lowered menacingly. "You lie to Great Eagle you get tongue cut out—"

"He works at the diamond fields *and* for the government," the boy said quickly, sweat pouring off him now, though it had turned very cold. "Ask Mr. Wentworth if you don't believe me. Howell is up here on field service for the British Government at the Cape . . ."

There wasn't a sound. The chief stood thinking, a thunderous frown knitting his brow, and after a moment when no one breathed he looked again at Olwyn, something like regret on his face. "White man no take good care of leopard woman. You want marry this man?"

She hesitated only a fraction of a second, then nodded.

M'Buru hunched his massive shoulders and sighed heavily.

"He no good man. You be sorry."

The Scobbies were in a high state of agitation when they were informed of the harrowing meeting with M'Buru, both James and Hannah insisting flatly that it could no longer be evaded. Olwyn must marry Maury Howell—if he would have her.

Harold, hating Maury as he did, had another suggestion. "Why can't Olwyn move to Teragno until after her baby is born? Mr. Wentworth wouldn't mind—"

"No!" Olwyn cried in horror. "I can't go there!" When Hannah gave her a funny, penetrating look she added hastily, "He's an outsider. I don't want him, or anyone else, to know about the baby."

James snorted. "Everybody will know soon enough. Look at you!" His eyes flicked to her stomach, then quickly away. "I just hope Maury will have you now."

"She's too good for Maury Howell!" Harold cried angrily. "If I were only old enough I would marry Olwyn myself," he finished wildly, giving his father a scowling, defiant look.

Olwyn stayed awake that entire night, her mind seething. Despite the fact that he was an opportunist, she liked Maury, and there was much to commend them as a team, but—

Justin came into her mind. His vibrant blue eyes seemed to mock her. "Howell can never make you happy," she heard him say, "never fulfill you, and never love you as I can. You know that, Olwyn."

Yes! God help her, she knew deep inside that it was true. Yet though he professed to love her, Justin withheld marriage. Olwyn knew that he didn't quite trust her and she, for her part, had doubts about him. It was significant, she mused, that he was prepared to make love to her, even to have her to live with him at Teragno, yet refused to dignify that love by giving her his name.

She would not go to him under those conditions! Never, she wept, never!

Harold said to her in the morning, "Stay here today.

You look terrible. Besides, we don't want another scene like yesterday with M'Buru."

He rode away alone to Moorelands but first he made a detour.

Olwyn spent the morning in her room, too weary and distracted to face anybody, torn one way and then the other as she tried to come to a decision, one she didn't want to face. She was still there when a rider galloped into the mission just before noon but she felt too exhausted to stir herself to get out of bed. Feeling as she did, she had no interest in visitors.

Then, through the window beside her bed, she heard the deep, familiar voice and bolted upright with her heart pounding.

# ——◇—— 25 ——◇——

**I**f Justin's manner had been warm, loving, tender, it might have changed everything that day but he stormed into Olwyn's room, slamming the door shut behind him, strode over to her bed, and demanded harshly, "Is the child mine? If it is, you can banish the thought of marrying Maury Howell. I wouldn't inflict him on a dog, much less any babe of mine!"

Olwyn was too overwhelmed at the unexpected sight of him to reply. She had never dreamed that Harold would take it upon himself to defy her wishes and contact Justin, and she could well imagine the blundering way Harold had broken the news to him. Now that Justin was here, big, handsome, glowing with vibrant good health and strength, Olwyn was rendered mute, thinking with an inward groan that if she lived to be ninety she would never be able to overcome the weakness and longing she always felt at the sight of this man. More than anything in the world she ached for him to take her into his arms and tell her once more that he loved her.

Instead, Justin growled, "Well, *is* the child mine?"

Olwyn frowned, hurt that he should even ask such a question; that he should doubt it. Just because she worked with Maury Howell, was friendly with him, and might be considering marrying him—didn't mean that she had already slept with Howell! She resented the inference, and now that she thought of it, she resented the way he had barged into her room daring to order her about, telling her who she could and couldn't marry.

"I would like to be treated with more respect." Olwyn had meant to sound cool and composed but her voice was shaking. "I—"

"Get dressed," Justin cut in. "I'm taking you back to Teragno."

He reached down and started to pull the quilt away from her and help her up but Olwyn clutched at it and dragged it up to her chin. "Why would I—I go with you to Teragno? If you think I'm going to live with you there like a . . . a common strumpet then you are mistaken, Justin Wentworth!"

He wrenched the quilt away from her, then came the words that Olwyn had been desperate to hear almost from the day she met him. "Get up. I'm going to marry you. Scobbie can perform the ceremony now."

Olwyn stared at him and his face suddenly went out of focus, the room blurring and spinning about her. Those words . . . those thrilling, wonderful words, "I'm going to marry you." But not spoken like that! Not made to sound like an obligation, something he was forced to do and, above all, not said in anger.

Olwyn opened her mouth to speak and instead began to weep harshly.

"Dear Christ!" Justin sat down on the side of her bed and took her shaking body in his arms. He had entered the room furious at her and what she planned to do. Now he was furious at himself.

Justin had had a stressful week. For the past month

Kelly and a geologist on his payroll had been on a diamond-finding expedition to farmland near the Vaal River, about a hundred miles northeast of Teragno. Rumors had been filtering down to them since the previous year that there was diamondiferous soil in that area and finally Justin had sent his men to explore. Kelly had reported back almost immediately that there were indeed diamonds—a few at least had been found—on a farm by the name of Driegraf, owned by a Boer. The farm, said Kelly, was only worth about fifty pounds. Justin sent a message back instructing him to purchase it and offer anything up to two thousand pounds, if necessary; thereupon the Irishman approached the farmer—only to learn that a syndicate from Natal had bought it for a thousand the previous week.

Kelly hadn't been able to resist adding a chiding postscript to his letter. "We were too slow off our mark. I warned you about this last October, if you remember, but your attention was taken up with something else—or *someone* else."

Justin wrote back telling him to keep looking, particularly at other farms near Driegraf.

That news had annoyed Justin but worse was to follow on the Thursday. This time it arrived in a letter from his lawyer in Scotland. The Wentworth Mills had been floundering for a year or more, and when he thought the time was ripe Justin, through his lawyer, had put in an offer to buy the mills and factories, masking his true identity under his company name, Teragno Minerals.

Christina had turned his offer down.

Justin's lawyer wrote: "Mrs. Wentworth informed me that she has received a better offer from another quarter, but has not yet come to a decision—even to whether she wants to sell at all! Of course she *has* to sell," the lawyer went on. "We all know that. As for the other offer, I'm convinced she's bluffing, hoping you'll come back with a larger sum. Well, my friend, I imagine you know your stepmother better than I do and the final decision on the matter is yours. I await your instructions."

He had given Christina an excellent offer for a business on the verge of liquidation! Justin was debating with himself whether to call her bluff and sit tight or go back to the leech with a larger figure—when Harold Scobbie came on the scene. After stammering out, red-faced, that Olwyn was pregnant, Hal said, "Would you have her at Teragno until she has the baby? She's going to marry Maury Howell otherwise, and Howell is an arse; he's not nearly good enough for her."

Justin had been stunned at the news of her pregnancy, though he realized that he shouldn't have been. He'd felt a burst of delight and pride . . . until it occurred to him that Maury Howell could be the father. Tondo had mentioned, during the time he was recovering from the gunshot wound, that he'd seen Olwyn with Howell at Klipdrift. That had been all the way back in January.

"When is the child expected?" he'd asked Hal, and waited tensely for his answer.

But the boy had just shrugged. "I'm not sure, probably August or September. We don't talk about it much at Nuruzambora."

"Does Olwyn know you intended coming to see me?"

Harold's round blue eyes had widened and he'd replied in his usual forthright way, little realizing how much his next words wounded Justin. "Oh, no! I suggested it but she nearly had a fit. She said she didn't want you to know about the baby." When Justin's face tightened he added, "I don't think she wanted to trouble you, Mr. Wentworth. Anyway, if you could just ride down and invite her, perhaps coax her a little—it would be terrible if she married Maury Howell! Olwyn doesn't know it but he drinks heavily and gambles and"—Harold blushed to the roots of his chestnut hair—"associates with those vile women who hang about the camps."

Justin had his horse saddled immediately.

He had ridden down to Nuruzambora in anger, deeply hurt that Olwyn would have kept the news about the baby from him, preferring to marry the likes of Maury Howell instead of the child's rightful father. He had burst into her room prepared to carry her back to Teragno with him kicking and struggling, if necessary. But she would not marry Maury Howell!

Now, with Olwyn in his arms, all his fury evaporated. He put his cheek against her hair and told her softly, "I'm sorry, my love. Don't cry. A girl shouldn't go to her wedding with tears on her cheeks. Olwyn"—he lifted her face so that he could look at her—"when is the baby due?"

Olwyn smiled at him through her tears but it was a cynical smile with no warmth in it. She felt that he was still trying to figure out if the child was his—before he married her!

"It's not yours," she said, pulling away from him. "Why do you think I'm going to marry Maury Howell?"

Olwyn and Maury were married on June fifteenth. It was a quiet ceremony conducted by James at Nuruzambora with a small feast to celebrate afterward. Both the bride and groom looked very sober; the bride also looked very pregnant. A new pink gown had been bought for the occasion. It would be useless for Olwyn once the baby was born since it was many sizes too large for her—but even then her swelling stomach was obvious.

"I shouldn't be surprised," Hannah whispered to James, "if she's going to have twins."

This proved to be quite correct. The girl was born first, at nine o'clock on the evening of August fifth, and two minutes later her brother arrived. Ariann came into the world with her tiny fists clenched, squalling at the top of her lungs. Aidan had a fierce scowl on his face. He looked exactly like his father had the last time Olwyn had seen him.

When Hannah, James, and the others had finally left them and they were alone in Olwyn's bedroom at Nuruzambora, Maury leaned over the bed and stared hard at the babies she held, one on either arm.

"*Now* won't you tell me who their father is?" Howell asked her.

Olwyn, pale and exhausted, shook her head. "You promised never to ask that question, Maury. You promised—"

He drew away, stood up, walked to the window, and stood with his back to her, remembering his shock when Olwyn had first broken the news to him. It had been as if she'd struck him in the face with a whip. Yet he supposed he should have guessed. Normally slim and willowy, Olwyn had suddenly started to gain weight, particularly in the region of her stomach, yet . . . the fact that she might be pregnant never once crossed his mind. Not his beautiful, pure, unsullied Olwyn! Not the girl who would hardly permit him a kiss! By then Maury had put her on a high pedestal; he viewed her as a kind of Madonna; a virgin goddess. Olwyn's announcement shattered Maury, blasting his near-saintly picture to shreds.

"Who is the father?" he'd cried, furiously jealous. "Tell me his name and I'll kill him!" At the same time Howell had quickly convinced himself that some swine had taken advantage of her, forced her against her will.

Olwyn refused to give him the name; she protected the scoundrel by her silence. Maury knew then that she had been a willing party to the affair.

Crushed, he choked out, "Do you still love him?"

She had hesitated, then said, "It's completely over, Maury. It was a dreadful mistake."

He rushed out then and embarked on a massive drinking binge that lasted five days. Once he had sobered up Howell was very sober indeed. He sat down and carefully reviewed the situation from all angles, particularly those pertinent to himself. He had an impetuous nature; he knew that. It had often cost him dearly in the past. But not this time. Maury swallowed his pride, his hurt and outrage, and returned to Nuruzambora to ask Olwyn to marry him.

To his utter astonishment and chagrin, she didn't immediately jump at the chance as any other woman would have done in her awkward situation. First, Olwyn admitted honestly that though she was very fond of him and liked him immensely, she wasn't in love with him. Then she said, "You must promise never to ask me the name of my child's father, or allude to the, ah . . . affair again. It's the only way our marriage could work, Maury! We have to forget the past and start fresh."

When he nodded, Olwyn's face softened and she reached for his hand, saying that she would promise in turn to do everything in her power to be a good wife to him; to help him achieve all of his many glowing dreams, and someday to bear his children. Then she leaned forward and put her arms around him and kissed him warmly on the lips—the first time Olwyn had ever initiated any physical contact between them other than a quick, friendly peck on the cheek.

But the birth of the twins stirred all Maury's hot jealousy, his feelings of hurt, outrage, and resentment. The question of the other man was never very far from his thoughts, and he'd done some fairly wild speculating. At one point Howell had even suspected James Scobbie! From there his seething mind had turned to Harold. Hal was a big, well-developed lad, he thought darkly. There were even younger boys at the diggings who associated with the whores who always hung about the various camps; boys as young as twelve and thirteen!

Finally, though, Maury came to the conclusion that it was probably one of the traders who'd stopped at the mission while covering their territory. For the last year or so their numbers had greatly increased, lured as they were to the diamond fields. There were also thousands of prospectors and various businessmen now crawling all over Griqualand; men who often stopped at missions, farms, and any hospitable spot they could find where they could safely spend the night. A faceless stranger was easier for Maury to stomach than someone he knew.

As he stood at the window trying to control his emotions, Olwyn said, "You gave me your word, Maury. I would never have imagined you'd break it."

A flicker of uneasiness crossed his mind. He warned himself to be careful. After a moment Howell turned with a lopsided smile, contrite and rueful. "I'm sorry. It's just—oh, never mind! A bargain is a bargain."

Olwyn held out her hand to him and after a slight hesitation he went to the bed and leaned down to kiss her, but he didn't kiss the babies or even look at them for the few remaining minutes he was in the room.

There was no question of Olwyn going to Moorelands for the next two months, and Maury was therefore solely in charge. During this time Harold saw much that infuriated him and one evening he returned to the mission to tell Olwyn, "The quicker you get back to the field the better," but she stopped him immediately.

"Maury is my husband now, Harold," she said quietly, but firmly. "You must never forget that. He has our best interests at heart and I don't want you ever talking against him, not to me or anyone else."

She pretended not to notice when occasionally Maury returned to Nuruzambora smelling of drink, nor did she kick up a fuss on the one or two occasions when he didn't return at all, and stayed away overnight. Olwyn accepted his excuses without question, reasoning that he was working hard and often found it easier just to stay at the field at night than make the long journey back and forth to Nuruzambora. Besides, deep down she felt she couldn't make too many demands on her husband. He, after all, had accepted her without question.

Olwyn became completely immersed in motherhood over the next few weeks, with diamonds taking second place to babies. The infants were not identical twins. Ariann was very fair, while Aidan had a soft cap of silky brown hair and slightly darker blue eyes. "Their coloring will probably change once they get a little older," said Hannah, clucking over the tots almost as much as Olwyn. Surrounded as they were with a doting family—except perhaps for Maury, who was usually too tired by the time he returned home to pay them any attention—Olwyn told herself over and over that these children were very lucky; that there was nothing in the world they lacked. James, always clever with his hands, made their cradles. Hannah made most of their clothes. Jamie, who had a very good singing voice, sang them lullabys and Hal—though too afraid to pick them up—spent a lot of time at their cradles entertaining them with his clever imitations of wildlife, from birds to elephants, and this was always guaranteed to quiet the babies whenever they were fussing. There were times when Olwyn was very thankful to see Harold arrive home at night. Ariann especially was a very restless, demanding baby. She was almost always the one to start her brother off.

Sometimes when she was alone wtih the twins, sitting between them rocking their cradles, Olwyn gazed at the babies, who had been registered as Aidan and Ariann Howell. Then their true father's face would loom up in her mind, hard and accusing, much as it had been the last time she saw Justin. Olwyn felt a terrible wrenching sickness of the heart so severe that tears flooded into her eyes. *Dear God, why?* she asked herself hopelessly. Why could Justin not have asked her to marry him that last day without subjecting her to a degrading interrogation? Why had he been so angry, so suspicious? To insinuate that she and Maury —how could she have married him after that?

But Olwyn couldn't help but wonder how Justin would react to the news that he had a son and daughter, not that he would ever know.

Life went on at Nuruzambora and Olwyn quickly recovered her energy and stamina and eventually the night came when an impatient Maury claimed his husbandly rights. The act was over astonishingly quickly. Olwyn was glad because it had left her totally cold, even though, for her husband's sake, she had pretended otherwise. Soon she grew to dread those nights, though she resigned herself to their inevitability with as much enthusiasm as she could muster.

James started preaching to the camp at Moorelands regularly, then was invited to preach at Klipdrift and Teragno. It was through James that Justin learned of the twins' births. Not long afterward the gifts arrived, silver cups for each of the babies with their names picked out in diamonds.

Those gifts almost broke Olwyn's heart.

Misunderstanding, Maury laughed at the look on Olwyn's face.

"Don't worry, Wentworth can afford it," he said with a shrug, never stopping to ask himself why Justin would have given such an enormously expensive gift to the offspring of mere friends. Howell had other things on his mind, like the argument he had had with Harold on the way home that evening. It was over a rumor that had been circulating around the camp— and Klipdrift and Teragno too—for weeks now, that diamonds were to be found away from the rivers entirely up on high farmland about eighty miles northeast of Moorelands. It seemed that some prospectors, unable to find good digs at the rivers, had wandered farther afield and happened on some remote farm owned by a Boer. The Dutchman had allowed them to dig for a small fee and within a short time a few diamonds had been found, or so the rumor went.

Maury, like most of the prospectors, scoffed at the

idea. Diamonds were always found near water, or where water had once been, and they were always close to the surface of the earth. It wasn't worth investigating, he felt, and he wasn't alone in his thinking, as most of the experts agreed with him. Harold, neither an expert nor very experienced, took the exact opposite tack—as was his habit when questions arose between himself and Maury. Harold felt strongly that it should be looked into, and even volunteered to go himself.

That night the boy couldn't hold his tongue a moment longer. As the family sat at their evening meal on the veranda overlooking the main kgotla fire, the soft voices of their native crew drifting up to them from below, Harold burst out, "Olwyn, something has come up that you should know about."

He told her of the rumor, adding, "If it's true, we might be able to buy the farms they're talking about and get them cheap. Surely it's worth investigating? Moorelands won't last forever." And he shot Maury a sullen look.

"Utter stuff and nonsense!" said Howell. "Diamonds are always found near watercourses. How on earth would they have got onto farmland many miles away from the rivers?" He glared at Hal. "You expect us to waste time and money tracking down every rumor that drifts through the diamond fields? Ha! We'd never get a stroke of work done!"

Privately, Olwyn was of the opinion that it wouldn't have hurt to send Harold and a few of their men out on an exploratory expedition—if only to give the lad a break and change of scene—but she couldn't take Harold's side over her husband.

In November young Jamie, the scholar of the family, was sent to one of the best boarding schools in Scotland at Olwyn's expense. Hardly had he left when the astounding news broke. A big new diamond strike had been found at Dutoitspan and Bultfontein on farmland more than seventy miles away from the Orange River, farms recently purchased from their

Boer owners by more farsighted men than Maury Howell.

The second big rush began. Prospectors left the river diggings by the thousands to surge in a frantic wave inland to the new strike, adhering to the tenet that the grass was always greener on the other side of the fence. In days the diggers at Moorelands were cut in half and dwindling rapidly, with a serious loss of revenue in claims. It was the same next door at Teragno and also at Klipdrift, even though Klipdrift, later to be renamed Barkly West, was recognized to be the best prospect of the three. Digging continued at Klipdrift long after Teragno and Moorelands were considered to be dug out, or at least the gems too scarce to make digging a viable proposition.

Harold was loud in his condemnation of Howell. So loud, in fact, that once more the men almost came to blows. And as before Olwyn defended her husband, while swallowing the alarm she felt at losing the money they received from the claims, not to mention the opportunity to purchase the farms where the new strikes had taken place. She felt almost sorry for Maury as he sat scratching his head, genuinely perplexed. "But . . . diamonds are *never* found away from water; they are alluvial," he kept repeating over and over until Harold exploded. "Well, they have been now! Get that through your head; *they have been now!*"

"Shut up!" Maury half rose from his chair, purple in the face with anger. "Who exactly do you think you're speaking to, some coolie on the site?"

Harold gave him a withering look. "Well, I'm not speaking to the owner of Moorelands, that much I know," he sneered.

"Stop it!" Olwyn cried. "Be quiet, both of you. Instead of immediately diving at each other's throats you ought to be sitting down with me trying to decide what best to do, and obviously we have to do something with the prospectors leaving our camp in droves."

What she did was consult two independent geologists about the advisability of investing in the new strikes herself. Both these men thought she should. Charles Butterfield, an American with more than twenty years' experience at diamond diggings all over the world, was especially helpful and took great pains to explain the difference between alluvial diamonds and those found inland. The gems themselves were exactly the same, he said. It was the ground they were found in and the method of recovery that was different.

Charlie explained that the inland, or dry strikes were confined to what he called pipes, conelike areas that appeared on the surface either as kopjes—low stunted hills—or circular hollows. In both cases the pipes, he felt, would go very deep into the earth and stood a good chance of producing more gems than the river diggings. Further, they would probably last much longer. "Of course we're talking about *mining* here," he went on. "It will be a different proposition from the river diggings; more difficult too."

Olwyn asked him a question she had always been curious about. "How exactly are diamonds made? I mean, how do they come to exist?"

"Ah . . ." Charlie grinned at her, "now that is a very big question. Nobody knows precisely the exact process, but diamonds are essentially carbon. It's fairly safe to say that it all started millions of years ago deep down in the bowels of the earth when carbon was exposed to intense heat and pressure. This is what makes the gems so hard. As you know, it takes a diamond to cut another diamond."

Olwyn nodded. "How did they get up to the earth's surface, or at least near the surface?"

"By internal explosions, to put it simply," said Butterfield. "The gems erupted into the air along with the molten lava, though obviously some didn't make it all the way through the earth's crust. Some of these eruptions set part way up; these are the pipes," he finished with a smile.

Maury was dispatched soon after this conversation to invest as heavily as they dared in the new dry strikes; also to sniff about for any other likely property where there could be diamondiferous ground. He was gone for a month. During the time he was away Olwyn returned to working at Moorelands, now greatly reduced camp-wise but still producing some good diamonds.

She took to appearing at the site in well-tailored English riding clothes, much more comfortable than long, trailing gowns, and again wore her hair sleekly pulled back from her face in a chignon. The prospectors gaped at her but covertly. No one dared leer or whistle at her now. Mrs. Howell had become a well-known and respected figure in the territory. That she was also young and very beautiful—and rich—only added to the fairy tale aura surrounding the first woman in the world to own a diamond field.

# 26

The following April Olwyn and Maury moved into their mansion on Moorelands. It had been built in the style of a planter's house with a long portico and columns across the front, and was filled with imported furniture from Europe. To Olwyn—who had once lived in a tenement—it seemed like the grandest, most beautiful house in the world. She couldn't believe it was hers; it all seemed too incredible. It had been constructed with a large addition at the rear but it was only after weeks of soul-searching that James Scobbie finally conceded defeat and resigned from his mission at Nuruzambora. "The Lord is pointing me in a new direction now," he said. "I can but go where He leads me."

The Scobbies moved into the spacious addition at Moorelands, Hannah with the utmost relief. The only one not too happy about the arrangement was Maury, who secretly wanted the entire property to themselves.

By now James was a familiar figure on the diamond

fields, and generally liked and respected by the prospectors. They were a rollicking lot and worked and played hard so James had plenty of sin to do battle with, such as drinking, gambling, fornication, and adultery, as well as thieving, cheating, or as Scobbie put it, "Every vice known to man or beast."

He also started counseling men suffering from stress. The diggers veered from being on top of the world one moment, when they found stones, to plunging into the depths the next when none were recovered. Few could afford to tarry very long unless they were producing, and since many had staked everything they owned on the venture the tension was overwhelming. Some went mad; others committed suicide. There was violence, even murder on the fields, though the crime rate was not excessive considering that there were now close to fifty thousand newcomers in what had once been an unspoiled wilderness.

One day James ran into Wentworth at the Dutoitspan mine. Scobbie thought that Justin looked a bit strained himself, and when he commented about it the younger man admitted, "I recently lost a good business opportunity at Driegraf."

At that very moment Justin was involved in another potentially good opportunity—if he could just bring it off. He had joined with a group of investors from Port Elizabeth in trying to buy a farm owned by the De Beers brothers, two stubborn, immovable Boers. Their farm was only a few miles west of Driegraf.

Through Kelly, Justin offered them three thousand pounds for their property, a fortune at the time since the land had originally cost them less than fifty pounds. Further, three thousand was more than the owners of Dutoitspan and Bultfontein had received for each of theirs.

"No, no," said the De Beers, shaking their heads. "We don't wish to sell."

Justin's instinct screamed at him to go all out to

purchase this property. He went back to the Port Elizabeth group and suggested they hit the De Beers with a stunning offer, one that would rock them back on their heels and be just too tempting to refuse. They instructed him to go ahead and offer the farmers what he felt would be necessary to acquire the farm.

Shortly after he saw James at Dutoitspan, in May of 1871, Justin and the Port Elizabeth syndicate bought the De Beers farm for just over six thousand pounds. His ploy had worked and the Boers went off rubbing their hands in glee, certain that Wentworth had lost his wits. Why, they could buy twenty farms with all that money! The brothers were overjoyed.

They had just made the mammoth mistake of all time. The De Beers departed the scene but their name lingered on. Ever afterward, it was to become synonymous with diamonds.

De Beers, Dutoitspan, and Bultfontein were all within a few miles of each other, the last two quite close. Mining towns rapidly sprang up around them, towns that would become permanent. Dutoitspan and Bultfontein would eventually take the name of Beaconsfield, and De Beers and a mine yet to be discovered would become Kimberley, named after the Secretary of State for the Colonies, John Wodehouse, the Earl of Kimberley.

But naming the towns was the least of the prospectors' concerns at that time.

While Justin was still haggling over De Beers in early April he bumped into Maury Howell in one of the shacklike taverns at Bultfontein. Taverns were always the first buildings, other than rough dwellings, to be thrown up at diamond strikes. Howell was with a group of his prospector friends from Colesberg, and he waved Justin over to their table, immediately bragging, "Take warning, my friend, Teragno is about to be eclipsed. The wife and I are moving into our new house at the end of the month, and I'll wager it will be the showplace of the territory." He went on in the same vein. "We are also building a house up here, off the Dutoitspan Road. A must with the mines opening up. Kelly was telling me you are doing the same."

"As you say, for convenience," Justin murmured. And he asked as casually as he could, "And how are Olwyn and the children?"

"Oh, splendid, splendid!" Then Howell made an announcement that cut Justin to the quick. "We have another babe on the way." Maury cast a bleary smile around the prospectors gathered at the table, saying, "Let's hope I can do it again and we have another set of twins. Got to fill up that big house we're moving into."

Howell's Colesberg friends laughed and thumped him on the back and, half drunk as they were, they expressed their feelings that Maury certainly had it in him in the crudest, most explicit language possible— and they included Olwyn in their remarks. Howell sat gloating, laughing with them.

Justin stood up abruptly. He had the choice of leaving immediately or murdering Howell on the spot, which would certainly raise a few eyebrows, for why should he, a mere acquaintance, do violence to a man for showing disrespect to his own wife?

"Hey, hang about a bit!" Maury grabbed his arm when he saw Justin was about to leave. "I have a proposition to put to you. The boys and I"—he nodded to the others—"are prospecting over by . . ."

Justin hardly heard Maury above the roaring blood in his ears. He gazed down at Howell stonily and felt nothing but contempt. When he'd first arrived in Cape Town Maury had been a fresh, good-looking young man, but already the signs of seediness were stamped on his features in spite of the expensive clothes he now wore. Somewhere along the line he had grown a raffish moustache and taken to wearing his curly, dark hair slicked back from his face, a face displaying the first marks of excess. His green eyes were bloodshot, with faint pouches beneath them, his skin mottled, especially over the area of his nose. And slim as he was, he had a paunch. He looked what he was, a degenerate.

". . . well worth exploring," Howell was saying. "The kopje is only about a mile or two from the digging going on at De Beers." He flashed what used to be a persuasive grin at Justin, and now struck Wentworth as merely oily. "Want to invest? We need more capital," he admitted, and continued before Justin could answer yea or nay, "The whole area looks promising. How much can you put in?"

"Not interested," Wentworth replied coldly. "I have another deal pending at the moment."

"Taciturn bastard!" Howell muttered as Justin walked out the door. "Probably jealous. He was the big man when things first started happening up here but times they are a-changing, and he doesn't like it. Bully to him!"

One of the Colesberg gang looked thoughtful. "I wonder what deal he was talking about. You should have felt him out, Howell. Could have been something worth getting into. That kopje we're working on . . ." he shrugged, "empty as the inside of an old beer keg, and as you know, lads, there just *ain't* nothing emptier than that!"

They all laughed and nodded affirmatively.

They didn't know it then but their luck at the kopje was soon to change dramatically.

In May Olwyn suffered a miscarriage. Maury took it as a personal insult. It didn't help his humor when, less than a week later, his wife's photograph appeared on the front page of *The Diamond News,* together with an article raving about her extraordinary success. The title was, "Queen of Diamonds—Olwyn Howell née Moore."

There was very little about Maury in the script.

He stamped home late that afternoon and banged into their twenty-room mansion on the banks of the Orange River, and tossed the newspaper across his wife's bed, where Olwyn lay recovering from what had been a severe ordeal and great loss of blood, not to mention a bitter disappointment.

"Do you know what I sound like in that?" he cried, jabbing a finger at the newspaper. "I come out sounding like a bloody appendage to you! A—a kind of gigolo, for Christ sake! Queen of Diamonds!" he spat. "I wonder how queenly they would think you were if they knew I'd married you when you were seven months pregnant!"

Olwyn's white face reddened, but she replied quietly, seeing how upset he was, "I'm sorry, Maury, but I didn't write that article—"

"Sorry! Much good that will do me now. I'll be a laughingstock at the diggings once this gets about. I can see it now; Maury Howell, court jester to the Diamond Queen!" He stepped up to the bed and glared down at her out of eyes that were moist and bloodshot. "You've turned me into a blasted fool!"

Olwyn could smell the strong reek of alcohol off him now that he was closer. It crossed her mind that if he'd been turned into a fool, then he'd done it to himself. His drinking, gambling, and wenching were now the talk of Griqualand West, as were his extravagance, boasting, arrogance, and penchant for fighting. Maury had made many virulent enemies through his antics, and the editor of *The Diamond News* happened to be one of them, a man he had once insulted in public by calling him "a nit-picking baboon living off the lice of others."

"Pay no attention," Olwyn soothed. "Everybody knows he—"

"Pay no attention?" Howell snarled. "And I suppose I should also pay no attention to the fact that you lost my baby?"

"Maury!" Olwyn gasped, "You make it sound as if I lost it deliberately!" Tears started up in her eyes and her lips began to quiver.

He put his hands on the bed and leaned forward, blasting alcohol fumes into her face. "You could carry twins for some—some filthy piece of scum, yet you couldn't even carry *one* for me. Maybe you did lose it deliberately. There are ways—"

"Get out!" Olwyn gasped, trembling with shock and disgust. "Get out of this room—"

He slapped her face, hard, the first time he had ever hit her.

It wasn't to be the last.

In July Howell's Colesberg cronies finally struck it rich at their kopje, some said the biggest strike yet. This started a mad stampede, a new rush to the area, a mine that was to be called variously New Rush or Colesberg Kopje, but eventually became Kimberley. The Howells had invested heavily; they were now among the mega-rich, or soon would be. To celebrate, Maury suggested a world tour that would include a gigantic shopping spree. He and Olwyn had hardly spoken since the night he hit her, but shortly after the strike at the kopje he came home one evening after an absence of several days and presented Olwyn with a kitten-soft sable cape and a huge bunch of red roses. He even had gifts for Ariann, Aidan, and the Scobbies. Once alone in their bedroom Maury took her in his arms and told her how sorry he was. "I've been a beast," he said. "Blame it on business worries, the fever"—Maury had recurring bouts of malaria—"or whatever, but I really *am* dreadfully sorry, Olwyn darling, and I'll make it all up to you, you'll see."

She nodded and tried to be enthusiastic, and Olwyn supposed that this was the time to tell him of her suspicion—that she might be pregnant again. But something warned her to wait to make sure it was true, and that she would carry this baby safely, remembering how Maury had reacted to her miscarriage. There was a definite risk involved in traveling while she was pregnant, but a bigger risk, Olwyn felt, in informing her husband prematurely.

The twins were walking now, Aidan a sturdy toddler with golden-brown hair and deep blue eyes. He had a cherubic smile that melted his mother's heart

and was a very affectionate child. Ariann, the one
most like her father, could rarely sit still long enough
to be cuddled. It was she who led her brother into
mischief.

A few days after the children's first birthday James
returned from De Beers with a huge grin on his face.
"Come outside," he said to Olwyn, "and bring the
tots."

In the back of their new carriage that James had
used that day were two huge stuffed animals, almost
life-sized; a lion for Aidan and a tiger for Ariann. The
children squealed in delight at the sight of them.

"From Justin Wentworth," said James. "It's good of
him, don't you think? I'm surprised a busy man like
Wentworth would remember the twins' birthday."

Olwyn wasn't. It was all she could do to hold back
tears. She was certain, too, that Justin suspected the
children might be his, even though twins often arrived
prematurely. If only he could see them! she thought,
then immediately checked herself. If he saw Ariann, in
particular, then he'd know the truth!

On August fifteenth the Howells departed for Europe. They visited Scotland, naturally, and it was very
difficult for Olwyn to return to the country of her
birth, to walk with a reluctant Maury through the
rough streets of the Gallowgate while shuddering and
casting uneasy glances over his shoulder as if he
expected to be pounced on at any minute. Olwyn
pointed out the tenement where she had been born,
their single-end apartment in the building, long-since
repaired following the fire that had killed her father,
but as mean as ever, even more so now.

She cried then, thinking of the quiet man who had
driven her to learn her lessons and succeed in the
world so that she wouldn't have to continue to live in
the Gallowgate, and how she *had* succeeded beyond
her father's wildest dreams! Had he sensed, Olwyn
wondered as she stood thinking while Maury stamped
up and down impatiently, that she had better learn to

take care of herself; that no one else would do it for her?

Gazing at the building, Olwyn sighed as she thought of the past, wishing her father could have lived to enjoy the benefits of her new life.

From there they went to the medical school. "Let's not go in," said Maury, glancing at the heavy gold watch on its chain across his vest. "Don't forget we have an appointment with the newspaper people at one o'clock."

Olwyn returned to visit the Copper Jug alone—only its name had been changed! It was now the Red Lion, a rather shabby-looking pub. Time marches on, she reflected, thinking that it was at exactly this spot where it all began. That rainy, bitter cold November night came back to her vividly; how she'd felt unappreciated and lonely, easy pickings for Devlin Sproat and his friends. How innocent and naïve she had been then!

The visit home left her feeling sad. It didn't help when an article appeared about them in a Glasgow newspaper asking about her: Is This the Woman Who Has Everything?

Maury laughed when he read that. "Well," he said, "sometimes they get things right!"

Olwyn smiled but thought privately, *No, not everything.*

They moved on to London, then Paris, which was perhaps not at its best as it was recovering from the recent Franco-Prussian war, but they went to the Opéra, the Théâtre Francais, dined in all the noted restaurants, and saw most of the famous sights. Olwyn, urged by Maury, visited the couturieres back in business following the war, and was fitted for many new gowns, which would be sent on to her in Africa. It was all so hectic and flurried that Olwyn made up her mind to return to Paris one day, at a time when she could enjoy it—savor the city—at a more leisurely pace. Maury was more interested in the nightlife than the sights, in buying up the contents of all the well-known shops in every city they passed through. Mountains of goods were purchased and shipped home ahead of them, much of it expensive trash Olwyn was certain they would never use, but if it made him happy . . .

From there they went to Venice and Rome, and naturally they traveled everywhere first class and stayed at the best hotels in the most lavish suites in those establishments. They also saw the inside of every casino en route, where Maury lost a great deal of money, accepting his heavy losses with a shrug and the remark, "Plenty more where that came from." And grinning: "Just have to dig it up!"

Everywhere they went they attracted attention, first because of Olwyn's beauty, well displayed now in gowns of the finest silk and lace, but also because of all the money her husband tossed about. Maury had a habit of carrying a pouchful of diamonds with him everywhere, and when he wished to make a particularly big impression, he would pour the gems out on a table in front of him—always when people of importance were with them or seated nearby—and once he even tossed a ten-carat diamond to a waiter in lieu of a tip, saying, "There you are, my friend! Now you can buy this place," with a wave around the restaurant they were dining in.

Olwyn was constantly embarrassed by his ostentatiousness. Though it had a big impact on many of the people they met, it repelled others. She couldn't understand how he could be so blind. The very people Maury most wanted to impress were revolted by his behavior. The others courted them, flattered them, and treated them to many lavish entertainments, but none of it was sincere and it sickened Olwyn, though she made no comment.

This holiday, the first part of a projected world tour, the other half scheduled to take place the following year, was supposed to have been a quiet, private affair. It turned into a circus. Thanks to some of the people they met and the many interviews Maury gave the newspapers, the Howells' notoriety preceded them and they were met at each new stop on the trip by a rapidly expanding army of sycophants.

By the time they returned to London, where a crowd of reporters were awaiting them, Olwyn was hard-pressed to hold her tongue and swallow her feelings when Maury announced that he was throwing a party for all their new friends, including a visit to the new Albert Hall. That night he wore a black dinner suit—but otherwise he blazed with diamonds —gems flashing from every conceivable part of his anatomy where a man might wear such things, including a few parts he himself had invented. Olwyn chose a beautiful, understated white gown but her husband immediately vetoed her selection, plucking from her wardrobe a magnificent silver creation he had had made for her in Paris. "I want you to wear this," he said firmly, throwing the white gown on the floor of her closet. "Everybody will be there tonight, including some of the royal family, and I won't have you put in the shade. Another thing," he added when she frowned, "put on your waterfall necklace. I didn't give you the thing to lie hidden away in a safe."

At that Olwyn's patience snapped. Her waterfall necklace, as he called it, could have lit up the entire City of London all by itself, a veritable cascade of brilliants that was so ornate and heavy that it almost broke her neck to wear it.

"No!" she snapped, "I'm wearing rubies tonight." And at his thunderous frown: "They look better with the silver dress and I wouldn't want to compete with the stones you are wearing," she added to humor him. "You know that fabulous necklace puts everything else in the shade, dear."

Mollified, Howell regarded himself approvingly in the mirror. "I'll wager your husband will start a new fashion tonight, Olwyn!"

"Oh, I'm sure you will, Maury dear." Olwyn could hardly keep a straight face but at the same time she felt sick at the thought of the evening ahead, one bound to end with Maury slobbering all over her in bed, reeking of alcohol, forcing her to intimacies that revolted her.

Olwyn told him about the new baby then, hoping it would have a steadying effect on him. He was delighted. "Fantastic surprise!" Then he gave her what almost amounted to a warning look. "Let's hope you carry it to term this time."

Rather than steady him, the news made Maury strut, boast, and drink more than ever. When Olwyn chided him he retorted, "Got to celebrate the big event."

"The baby isn't here yet—"

"Enjoy it while you can, that's my motto," he interrupted. "Besides, with you"—he shrugged—"anything can happen, as we well know."

They returned to Cape Town at the beginning of December. To Olwyn's surprise Maury was all for continuing on home at once, even if it meant missing the Governor's Ball, to which they had been invited. This was most unlike Maury Howell! He loved city life and could be assured of all the attention he craved now, even at the highest level, and Maury never forgot how he'd once been treated like a common plebeian at the start of his career in Africa. He took every opportunity to gloat.

Yet . . . he wanted to be home. Olwyn couldn't understand it.

She was anxious to return to Moorelands too. The trip had exhausted her in her present condition and she was beginning to show now. Besides, she missed the twins and the Scobbies desperately and couldn't wait to see them again. But they had important business in Cape Town that must be attended to, including a visit to Fabien Precious Gems, Ltd.; she was most anxious to meet Mr. Fabien himself at long last.

"You concern yourself with business when I'm about to come down with another attack of malaria," Maury grumbled, shivering ostentatiously and refusing to get out of bed that morning. Olwyn had been up for an hour and was fully dressed, anxious to visit Fabien, discuss a few points of business that puzzled her, then hurry on home to her family.

Well aware that her husband often used attacks of fever to worm his way out of doing something he didn't want to do, she marched back to the bed and laid her hand on his brow, but Howell angrily jerked away, slapping her hand so hard that he broke her little finger. Olwyn cried out in agony and stumbled back from the bed, the blood draining from her face. Howell jumped out of bed, instantly contrite, took the injured hand and kissed it again and again, then announced that they would find the best doctor in Cape Town. When they left the doctor's surgery just before noon he put his arm around her waist and said, "Some lunch, then home!"

Olwyn turned and gave him a long, searching look, thinking that his attack of fever had been short-lived—if he'd had it at all. In fact, he looked fitter than he had for a long time. The holiday had done him good. All the more surprising, then, she mused, that he was so anxious to forego the amusements of Cape Town and bring it to an end.

"Maury," she said patiently, "I'm as eager to be home as you are, but first I *have* to see Fabien—"

"Why, in the name of God?" he cut in, his temper flaring instantly.

"Why not?" Olwyn asked him quietly.

Less than two hours later the Howells were seated in the opulent offices of Fabien Precious Gems, Ltd., ensconced in plush leather chairs in Mr. Fabien's spacious private domain. Fabien turned out to be much younger than Olwyn had been expecting, surprisingly young to have had time to build up such a supposedly reputable firm, something that usually took a very long time, if not several generations.

The moment she set eyes on the gem dealer Olwyn thought he looked familiar. As Maury introduced him simply as, "My friend, Fabien," and they shook hands, Olwyn smiled and asked, "Is it possible that we might have met before? I seem to know your face?"

Fabien was short and broad, his width disproportionate with his height. He had sallow skin and bulbous eyes that were set very far apart and his smile, Olwyn thought, seemed ingratiating and rather oily. The Frenchman—

"No, Madame Howell, we cannot have met before," the gem dealer assured her smoothly, at the same time flicking a glance at Howell, who was acting peculiarly stiff and ill-at-ease. "You see, I've never had the pleasure of visiting the diamond fields, though I mean to rectify that shortly. Your husband and I are old friends, as I imagine he has told you. We met shortly after Maury arrived here from Britain." His moist, reptilian eyes touched on Howell and he smiled. "Many good things have happened since then, eh, Maury?"

"Ah . . . quite. Quite!" Maury replied, shifting about in his chair.

He offered them refreshments, saying, "I have some excellent wine?"

Olwyn requested coffee; Maury whisky. "And make it neat," he said.

"Have you heard the big news?" Fabien asked them as they waited for the various beverages to be brought to his office. When they shook their heads, explaining that they had only arrived back in Africa the previous morning, he said, "Well, the boundary dispute has finally been settled. Griqualand West was made a Crown Colony in October."

Maury came alive then. "Topping news! This does call for a celebration!"

"You'll perhaps excuse me if I don't join you," the dealer replied with a rueful grin. "Have you forgotten I'm Dutch?"

Dutch? Olwyn stared at him with her original sharpness. She'd thought—Maury had told her that Fabien was French; that his parents still lived in Paris. But his information did prove distracting and

Olwyn sat for a moment considering what it would mean to them.

Four different factions had been involved in the dispute over the diamond territory, territory nobody much cared about only a year or two ago, but land that had suddenly become hot property with the start of the inland diamond mining. Unlike the river diggings, the dry pipes showed every indication of lasting much longer. Already a permanent settlement was growing up around these mines and at least fifty thousand newcomers had arrived in the area and seemed quite prepared to stay.

The different claimants for the mines were President Pretorius of the Transvaal, Brand from the Orange Free State, then a Griqua chief, Nicolaas Waterboer, and finally Britain.

As the three of them discussed it over their drinks, Fabien made it sound as if Britain had won by scheming and trickery. If they could believe him, the British had sat back and cunningly pitted the other three against each other, then announced that the question must be settled by arbitration, since they obviously couldn't agree. There were very few high officials able to handle the proceedings in the hinterlands of Africa at that time, and it was difficult to find an arbitrator not himself involved in the dispute. Finally Sir Richard Keate, the Governor of Natal, was chosen, and asked to set up a panel to hear the various cases. His final decision was that the territory belonged to the Griquas.

"Keate is British," Fabien pointed out unnecessarily, "and he knew that the Griquas always side with the British against the Dutch, so it's hardly surprising that Waterboer subsequently turned to them for protection when it became known that neither Brand nor Pretorius were satisfied with the outcome. Therefore"—he shrugged—"Griqualand became a British Protectorate in October. Clever, eh?"

Though the dealer laughed and shrugged, Olwyn saw a resentful glint in his eyes, understandable enough, she supposed, since he himself was Dutch. Yet she couldn't help wondering just how good a friend he really was to Maury, or how wise a choice as a business associate; if a man like that could have their best interests at heart. And thinking of business—

Olwyn regarded him soberly. "Since we won't be spending much time in Cape Town there are several business matters I would like to discuss," she said. "Certain things that have puzzled me, Mr. Fabien—"

"Oh, just Fabien, please!" he beamed, and though he seemed to have turned a shade paler, he rushed on heartily, "I sincerely trust we have been of satisfactory service to you?"

Maury gave a start and sat forward. "Oh yes, yes indeed!" he answered for her. "Perfectly satisfactory. Couldn't ask for better!"

Howell stood up suddenly with his empty glass in hand and nodded to the nearby sideboard where several decanters and bottles stood on an enormous silver tray. "May I?"

"Most certainly!" Fabien nodded, and as he did so a drop of sweat fell from his face onto the papers scattered in front of him on the desk. Both Olwyn and the gem dealer stared at it, then both raised their heads at once and their eyes clashed. The man was perspiring heavily. As he lifted his head Olwyn's mind jumped back to the time she had gone to see Knute Bleur with what she thought was a piece of graphite, and after examining the stone she recalled the way Bleur's froglike eyes had peered at her over the stack of books on his desk.

A hideous suspicion surfaced and then swelled in Olwyn's mind, though she made no comment. Instead, she enraged Howell by suddenly demanding all the figures pertaining to the transactions Fabien had made for them from the start of the business, saying coolly, "They will be turned over to my accountants and lawyers for thorough examination."

Howell swung around from the liquor cabinet, the whisky in his glass splashing all over his hand and clothes, his green eyes wide with feigned hurt and affront. "Now see here, Olwyn—"

"Madame Howell!" Fabien too was now on his feet, his hands fluttering, striving hard to look indignant. "I hope you are not suggesting—"

"The figures, please," Olwyn interrupted grimly. "I have no intention of leaving this office without them."

Then she waited, turning a deaf ear to both of them.

It was almost two hours before the Howells left Fabien Precious Gems, Ltd., Olwyn with a sheaf of papers clutched tight in her hand. She asked their coachman to take them directly to their Cape Town lawyer—not that she needed the lawyer to tell her that she had been robbed; that Maury—her own husband —and Fabien had conspired between them to swindle her out of a fortune.

Once inside the coach Olwyn collapsed back against the seat, sick to the bone. Howell turned to her, his face engorged with livid blood, and snarled, "You bitch! You arrogant, emasculating bitch! I—I could—"

He struck her a vicious blow across the face and blood spurted from her nose, her lip splitting like a ripe peach. He seized her wrist in both hands and twisted it until the incriminating papers fell from her nerveless fingers and skidded all over the floor of the vehicle. Then, hurling her back against the window, Maury got down on his hands and knees, scooped up the papers, and tore them to shreds, panting all the while, "You'd make trouble for me! You'd embarrass me in front of Fabien . . . threaten . . . you'd dare— dare, for Christ sake, to threaten me! I'll conduct this business as I see fit!" he roared, rolling down the window and tossing the fragments out into the street. "I'm your husband, head of this family . . ."

Olwyn lay slumped against the side of the coach, her head swimming, his voice seeming to come to her from a great distance. But even then, dazed as she was, Olwyn knew that she would never trust Maury Howell again. She also knew, as she touched trembling fingers to her lips and they came away bloody, that she hated and despised him; that she was married to a violent man who was half mad and quite capable of killing her in a fit of ungovernable rage. Though she was seething herself, self-preservation warned Olwyn to swallow her ire and say nothing—at least for now—but she knew that something would have to be done.

Under the circumstances, her suspicion that Fabien might be connected to Knute Bleur seemed incidental to Olwyn at that fraught moment. She supposed it was possible that Maury didn't know about her ordeal at the hands of the mineralogist; even Fabien might be unaware of it. After all, she had been Oliver Moore then. One thing was certain: both these men had conspired to cheat her, that much she knew for a fact. Any slight affection she had left for Maury Howell flickered out and died.

Olwyn leaned her forehead against the window and closed her eyes, wishing fervently that she had never married him, asking herself for the hundredth time why she hadn't married Justin instead. Pride! she thought bitterly; she had allowed pride to get in the way of the love she felt for him, but where had that pride gotten her now? Instead of elevating her, it had brought her low.

Olwyn's face was marked and because of it the Howells had to delay their departure from Cape Town. Maury amused himself by gambling, drinking and, Olwyn was certain, whoring about town. While he was out she took the opportunity to consult with her lawyers and accountants and made arrangements for their gems to be shipped directly to an old, renowned diamond merchant in London from now on.

She also found out that Fabien's father was Knute Bleur.

Olwyn sat down then and coldly reviewed the situation, deciding that she had struggled too hard all her life to cower back now and watch a raving degenerate destroy the future security of her children

—Justin's children! She had sincerely tried to be a good wife to Maury, to overlook his distasteful and often cruel behavior, and felt that she might have grown genuinely fond of him if given half a chance. Now it was obvious to her that their relationship could only go in one direction, and that was down.

Olwyn rose and walked to the window of her hotel suite but her mind was turned inward and she hardly noticed what was happening in the street below. She was thinking of what her lawyer had said to her. "I don't hold with this myself, mind you, but there are those who believe that a husband has a right to beat his wife if she goes against his wishes. I'm truly sorry, Mrs. Howell." His eyes touched on her bruised face, then dropped to her stomach, and he sighed and shook his head. "I can see for myself what you've been through and I think it's detestable, but . . . I must tell you that under the law you have no grounds for divorce. I'm most dreadfully sorry . . ."

The Howells returned to Moorelands, not at Christmas as Olwyn had hoped, but in February of the following year, via one of the new fast coaches pelting between the Cape and the diamond fields. On the way back Maury drank from a constantly refilled whisky flask and at one point slurred, "What I'm gonna do sh-shortly is rid the house of that Scobbie crew." His bleary eyes goaded her. "Parasites, the lot of them . . . 'specially that young pup, Hal." He lurched forward and glowered into her eyes. "You shleepin' with Harold, wife? He shlippin' into your bed when I'm out . . . filthy young hound . . ."

Olwyn gave him an icy stare and turned her head to the window, thinking that the best thing she could do was ignore him. But he wouldn't force the Scobbies out of Moorelands, even if she couldn't find a way to force him out of her life! The property was hers, or had been. Taking the advice of her lawyer while at the Cape she had deeded it over to her children with a proviso that she would administer the estate until they came of age. So if anything were to happen to her, Moorelands would go to Aidan and Ariann, and in the meantime the Scobbies would stay, of that Olwyn was determined. She wouldn't be cowed!

She could see the other passengers glancing furtively at Maury, who in every way looked like the degenerate he was, his eyes puffy and red-rimmed and his skin blotchy, his expensive clothes disheveled and splattered with snuff and spilled alcohol, his manner belligerent and coarse.

Olwyn could well imagine what they were thinking. "Surely this cannot be *the* Maury Howell, the diamond magnate? Not that morose, drunken tramp!"

In two months she would have this man's baby!

The Scobbies were amazed when they saw Olwyn's condition, which was obvious now, though she wasn't nearly as big as she had been with the twins, and oh, how Olwyn needed to hold her children at that moment!

When they burst into the room, Aidan with his plump little arms outstretched, Ariann flashing her bright, impish smile, Olwyn's heart melted, and as always when she looked at her children she thought of their father.

The little girl stopped some distance away and said, "Welcome home, Mother and Father," repeating the greeting her nurse had been teaching her for the past few days.

Aidan, as if he sensed what she *most* needed at that moment, raced to Olwyn and dove into her arms.

The following evening Harold brought a new friend home to dinner, a tall, plumpish young man of nineteen who had recently arrived to try his luck on the diamond fields.

"This is Cecil Rhodes, Olwyn," Hal said, introducing them. "Cecil is from England and his father is also a minister. He came out to his older brother's farm in Natal, but when Herbert decided to seek his fortune at

New Rush, Cecil soon got the fever and followed him," Harold told her with a grin.

"Actually, I came to Africa for health reasons," young Rhodes explained gravely, his voice high-pitched and his eyes, when he regarded Olwyn, betraying none of the sudden interest and admiration she had grown used to from every man who beheld her. "Though now that I'm here, well, why not give it a try? My brother and I are working a claim at New Rush and doing fairly well," he went on with no pretense at false modesty. "There's lots of scope here for enterprising young men, I've noticed. For instance, the heat. It's appalling. So . . . I bought one of the new ice-making machines with some of our profits and the cold drinks and ice cream have been a topping success. I've other ideas too—"

"Cecil thinks he's solved the problem of water seeping into the mine at New Rush," Harold cut in, clearly very impressed with his friend. "He's searching about now for a steam-driven pump which he feels will do the trick."

"You'll never find anything like that in Griqualand," Maury snorted, taking an instant dislike to the youth whom he soon nicknamed "the Cold Fish." "Aside from that, it would be prohibitively expensive for a lad in your position."

"Oh . . ." Rhodes gave Maury a reserved stare down his long nose. ". . . I'll find one somewhere," he assured him, coolly confident. "As for the expense, well, I can always take out a loan. I certainly won't let the money stop me."

"That's the spirit!" Hal approved, slapping him on the back. Then he made what was to be a very prophetic statement. "Cecil is going places over here."

They didn't know it then, but they were looking at the future prime minister, a man who thought on a mammoth scale and would one day give his name to a country—and who would eventually dominate the diamond industry.

356 ◊ CATHERINE LINDEN

Cecil intrigued Olwyn. He was so thoughtful and serious by comparison with the other young hopefuls on the fields, who were rowdy and wild-living in the extreme, squandering any profit they made on drink, dice, and women. She noticed, the more she got to know Rhodes, that he seemed uncomfortable in the company of women and showed no interest in them, but that he was very interested in business and the country as a whole. She agreed with Hal that Cecil seemed destined for resounding success, providing his delicate health didn't ruin his lofty plans. Hal had confided that Rhodes had always had lung problems, and at various times had been given only months to live. "But he's determined not to let that stop him."

Olwyn admired his force of will. At that moment her own was at its lowest ebb. If it hadn't been for the children, she thought, she would have had nothing to live for—for all her great wealth—tied as she was to a man she detested for the rest of her life. The prospect chilled her. Olwyn glanced around her luxurious home, now filled with priceless objects from every corner of the globe; she thought of her jewels, the type royalty would envy; her clothes, furs, and all the rest of it—and these things meant nothing when she lacked the thing she most yearned for.

In this tired, discouraged state Olwyn went into labor on April first. The following morning Harold galloped into Kimberley in search of one of the genuine doctors who had recently moved to the area, while Maury, after one look at his wife and convinced she was dying, shut himself up in his office and beat his own record in speedily drinking himself into oblivion.

Thanks to the skill of Dr. Sanders Olwyn didn't die, but when it was all over the doctor told her sadly that she would bear no more children. Her second son, Gerard, was born at eight o'clock on the evening of April second, and the first thing his father did upon sobering up was to take an uncut diamond from his desk drawer and go around the house scratching *his* child's name on every window with the sharp cutting edge of the rough gem. "That'll show 'em," Howell muttered to himself as he examined his handiwork in satisfaction. "That'll show 'em who's the real heir here."

Then Maury embarked on a gigantic drinking binge with his friends to wet the child's head, as he put it, though as James said dryly, "The bairn could well drown in the amount of alcohol his father consumes."

For a month afterward Olwyn lay exhausted and withdrawn in her bedroom. Lifeless as she was, she found it difficult to take an interest in anything or any of the many visitors who stopped by with gifts for the new baby. Hannah and James did their best to cheer her up; Harold came to her every evening after work to report on the day's activity at the Moorelands diggings several hundred yards upriver from their home. It was much smaller now that the mines had opened, but there were still about a thousand men digging at Moorelands. For one thing, the claims there cost vastly less than the mines, where it was hard to buy into a plot for less than a thousand pounds. The better claims at Dutoitspan and Bultfontein went for much more than that and at De Beers and New Rush the best fetched up to five thousand.

Harold, when he came to her each evening, concealed the problems at the diggings and told her the amusing, interesting details instead. Occasionally he visited the mines and expressed great enthusiasm. "And your house up there is beautiful!" he said, striving to rouse her out of her torpor. "Hurry and get well so you can see it! Lots of people are building now. Justin Wentworth's new place is just down the road . . ."

At that Harold thought he spied a tiny flicker of interest at last in her eyes. He nodded, rushing on. "You'll be surrounded by good friends up there, Olwyn. People are calling it the pioneer district." He chuckled. "The people who started everything are all there, or planning to be."

In the end it was the twins who gave Olwyn the jolt she needed.

It happened after breakfast one morning. The men had already departed for work. As she lay in her bed staring into space Olwyn heard Hannah scolding the twins somewhere beyond her room, and got up to see what it was all about. The door to the big office she shared with Maury was wide open, though it was supposed to be kept locked. All their private papers were in there, also a metal box containing all the diamonds brought back from their own diggings at Moorelands, eventually to be sent by courier to London.

Peering into the office, Olwyn saw the twins sitting on the floor with the upturned box of gems between them, gaily tossing the glittering stones all over the room. She had already noticed how attracted the tots were to the sparkling objects and they liked nothing better than when Maury amused visitors with his standard party piece, demonstrating his original method of testing them to make sure they were the genuine article. How the twins laughed when he bit down on them, bashed them with a hammer, and finally wrote with them on a piece of glass.

"That's very naughty!" Hannah was saying when Olwyn appeared in the room. "And look, Ariann, you've cut your finger! Some of these stones have very sharp edges—"

"How on earth did they get in here?" Olwyn asked.

Hannah sighed, her eyes flickering away. "Well . . . Maury must have forgotten to lock the office door." What she didn't say was that Maury frequently forgot to lock the door; that only the previous week Hannah had caught one of the servants loitering suspiciously in the room. She and James, well aware of the state of the Howells' marriage, had made a pact not to interfere, though it was becoming increasingly hard when Maury left lighted cigars lying around, or his pistol, and wasn't too careful of what he said and did in front of the children while under the influence of alcohol.

Hannah knew for a fact that he was carrying on with one of the servant girls—oh, it was difficult to hold her tongue!

"Has this happened before?" Olwyn asked tersely.

Hannah nodded. "He's been especially careless over the past month."

The month when she was in bed, Olwyn thought with a groan.

She was up and dressed when Maury arrived home that night, and she didn't mince words. "I want you to promise me never to leave that office door unlocked again," she said, her voice tight with anger. "You know how the children like to explore, and how some of the servants can't resist pilfering."

Maury hardly listened to what she said but he couldn't take his eyes off her. As Olwyn stood shaking with anger before him, her full breasts rising and falling provocatively with every breath under the white satin bodice of her gown, he felt a sudden, vaulting desire. Where before her cheeks had ben pale, now they were flushed a deep pink, so delicate against her shining black hair. And her eyes flashed with more fire than any diamond.

He walked up to her and pulled the pins from her hair and let it cascade through his fingers but when he went to take her in his arms Olwyn jumped back.

"Did you hear what I said?" she asked him breathlessly.

Maury seized her roughly and silenced her by grinding his mouth against hers, then he threw her across the bed and ripped her gown down the middle. "This is how I like you to welcome me home," he said, rubbing his stubbly cheek against her swollen breasts. "I prefer you in bed with your clothes off and your mouth shut. Remember that from now on."

Olwyn fixed her eyes on the ceiling while he ravished her, willing herself not to feel pain or disgust or anything at all, nor to hear the vile things he had started to say to her every time they made love; things that seemed to drive him to sexual frenzy.

But after a moment or two it was too much. *I can't stand this,* she thought, a scream of outrage rising inside her. *I can't stand this anymore . . .*

Suddenly she cried aloud, "Leave me alone! I—I hate you! I never want you to touch me again."

A female servant passing in the hallway outside paused and listened, her black eyes huge, gleaming in the semi-dark above the stairs. She heard what sounded like a slap, then the master growling, "Time I taught you how a loving wife should behave . . ."

# Cutting Edge

# 27

Seeta, the children's nurse, seemed slightly flustered when she returned to their town house after taking the twins for a stroll in their carriage.

Olwyn was on the point of leaving for the mine to meet Maury. He had ordered her to join him for lunch at Benning's Hotel, grumbling, "People are beginning to think I don't *have* a wife!" Following luncheon they had an important business meeting.

When Seeta returned with the twins Olwyn was fussing with her new hat in front of the hall mirror. Frowning at her reflection, she tugged it this way and that. Finally she tossed it onto a chair and decided to go hatless. Secretly she had no desire to lunch with Maury at all.

She kissed the twins, now two years old, and watched them scamper off to the nursery, then she asked their nurse if they'd had a nice walk. Seeta was a statuesque young Griqua girl, six feet tall and broadly built for a woman, or as Maury had remarked lewdly, "a challenging armful." Olwyn strongly suspected that Maury himself had succumbed to the challenge.

Seeta frowned. "That man speak to me and the children."

Olwyn's heart gave a leap. "What man, Seeta?"

"The one with yellow hair, Mr. Wentworth."

The girl eyed her mistress nervously. "I no chatty to him. He speak to me," she stressed, afraid of getting into trouble. Mrs. Howell constantly warned her not to speak to strangers. She scolded her, too, about her penchant for tarrying at the market or stopping at other houses to gossip with the servants there. Once, when Seeta popped over to the mine to have a few words with Shingo, her betrothed, Mr. Howell had seen her and given her a terrible thrashing, threatening to kick her out of the house if it ever happened again. In light of all that, the nurse wouldn't have mentioned the present meeting at all but Mr. Wentworth had given her a message for her mistress. "He say to tell you, uh . . . he say everything clear now."

Olwyn dropped into the chair, smack on top of her new hat.

Well, Olwyn thought, it had finally happened. Of course it had to sooner or later, since they spent most of their time at Kimberley now. Though there were now about fifty thousand inhabitants in the area it still had a small-town aura about it, and all the influential people in the diamond industry knew each other and met frequently in the course of business. For the past five months she had made excuses to stay on at Moorelands, leaving Maury to attend to things in town. Finally, though, her husband had exploded and threatened to drag her to Kimberley by the hair of the head. She had only arrived in town a week ago.

When she felt her emotions begin to run riot inside her Olwyn straightened in her chair and squared her shoulders. She couldn't, wouldn't fall apart now! Maury was drinking heavily. He was often forgetful and careless. Many mistakes had been made both at Moorelands and their new company, Howell Central

Mines, and it had cost them dearly. Bad enough as that was, there had recently been a sharp drop in the diamond market, yet ominous as that was, Maury continued to drink, gamble, and squander money with no thought to the future. At the rate he was going, Olwyn thought grimly, there would be nothing left to pass on to their children.

And she couldn't keep the twins prisoners inside the house. On the few occasions when she herself had run into Justin Wentworth during the past two years, Olwyn felt that she had handled it quite well, at least outwardly. It helped that they had never been in a situation where they had been alone together; that was what she feared most now, that he'd find a way to get her by herself and force the truth out of her about the twins.

Olwyn jumped when Sam, their coachman, banged on the door, calling, "We go now, mistress. It time."

Olwyn stood up stoically and smoothed down the folds of her mist-green gown, determined to put a brave face on it and behave as if nothing out of the ordinary had happened, yes, even if she ran into Justin. Above all, she must avoid behaving in a manner that might arouse Maury's suspicions. He was fiercely jealous, quick to violence as she well knew, and Olwyn shuddered to think what would happen if he ever had reason to believe that Justin Wentworth, perhaps their chief competitor in the diamond business, had been involved with his wife.

She took one last look at herself in the mirror, stunningly beautiful in the delicate soft green gown, a color that lent her tawny eyes a provocative hint of green. Her hair was fashionably dressed in clusters of ringlets; they glistened black as jet against the dusky pink of her cheek. Careful as she was to protect her skin from the sun, rarely venturing out without a hat or parasol, it had still caught a light, creamy tan. Olwyn frowned at the sight of it, little realizing that it gave her an exotic look that men, at least, found appealing.

Snatching up the hat and knocking out the flattened brim, Olwyn irritably wrenched her mind away from Justin Wentworth and back to business. After lunch they were meeting with a syndicate to discuss amalgamating to buy up all the claims that had become available following the recent slump in prices, wiping out many of the smaller prospectors. Maury had been all for tightening the belt and standing fast to see how the wind would blow, but Olwyn agreed with Cecil Rhodes when he said, "The slump is a good thing in the long run, I assure you. There are just far too many small-time speculators in the business, and too many diamonds flooding the market. If the output were restricted, then the price of the stones would go up, but of course you can't do that with so many independent diggers cluttering the fields, churning up diamonds faster than you can blink—"

"Well, they have to, for God's sake!" Maury had cut in. "These fellows have to eat and pay their expenses or lose all they invested."

"They should be weeded out!" Rhodes retorted brutally, with a scornful glance at Maury. "It's not the way to conduct business. Supply and demand must be carefully controlled. Now . . ." he stroked his full-blown moustache, which made him look much older than his nineteen years, ". . . what's got to happen is a monopoly wherein production and prices are carefully structured with a view to increasing the price per carat of every stone mined, *then* you'd seen this business finally stabilize." His bulbous blue eyes gleamed as he added, "And it will come, make no mistake about that. It has to."

"Overblown buffoon!" Maury snorted when Rhodes and Harold left the office. "He's a blasted child, yet he thinks he has all the answers! I'll be glad when he returns to Oxford to finish his education— and let's hope he stays in England! He would give James Scobbie a good run for his money with his sermonizing."

Olwyn had not been able to take to Rhodes either,

though she had tried for Harold's sake. The lad was as cold and ruthless as he was clever. In the short time he had been in Kimberley he had done incredible things. The claim he worked with his brother was producing reasonably well—but Cecil hadn't contented himself with that! Oh no, with the money he made from the claim he'd immediately forged into several related businesses—ice-making, very welcome during the broiling summers, and pumping water from the mines, also very welcome to the harassed diggers, many of whom now found their expensive claims completely flooded the lower down they dug. Though she didn't particularly like Rhodes as a person, Olwyn, like Hal, greatly admired his enterprise and business acumen. She found it hard to believe sometimes that the boy was in ill health; he displayed more vigor and drive than a dozen men put together.

Maury was very leary about buying up the newly available claims floating about, particularly as each of these claims cost upward of five thousand pounds. It had taken weeks to convince him that they should at least get together with their advisers and associates to discuss it, and it was only when he discovered that one of his Port Elizabeth friends was interested that Maury finally agreed to the meeting, scheduled to take place after lunch that day.

Olwyn, in great awe, stood on the huge dusty plain beside New Rush, or Kimberley Mine as it was starting to be called, and gazed down into what seemed to her a steaming inferno where the damned —the diggers—scurried about like mad ants far below, all working on squares of ground like so many building blocks of hundreds of different heights. Each claim was excavated at varying rates depending on the desperation or industriousness of its owner, or owners. By bucket or wheelbarrow the yellow earth was brought up to the surface where carts and wagons waited to haul it away to be washed and sorted. Each claim holder, or group of claim holders, had his own sorting area set back a little way from the perimeter of the mine. The dirt, noise, and dust was dreadful. The working conditions, Olwyn saw, were dreadful too. The pipe was about six hundred feet in circumference and within the giant hole were hundreds of claims worked by thousands upon thousands of men, the majority of them the black employees of the prospectors.

Maury had told her about some of the problems—landslides when tons of earth and equipment toppled over onto the hapless men working below; vicious fights when one digger accused another of infringing on his particular building block, or claim; stealing, which was rife, then a more recent one brought about when they reached the underground water table, murky, vile-smelling water flooding the deeper plots. Cecil Rhodes and his pumps could hardly keep up with the demand from the frustrated prospectors all clamoring to rent his machinery. Olwyn could well see how Rhodes had already made a small fortune, and why the Diggers Committee were investigating safer methods of recovering the stones, including the idea of erecting platforms around the crater's edge and whisking the earth up to the surface using ropes and winches. Already two such platforms reared dark against the vivid blue of the sky. Olwyn knew from Maury that one of them belonged to Justin Wentworth.

Glancing at it, she spotted Kelly and Tondo and her heart fluttered madly. Hastily she turned away in the opposite direction, but had only taken a few steps when she heard a loud commotion from the other side of the mine, shouting and screaming and a cracking sound akin to gunfire.

Certain that somebody had been hurt and that she might be able to help, Olwyn picked up her skirts and ran around the enormous cavity of the mine, the red dust and clouds of lime always hanging over New Rush quickly coating her face, hair, and gown. The workers, black and white alike, gaped at her, but many of them, too, were converging on the spot where all the noise was coming from. When Olwyn finally reached the spot, panting and pushing her disheveled hair back from her face, quite a large crowd had gathered.

Pushing her way to the front of the crowd Olwyn was aghast to see Maury standing in the center of the small clearing with a whip in his hand. Sprawled at his feet was what at first looked to be a huge lump of bloody meat, soon identified as one of the Kaffir laborers working at New Rush.

"Filthy scum!" Maury bellowed, giving the man a savage kick. "Caught him red-handed this time." Spittle flew from his lips as Maury's glittering eyes roved the circle and he added, "Just as well I came down here today. I've had my suspicions about the crew working next to mine. Well, I happened to glance down and saw this bastard"—he gave the man another kick—"scoop earth out of my claim while my own men's backs were turned, pick up a stone and pop it into his mouth." He ran an arm across his sweating face and continued the tirade. "This is what comes of allowing non-whites to hold claims, and you wonder about the prevalence of illicit diamond buying!" he sneered.

Somebody shouted, "That Kaffir doesn't work for a non-white, Mr. Howell. He's employed by Roy Jordan, the American."

Maury let out a scornful laugh. "Well, we all know it isn't just the coloreds who indulge in IDB, though they are the worst offenders and ought not to be allowed to buy claims. Maybe now the Committee will get off their fat arses and do something about it. Do you men want to see all your profits go up in smoke?"

Olwyn couldn't move. Horror froze her to the spot. She knew well enough about the continuing scourge of illicit diamond buying, or IDB as it was referred to at the mines, a practice that resulted in horrendous loss of revenue to the honest prospectors and investors, who paid dearly for the privilege of digging in the first place. It was held that the native workers were the culprits—though the real criminals, the powerful dealers behind it all—stayed well in the background. It began with a worker picking up a diamond and hastily concealing it in his ear, hair, mouth, or another part of his anatomy or clothing, then, when he had the opportunity, running with it to his first contact, often a trader or small businessman near the diggings. Then he in turn would ship it out to Cape Town or Port Elizabeth or elsewhere to the faceless and often outwardly respectable gem dealer for eventual shipment to Europe or America. Many of the native thieves simply swallowed the stones, the safest way to get them out of the mines, for even then brutal punishment was meted out to any native caught stealing, punishment Olwyn was now witnessing for herself.

It made her sick. For a moment the sight of that poor, lacerated creature paralyzed her. The cat-o'-nine-tails in Maury's hand was tipped with metal—

Olwyn suddenly dashed into the clearing and sank to her knees beside the fallen Kaffir, her stomach lurching when she saw the state he was in. A sudden silence gripped the crowd as she put her fingers against his neck—and felt nothing, not the slightest flutter. "My God!" she breathed, a chill sweeping through her. Olwyn raised her head to where Maury was looming over her, the whip still twitching in his hand. "He's dead!" she cried, her face suddenly ashen in the bright sunlight. "He's *dead,* Maury! Dear God in heaven—"

"Get away from here!" Howell snarled. He bent down and with his free hand grabbed Olwyn by the arm and jerked her to her feet. "Go home, damn it! This is no place . . ."

But he got no further. A newcomer suddenly barged into the circle, a man of about forty dressed in twill trousers and a sweat-soaked blue shirt. Harried brown eyes jumped from the Howells to the dead laborer, then he spun on Maury, yelling, "What have you done? This is one of my best men and he would never—"

"He's a thief, Jordan, and got his just deserts," Maury yelled back, too enraged to be intimidated by the tall, powerfully built American, and too secure in his own exulted position in the diamond community to feel threatened by one he considered to be an inferior. People bowed and scraped to Maury Howell; they courted his favor, flattered and cajoled him, and never dared question his judgment or contradict him regardless of how they felt about him privately.

Therefore Howell almost choked on his wrath when Jordan demanded, "Let's see the stone he supposedly stole off you? Shingo has been with me for—"

"He swallowed it, you stupid arse!" Maury roared. "What d'you think he did with it, waltzed out of the mine with it stuck in his belly-button?" He glowered at the American from under his brows. "I'd be careful if I were you, Jordan. Some might wonder why you'd defend a thief, unless the pair of you are in cahoots—"

He got no further. With an enraged howl the American lashed back and struck him a resounding punch to the side of the head that sent Maury reeling to the dust, then Jordan launched himself upon him and proceeded to give him a taste of the same rough treatment Howell had accorded his dead worker, kicking and punching for all he was worth.

"Stop it!" Olwyn screamed, running around them as they battled it out on the ground, trying unsuccessfully to pull one back from the other and in the process falling victim to a few random blows herself.

Nobody tried to intervene. Some of the onlookers were afraid to get involved with a volatile character like Maury Howell. Others thoroughly enjoyed the unexpected treat of watching a man many of them secretly hated getting the stuffing knocked out of him for a change. Howell doled out ferocious treatment to his black workers, though not at Moorelands, where it would be immediately reported back to Olwyn. This was the first time Olwyn had come to the mine.

Then, too, some of the crowd were titilated by the sight of the beautiful Mrs. Howell, the First Lady of the diamond industry, struggling like a barmaid in her hopeless efforts to separate the men. They licked their lips as her long black hair lost its pins and tumbled down her back and over her shoulders in wild disarray, and felt their pulses leap as her green gown ripped, exposing one creamy shoulder and half a succulent breast. God no, they certainly wouldn't interrupt that! It was even better, vastly better, than the main event. Under her ladylike exterior, they saw, lurked a tigress. They stood watching, spellbound, until a tall, blond man on horseback burst on the scene.

As Olwyn bent over Maury and Jordan, screaming at them to stop, she suddenly felt herself plucked up into the air and carried back a little distance, then set down on her feet. Justin strode away without even a glance at her and plowed into the brawlers, wrenching them away from each other and hurling them in different directions. The American took one look at the President of the Diggers Committee and instantly backed off, but Maury, snarling like the savage animal he had become, launched himself at Justin, yelling, "Who do you think you are?"

Wentworth knocked him out with one blow.

The crowd slunk away under his icy stare, thinking belatedly that perhaps they should have done something, especially for the sake of the woman. While the dead Kaffir's friends ran to get his body, Olwyn sat down in the dusty earth and buried her face in her hands, but not for long. A shadow fell across her as she sat in the brilliant sunshine. Looking up, tears streaking the dirt on her face, she encountered a pair of frigid blue eyes. They sliced through her accusingly like the cold blade of an open razor; they might just as well have carved out her heart, Olwyn thought dismally. It was mortally stricken anyway.

Without a word Justin lifted her to her feet, whistled up MacBeth, and tossed her up into the saddle, then vaulted up behind her. Olwyn glanced back and saw that Maury hadn't moved; he lay where Justin had dropped him, fully exposed to the broiling sun without even a hat for protection. It lay trampled into the dirt about twenty feet away.

Nobody made any attempt to help him or even go near him. Maury might have been a leper the way the diggers shunned him now. Before long he would be badly burned, Olwyn thought, her mind fractured with everything that had happened, or he might die of sunstroke. She detested Maury now. Still . . . he *was* her husband and Gerard's father. She couldn't just ride away with another man and leave him to roast.

"Let me . . . wait a minute!" she gasped, twisting around in the saddle to appeal to the hard-eyed man behind her, at the same time suddenly acutely aware of his muscular body pressing against hers. "I've got to go to him. I—".

"Look at yourself!" Justin interrupted harshly, his eyes burning over her bare shoulder and the velvety swell of her breast. "I think you've given the diggers enough of a show already."

With that he spurred the horse forward and Mac-Beth broke into a canter, his nose pointing out into the vast plain. Olwyn, panting with indignation at this hasty abduction, and abduction it was since Justin hadn't even said as much as, "By your leave," struggled to throw her leg over the side of the horse and slide to the ground. Instantly a bronzed arm snaked around her waist and tightened to weld her against his body, and at the same time he spurred MacBeth to a gallop, red dust spiraling up in a cloud behind them as they streaked across the veld.

Olwyn squirmed and writhed in vain. Justin merely tightened his grip on her until she could barely draw breath. His rocklike chest ground into her back and shoulders, his hips and thighs imprinted themselves on her buttocks, the plunging motion of the animal under them thrusting them against each other in a way that caused Olwyn's racing blood to veer suddenly in a different direction. It brought back fiery memories that made her mouth go dry and her senses pound.

Soon they left the sprawling camp town behind them. Justin steered the horse into a grove of mahogany and ironwood trees and there brought him to a halt. Slapping his hands away, Olwyn tumbled to the ground, but she was back on her feet in an instant, wheeling to face him with her eyes blazing, her breasts heaving as she panted for breath.

"What right have you to bring me here against my will?" she cried, at the same time thinking of all the people that had seen them ride away together—and gossip was rife in Kimberley. If this ever got back to Maury—

"It's time you and I had a talk," Justin replied, his tone maddeningly reasonable, his eyes moving all over her face and body.

"We've nothing to talk about!"

"We both know that's not true—"

"Then I'll walk back," Olwyn cut in angrily, but now her anger was mixed with trepidation, and she could well imagine what he wanted to discuss. As she started to march away Justin caught her by the arm and pulled her down beside him on a moss-covered rock, holding her there when Olwyn tried to spring up.

"I'm going to give you a warning," he said coldly, "though God knows why I'm bothering to stick my own neck out." His eyes rasped over her face and he added bluntly, "Your companies are about to be investigated."

Olwyn just stared at him, speechless, thoroughly taken aback. She had been so sure Justin was about to launch into a diatribe concerning the twins. It took a moment or two for the information he had just given her to sink in, and when it did she scoffed, "What on earth are you talking about? Why would we be investigated?" He was only trying to scare her, Olwyn told herself. Perhaps this was his way of getting his revenge, though it surprised her that a man like Justin Wentworth would stoop to such tactics.

"You deal with Fabien Bleur in Cape Town," he stated.

Olwyn felt as if she'd been punched in the chest. All the indignant color ebbed from her face, taking her anger with it. Justin was President of the Diggers Committee, she was thinking. He was also on the board of the Diggers Mutual Protection Society. Aside from that, he was the most influential figure in the entire diamond-mining industry and had powerful connections throughout Africa and overseas.

Suddenly Olwyn knew, with a terrifying sinking of the heart, that he wasn't jesting. So shocked and frightened was she at that moment that she could find no words to say.

"Bleur has been arrested," Justin continued in the same deadly voice, "for fraud, dealing in stolen gems, bribery, kidnapping, and a host of other charges as long as my arm. Those who have been involved with him, who *supplied* him with stolen diamonds"—here he stared at her hard—"will tumble with him. Bleur isn't the sort to keep his mouth shut and take it on the chin," he added with a frosty smile. "He'll talk once they start applying the pressure."

Olwyn was numb with fear, remembering her discovery last December, her shock and hurt upon learning that Maury and Fabien had cheated her out of a fortune.

"You've been involved with Bleur from the start, haven't you?" Justin's deep voice broke into her thoughts. "You lied to me all along." He shook his head, marveling, "What an extraordinary woman you are! I've known some ruthlessly ambitious men in my day; men who would stop at nothing to get what they wanted, but you . . . you make them all look like soft-hearted drones. You are the most merciless, relentlessly determined lady I have ever encountered."

Justin got up suddenly and walked a little distance away as if he couldn't bear to be near her. He stood with his back to her gazing through a break in the trees that afforded a view out over the plain.

After a moment he glanced back at Olwyn over his shoulder, and said contemptuously, "Diamond Queen! I imagine that must be your favorite role so far—the best of many. Christ, woman, you ought to write a book! It would probably make a fortune. You could call it, let's see . . . *The Chameleon*."

Olwyn flinched. She sat on the rock where he had left her, her head bent, her eyes fixed on her hands clasped tightly in her lap. There was no use in trying to defend herself, she mused hopelessly. Justin knew about their involvement with the Bleurs and would never, ever believe now that it had been none of her doing. And as for his remark about her being a chameleon, well . . . she could well understand why he would think that.

He turned to face her. "It's about to end," Justin said curtly. "You'll lose your companies—"

Her eyes jumped to his face, wide and aghast.

He nodded, thinking that this was his moment of triumph; his moment of sweet revenge. She had stolen his diamond on the ship, sold it to Knute Bleur, together with the exact location where it had been found. Bleur had come to Teragno looking for more of the same and in the resulting fight one of his men had been killed and his property almost burned down. Then, as if that wasn't enough, she had somehow or other managed to get her hands on some of Jonus van Klerk's diamondiferous land—land he himself had wanted to buy—and proceeded to set herself up in direct competition with him, rapidly expanding until she was his chief rival in business. She was—was truly fantastic!

Justin knew he should have been gratified at the way

things had turned out. Instead, he only felt a bitter regret.

"Why are you telling me all this?" Olwyn whispered.

He threw up his hands, admitting, "I don't know . . . I honestly don't know."

She ventured, "Please believe me, we don't deal in stolen gems—"

"Oh, for God's sake, Maury Howell is up to his chin in IDB!" Justin almost shouted, his voice harsh with impatience. "We've been watching him for some time." He hesitated, shrugged, and decided to tell her the truth, since it couldn't make any difference now. "His courier was intercepted two weeks ago with a shipment of stones for Fabien Bleur, and Howell has the gall to accuse others. He killed a man today for that very reason!"

Olwyn almost fell off the rock. Intercepted a courier two weeks ago? Two weeks ago! She couldn't believe it. They had stopped associating with Bleur the previous December and this was September of the following year—

But, her heart plummeting, Olwyn knew that Justin spoke the truth.

"Oh, my God!" she whispered. "Dear God . . ."

Justin stared at her. She had gone very pale under her light tan. Real shock and horror brimmed in her beautiful golden eyes; eyes that could still, after everything that had happened, captivate and thrill him with their spellbinding allure.

At Christmas he was pledged to marry a woman he didn't love, though he was very fond of Kate D'Lyon, and when had love been any guarantee of a perfect marriage? Still, Justin had felt honor-bound to be honest about his feelings to the woman he planned to make his wife. Of the many that had passed through his life in the last two years Kate was the one who most interested and appealed to him.

He had met her in Cape Town, where she was staying with her brother, and in many ways he'd felt sorry for her, widowed as she had been at a very early age and left with a young son to support. An Englishwoman herself, she had been married to an obscure and impoverished Italian count who'd managed to get himself killed in a duel, leaving his wife and heir, a boy now eight years old, with no money to support them. One of the things he had promised Kate was that he'd restore the D'Lyon castle and vineyards once they were married and turn them into a holiday home. Little Max, of course, would be sent to the best boarding school in Britain.

Yes, Justin convinced himself, the marriage would work well enough. Yet . . . the things he really wanted in life continued to evade him. Olwyn had married another man, and Christina—he felt a stab of anger and frustration—Christina had wormed her way out of financial ruin by becoming the wife of a man old enough to be her grandfather! Richard Armstrong, his lawyer, had written: "I fancy the fellow isn't quite as wealthy as she thinks he is; one hears rumors. However, this doesn't alter the fact that she won't be obliged to sell now. I'm sorry, old friend. I know how much it meant to you."

There was also something else . . .

Justin crossed the glade and stopped before Olwyn. She sat with her head bent, the very picture of dejection, but the instant he felt his heart begin to soften Justin reminded himself of what a clever actress the woman was, how, when she set her mind to it, she could make one believe almost anything.

"I want my children," he said. "They should be raised in their father's house. I won't have them stigmatized through any connection to Maury Howell, and I'm prepared to fight through the courts, if necessary . . ."

Olwyn raised her head then. Her eyes were swimming with tears.

"Please . . ." she whispered, her lips trembling, "I'll give up anything . . . but not my children."

## 28

Justin studied her appraisingly, struggling to do so with a cold eye. It was well nigh impossible, especially when she looked so defenseless and vulnerable, her ebony hair in a fetching tangle, eyes drowning, the cleft between her breasts deep and full of mysterious promise in the shadows under the trees.

"You'd leave Howell?" he queried, his pulses jumping.

Olwyn nodded. "I loathe him!" she replied vehemently.

"What about the mines and Moorelands?"

Here she hesitated. The companies were her life's blood. She had started them, one of the pioneers in the diamond industry, and plunged everything she had, mentally and physically, into making them something she could be proud of. But—

Olwyn nodded.

There was a silence as he stood gazing down at her searchingly, a tall, broad figure in tan riding breeches, polished boots covered with a thin film of dust, his

open-necked white shirt exposing a wedge of darkly
tanned chest that Olwyn knew was warm and smooth
and powerfully muscled, and so stirring to the touch.

As they looked at each other Justin saw an almost
imperceptible change in her expression, especially in
her eyes, and he felt a change in himself too—a
sudden pounding awareness. It seemed to grow very
quiet, as if all sound had been sucked out of the
countryside around them, locking them into a vacu-
um where only he and she existed. It became difficult
to breathe.

Justin started to say something to break the spell—
and reached for her instead, wrenching her upright
and hard against his chest so that she gasped at the
impact. For one second he glared down into her eyes,
as if to say that this was happening against his will,
then he bent his head and ravished her mouth in a
brutal kiss that had her knees buckling beneath her.

The instant they touched Olwyn's starving body
was on fire. Blind and desperate desire shuddered
through her in waves, a release of the great and
persistent longing that she had suppressed for almost
three long years, now bursting forth from every pore
in her body. But at that electrifying moment Olwyn
gave no thought to the past or future, to right or
wrong, to anything but the here and now. It didn't
even matter that Justin's lovemaking was savage rather than tender. All that mattered was that he should
appease the deep and driving need that cried out
inside her.

He grasped what was left of the top of her gown and
impatiently pulled it down to her waist, watching as
her breasts sprang free, hot and dewy with lustful
expectation, the dusky brown of her nipples already
stiffly erect. With a muffled groan Justin lowered his
head, tasting and devouring her with hungry lips,
roving her face and ears, mouth and throat, the
slightly rough moistness of his tongue licking the full,
taut mound of her left breast, inexorably circling

inward to flick the nipple, then, with a sudden tug, draw it into his mouth.

Olwyn's senses reeled with unbearable pleasure as he moved from one breast to the other, his burning hand at her bare back, the fingers languorously caressing satiny skin that was exquisitely sensitive to his touch, quivering at the slightest pressure. Mindlessly, she ripped open his shirt and slipped her hands under the garment to stroke his chest and back, to tighten over the bulging muscles of his shoulders, to tease the curling golden hair on his chest, and as her own need beat in her blood like a pulse, she shamelessly thrust herself against his throbbing member, her arms flying up to encircle his neck.

Justin threw her back on the long grass and his hands went to his belt buckle, his eyes never leaving her flushed face as he undressed, the sight of his rodlike hardness almost making her swoon in eager anticipation. Then he was beside her, pulling the gown down over her hips and off her body, nuzzling and kissing her breasts, her stomach, tickling the inside of her thighs with his tongue. When he slipped his hand between her legs, separating and probing until he felt the wet little nub he was seeking, Olwyn arched against him and cried, "You know! Oh God . . . you know!"

"Yes, I know," he said, his voice very deep, as if it came from the bottom of a well. He should know, Justin thought. He had been the one to first awaken her to the joy of lovemaking. And he should have been the last!

At first his touch was light and playful as he stroked her most sensitive part like a feather, the voluptuous tingle it aroused in Olwyn, breaking her out in a sweat. Hardly aware of it, she began to jerk and writhe, her breath spurting in choked little gasps. She wanted to cry out as rapture flooded through her; she wanted to scream, to beg, to—

She clutched his hand and pressed it harder against

her, moaning, "Oh, don't tease!" Then, as she felt a thrill rocket through her, more frantically, "Justin! I—I'm going to . . ."

He was suddenly on top of her, plunging downward in a fury of passion, then withdrawing, and thrusting harder. Each time Olwyn trembled on the brink of that magical, breathtaking void, he'd withdraw, pause for an instant as he watched the anguish in her face, her nails digging into his shoulders as she sobbed, "Oh God don't stop! Don't torture me, my dearest love. I need you so . . ."

And Justin found himself wanting to believe it.

Then, his control crumbling, even he couldn't hold back. The ecstasy came in a rush, like a fire sweeping across the veld, and Olwyn shuddered uncontrollably in his arms, crying, "Oh, darling! Darling, I do love you. I love you so much."

But Justin murmured no endearments.

For several minutes they lay together without speaking while their breathing slowed, Olwyn's head cradled loosely on his arm, their bodies just touching. He neither kissed her nor hugged her tight as he used to do after lovemaking. And he didn't tell her that he loved her too.

From burning heat Olwyn felt as if she had been plunged into ice water. For a second she felt crushed, terribly wounded, ready to weep. Then came embarrassment, mortification at the way she had revealed herself by crying out that she loved him, needed him, and her wanton hunger, her uninhibited joy at being with him again!

How he must be laughing at her now!

Olwyn sat up, her lips pinched and face sober, and reached for her gown. She felt Justin looking at her as she slipped it over her head, pulled the ragged sides of the bodice together, and did her best to make herself look as respectable as it was possible to look when the thing was in shreds. Then she ran her fingers through her hair until she felt a couple of stray pins, and drew it all back from her face and fastened it behind each ear. And all the time she was attending to these mundane tasks her heart was breaking. He didn't love her anymore! Animal lust was what he'd shown a few minutes ago. And she—she had made a ridiculous fool of herself!

Her pride stung and she felt a searing twist of anger, but almost at once it evaporated. She and Maury were in grave trouble. Olwyn wondered if Justin imagined that that was why she had been so eager and ardent in her lovemaking—hoping to persuade him to use his influence to bail them out of their difficulties! Yes, she mused bitterly, that was exactly what he must be thinking.

Gathering the remnants of her pride together, Olwyn turned to him and said coldly, "Thank you for warning me about the investigation, but I assure you that *I* have had nothing to do with illicit diamond buying—"

"Ah, but your husband has." Justin's lips twisted over the word *husband*. "Your only recourse is to liquidate what you can and get out of the country, and hope you make it away safely. Perhaps you can don one of your clever disguises," he suggested sarcastically. "They've been successful in bailing you out of tight spots in the past."

He saw her wince and her face tighten, and Justin felt a stab of self-disgust.

"If I go," she said, "I'll be taking the children with me. And if you try to prevent me I—I'll—"

"Stop it, Olwyn," he interrupted wearily, running his fingers through his hair. "Enough!"

Justin couldn't believe they were having this bitter conversation only moments after making love. It sickened and saddened him, and he was suddenly tired of the constant sparring between them, the accusations and recriminations, the doubts, suspicions, the constant strife. It was all so futile and senseless. It accomplished absolutely nothing. But one thing was abundantly clear, clearer now than it had ever been: he loved this woman. Yes, loved her regardless of any flaws she might have—and he had plenty of his own!—and greatly admired her and what she had achieved. That was fact. The rest was merely worthless speculation.

He felt a tremor of excitement go through him, remembering what Olwyn had said earlier. She loathed Maury Howell and was prepared to leave him. She had said that she loved him—Justin—and needed him. And she had been hurt, sincerely hurt, at his coolness; he despised himself for that now, yet as glowing ideas came into his mind his senses soared, and he almost jumped to his feet and swept her into his arms, promising to love and cherish her and do everything in his power to smooth over her business problems. He was not without clout. Many in positions of power were indebted to him. But—it was no longer just a matter of himself and Olwyn and the conflicts in their relationship, which he was now convinced could be worked out. Nor even the serious charges that could be brought against Howell Central Mines and also Moorelands if Fabien Bleur had kept written records of his illegal transactions and they had fallen into the hands of the authorities. Worse, in Justin's estimation, was Maury Howell himself. He was Olwyn's husband and, knowing Howell, he would never let her go. Never! Then—then there was Kate. Justin had pledged himself to marry her in December. It was as good as a legal contract, even though nothing had been put in writing.

With difficulty Justin curbed his fierce impatience, warning himself that he must give the miserable tangle sober and serious thought and try to find a way to work things out—if they could be worked out at all! In the meantime he was in no position to make promises to Olwyn, promises he might not be able to keep. Then there was another thing; would she want him now after the callous way he had behaved a few minutes ago?

She stood up and glanced at him sideways. "I must get back."

Justin rose and pulled on his breeches. He had an intense urge to take her in his arms but she looked cool and aloof now. Instead, he said, smiling, "The twins are beautiful! They are marvelous little rascals, so bright and inquisitive."

Instantly a wariness came into Olwyn's eyes. She went very tense, wondering what was coming. But he continued in the same conversational vein, "Ariann has your eyes."

That startled her out of her uneasiness. "Justin, her eyes are blue, or bluish-green!"

"Oh, I wasn't talking about their color," he said, fastening his belt. "I meant their shape, their expression; exactly like her mother," he said firmly. "One day in the future that girl is going to be sensational," he predicted. "She'll make heads spin; male heads."

Olwyn had to laugh at that and some of the apprehension drained out of her.

"And Aidan?" she asked him, interested to hear what he would have to say about his son.

"Oh, he's a rugged, handsome fellow just like his father!"

Olwyn's smile faded and she was gripped with a sudden feeling of guilt. The twins were past their second birthday now and their own father had only seen them once! She was touched at how tenderly and proudly Justin spoke about them, essentially little strangers to him, all on the strength of that one brief meeting. Dear God, she groaned inwardly, why did it have to be like this?

Justin turned away to scoop up his shirt, and Olwyn's dreary thoughts were banished abruptly when she spotted the scar on his back, a pearly white circle against his deep tan.

"What's that scar?" she blurted. "It wasn't there before."

For a moment he tensed. Mention of the scar brought back painful memories for Justin, not of the wound itself, bad enough as that had been, but of the letter waiting for him when he'd recovered enough to read it. But he didn't want to talk about it, to stir up fresh awkwardness between them.

Olwyn stared at him curiously, waiting for an answer.

He shrugged and tried to pass it off lightly. "Oh, I caught a stray bullet while out riding—"

"When?" Olwyn interrupted worriedly. "Was it a serious wound? It looks as if it must have been considering its position. Justin . . . you don't think it was deliberate, do you?" The anxious questions fairly bubbled out of her, and he couldn't fail to catch the genuine concern in her voice.

"No, no, and no!" Justin laughed, and impulsively leaned down and kissed her. When they drew apart they gazed at each other uncertainly, probingly, each trying to gauge the other's deepest feelings. "Take good care of my children," he said gently, huskily, and saw vast relief shine in her eyes.

"I—I will," Her voice was unsteady. He saw tears rush into her eyes.

Justin closed the brief distance between them and put his arms around her. He yearned to say so much, to ascertain exactly how she felt about him, to make plans for the future, but it wasn't the right time. Instead, he spoke to her very low, his cheek against her hair. "I *do* love you, my darling, and always have. And I'm going to do everything in my power to help you. Trust me, Olwyn?"

She looked up at him, her eyes swimming, and nodded.

Then they kissed deeply.

Olwyn almost managed to sneak into the house without the servants seeing her, but as she passed the upstairs nursery a tall dark shadow stepped from the doorway, closing the door softly behind her.

It was Seeta, the children's nurse, and her black eyes went huge as they crawled over her mistress, taking in her wild, unbound hair, the beautiful gown all torn to shreds, the worry in Olwyn's eyes.

"Mistress!" the girl gasped, "what happen?"

"There was a—an incident at the mine," Olwyn replied, brushing past her. She felt a stab of annoyance. Seeta was forever creeping around. More than once she had caught the nurse eavesdropping and had wanted to let her go, but Maury had intervened. Olwyn was positive Maury and the nurse were having relations. Not that such arrangements were uncommon in Kimberley; far from it! Seeta was extremely inquisitive and she liked to gossip. Olwyn could well imagine some of the tales she had to tell her friends about what went on in the Howell household.

"Is Mr. Howell at home?" she asked the girl nervously, terrified that Maury would come on the scene and demand to know where she had been for the last hour or so, but the nursemaid shook her head.

"And nobody else has come to the house?"

"No, lady."

"Then tell Sam to be ready to take me back to the mine in ten minutes."

Olwyn hurried along the corridor to her own room, closed the door, and sagged against it. Her emotions were in a turmoil, the events of the morning churning through her head—the wonderful yet disturbing meeting with Justin, his warning about the possibility of an investigation into illicit diamond buying, and Maury's involvement. And where was Maury himself?

She was his wife, Olwyn reminded herself grimly, and she couldn't just stay put and do nothing.

Quickly she stripped off her ruined gown and dropped it on the floor. There was no time to bring up water for a bath, so instead she hastily washed herself and plucked riding breeches and a shirt from her wardrobe and pulled them on, then ran a brush through her hair and pinned it back in a chignon. Catching sight of her reflection in the cheval glass, Olwyn remembered the stir she had caused when she'd first appeared at the diggings in her breeches, rather than the long flowing skirt more expected of ladies when out riding. She preferred the breeches.

They were much more comfortable and allowed more freedom of movement. Besides, they always gave her a chuckle and made her think of Oliver, the poor little urchin from the Gallowgate, and how different her life was now.

Harold had just arrived with a packet of diamonds from Moorelands when Olwyn hurried downstairs. All the stones were shipped from Kimberley now. Quickly she explained to Hal what had happened as she took the gems into the office and locked them away in the safe. She couldn't lock the door. Maury had lost one of the keys and had confiscated hers until he remembered to have another made.

Harold, now a strapping, powerfully built young man of seventeen, announced that he would accompany her to New Rush. Instead of taking the trap, they rode over on horseback. The town of Kimberley was expanding by leaps and bounds, and it was a place of violent contrasts, with a few very grand houses—like Olwyn's—surrounded by a sea of tents and shacks, tumbledown taverns, hotels, restaurants, and gambling halls smack next to the newer elegant shops and offices, exclusive clubs, and casinos. Everything in town was horrendously expensive. Water—the water used to wash the sludge brought up from the mines— cost almost as much as champagne. As well as the prospectors and businessmen and the various and sundry attracted to the diamond fields, had now come doctors, lawyers, accountants, and men of high finance; some very high indeed, such as the Lipperts, Jules Porges, a firm from Paris, perhaps the most important diamond merchant in Europe. Of course there were now many banks, and in the near future even the fabulously wealthy Nathan Rothschild would become involved. But for all this heady mixture of power and influence the people most looked up to and respected at Kimberley were the original few, the courageous, determined men—and woman—who had started it all. The pioneers.

Once at the mine Olwyn learned from a foreman at

their own diggings that Maury was all right, at least physically. "He's awa fur a dram," the Scotsman told her with a grin. Jake Cameron had been with them almost from the start and he knew his employer's habits well. "Ye ken whit he's like, Missus? He'll bide awa till he's foo, then ye can expect him hame. A widna waste ony time worrying aboot him," their head foreman went on in his usual blunt manner, and joked, "He's still got at least twa o' his nine lives tae use up."

Harold laughed. Olwyn had to smile a little too. It always astonished their team that Maury, always so hot-tempered and touchy, tolerated Jake Cameron, who never minced words, even to his face. Perhaps it had something to do with the fact that Cameron was a huge, burly Highlander, Olwyn sometimes mused, but more likely because he was scrupulously honest and loyal and recognized to be the best foreman in the business.

They eventually tracked Howell down in the Gilded Lily, one of the many bars in town, where he was drinking with a group of friends. They had been working themselves up to a fine lather against the non-white claim holders, grumbling that they were the ones at the core of IDB. Further, the non-whites undercut their prices at every turn, selling off the stones they found far cheaper than they could afford to for the simple reason that they were able to live much cheaper, or as Maury put it, "like swine."

Something would have to be done about it, they all agreed with each other dourly, and since the Diggers Committee were dragging their feet . . .

They put their heads together and made a plan, deciding to take matters into their own hands. In fact, they would take care of it that very night.

When Harold Scobbie walked into the tavern it was to find Howell and his cronies hunched over a table muttering together under their breaths, which certainly wasn't like them. Normally this bunch were loud, often disruptive, but strangely, their unnatural behavior made the bartender even more nervous, and as he washed and dried his glasses he kept shooting them uneasy glances, expecting trouble to erupt at any moment. Though Mr. Howell was a big man at the mines he was far from dignified, he was thinking, and once in his cups anything was liable to happen.

Surprisingly, Maury returned home with them without protest, even though Olwyn could sense that he was in a morose mood. Once inside the house he pulled a small pouch of diamonds out of his jacket pocket, the stones dug up that day from their various claims, took them into the office just off the hall, and tossed them on the desk. Then he walked out, banging the door shut behind him.

"Don't forget to lock the door," Olwyn prompted.

He stopped and felt about in his pockets for a moment, shrugged, and started for the stairs.

"Where's the key, Maury?" Olwyn called after him. "We can't leave the door open like that."

He kept going, calling back, "Bugger the key! I seem to have misplaced it," he slurred. Without looking around he waved for her to join him. "Want a word with you, wife."

Olwyn and Harold exchanged a long-suffering look. Harold was about to leave for the long ride back to Moorelands. Late in the afternoon as it was, now he'd barely make his first stopover spot—a Boer farmhouse—before sundown, and it was very dangerous to travel in Africa after dark. But he offered quietly, "I'll stay if you feel you need me?"

Olwyn thought a minute and shook her head. "No, no, I can handle him. As a matter of fact"—she frowned, thinking about it—"he doesn't seem quite himself; perhaps it was that punch in the head . . . no, go along, Hal, I'll manage."

Still the youth hesitated. He found himself wondering what Howell and his cohorts had been discussing when he walked into the Gilded Lily. They had seemed secretive, furtive, and had broken off the moment he entered. He'd gotten a feeling . . .

"I think I should hang about, Olwyn."

Olwyn took his arm and marched him to the door. "Go! If you don't return home tomorrow your mother will be frantic."

Reluctantly, Harold left.

Olwyn climbed the stairs to their bedroom with some trepidation, wondering what Maury wanted to talk to her about, fearing that somebody had told him about her leaving with Justin—the man who had knocked him out.

Howell was sprawled across their bed when she walked in, his arms folded behind his head, his eyes half closed, as if he'd been dozing. He was a mess, Olwyn thought in disgust. Maury was still dressed in the same clothes he'd worn to the mine that morning, clothes that had suffered in the course of the fight he'd had with Roy Jordan. They were also caked with dust and stained with spilled alcohol and reeking with sweat.

"Give the servants the evening off tonight," Maury ordered her. "I'm going out later but I don't want them to know about it."

Olwyn frowned, puzzled as to why he would care whether the servants knew he was out or not. It had never bothered him before.

Maury chuckled slyly. "Big things happening tonight, wife, but that's all I can tell you for now." He dismissed her with a flick of his hand and turned over on his side, settling himself to sleep. "Just be sure to get me up for seven o'clock."

Olwyn stared at him curiously for a moment, then shrugged. Maury liked to make mysteries. He liked to try to make her jealous by hinting about all the exciting things he got up to when he went out without her—as if she cared!

There was a more important reason she hesitated. Now was the time to tell him about the possible investigation. Certainly he would have to be warned. She could always say she'd heard a rumor about it while at the mine today.

But . . . Maury was in a surly mood and under the influence of alcohol and there was no saying how he might react. What if he started asking her awkward questions about riding away from the mine with Justin, for instance? Olwyn shuddered at the thought. She just wasn't up to another scene. After everything that had happened she was worn out herself, and wanted nothing more than a hot bath and a nap, when for an hour or two at least she could forget all her problems.

She went out, closing the door quietly behind her.

As she passed the nursery she could hear the baby wailing fretfully. Little Gerard was teething. At five months he already had two teeth, with two more on the way. Perhaps, she thought, he needed more of the paste she mixed up to soothe his gums.

Olwyn ended up staying in the nursery until after five o'clock, rubbing the cooling ointment on the infant's gums, then rocking him to try to get him to sleep while Seeta played with the older children. Olwyn gazed down at the beautiful dark-haired baby boy and prayed he would never turn out like his father, even if he looked like Maury, with his black curls and bright green eyes, or as Maury used to look. Normally Gerard had a sunny, placid nature, and Olwyn doubted that her husband had ever been placid, even as a child.

She fell asleep with the baby in her arms.

At eight o'clock that night Olwyn intercepted Maury as he was trying to slip out of the house. Everything was unnaturally quiet with all the servants away and the children asleep in bed. The couple faced each other tensely in the big downstairs hall.

Maury, Olwyn noticed, was not wearing his usual evening finery. He was dressed in the tough cord breeches that he wore to go to the mine, high boots, and a tan safari jacket. He had a wide-brimmed hat pulled well down over his eyes. As her eyes moved over him in surprise, Olwyn detected the bulge of a pistol under the flap of his jacket. That in itself wasn't unusual; Maury always carried the weapon on him somewhere—but he also had a chunk of wood like a club in his hand and his manner was furtive.

"What are you up to?" Olwyn challenged him, her voice shrill with alarm.

He looked her up and down as she stood in her pink silk robe, fresh and glowing from her bath, her hair loose and falling like fringes of a Spanish shawl over her shoulders.

"Do you actually imagine I'm the kind of man to take these insults today lying down?" he growled.

Terror surged inside her as her eyes went to the club in his hand and a terrible suspicion sprang up in her mind. "Are you out of your mind?" she whispered. "Don't you realize that you're in enough trouble as it is after killing that Kaffir? There will be an inquest and—"

"Not to worry, my dear," Maury interrupted complacently, "that has all been taken care of. The fellow isn't the first Kaffir to have died on the job and he certainly won't be the last. These natives"—his hand tightened on the club—"need to be taught a few hard lessons about honesty. The same goes for the colored claim holders undercutting us at every turn." He scowled at her. "You of all people ought to be in agreement there, or do you want to lose all we've invested up here?"

"These people have a right to hold claims; it's their country!" Olwyn hurled at him. "And if you think you can take the law into your own hands—"

"Oh, for Christ sake!"

He dropped the club then and seized her by the shoulders. With a glance up and down the hall, brightly lit but eerily silent, Maury hurried her forcibly ahead of him down a corridor leading to the kitchen and thrust her into a small pantry and turned the key that was in the lock. "That will keep you out of mischief until I get back." He laughed from the other side of the door.

Then he left, hurrying back to the foyer.

Olwyn screamed and battered on the door, yelling at him to come back, reminding him that she was the only one in the house to keep an eye on the children, but moments later she heard the front door bang shut.

Olwyn, left in the dark, stuffy little pantry, was frantic. Somehow she had to get out! She had to warn Justin and that American prospector, and somehow get word to the sprawling native camp on the outskirts of Kimberley. Knowing Maury as she did she knew he wouldn't venture out to seek vengeance alone; that wasn't his way. No, he'd have a posse of his drunken friends with him, men as corrupted with power, as obsessed with wealth as he was, wanting it all to themselves.

She battered the door until her hands went numb. She shouted until she was hoarse. Nothing happened.

Upstairs in the nursery Gerard began to wail, disturbed by all the noise. Through a connecting room the twins sat up in bed and began to howl with fright, calling for their nurse, and when Seeta failed to appear they got out of bed and made their way downstairs, attracted to the sound of their mother banging the pantry door.

"Mama, what you do in there?" Aidan cried. "Come out, come out! Mama—"

"Turn the key in the door, darling," Olwyn coaxed, struggling to control her panic. "Turn the key and Mama can get out."

"I do it!" Ariann announced, and clutched the big key in her tiny hand, but her brother, an inch taller than her now, pushed her aside. For a moment or two they fought to see who would have the honor of releasing their mother from the cupboard, and as they pushed and shoved each other the key fell out of the door onto the floor.

"Don't fight, children!" Olwyn scolded from her dark little cell. "Take turns. Ariann, let Aidan try first."

"No!"

"Ariann, don't be naughty!"

Olwyn felt hysteria rise in her when she heard the tots struggling with each other again, but finally she could tell that bigger, stronger Aidan had the key, and as it rasped about in the lock she held her breath. But the two-year-old, smart as he was for his age, couldn't manage it. Within ten minutes the twins tired of the game and wandered off to explore, turning a deaf ear to their mother calling to them to come back. Their first port of call was the kitchen, that intriguing room where all the delicious smells came from and tasty treats were made, a room usually off-limits to them. Then with chunks of gingerbread in their plump little mitts they made for another room that was taboo— the office.

Aidan was the one who found the small pouch of diamonds on the desk, still lying where Maury had tossed them. In all the hubbub and distractions of the day neither of his parents had remembered to lock them away in the safe.

The twins were greatly attracted to the glittering stones. They remembered the funny game their father often played, when he'd strike them with a hammer, scratch marks on a piece of glass—a hideous sound that made them cover their ears—and bite down on them, almost as if they were sweets.

"See!" Aidan held up the pouch triumphantly.

Ariann tried to grab it from him but he pushed her away. In the light pouring through the open door from the hall Aidan paused for a moment and glanced around, then he ran to the desk and climbed up in the big leather chair.

"Watch me," he told his sister, and dumped the contents of the bag onto the desktop.

# 29

In the Gilded Lily thirty men clustered around tables at the back of the room, a smoky, noisy room crowded with prospectors and their laborers. Thad, the bartender, noticed that the group held themselves apart from the rest of the customers, which wasn't like them. Normally this bunch were the first to get into the swing of things.

They drank steadily for an hour then, silent and grim, got up to leave.

Watching them go, Thad remarked to a young lad who materialized out of the smoke to request another beer, "What's up with Mr. Howell and his mates, I wonder? Ain't like them to be so snooty and quiet."

The youth said, "Forget the beer, Thad. I just remembered something I forgot to do."

Once outside in the velvet dark of the African night, Harold Scobbie gazed after the posse riding away in the direction of North Kimberley where, on the fringes of town, the black claim holders and laborers had their camp. Harold had had ample opportunity to learn how Maury Howell's mind worked. He was a man who never forgot a slight or an insult; he was also a man who felt non-whites should not be allowed to hold claims—though he was not alone in this. Howell was out to kill two birds with one stone, Hal reasoned anxiously, debating what he ought to do first. He would make trouble at the native camp, the youth was convinced, then strike back at Wentworth and Roy Jordan, and in all the resulting turmoil the blacks, as usual, would end up getting blamed for everything.

Harold was glad now that some instinct made him linger on in Kimberley. He decided that the best thing he could do was ride out and warn Wentworth, then Justin could alert the rest of the Diggers Committee and gather a posse of their own together. He hoped they wouldn't be too late.

As he rode past the Howell residence, brightly lit from the light pouring through the windows, Hal wondered if he ought to stop for a minute and tell Olwyn, then concluded that it would only cause her more worry, and she'd had her fill of that as it was. He rode on by.

In a gully half a mile from the native camp Howell and his companions found the pitch-impregnated faggots where they had concealed them earlier in a hollow under a gigantic ironwood tree. They paused only long enough to pass several flasks around and, once the flasks were emptied, they drew masks from their pockets and put them on, then lit the torches.

They were all quite drunk by now and excited as they contemplated the fine sport ahead of them, all except one of Maury's Colesberg friends. This man harbored a secret grudge against Howell, convinced that Maury had recently connived to exclude him from a very lucrative deal—this after he had cut Howell in when they struck diamonds at New Rush! So much for gratitude! Howell had made a fortune at New Rush.

They had crossed the plain like shadows, but when

they burst out of the gully with their masks on and torches flaring, they were like fiends erupting from the jaws of hell. Roaring, shouting, howling obscenities, the posse thundered into the native camp, setting fire to the flimsy shacks, clubbing the unfortunates who tried to flee to safety, beating, trampling, and in two instances shooting, the terrified diggers who tried to escape.

The wind sweeping across the veld fanned the flames into an inferno that quickly illuminated the scene of carnage and threw a dull red glow into the sky. That glow was like a warning light to those in the white camp closer to the mine, and destroyed the element of surprise.

"Hey! What's going on over there?" an English prospector shouted to his neighbor in the next tent. "Something's burning—"

"Cor, mate, it looks like the whole camp is burning!" the other yelled back. "And don't that sound like gunfire?"

Maury and his friends got a surprise of their own when they galloped into the white camp looking for Roy Jordan. Greeting them were a solid phalanx of grim-faced diggers with various weapons in their hands. The diggers took one startled look at the posse hiding behind their masks and instantly set about defending themselves. In the resulting battle Maury Howell was knocked off his horse.

Howell slunk away into the trees, aware that they were vastly outnumbered and couldn't hope to win. Furious, he cursed his friends for not heeding his advice. His plan had been to attack Justin Wentworth first, a suggestion that alarmed them. Then, by using stealth rather than intimidation, slip into the white camp and hunt down Jordan, and once that was taken care of, read the riot act to the black diggers. But no, his friends were secretly afraid of Wentworth. The spineless bastards were even loathe to touch Jordan. Far better, they said, to stir up a revolt—black against white—and while it was raging follow through with their plans for Wentworth and Jordan. Afterward it would be impossible to determine who had been to blame, and they'd all get off scotfree.

Ha! sneered Maury, glancing back at the ruckus over his shoulder. His friends had about as much sense as Harold Scobbie's mule! Now the entire camp was seething, the very air resounding with shouts and screams, cursing and swearing and blood-curdling shrieks as the fight spread, everyone getting into the act now. It seemed that the entire African sky was ablaze. It would be a miracle, Howell mused as he made for the nearest concealing dip in the land, if anything was left standing by morning. For just a second, as he hurried away, Maury felt a touch of fear at what he had started, thinking that he must not be found here, caught in the act, as it were.

He inhaled sharply and threw himself flat on the ground when he spied a group of riders thundering across the veld from the direction of town. In the eerie glow from the fires he recognized the leader as Justin Wentworth. Once they passed by Howell looked about frantically for a place where he could conceal himself until it was safe to slip back home, but there were few such places on the open plain; even very few trees. Virtually crawling, terrified of being seen, he scuttled like a crab in the direction of the gully where they had hidden the faggots earlier, and tumbled down the shallow ravine and hid himself in the shadows under an ironwood tree.

It took Justin and his men half an hour to restore order, though many of the fires would rage all night. It quickly became obvious that they would never be able to round up all the instigators. True to the code of ethics that prevailed at the mines, no man would implicate another.

But Justin knew the name of the chief instigator, one who had committed murder earlier that day, and he was determined that this time Howell wouldn't wriggle out of his clutches. Turning to his second-in-charge, a prospector called Morrison, he said, "You stay here with the others and try to contain the fires. I'll find the bastard; he can't have got very far." Justin's eyes shone cold as steel in the glow as he added, "And when I find him he'll curse the day he was born."

He rode away alone out onto the veld.

"Children, what are you doing?" Olwyn called through the door to the twins. "Come over here and stay near Mama. Children?"

In her stuffy, dark, little prison Olwyn streamed with sweat. If she didn't get out soon, she thought, she would suffocate. But worse than her own discomfort was the fear that the twins would manage to open the front door and get out of the house, or wander into the kitchen where there were knives and cleavers for cutting meat, the hot oven that the servants would have left banked down until morning, and countless other potential hazards that could cause injury to the inquisitive pair.

Using jars of preserves and anything reasonably heavy that came to hand in the pitch darkness, Olwyn had tried mightily to batter down the door, or at least break it enough so that she could somehow manage to open it, but she hadn't been able to make as much as a chink in the solid mahogany. Now, her hands cut on the broken jars, the floor beneath her slippery with the sticky jam that had spilled out, Olwyn clamped an ear to the door and tried to determine what was happening with the children. Very faintly she could hear Gerard crying upstairs; she thought she heard the twins moving about somewhere near the hall, though the baby's cries made it difficult to determine exactly where or what they were up to.

They were playing a game with the pretty stones they had found on their parents' desk. Selecting the largest of them, Aidan grabbed a heavy paperweight on the desk, in lieu of a hammer, and struck the stone a couple of heavy blows.

His sister laughed merrily. "Like Papa," she said,

eyeing her brother sitting importantly in the big leather chair in his blue linen nightshirt, his golden-brown hair rumpled, blue eyes sparkling with mischief.

He glanced about and, finding no glass, proceeded to carve marks onto the outer rim of the desk top, the part framing its leather surface. "See?" he kept saying, "See what I do?"

"Me try." But when Ariann tried to grab the stone he pushed her hands away.

Then he put the diamond in his mouth, gripping it between his front teeth. Ariann began to laugh again. "Bite, Aidan, bite!" She giggled.

He did, and the stone fell down his throat and he began to gag, then cough. In a moment, while his little sister watched him, open-mouthed, Aidan tumbled from the chair and thrashed about on the floor. Ariann squatted beside him, puzzled as she gazed down into his face, rapidly turning blue.

He held up his hand to her in mute appeal. The little girl grasped it and shook it, as they'd been taught to do when they met someone for the first time. She was too young to know that in this case they were bidding each other good-bye.

Close to an hour went by and still Maury cowered in the gully, watching the flames light up the night sky. The ruckus from the camp was beginning to die down at last, much to his relief, and hopefully, once most of the fires had been put out it would be safe for him to crawl out of his hiding place and hurry home across the plain, on all fours, if necessary, he decided.

He had to be home before dawn. Come daylight it would be impossible to conceal himself up on the open veld, where there were few trees and almost no cover.

Though it was September and the beginning of spring, the nights were still very cold and he began to shiver, hugging himself to keep warm, thinking longingly of his warm, comfortable bed—

Somebody was coming! Or something . . .

Maury pressed himself against the sturdy trunk of the tree, his heart thudding, eyes apprehensively circling the rim of the gully. He strained to listen, his mind leaping from Wentworth and his crew to predators, and if it were one of the latter he wondered how quickly he could climb up the tree he was sheltering beneath. With a quick glance upward he saw that there were no stout branches within eight or ten feet of the ground, so it would mean jumping and hoping for the best.

He started sweating profusely, cold sober now, hand fumbling under his jacket for his pistol. It wasn't there. His heart gave a sickening lurch of terror, his very bowels seizing up in a spasm of pain that made him gasp and turn pale. The gun had either been knocked out of its holster when he'd parted company from his horse or had somehow fallen out when he'd thrown himself to the ground at the approach of Wentworth's posse. Either way, it was gone.

Everything seemed to go very quiet, the sounds from the camp muted now. The sky darkened as one by one the fires were doused. Night sounds took over, the chirring of crickets, the thin, shrill cry of a galago in one of the acacias in the thicket, and the eternal dry sobbing of the wind restlessly sweeping across the veld.

Howell had just started to relax a little, telling himself that he was imagining things, when a figure loomed up on the lip of the ravine, outlined against the sky. It was impossible to identify the figure in the darkness, and Maury had a choice to make then. Should he stay put, hoping he wouldn't be seen, or make a dash for it?

He decided to stay where he was, and thereby made a fatal mistake.

# 30

With her husband and son both dead, Mrs. Maury Howell went into deep seclusion, and for the next year diamonds ceased to be the prime topic of conversation in Kimberley. Death, destruction, and a major scandal rocked the frontier town. Newspaper reporters flocked to the area from all corners of the globe, avid to ferret out the juiciest stories for their readers, yet finding it frustratingly difficult to persuade the local people to talk, especially about their own particular royalty, as Howell and many of the others involved were.

But they had plenty of material to work with, and the facts spoke for themselves. Kimberley, one correspondent wrote in a dispatch home, was a seething cauldron of great wealth and corruption, degradation, and squalor. So much had happened that they hardly knew where to begin.

First, there was the official inquiry into the death of Maury Howell, one of Kimberley's leading citizens and Africa's richest men. He had been stabbed to death, with over forty wounds on his body. Also, his throat had been cut.

One reporter remarked dryly, "Somebody really wanted that fellow dead!"

Among those called to account for their movements on that fateful night in September was Justin Wentworth, the most influential figure in the diamond industry. It was known that Wentworth had confided to another member of his posse on the evening in question, that when and if he found Howell "he would curse the day he'd been born." Harold Scobbie was also questioned. It was common knowledge around the mines that he hated Howell; they had fought on numerous occasions and constantly disagreed. Scobbie had been seen in the vicinity of the white camp at the time of the riot, and he did not attempt to deny it.

There were other suspects, and here the proceedings began to take on the aura of a circus. Business rivals were brought forward, then the editor of a local newspaper, a man Howell had insulted in public, and countless Kaffirs and non-white claim holders, all sworn enemies of the dead man. As the presiding official remarked to his assistant when the inquiry was only part way finished, "It's a damned miracle that the fellow managed to live for as long as he did!"

The magistrate found himself in a unique position. Instead of having a dearth of suspects, as was usually the case, he had a surfeit. At least a hundred people could have killed Maury Howell. They all had motive, means, and opportunity; more than half of that number had been at the camp while the fighting was going on and the rest had been in the nearby town.

The inquiry ended in a shambles, but the case was left open pending new evidence coming to light at a later date.

In the course of the inquest the sordid private life of the dead man was brought to light and thoroughly raked over by the press. Lurid headlines sprang from the front pages of newspapers: MAURY HOWELL'S HAREM CROSSED THE COLOR BARRIER! And HOWELL DRANK AND GAMBLED AWAY IN ONE NIGHT ENOUGH MONEY TO FEED TEN FAMILIES FOR A YEAR! Then darkly, HOWELL A VICIOUS KILLER IN HIS OWN RIGHT!

But time passed and the public, fickle as always, stopped buying newspapers to read about Maury Howell. By the end of that year, 1872, there was precious little left to reveal about him anyway, and that seemed to be that.

Then a new scandal erupted in Kimberley. This time it concerned one of the chief suspects, Justin Wentworth. In February of the following year, Wentworth was sued for Breach of Promise by one Kathryn D'Lyon, a Cape Town widow and the mother of a nine-year-old son. It was revealed that Wentworth had promised to marry Mrs. D'Lyon in December, and had reneged.

The newspapermen were back in business and back in Kimberley en masse, delighted and amazed that the small frontier town could provide so much fodder for their various gristmills. Wentworth refused to comment and gave no interviews to the press. His friends and associates were equally tight-lipped. Thereupon the reporters rushed to Cape Town and there they fared considerably better. Kate D'Lyon, incensed, virtually frothing at the mouth at having been scorned —and by a multimillionaire—was all too eager to discuss the matter if the price was right. Justin had, through his lawyers, already settled an enormous sum of money on the woman, more than enough to build a castle, let alone restore the moldering D'Lyon stronghold in Italy. He had also written Kate a long, regretful letter wherein he had tried to explain his change of heart, careful to stress that it was through no fault of hers that he could not go through with the marriage. Kate tore the letter to shreds but kept the money. When the reporters started banging on her door she saw no reason why she shouldn't at least profit financially, and make up in some small way for the great fortune denied her now, not to mention the dreadful blow to her pride.

She granted an "exclusive" interview to the *Times* correspondent—he had outbid all the others by far—and began by stating haughtily that she wished to be called by her proper title, the Countess D'Lyon, both in and out of his newspaper. She had enjoyed a whirlwind romance with Wentworth, Kate began. He had "swept her off her feet, showered her with expensive gifts, and promised her the world if she would only marry him."

"He seemed like a gentleman," she said, "and naturally I took him at his word. Even after he became involved in that hideous murder I continued to stand by him; then at the last moment he practically left me standing at the altar!"

She continued in the same bitter vein. Everything he had said to her was lies, all his promises empty ones, his word worthless. Anyone who believed him now was an idiot. "He's very clever, you see; very persuasive and convincing. And of course he has great wealth and they say money can buy anything."

The reporter leaned forward and asked her bluntly, "Do *you* think he killed Maury Howell, Countess?"

Kate's lids lowered slightly over her pale blue eyes. She was no fool. It had been a long, rough climb from a small English market town to a castle in northern Italy, and she had learned a lot along the way. Wealth also had a long reach, she was thinking, and a viselike fist that could grasp and crush. It was one thing to blacken the character of a man who had spurned you—that was only to be expected—but to go as far as to call him a murderer—

"I have no comment to make about that," she replied stiffly.

The reporter apologized and steered the conversation back to the original subject. "And you have no idea why he changed his mind about the marriage?"

Kate said something then that had him panting like a hound on the trail of a fox. "All along I had the impression of a shadowy woman lurking in his background. I felt that perhaps this lady was not free, that she might have been married herself at the time we became engaged, then later became, er . . . available. It was something I sensed from the start, though, naturally, I told myself I was imagining things, especially when he asked me to marry him."

"Do you know the identity of this woman?"

Kate smiled slightly and shook her head.

Thereupon the press had another unsolved mystery on their hands. Frustrated, two newspapers offered a reward to anyone who could supply the name of the woman in question. Many names were forthcoming, all women Justin had been involved with briefly in the past, but the identity of the woman remained elusive.

In time everything died down, but a few canny reporters decided to stay on in Kimberley for a while. It had proved to be a veritable Pandora's Box bulging with exciting copy, the type that made headlines. It wouldn't hurt, they felt, to keep a sharp eye on the principals surrounding Howell's murder. They were convinced that one of them was the killer. Perhaps he would eventually make a mistake. They always did, sooner or later.

Under all this hullabaloo life in the diamond town went on as usual. A scant year after Maury Howell's death great improvements had been made in mining techniques. Now almost all the prospectors brought up their diamondiferous earth from stagings, tall platforms ringed around the lip of the mines, one standing behind another "like guillotines against the innocent blue African sky" as one newspaper put it, tongue-in-cheek. From the stagings long ropes or chains with buckets attached snaked down into the mines, there to be filled with kimberlite or hard blue ground before being hoisted back up to the surface to be washed and sorted. At first Kaffir labor had been used to do the pulling, then donkeys and horses, but by the end of 1873 the steam-driven engine had almost supplanted them everywhere. The engines were expensive—but so was the cost of time in Kimberley—and speed won out.

Not too far in the future dynamite rather than hand-held picks would be used to break up the kimberlite, and massive engines would be put into operation to bring the broken ground flying up to the surface by the ton. Aerial tramways would transport the miners to and from their work, but by then there would be far fewer diggers to transport. Amalgamation would have taken place and the small, independent prospector squeezed out, a process already underway by the winter of that year—the year a cocky little Jewish boy from Whitechapel in London arrived to try his luck at the mines, with nothing but a few pounds in his pocket and forty boxes of what one digger called "putrid, god-awful cigars."

The newest hopeful was Barnet Isaacs, or as he preferred to be called, Barney Barnato, a third-rate boxer and would-be music-hall artist who felt in his bones that he had yet to find his true niche in life, which he did, magnificently, in Kimberley. He was twenty years old when he arrived.

Barney Barnato and Cecil Rhodes were eventually to challenge the Howells, Wentworths, Robinsons, and Beits for supremacy at the diamond mines, but their time had yet to come, and like all the others there before them, they too would pay a severe price for prosperity.

In June of 1874, Mrs. Maury Howell finally emerged from seclusion. She had decided to take a holiday. Leaving her companies in the capable hands of her many executives, her accountants and lawyers, she moved with her two young children to a palatial home in Belgravia in London. She spent a month there before traveling on alone to a home in Glasgow,

Scotland, but there she only tarried for a few days. Then she vanished, destination unknown.

Olwyn's hideaway cottage in Ayrshire, thirty miles south of Glasgow, drew no special interest from outsiders and locals alike. It was a very ordinary house, built of granite with a peaked roof and small windows and only seven rooms in all, but it was at the end of a long, private road through a field and surrounded by a wood. The back of the house overlooked the Firth of Clyde and had a beautiful view across the sea to the island of Arran. Above all, it had complete privacy.

She had leased the house under the name of Douglas and informed the solicitor that she was a widow and still recovering from the shock of her husband's death. Naturally, she wished to be alone at such a time. Olwyn only engaged occasional help to run the place, a scrubwoman and gardener when needed. To the villagers of Dunure, a few miles away, she seemed a tragic figure, invariably dressed in black, with no jewelry or adornment of any kind. They could see that she was a gentlewoman from her speech and manners, but they felt from her dress and the fact that she employed no full-time servants that she had been left in rather straitened circumstances. They respected her obvious desire to be left alone.

Olwyn had been at Arran View two weeks when she had a visitor.

He arrived late one blustery Friday evening, a lone figure on horseback, bundled up in a hooded cloak against the rain. Had anyone seen him arrive they would have wondered at his choice of transport on such a stormy night, especially when he could have taken the public coach that plied between the town of Ayr and Dunure every evening. But the only person to see him was the woman standing at an upstairs window inside the cottage, where she had kept vigil every night for the past two weeks. Olwyn's heart gave a mighty leap when she spied him riding down the private road, illuminated in a flash of lightning. She flew downstairs, threw the front door open, and hurled herself into his arms.

"At last!" she wept. "Oh God, I'd almost given up!"

"Not you, my darling." Justin swept her off her feet and showered her face with kisses. "Not you . . ."

It was the first time they had spoken to each other in two years.

# 31

They clung to each other for many minutes, too overcome to say a word. There were so many things they wanted to say, things they had to talk about, but mere words could not have described the intensity of their feelings at that moment, especially how they felt about each other, about being together again.

Dimly, over the mad beating of their hearts, they could hear the waves crashing against the foot of the cliffs, the wind howling in the trees surrounding the house, but inside all was warm and still, except for their own harried breathing.

Eventually they drew back and looked into each other's eyes.

"If you hadn't come!" Olwyn cried, her voice cracking.

"But I did!" Justin caught her cold hands and raised them to his lips. "Of course I had to come; I've thought of nothing else for the past two years. But darling, you know about the circuitous route I had to take—"

"Yes, I knew—but I wondered." Olwyn swallowed and tried to control her trembling; tried not to think of the dread worries that had plagued her constantly. "Every night I waited—I was so afraid, Justin!"

He kissed her fears away, his eyes devouring her over and over, embracing her, drinking in the scent of her, still not quite able to believe that at long last they were together—and completely, blissfully alone!

Justin had noticed while riding to the cottage that miles and miles of deserted countryside stretched away in all directions, with only the odd crofter's house or farm dotted here and there. The only signs of life he had seen on that ride through what amounted to a gale, were sheep; hundreds of sheep huddled by stone dykes and hedges, seeking shelter from the elements. Gazing at them in the flashes of lightning streaking through the dark sky, Justin had sympathized, thinking that he, too, was seeking sanctuary from the storms in his own life.

Well, now he had found it. He had felt the welcoming warmth the instant he stepped inside the cottage. Through a door leading off the hall he spied a room with a blazing fire. The house was filled with a wonderful aura of tranquility. He had the woman he loved in his arms, and that made him ecstatically happy. This is all I want, he thought, feeling the dank weight of the past two years begin to slip off his shoulders; this is all I've ever really wanted. Why has it taken me so long to know?

"Come in to the fire." Suddenly Olwyn was smiling through her tears, hugging his arm, a great burst of joy sweeping through her each time their eyes met. Yes, she thought, he's here; he's really here. The miracle had happened. It gave her sudden strength, having him beside her; it gave her the confidence to think they could work all the rest out, that happiness was still possible.

Arms around each other, they walked into the small, square sitting room where an enormous fire crackled in the hearth. It sent out a great heat into the room, and tongues of flame flickering up the walls in the shadowy corners. Two pink-shaded lamps glowed; a small table had been drawn up to the fire and set for two; it had a vase of peach-tinted roses in the center of the table, their perfume heavy in the warm room.

Justin glanced about, his eyes very bright. "My Lord, this is wonderful! How did you ever find such a place?"

The room was furnished simply and gave off a settled, comfortable aura. There was nothing of the usual Victorian extravagance and vulgarity here, Justin noticed as his eyes roamed the room. The tall sideboard of mellow dark oak, with its row of blue-and-white Delft plates, had come down from a bygone era; the Turkish carpet in muted shades of rose, blue, and gold, was almost threadbare, and the wing-back chairs drawn up on either side of the fireplace were covered in faded wine-colored velvet, the knap long-since flattened by all the people who had sat in them through the years to warm themselves by the fire.

Everything about him was quiet and serene, startlingly so when contrasted to what they were both used to now, yet it struck Justin as being the most beautiful, most desirable, and most welcoming room he had ever set foot in.

Olwyn drew him over to the hearth, where they kissed and embraced once more, then she pushed him into one of the chairs, saying, "You must be famished. I'm going to serve supper at once."

He was indeed famished but not for food.

He grabbed her as she made to walk away, and pulled her down on his knee and buried his face in her neck, his senses reeling at her warmth, her sweetness, the wonderful feeling of her body against his. After a moment Justin drew back and looked at her; he couldn't seem to stop drinking in each feature of her face, her hair; even her soft breath he drank in. This was food, he found himself thinking; this was nourishment! But . . . he saw a great change in Olwyn, and it hurt him deeply. She was like a mere husk of her former vibrant self, so thin and pale, and the second she stopped smiling, her eyes were sad, wounded, some of their brightness dimmed now. He touched her trembling lips with a gentle finger. "If you only knew how much I've ached for this moment," he said, his voice unsteady, moved and struggling futilley to control his emotions. "I would have given a king's ransom for one sweet kiss." Then he did kiss her, so tenderly, his fingers moving caressingly through her hair, then moving down her arms, over her body as if to make sure that she really was there, for even yet, after all his dreaming, Justin half expected to wake up and find himself lying alone and bleak on his bed, a pillow held close in his arms—then hurled against the opposite wall with all the disappointment and frustration in his body.

Olwyn knew she had changed and that it had deeply affected him. She took his face between her hands and smiled into his eyes, determined to cheer him up; that this should be a bright, glowingly happy moment. Nothing, nothing must mar it tonight, even if they would have to talk more seriously later. Tonight, she thought firmly, they would celebrate their love, and how that love had triumphed in spite of everything that had happened to them.

Justin, too, had changed, she saw with a pang. Though still a handsome, vigorous-looking man, his golden hair glistening in the firelight, his face wet from the rain outside, ruddy and tanned, like polished dark copper, still . . . the signs that he, too, had suffered greatly were obvious. His face was leaner, the strong bones more pronounced, and there was a tightness around his eyes and mouth that hadn't been there before.

"I'm going to feed you," Olwyn told him, a little of the old seductiveness coming back into her eyes. "And then I'm going to love you."

"In that order?" His own eyes suddenly flared, reflecting hot sparks from the fire.

"Yes, sir, in that order, otherwise I fear you won't have the strength to keep up with me later."

Justin chased her out into the kitchen, delighted with her teasing, playful mood, even while aware of what it cost her. But he'd always known she had great strength; it was one of the things he most loved about her, most respected. One of the many. And he'd had ample time over the last few years to think about this woman and appreciate her. Time, too, to realize what a blind fool he had been when he first met Olwyn; how he had allowed his experience with Christina to warp his thinking.

But Justin eagerly caught her light-hearted mood and hung on to it, ignoring the sword that dangled over his head, or rather, a noose, if this rendezvous were ever discovered, something that would be bound to be viewed with the greatest suspicion, and might well lead to his arrest, since he'd been one of the prime suspects in Howell's murder. As he helped Olwyn prepare the tray to be carried into the sitting room, stopping constantly to kiss, touch, laugh, and tease each other; under all this hung the question: Who had killed Maury Howell?

A scant three months after Maury's death, after the death of their baby, Justin, unable to bear it any longer, sure she must be in anguish just as he was, risked sending her a note through Harold Scobbie. In that note he asked Olwyn if she would be interested in meeting him at some location suitable to both of them, at which time they could discuss their future plans. He wrote: "It cannot be for some time, under the circumstances, but are you agreeable to us meeting at a future date?"

That note had saved Olwyn's sanity, even though it had taken almost two years to arrange their reunion; to risk being away from Kimberley at the same time.

They dined cozily at the small table beside the fire, Justin wolfing down roast beef, humble potatoes, and salad greens, and it all tasted like nectar from the

Gods. When he noticed that Olwyn ate very little he kept leaning over demanding that she open her mouth, then popping some tasty morsel inside, scolding, "You are far too thin! My prime objective over this two-week period is to fatten you up, beautiful lady. I like a lot of you in my arms."

She grinned. "Your *prime* objective?"

"Well . . ." he said, desire smoldering in his eyes, "perhaps not my main objective . . ."

The small bedchamber upstairs had a steeply sloped ceiling and a patchwork quilt on the old brass bed. A fire in the grate filled the room with a warm orange glow and sent flickering shadows leaping across the plain white-washed walls, twinkling on the metal posts of the bed. Naked, skin touching, breath mingling, eyes speaking far better than words, they lay together looking into each other's eyes. Olwyn could feel his fingers playing over her lightly, so soft and gentle they felt, like whispers, telling her of the delights to come.

"Why did we make it so hard for each other?" Justin asked suddenly, speaking the thought as it entered his mind.

Olwyn smiled wistfully as she ran her fingers through his hair. "I suppose that's just the way we are, darling; not the types to take the easy route."

"I love you so much, Olwyn . . . and we've wasted so much time—"

She closed the few inches between them and kissed him quickly, and when they drew back she said, "We can't change it, Justin, so please—let's not talk of it tonight."

All the time their bodies had moved closer, brushing, caressing, fitting together in their own perfect way. Justin restrained the pounding urgency inside him, wanting to taste, to savor every second of this first union after such a long time, to fully relax her—she had been taut to the snapping point when he arrived—with tender kisses and murmured endearments, the light stroking she enjoyed so much; all this he did while the hunger built up inside him, flames kindling as Olwyn pressed her breasts to his chest, and ran the tips of her fingers in circles across the hard muscles of his thigh. "I want to be with you every second for the rest of my life," she told him softly.

"You will be, my love," he said. "In my heart."

"Justin"—a tiny frown ruffled her brow—"I wonder how long it will be before that can happen. How long we'll have to keep up this—this chasing about?"

"As long as we must."

She nodded.

Olwyn inhaled sharply when she felt his fingers trace a path from her breast to her hips, then move inward, deeper, deeper, until he encountered moist, velvety flesh. Stroking her, teasing her, Justin bent his head and kissed her breasts, his touch unlocking feelings and sensations inside her that Olwyn had begun to fear had withered up and died, releasing her from the tomblike coldness that had frozen her blood. She felt the ice begin to crack and melt under the burning onslaught of his passion, each kiss, each cherishing caress, stirring her more, pulling her back from the dark abyss into warmth and light—into life.

She threw her arms around him, quivering inside as his hands wandered down her back to her hips, stroking every inch of her to throbbing awareness, to heart-stopping desire. With his hands at her hips he drew her tight against his hardness. "Oh, my love!" she gasped, her legs rising like wings to encircle him, to draw him to her urgently, impatient now, moist and ready.

Distantly they could hear the beat of the waves against the cliffs, a steady, pounding rhythm that echoed in their blood as with hands and lips and feverish bodies they sought and found the confirmation each was seeking from the other. They found it in dewy, love-washed skin, devouring lips, and saw it in eyes glazed with need for each other in the light from the fire.

Justin felt her senses quicken, felt the heat fanning

and pulsing between them, and joined, moving together in a sensual dance, they surged in a final, bone-melting burst of rapture, then fell back against the pillows, breathless, deliriously happy, neither wanting to separate.

In the days that followed they walked the beach, climbed the cliffs, and explored the many caves where in times past pirates had hidden their illicit goods. They took picnics into the verdant, green countryside, now blazing with the russets, golds, and deep reds of autumn. When the days were sunny they often lounged indolently in the garden, and when it rained —they almost enjoyed those times best—they cozied up inside the stout little cottage in front of a roaring fire.

And they talked.

Finally, belatedly, they shared the heartbreak of Aidan's death. The little boy would have been four years old now.

"I wanted to die too," Olwyn wept, all the agony, the pain, the guilt came pouring out in Justin's arms, feelings she had never really been able to share with anyone; her deepest, sometimes darkest emotions. "I thought of killing myself; I might have, too, if it hadn't been for the other children. And I was determined to get rid of the businesses. I never wanted to see another diamond for as long as I lived!

"It was James who pointed out that it wasn't really the diamond that had killed Aidan," she went on, her voice thick, breaking. "It could just as easily have been anything else in the house that night—a knife in the kitchen, for instance, or fire. Or he could have fallen down the stairs. He—"

"Maury Howell was responsible!" Justin broke in harshly. "Howell killed our son!"

At the look in his eyes, so cold, so merciless, Olwyn shivered. "One of the worst things for me," she went on very low, "was that you never got to know him,

Justin. And he never had your name. Oh God, how I blame myself for that!"

He drew back and looked at her in astonishment. "You blame yourself! Olwyn, I'm the one to blame, make no mistake about that!" he said grimly. "I allowed stupid trivialities to come between us; to keep us apart. I based our relationship on past experience, things that had happened to me long before I met you. I was a fool!"

Olwyn could feel that his muscles were rigid, that he was tense and angry, disgusted with himself. But after a moment he relaxed, sighing. "One thing finally sank home. No matter what, I never stopped loving you. I'll admit I tried to"—he looked at her to see how she would take that—"but it didn't work. The meaning of it became clear then, that you were the most important thing in my life, but . . . " his voice dropped, ". . . by then I had asked Kate D'Lyon to marry me."

Justin, obviously embarrassed, tried to explain about Kate. It was made more difficult since now, looking back, he found it impossible to understand himself.

"Call it a mad impulse," he said ruefully. "Call it loneliness, pity, call it what you will, but this I can tell you, I was never in love with her, not remotely, and I made that clear." He thought a minute, looking troubled. "I liked the woman; I felt sorry for her, I suppose; she'd had a hard time of it."

Olwyn listened in silence while he told her about Kate's background; the death of her young husband in a duel, her impoverished circumstances, having to eat humble pie in the house of her brother and sister-in-law, and being left in charge of a young son she was already finding hard to handle. "I managed to convince myself that in many ways we suited each other well enough," Justin went on with a wry smile. "I told myself that countless marriages were contracted for reasons other than love; I told myself it would work." Then he said something that made Olwyn sting with jealousy, though she knew she had no right to, since by then she herself was married. "She appealed to me more than any of the others—"

Suddenly realizing what he'd said, Justin broke off and gave her a quick kiss. "What I was looking for and never found," he said, "was another you."

Olwyn relaxed then. "Go on."

"Well . . . I think you know the rest. The lawsuit."

"Is it settled?"

He nodded. Then he turned right around to face her and swept her against him in a bear hug that took her breath away. "Thank God I didn't marry her!"

"Thank God our love survived, that it's so indestructable."

"Yes," he nodded, "like diamonds."

The following afternoon they were sitting on rocks at the entrance to a cave, Justin idly tossing pebbles into a pool of water, Olwyn examining several pretty shells she had picked up along the beach, when he suddenly turned to her and said, "I didn't kill him, Olwyn."

She looked up with a start, and all of a sudden she noticed a chill in the atmosphere, that the sun had gone behind a cloud and the breeze had grown cold. The pleasant, relaxing afternoon they had just spent together disintegrated, and she shivered. "Good God, Justin," she said, "I never once thought you had!"

He looked away, and pitched a stone into the pool with some force, sending up a shower of cold sea water. Then he turned to face her again. He looked hard, defiant. "But I might have," he said, his voice like flint, "if I'd found him that night."

"Don't talk like that, Justin. It . . . it frightens me."

He turned away from her and gazed out to sea. "I hated the man. If I'd succeeded in hunting him down that night I can't honestly say what would have happened. I know that I was furious enough to kill—"

"Don't, Justin!" Olwyn stood up, the shells tumbling. She started to walk away along the beach, walking quite fast, a terrible clutching fear at her breast, his last words ringing in her ears. "I was furious enough to kill." She couldn't bear listening to him talking like that. It brought everything back, Maury's death all mixed in with Aidan's, the choking, crushing horror, and always the knowledge that Maury's killer had never been caught.

In a moment or two Justin reached her side, and for a little distance they walked along in silence, not touching; then, as they started to climb up the hill to the cottage, Olwyn felt his arm go around her. She looked at him and suddenly thought, "What would I do if he confessed that he *had* killed Maury?" The answer came at once. "Nothing." And God help her, it was true.

She reached up on tiptoe and kissed him, and they walked back to the house together arm-in-arm.

Over that two-week period they aired everything, and Justin finally told her about Christina. Perhaps more than anything else, learning about his stepmother helped her understand Justin better. But there was one small secret that he didn't confide, something that had happened a few months ago. At that time he learned from his lawyer in Scotland that Christina's elderly husband had died of a stroke and the factories and mansion were up for sale. What sort of offer should he make on Justin's behalf? his lawyer asked.

None, Justin wrote back.

The properties were of no use to him now. He had never wanted them back for himself, but for his son, and his son was dead. From Scobbie he had learned that after the birth of her last child, Olwyn had been told by her doctor that she could never get pregnant again. So, if the day ever came when they could finally marry, they could not look forward to extending their family.

Ariann, his daughter, was now his heir. But he never wanted Ariann out of his sight! Certainly not far away on another continent.

None of this he told Olwyn, afraid of making her

sad again. She was gradually starting to be happy, to find fresh hope, even starting to cope with the sorrow of losing Aidan. They must go forward! Justin felt that strongly. And to go forward they would need all the strength, fortitude, and confidence they could muster. They had to let the past go. Above all, they had to go on believing that one day they would all be together.

Time, that merciless enemy, quickly snatched them away from each other. Justin would depart first, as they'd arranged, and Olwyn two weeks later. The night before he left they made desperate love, again and again until they were exhausted, enough lovemaking to last them for a year.

When Olwyn broke down Justin caught her by the shoulders and tried to impart some of his own strength into her. "We must go on as usual," he told her determinedly. "We will not let this defeat us. Think, my darling, we have our love to sustain us! Nothing can ever destroy that. And one day," his deep blue eyes willed her to believe what he was about to say, "one day we will live together openly. Have faith in that, Olwyn. Live for it!"

She nodded, her smile wobbly. "I'll try."

They made their plans then. Once back at Kimberley they could have no contact except through business, and when the time came to plan their next meeting that would be done through Harold or James, as usual. The Scobbies knew the truth now; they could be relied upon to keep their secret and to help them all they could. Finally Justin said to her, "And you must get involved in the business again, Olwyn." When he saw her reluctance he grinned. "That's one way we can meet without raising eyebrows."

"But it's such torture, having to be so cool and detached with each other."

"Sweet torture." Justin smiled, his eyes roaming over her. "I can at least look at you and let myself imagine . . ."

Olwyn cuffed him lightly, then immediately kissed the spot she had slapped.

Every year—and they hoped there would be no need for this—they would meet in a different country. Above all, they had to be careful, and never by word or deed give anyone reason to be suspicious.

"But think of the eventual reward!" Justin said when he saw she was about to weep again.

It was the eventual reward that kept Olwyn together when she saw him away the following evening. The last thing she said to him before he rode away was, "I'll go back to work. I know you are right about that. And don't worry, my love, I'll manage."

"I never doubted it," Justin replied.

# 32

The snake led them to find the key.

Like children everywhere, the Howell youngsters loved to play tricks on their nurse, the more so since Seeta tended to be dour and cantankerous, and had changed a lot from the bright, chatty young girl she used to be. Olwyn put it down to the fact that, like everyone else, Seeta was getting older. She had passed her thirtieth birthday now and was still unmarried.

"She's just a cranky old maid!" Gerard complained whenever his nurse scolded him. "Thank goodness I'll soon be off to school and won't need a silly nursemaid fussing over me."

That always brought a pout from Ariann. "I don't understand why Mother refuses to let me go off to school. I'm ten years old now, and all my friends have gone. It isn't fair!"

"You are a girl," her half-brother pointed out. "That makes the difference."

"Charlotte Robinson is a girl!" Ariann retorted.

"And Beth Hayes and Maryellen Stockwell, and all of them are away at boarding school."

The day their gardener killed a serpent in their strawberry patch, Gerard talked him into letting him have the carcass. The children then waited until Seeta had gone to market, and the moment she left they sneaked up to her tiny attic room, laughing and whispering, Gerard with the dead reptile inside a paper sack, and slipped inside their nursemaid's private domain, quietly closing the door behind them. All the other servants lived in the extension at the back of the house, but Seeta, who had become something of a recluse, had requested to be allowed to stay in the attic, even though that part of the house was stiflingly hot in summer and freezing during the winter nights.

Ariann and Gerard glanced around the chamber without much interest. They had been here a few times before when Seeta had been with them. The small room was clean but very cluttered. Their nurse was the type of woman who liked to hoard things and never threw away anything, however small or unimportant. The room had a narrow bed covered with a yellow quilt, a chest of drawers with dozens of items displayed on the top, an old rug, a chair, and a wooden kist or blanket chest under the tiny dormer window. The kist had been hand-made and looked it; it had been given to the owner by a former suitor. Made of rough wood planks, some of which didn't fit too well together, it had a crude picture engraved on the top of an eagle, a tree, and an elephant.

"Where shall we put the snake?" Ariann wondered, looking about.

"In her bed, of course!" came the prompt reply. "Oh, won't she get a rare surprise? I wish we could be here when she finds it."

"Ger . . ." the little girl frowned, thinking of how she would feel upon climbing into bed to find a serpent there, ". . . perhaps we shouldn't—"

The boy gave her an impatient glance over his shoulder. "Oh, don't be such a spoil-sport! It's just a prank. The snake can't harm her now, can it?"

At that he grabbed the bed covers and wrenched them back, sending the pillow toppling over onto the floor. Both of them gazed in surprise at a large black iron key that had been concealed there.

"What's that for, I wonder?" Gerard said after a moment. "It's too big for the door."

Ariann pointed to the kist. "That has a lock on it, Ger." But when he darted across to it, she cried, "No, don't open it! It must be private, otherwise she wouldn't keep it locked." But already he was down on his knees, fumbling to turn the key, which was rough and an awkward fit. He laughed. "We'll just see what Seeta has in it. Let's hope this is where she keeps her sweets."

Ariann walked over beside him, half curious, half afraid. "Mother will be angry if she finds out what we've done."

"Mother is out," Gerard shot back.

The kist clicked open.

Olwyn had gone out to pick up a few last-minute things for her holiday, the ones she took alone. Only the previous day Ariann had inquired, "Mother, why do you take these holidays alone every year? It's not really the done thing, you know, for ladies to go off on their own. That's what Mrs. Robinson says."

Then she giggled and put a hand up to her mouth. "I think some people have the notion that you must be sneaking off to meet a lover."

Olwyn felt as if ice had been poured down her spine. She was amazed at how calm her voice was when she inquired. "And who do you think my lover is?"

"Oh . . ." her daughter shrugged, "I don't think they know—but they would like to find out! You know what a lot of gossipy biddies they are, at least that's what Uncle James calls them."

Olwyn did indeed know. And she felt a touch of alarm. They had been so careful, but—

"*Do* you have a lover, Mother?" Ariann asked, watching her face.

Olwyn evaded an answer by scolding. "What a thing to ask your own mother! It's certainly not a subject a girl your age should be interested in. Lover, indeed!" But inside she was quaking.

Ariann was growing up, Olwyn noticed. She was tall for her age, long-limbed, perhaps a bit too thin and lanky. But she had beautiful turquoise eyes and full, well-defined lips, and thick blond hair that tumbled down her back in riotous waves and curls, a style very popular in 1880. Recently she had become very interested in fashion, in fixing her hair, using scent, and now . . . talk of lovers!

Olwyn frowned. "You'd do better to pay more attention to your lessons."

"Lessons are dull." The girl gazed at her with eyes full of secrets, and repeated, "Are you sneaking off to meet a sweetheart?"

She was, and had been for the past six years.

Names, places, and times flew through Olwyn's mind then—Italy, Spain, Denmark, Morocco, Egypt —her life crammed into two-week periods. Only during those brief holidays was she truly, fully alive. And soon another one, this time Ireland. As the departure time neared, Olwyn felt her deepest, most vital senses beginning to awaken, to flex and stir in joyful anticipation. It was like coming out of an emotional coma; like being reborn once a year. But after their meetings . . . despair and depression, anger, frustration and, lately, defiance that they had to conduct their lives like that, and always the frightening awareness that time was passing, that every time they met the risks increased.

The whole world was changing around them and their situation remained the same!

Kimberley itself had changed greatly. It had grown into a proper town, with permanent brick buildings rapidly replacing the shacks of the early days. The fortunes of the prospectors had changed, too, mostly for the worse. Diamond mining was now largely in the hands of the magnates, men like Cecil Rhodes, Barney Barnato—the cocky little Jewish boy from Whitechapel in London—people like Alfred Beit and brawny, clever Julius Wernher, originally from Prague, and, of course, Robinson, Howell, and Wentworth.

In every slump in the market, and there had been many throughout the seventies, more and more of the small, independent diggers had been weeded out, leaving the new magnates to snap up their claims. Now even the magnates were joining forces to increase their strength and bargaining power, and many outside investors had come in. The real power in Kimberley had all come from elsewhere—Scotland, England, Germany, France, America, and a host of other places.

The previous year Olwyn's own companies had united with Teragno Minerals, Hawkins & Lange, Maritz, and Druce, to form the Central Diamond Syndicate. Amalgamation was taking place in Kimberley, the aim to control the output of diamonds and thereby stabilize and increase the price per carat.

With fewer people in control it was easier to stamp out the problem of illicit diamond buying, or IDB. Though Olwyn had been very much against it, nonwhites were no longer permitted to hold claims in the mines, nor were the Kaffir work force allowed to wash and sort kimberlite. The natives now were required to show passes when entering or leaving the mines, and they were kept in closely guarded compounds for the duration of their contracts. They were also subjected to periodic spot-checks, when every nook and cranny, every orifice of their bodies were examined in a bid to eradicate stealing.

The new working conditions were harsh, yet thousands upon thousands of natives still arrived at the mines looking for work. The pay was good. In the compounds they were taken care of in every way—fed, clothed, given medical attention when needed, even recreation was provided. Honest workers had nothing to fear. For the dishonest, those found stealing, the punishment was savage. But when Olwyn had protested about that during one of their board meetings, the majority vote had prevailed. IDB must be wiped out. It was as simple as that.

One of her pet projects, something she'd worked on with James and Hannah, had been building a church in memory of Aidan. Now James had his permanent niche at last! Hannah and Harold paid yearly visits to their relatives in Scotland, and their relatives came to see them. Jamie, now eighteen and reading law at Glasgow University, would eventually return to Kimberley to join their legal team.

Taking Justin's advice, Olwyn had diversified into other minerals, into property—in London, Paris, the Cape—investing in textiles, transport, steel, and cotton farming. Recently a British magazine had featured an article about her. Under a photograph of Olwyn the question was asked: Is This the Face of the Richest Woman in the World?

That had brought a bitter smile to her lips.

"It depends on by what standard you measure riches," she'd remarked to Hannah.

The older woman had squeezed her hand. "You mustn't ever lose hope."

But she was! Bit by bit, it was being chipped away.


"What's all this rubbish?"

Gerard leaned over the kist and pawed about among the contents, his sister hanging over his shoulder. Ariann pointed. "Is that an ax?"

Gerard fished it out somewhat gingerly. "It's one of those native things, I forget what you call them."

"It's got something on it . . ."

The boy held it up to the window and immediately

both of them spotted the brown stains, lots of them, thickly coating the blade.

"That's blood!" Gerard cried, and dropped the assegai back into the kist with a grimace of disgust. "It's dried blood, Ariann. Ugh! I hope I didn't touch it. It's got some on the handle too."

Ariann didn't answer. She was staring at a yellowed newspaper neatly folded under where the assegai had originally been. Then Gerard spotted it too.

"That's a photograph of my father!" he cried. "It's just like the one in the album downstairs. Why d'you think Seeta kept it?"

"Ger," Ariann put a hand on his shoulder, "I think we should go."

"Yes!" he agreed at once, and jumped to his feet, but when he turned around the boy froze.

Ariann looked behind her then and saw Seeta standing silently in the doorway.

Olwyn returned to the house at noon. When the children didn't put in an appearance at lunch she was very surprised. Usually they were the first at table. She questioned the servants but none of them had noticed the youngsters leaving the house, nor did they know where their nurse might be.

At two o'clock Olwyn ordered a search of the house and grounds. Nobody thought of checking the attic. Aside from Seeta's small room, it was only used for storage, and Seeta rarely went to her room unless to sleep.

They weren't on the property, that much was established soon enough.

"Then I want all of you to go off in different directions and search the town," Olwyn told them worriedly. "Sam, you call in at the homes of their friends. I'll stay here in case they come back."

She was still there at four o'clock when Harold Scobbie arrived to tell her about a problem at the mine, but he forgot all about it the instant he saw Olwyn's ashen face and listened to her frantic story, for by now she was convinced that something awful had happened to the threesome.

"Hal, you don't think . . . you don't think slavers might have caught them?"

He gripped her hand tight and shook his head. "No, of course not. Nobody has seen slavers in this area for years. Too risky for them with all the security around the mines." He squeezed her hand, adding, "Try to stay calm. They'll come back, never fear. They've probably gone somewhere and forgotten the time."

"No, Hal." She shook her head, her stomach in knots. "Seeta would never have taken them anywhere without telling me first. Oh, Hal . . . I have such a terrible feeling!"

He sat her down in a chair and told her to think carefully. "Chances are Seeta might have told you where they were going and it has slipped your mind. Or you might come up with a place we haven't looked. I'll go and take a wander around myself," he said. "I know of a few places that Gerard in particular likes to go. I won't be gone for more than half an hour."

Olwyn didn't sit long after Harold left. In a moment she was up pacing around the silent house, wracking her brains for where they might have gone; for a place they'd forgotten to search. Systematically she ran every nook and cranny of the house and grounds through her mind, mentally ticking them off one by one.

Finally she came to the attic.

No, Olwyn thought, the children had lost interest in poking about the attic long ago. Seeta's little room was there but the nurse only went there to sleep. All three of them certainly wouldn't have spent an entire afternoon—and part of the morning too—inside that stuffy little room.

But it was the only place they hadn't looked.

Olwyn hurried upstairs and along the corridor to the narrow door leading to the short flight of steps to the attic. At the top there was a door, and lying beside it, tumbled over, was Seeta's basket. Some of the contents had spilled out; an orange, bundle of leeks, a small can of something or other—all left where the nurse must have dropped them.

Olwyn stared at these things dumbly—then felt a sudden, numbing chill.

They were in there! All three of them! Somebody had stolen into the house while she was out and herded the children and their nurse into that musty little room and—and—

Blindly, breathless with terror, Olwyn turned the handle and opened the door, flew across an open space and into the nurse's room. Seeta lay on the floor by her old kist, a bottle upturned beside her. Gerard, too, lay on the floor, his face white, a dark sticky liquid smeared around his mouth. Ariann was sprawled across the bed, her long blond hair dangling over the side, her pretty mouth blackened with the substance that had been poured down her throat.

The air in the room reeked of something tarry and pungent. The look of it and smell of it was familiar to Olwyn, and she identified it with a potion M'Buru had once shown them, a deadly poison made from wild berries, the same poison some of the more primitive tribes used to dip their arrows in.

A shriek tore out of her then.

All three were dead!

# 33

Screaming, every thought in her head splintering, Olwyn acted on instinct. She picked up her son from the floor and carried him to the bed and set him down gently. Then she got onto the bed herself between the two children and took each of them in her arms, her tear-drenched eyes moving from one to the other.

No one ever lived, M'Buru had said, who took that poison into their system. It was swift, and absolutely lethal. Her darlings were dead. Dead! "Oh God! Oh dear God . . ." She choked, unable to cope with it. "Oh, no . . . make this be a dream; make it not be real."

For a minute Olwyn thought she was going to be sick. Her eyes wandered the room like a drunk person, washed over with tears and seeing nothing. Only feeling, and she couldn't stand the pain. Not again!

Quite suddenly Olwyn stopped crying. Everything in the room went very still. Her mind became pristine clear and sharp, like a diamond. Yes, yes, she thought, it all made sense now. It was the only course open to her. She was like an hour glass and hadn't known it, even when, the last year or two, she had become so extremely conscious of the passage of time. Her mind had been trying to tell her something; now she knew.

Peace. It opened out like a flower all around her. It beckoned, and she went to it willingly, thankfully, easing the children out of her arms, saying softly, almost lightly, "Don't worry, my angels, I'll be back."

When Justin and Harold burst into the room it was to find Olwyn on the floor by Seeta's body, a bottle in her hand. Justin recognized the odor that filled the small room and roared, "Don't touch that! Olwyn . . . darling!"

Furtively, animal-like, she tilted the bottle to her lips—but nothing came out.

Justin sprang across the space that separated them and knocked the bottle out of her hand, but some of the gluey black poison from the neck of the bottle had rubbed off on her lips. Desperately Justin tried to wipe it off using the sleeve of his shirt, but Olwyn pushed him hard and turned her head away, screaming, "I want to die! Let me alone! Peace—give me peace . . ."

He grabbed her roughly by the head and held her until he had cleaned the area about her mouth, then he took her in his arms and held her tight, afraid to release her lest she dive for the bottle again. Every muscle in his body quivered. He could hear his heart pounding like a drum in his ears. He was afraid to look at the children.

"Come over here," Harold called from the bed. "See what you think of the bairns."

Justin knew from his own travels around southern Africa that the poison attacked the respiratory system. A small drop, he had observed in animals, acted as a kind of anesthetic. A larger dose put them into a deep coma, and a bigger dose yet paralyzed the breathing apparatus altogether and brought death. He glanced over his shoulder at Hal while keeping a firm grip on

Olwyn, who continued to moan and struggle in his arms. It was the blackest moment of Justin's life. "Are they dead, Hal?" he finally asked, his voice shaking.

There was a silence, then, "I—I can't tell. They feel cool, but not really cold; at least not yet."

Justin scooped Olwyn up and carried her to the bed. His face was gray beneath his tan as he gazed down at the children. "Harold, get Dr. Brinkley up here immediately," he said. "If he isn't in, try Dr. Jacobs, but for God's sake get somebody!"

Harold nodded and left, his heavy work boots clattering on the stairs. Justin sat down on the edge of the bed with Olwyn on his knee and, keeping one arm around her, reached with the other and felt for the pulse at Ariann's neck, then Gerard's. Nothing.

"They're dead!" Olwyn shrieked. "Can't you see they've taken the poison." In a paroxysm of grief she beat her forehead against Justin's shoulder, crying hysterically, her whole body shaking violently.

"Stop it!" he shouted, afraid she was losing her mind. He caught her face in his hand, his strong fingers biting into her chin, making her look at him. "Listen to me, Olwyn. It's possible they might still be alive. Their skin is cool, but it isn't cold. This poison can cause a deep coma that seems like death. While moving about the country in my trading days I've seen its effects more than once, both in animals and humans. In one village I heard of a man who was about to be buried but suddenly he started to move—"

Olwyn sat bolt upright on his knee, her eyes riveted to his face.

"Don't lie to me, Justin."

"I'm telling the truth," he assured her. "And if you would calm down and promise not to do anything foolish, then we might be able to help the children. As it is, I don't dare let you go."

Olwyn was off his knee in a flash, rushing for the stairs. "I'm going to fetch my old medical bag," she said. "You get water from the kitchen."

For the next half hour, until Harold finally came back with a panting Dr. Jacobs, Olwyn and Justin fought desperately to get some response out of Ariann and Gerard. Olwyn had noticed, upon lifting their eyelids, that the pupils of their eyes were reduced to little pinpoints. Belladonna! she had thought then. If only she could get twenty drops of belladonna inside them, but of course she didn't dare. They were in a coma—she made herself believe that—and it was dangerous to give anything by mouth in that condition. She had to content herself by breathing into their mouths, with Justin working on Ariann and she on Gerard. They applied mustard poultices to their limbs, doused their heads with cold water, and only a moment or two before the doctor arrived Justin lifted his head and shouted, "Ariann is alive! I'm sure of it. I felt something . . . like a whisper go through her. She's alive, Olwyn! Oh, thank God . . ."

Laughing, crying, they bumped heads over their patients and kissed, but almost immediately went back to work on them. Dr. Jacobs looked startled when he and Hal rushed into the room to find the two adults kneeling on the bed over the youngsters, when he had fully expected them to meet him at the door, wringing their hands.

In three days Ariann was completely out of her coma, though still very weak. Gerard took longer. It was a month before he could even sit up in bed, and for months after that his locomotion was affected. Until he was sixteen Gerard suffered from periodic convulsions, occasional loss of power in his legs, and headaches, though they were to lessen as he grew older. But Gerard was never to be quite the same little boy again.

Ariann told the story of finding the incriminating evidence in Seeta's kist but insisted that their nurse had not wanted to kill them. "She only wanted to make us sleep, she said, until she took the drink herself. She told us that she'd go mad in prison, that she couldn't bear being locked up." She paused, then added, "Of course she told us all that after we'd tried a sip of her special wine, otherwise we wouldn't have touched it." Ariann reached for her father's hand. "The next thing I knew I woke up in this bedroom."

He kissed her. "Thank God you did, both of you!"

Opening Seeta's kist was like opening a book. The contents told their own story, how her betrothed had been beaten to death that day at the mine, and how she'd bided her time and gone after Maury with the assegai the moment the right opportunity presented itself. A photograph of Seeta and Shingo together was in the pocket of the trunk, carefully wrapped up in tissue paper. Shingo's picture was also in several of the old newspapers she had saved, the man Maury had killed for supposedly stealing.

"I knew almost nothing about her private life." Olwyn sighed. "If only I had! For the last few years she kept everything to herself. But I can understand why she took the poison now. She liked to go her own way, to be free."

Justin drew her into his arms and smiled at her tenderly.

"We, too, are free," he reminded her.

"Yes," Olwyn nodded, a glint springing up in her eyes. "We've been free for a whole week now and you still haven't asked me to marry you, sir!"

"Oh," he grinned, "I thought that was a foregone conclusion."

# SUMMER STORM
## Catherine Hart

"Hart offers a gripping, sympathetic portrait of the Cheyenne as a proud people caught in turmoil by an encroaching world."

*—Publisher's Weekly*

SUMMER STORM. Soft and warm as a sweet summer rain, Summer Storm could be tamed only by Windrider, a brave leader of the Cheyenne. Though she had given her heart to another, he vowed their tumultuous joining would be climaxed in a whirlwind of ecstasy.

_____2465-9                          $3.95 US/$4.95 CAN

## AUTOGRAPHED BOOKMARK EDITIONS

Each book contains a signed message from the author and a removable gold foiled and embossed bookmark.

### PASSIONATE INDIAN ROMANCE
### BY MADELINE BAKER

"Madeline Baker proved she knows how to please readers of historical romance when she created *Reckless Heart* and *Love In The Wind.*" —*Whispers*

**LOVE FOREVERMORE.** When Loralee arrived at Fort Apache as the new schoolmarm, she had some hard realities to learn . . . and a harsh taskmaster to teach her. Shad Zuniga was fiercely proud, a renegade Apache who wanted no part of the white man's world, not even its women—but he couldn't control his desire for golden-haired Loralee.

_____2577-9                                   $4.50 US/$5.50 CAN

# FOREVER GOLD

**Catherine Hart's books are "Beautiful! Gorgeous! Magnificent!"**
— *Romantic Times*

FOREVER GOLD. From the moment Blake Montgomery held up the westward-bound stagecoach carrying lovely Megan Coulston to her adoring fiance, she hated everything about the virile outlaw. How dare he drag her off to an isolated mountain cabin and hold her for ransom? How dare he kidnap her heart, when all he could offer were forbidden moments of burning, trembling ecstasy?

_____2600-7                         $4.50 US/$5.50 CAN